False
Gods

L. R. TROVILLION

Hippolyta Books
P. O. Box 31
Glenwood, MD 21738

Printed in the United States of America

Library of Congress Control Number: 2014919648

ISBN 978–0-9908995–0-1

Being defeated is often a temporary condition.
Giving up is what makes it permanent.
~*Marilyn vos Savant*

Part I
Autumn

She clothes herself in rust and brown
Gathering the leavings from the fallow earth.
And huddles in the advancing darkness,
Against the coming frost.
–From the journal of Cory Iverson

Chapter One

CORY SLUMPED ON the shaded bench at the school's front entrance, hoping to avoid the rest of the girls leaving for the cross-country team tryouts. Leaning back deeper into the shadows, she watched the stream of girls jog down the hill, turn onto the road, and disappear. She'd intended to run with them, to try to make the team, but . . .

Why was it still so hot in September? Not at all like back home in Massachusetts. Home. It had only been three weeks since school had started, eight since her family had moved to Maryland. Except Dad. He had left her mom, Roni, and Cory knew her mom would sooner wear white shoes after Labor Day than be known as "the abandoned wife" among her friends back home in Wellesley.

Things would be different if she were still going to school in Wellesley. Cory recalled it was the start of the school season in Massachusetts when women removed their hot pink toenail polish, packed away the Nantucket wicker pocketbooks, and pulled out chests of mothball-infused woolen sweaters. In other words, in the fall. Here in Maryland school started in August.

A group of girls passed by, their rubber flip-flops flapping against heels, bare legs under short shorts. Cory tucked her legs under the bench. When she picked out the new shoes at the store she thought they looked great. Now she wasn't so sure. She realized she stood out, and maybe not in a good way.

The buses were late. Cory unzipped the gym bag at her feet and pulled out a slim paperback of *Candide*. The words on the page swam before her eyes without comprehension. Over the top of the book, another set of eyes met hers.

The boy had on jeans with a slit over each knee, topped with a polo shirt. A lacrosse stick rested on his right shoulder. She recalled seeing him during lunch periods, but he wasn't in any of her AP classes.

David Randall. Though she had only been at Glenwood High a few weeks, she already knew who *he* was. Everyone did. David, like the famous statue. He was always followed by a group of other guys who hooted and cheered when he slapped a girl's butt or made jokes about some geeky kid. His own Greek chorus. But sometimes he was kind of funny. Yesterday in the cafeteria he invented a tater-tot tossing game. He lobbed ketchup-laden tots at the dropped ceiling, and allotted points for ones that fell directly in cups of water placed underneath. It was popular, that is, until the lunchroom monitor stopped him.

Cory dropped her eyes to the page, but every skin cell prickled on high alert as he approached.

"Hey, I read that."

Cory lowered the book.

"Want to know how it ends?" he asked.

His brown eyes looked at her from under a sweep of overgrown bangs. She wasn't sure what to say. "I read it already. In French class, last year."

The confident look on his face seeped away.

"But I don't remember much about it."

"Slide over," he ordered.

He sat on the bench and carefully propped his lacrosse stick against the arm. Her leg was nearly touching his, warmth permeated through his jeans. She studied the shape of his sharp knee jutting through a hole. He spoke in a low voice, leaning in to her as if imparting some confidential information.

"See, this guy, Candide—I thought that was a girl at first by his name—anyway, he gets caught by this girl's father . . ."

His lips moved, telling a skewed and partially made-up version of a book she knew by heart. A shadow of stubble above his top lip changed in definition and hue as he formed the words. She fixed a look of interest on her face.

" . . . and then Candide ends up marrying this girl, even though she's turned into an ugly skank. Then, after killing all these guys to get her, they end up being farmers."

David shrugged. Cory could think of absolutely nothing to say about his strange rendition of the story. She could point out it was a social satire on society at that time, but figured it would be lost on him. She couldn't resist, however, remarking, "Ignorance is bliss." David's eyes narrowed.

A bus pulled in to the parking lot and angled into a slot. Other buses lined up nose-in facing the school like a herd of yellow wildebeests gathering at a watering hole. Students reached for backpacks and slowly made their way toward them. Cory shouldered her backpack and bent over to grab her gym bag.

"Only losers ride the bus. Look at them!" David sprawled on the bench, his left arm snaking behind Cory's shoulders, his legs spread wide. "Just freshmen and losers. I wouldn't be caught dead riding the bus." He watched the lines of students boarding and shook his head.

Cory leaned back. She didn't want to be thought of as a loser. She didn't move as the kids on her route filed onto bus sixty-seven.

David's attention snapped back. "Right. Hey, um . . . what's your name?"

"Cory. Cory Iverson."

"Yeah, Cory, you play sports or something? Got that huge gym bag and all."

The bus began to pull out of the school's parking lot. Her neighbor, Adam Hollis, had his face pressed against a window, staring out at her. Cory swallowed, wondering what the heck she was doing still sitting there and how she'd get home now. "Nope. I don't play any sports." She hurried to add, "Not at school." She thumbed the pages of the novel. Her feet rested evenly on the pavement, her knees pressed together.

"What are you carrying in this bag then?" He smiled as he hooked the strap with one hand and hauled the partially open bag up onto his lap.

A twinge hit the bottom of her stomach, like a creature with a lot of little, hairy legs was crawling around down there. "Nothing. Really." She pulled the bag gently over onto her own lap. "Gym clothes and stuff."

He stuck his arm elbow-deep into the bag and fished around in it. His hand, rooting in the bottom of the bag, brushed against her thighs.

"What are these?" He pulled out her new running shoes. Not sneakers. She had begged for real running shoes in order to try out for the cross-country team. Her mom had gasped at the price, complaining that Cory already had perfectly good sneakers.

"In my day," her mom said loudly in the shoe store, "we used things up, wore them out, or did without."

Cory winced, recalling that embarrassing scene. Roni talked as if she had lived through the Depression or something. Truthfully, her mom never reused anything, not even a pair of pantyhose.

David stood, holding the new, neon-white, and incredibly expensive running shoes by their laces. He swung them back and forth, dangling from one finger. Cory reached out to grab them, but he snatched them away.

"Nice shoes. You run?"

"Yeah, well, kind of." Cory used to run with her dad back home. He was the one who got her into it. She should have been at tryouts now, not ditching the practice because she was afraid she couldn't do the 5K in time to make the team. When she looked at the shoes dangling in his hands, she heard her mom's voice, "But you're not exactly the athletic type, are you?" Maybe she wasn't.

David took a few steps toward the parking lot with her shoes. Cory leapt up after him. He turned, smiled at her, striding backwards. He swung the shoes, tied together by their laces, in a wide arc.

"Hey," Cory called tentatively. "Wanna give those back?"

A few faces turned their way. Some kids, waiting for rides, jostled each other for a better view. David's smile broadened. His Adam's apple bulged more prominently as he tilted his head back and looked up. In an instant, his arm swung, his shoulder muscle rippled under the light t-shirt, and at the top of the arc, his fingers spread open wide like a Chinese fan. He held that position, arm in midair. The shoes flew upward in a straight trajectory, like a pair of matched doves.

Cory lost sight of them for a split second when the sun's glare caused her to look away. She anticipated the thud, signaling their return to Earth, but there was none. The shoes caught on the overhead power lines, one on each side of the wire. They spun in their individual orbits, hopelessly twisting the laces, entangled with the wire. They eventually stopped twisting and hung, toes down, like her sister's ballet slippers.

"All right!" David pumped an elevated arm. "First try!"

"Why did you do that?" She stood on the spot, gaping at the trapped shoes. Explaining the location of her brand-new running shoes to her mother flashed into her head. "What am I supposed to do now?"

Laughter exploded behind her. She spun. Enter the Greek chorus.

"Hey, sorry," he said in a way that showed he wasn't sorry at all. "I've never got them up there on the first try before." He walked over to the bench to retrieve his lax stick.

"Today's your lucky day, I guess."

A bright yellow car pulled up, and he yanked open the passenger side door.

"See you around, Carrie!"

"Cory," she said under her breath as the car sped off.

In the distance, the first few runners circled back from the first lap of the cross-country run. Cory went back to the bench and stuffed *Candide* into her bag. She stared up again at the dangling shoes and had to turn away, as if the sun were in her eyes. She hefted her backpack on one shoulder, the gym bag on the other and headed down the sidewalk, anticipating how sore she'd be after the half-hour walk home.

Chapter Two

CORY STOOD IN front of the full-length mirror, grabbed and held back the excess flesh at the top of her thighs, and studied the effect.

"See, this is how they should look." She cocked her head. "If I could lose the weight right here, it would be perfect."

She twisted around to check if her sister was listening. Jessica didn't look up. She lounged on one of the twin beds in their room, flipping through a dance magazine.

"That's it. I'm starting a diet tomorrow," Cory said, releasing her captive thighs. She sat on her bed facing Jessica. "You don't believe me."

Jessica closed the magazine and looked up at her older sister.

"I believe you'll *start* tomorrow." She swung her legs—her long, thin legs—over the edge of the bed and sat up. "It's just that you never *finish* anything."

Cory moved away and sat with her back against the wall. "Thanks for the encouragement." Her gaze floated past Jessica out the window.

A neat row of townhouses almost identical to hers stood in three rows. The neighborhood was so different from the big, old Colonial in which she grew up. Just beyond that, another row was under construction. The red clay earth surrounding the site was torn up with crisscrossed tractor treads, which threaded their way to a thin border of trees. Beyond the trees, Cory could make out a field enclosed by a white three-rail fence. The peak of a roof, maybe a barn roof, was barely visible through the trees. She leaned toward the window, hoping to spot horses.

The phone rang downstairs and her mother hollered something. Cory and Jessica looked at each other, but didn't move.

"Did you hear me?" Roni's shrill voice sounded from the bottom of the stairs.

Cory rolled off her bed and followed Jess down the stairs. They trudged into the kitchen where their mom was rinsing out a saucepan. Her flushed face clashed with her hot pink Chanel suit. Makeup, carefully applied that morning, had slid into blue-gray creases on her lids and a smudge of black mascara hung under each eye. Roni shut off the faucet with a sharp turn of her wrist.

"You would think," she began, as she often did. "You would think that knowing all I have to do around here I'd get a little help from you two."

She stared at them in turn, a wet hand on one hip, staining the suit.

Cory shifted to the other foot. Roni was great at making her feel guilty, and even though she didn't know why, that seldom mattered. When she tried to help out, her mother ended up redoing whatever it was Cory had done. Cory took shallow breaths as she waited her mother's next words, as if breathing itself might offend her.

Jessica twisted a strand of blond hair around her index finger, rolling it tight up to her head, then unrolling it. She asked the dreaded question: "What do you want us to do, Mom?"

"Do you want us to set the table?" Cory offered.

"I don't need you both to set the table," Roni said. "Cory, you go get that damn dog of yours, and Jess can take care of the table."

"What do you mean go get him?" Cory's voice rose. "Where is he?"

"He's wandered off again, and now we're getting complaints." Roni rummaged in the pantry, pulling out a jar of spaghetti sauce.

Spaghetti again, Cory groaned inwardly.

"Some woman just called and said to come get him; he's at her place. And she wasn't very nice about it, either."

"Oh, great. So I get to go."

Roni spun around. Her eyes narrowed. "He's your dog, isn't he? You begged for him. You promised you would always take care of him. Am I right?" Her hand went to her hip.

"Yeah, yeah," Cory mumbled. She was tired of this argument about Hershey. She figured her mother hated the chocolate Lab because getting him was something she and her dad had done. Almost seven years ago, they had decided to get a dog and picked him out at the animal shelter. Her dad wanted a Lab to train for hunting, but Hershey turned out to be afraid of loud noises. He gave up on the dog, so he became Cory's responsibility. "Where is he?"

"That farm down the road. Said he'll be in the barn. Bring him home and hurry right back here. I've got lots to get done tonight."

She always has lots to get done. Like getting dressed up to leave on a date.

Cory grabbed the leash by the front door and called back into the kitchen, "It's the farm down the road?"

"How many other farms do you see?"

She slammed the door behind her.

As soon as she stepped outside, the heat and humidity hit her like a heavy, wet blanket. When she walked past the last row of townhouses, the scenery changed. Huge, round bales of dried hay were lined up along the edge of the trees, like giant rolls of shredded wheat. A fence line ran the length of the road, holding captive tall stalks of tired-looking, dry corn. The humid haze carried the earthy, sweet smell of rotting crops and recently spread manure. A shrill birdcall punctuated the air.

The road followed a gradual left turn, delineated by the fence, to the head of a gravel driveway. A dented, metal mailbox painted with number 1325 and the name "Safe Harbor Farm" marked the entrance. Cory looked along the length of the drive and hesitated, imagining some vicious farm dog tearing out from behind a tree. She'd been to plenty of horse barns when she was taking lessons back home and they all had a pack of dogs around somewhere. And not all of them were friendly.

Cory took a deep breath and turned down the gravel entrance. The farm was deserted. No animals—meaning no horses—grazed in the fields that lined the driveway or in the paddocks alongside the barn. A little balloon of hope that had floated in Cory's chest deflated. Not a horse farm after all. Nothing moved in the stifling afternoon heat. A trickle of sweat ran down her side as she lifted a hand to swat a fly buzzing by her ear. The barn, straight ahead, was half-built into the side of a grassy hill. The bottom half was all stone, with tiny windows along the side. She approached the large, open doorway.

She called out a tentative "hello." Silence. Just inside the entrance, she was relieved to find it was much cooler. Walking down the barn's dim center aisle, a sweet scent like newly cut grass saturated the air. There was a steady, pulsating hum from a large fan somewhere farther within and the rhythmic munch-munch of animals pulling at hay nets and bumping up against feed buckets. The dark forms in the stalls became clearer as her eyes adjusted to the dim light.

Horses. Lots of them. Stalls lined each side of the aisle, at least twelve on each side, and every one was occupied. Occupied by horses.

Cory spun around, taking it in. One dark horse in a stall near the entrance moved from the shadowy recess to the iron grill that separated it from the aisle. A velvet muzzle covered with prickly whiskers thrust through the bars. Cory stroked the soft nose with two fingers and sucked in the familiar scent. The horse pulled his head away and raised its upper lip, showing a line of yellow teeth, then poked his nose through the bars again and grabbed at Cory's hand. She pulled away. The rubbery black lips made a flap-flap hollow noise as they slapped together. The horse turned its head sideways in an attempt to get more of his enormous head through the narrow opening.

"He wasn't trying to bite you." A woman appeared at the barn entrance. A pack of small white dogs milled around her, their toenails clicking along the cement aisle.

The woman approached. Her hair was pulled back under a baseball cap that shaded her eyes. She wore a loose tank top, breeches, and heavy boots.

"He's spoiled. Gets far too many treats handed to him." She turned her attention to the horse with the black lips. "Isn't that right, you spoiled thing? You expect everyone you meet has a carrot to hand you. Let's see, do you need some more water?"

She ignored Cory, walked farther down the aisle, and hooked a black bucket under the water spigot to fill it. When the water reached the brim, she carried it to the stall, slid the door open, and swung it onto a hook halfway up the wall without spilling a drop. The muscles along her forearms were threaded with veins.

"You must be here for the dog," the woman said.

Cory breathed a sigh of relief and nodded. *Get Hershey and leave.*

The woman walked down the long aisle of the barn and called over her shoulder, "Well, do you want him or not?" She didn't wait, but opened a door and disappeared inside.

It was a moment before Cory's feet obeyed and she followed. Beyond the door was a small office, dominated by a huge desk. Faded ribbons hung on a drooping string just below ceiling, and a heavy coat of dust and fly droppings covered everything. Behind the desk, Hershey rested in the corner on a small rug. A bowl of water lay within easy reach.

Cory snapped the leash onto the ring of his collar. Hershey thumped his tail rhythmically against the floor but made no effort to get up. She gave a little tug on his collar.

"C'mon, Hersh, let's go."

The dog heaved himself to his feet.

Cory remained by the door and adjusted Hershey's collar. "Thank you for taking care of my dog."

The woman swung the door open and held it with her arm extended, blocking the way.

"I wasn't taking care of your dog. I was keeping him from following after my female and from getting run over. There's a lot more traffic on the roads around here nowadays."

Cory braced for the lecture. She stood still, held her breath, and waited for angry words to wash down around her. She was used to it.

A fly buzzed by. Hershey's lolling tongue dripped a few drops of saliva onto the floor. He looked up at Cory.

"Well, take him home." The woman pushed the door wider.

Cory dived under her arm and down the long barn aisle.

September 18

This was probably the suckiest day so far. First, some lax bro tossed my new sneakers up on an electrical line where they are now permanently stuck. Of course, that wouldn't have happened if I weren't such a loser and had gone to cross-country tryouts after all. But oh well, another thing to hide from Mom. Not like she doesn't have tons of stuff she's hiding from us. Good news, found out we live near a horse farm. Bad news, the lady there, I guess the owner, is not very friendly. Understatement.

Chapter
Three

CORY STOOD IN front of the bulletin board outside the high
school music suite. A cacophony of instruments warming up
in the band room seeped under the door. She reread the notice
on the bulletin board while she debated going in.

All-Star Band Tryouts
September 23, 3:30 p.m.
Band room

It was already quarter past three. Gripping her clarinet case in one
hand, she wiped one palm down the front of her pants and switched
hands before pushing open the door. Cory scanned the room to find an
empty chair in the clarinet section and headed toward it. Once settled,
she propped her sheet music on a stand, flipped open the case and without having to look, grabbed the instrument's familiar pieces, and started
pushing them together. She popped the reed in her mouth to moisten
it and only then took a moment to look around. She knew most of the
kids from regular band, but now they were all here to compete for a
few seats in the All-Star Band. She counted five clarinet players. Good
thing she didn't play the flute—there were at least twenty of them. The

flute group on the opposite side of the room centered around one girl wearing a brightly colored sweater and talking with exaggerated hand gestures.

Cory turned her attention back to the sheet music in front of her and played the first measure of the piece she'd prepared for the audition. At home, she could do it without the music. She had played it repeatedly so many times her fingers flew over the keys from memory. Now the sound that came out was thin and wavering, the notes breathy. She inhaled deeply and started over. A high note squeaked. As she squirmed in the metal chair, the double doors opened and Mr. Schroeder, the band director, walked in. It felt like a ball was wedged under her ribcage making it difficult to breathe.

The director stood in the center of the room, placed a fat notebook with papers spilling out of it on the conductor's stand, and drew a baton out of his suit coat pocket. He tapped the edge of the metal stand. Dozens of eyes fixed in his direction and the room fell silent.

"Let's get started," he said.

He looked like some sort of predatory bird with small, black eyes sweeping over the musicians as if sizing them up for his next meal. His mouth, partially hidden below a thick mustache and a beaklike nose, opened again. He shuffled papers as he spoke.

"This is how it goes, for those of you who haven't been through it. Woodwinds first, then brass, and percussion. You play a prepared piece, then I pick a piece for sight reading. Okay?"

He sounded bored already.

"First up, flutes." He pointed the baton at the flute players.

The girl in the bright sweater sat up taller. Cory released her death grip on the clarinet and glanced down at the pads of her fingers. They were imprinted with little rings from holding them so tightly over the keyholes. *Maybe I don't belong here.*

The sweater girl volunteered to go first. She straightened the sheet music on the stand in front of her, wriggled into an upright position, and brought the flute to her lips. After a deep breath, she began to play. The music was steady and full. She played her piece without faltering over any of the fingering, but at the same time with pauses and crescendos that gave the music depth. Cory methodically fingered the notes of her piece, the tips of her fingers flying over the holes of the instrument, over and over.

The sweater girl finished. A redheaded boy in the flute section was next. Cory had been so intensely concentrating on her piece, she was startled when a tall, thin guy next to her leaned over and whispered in her direction.

"Watch, this will be painful. Mr. Schroeder hates this guy and always picks on him."

The whisperer nodded toward the redhead. The boy lifted his flute to his mouth, the end of it wavering with a constant tremor. A thin sound wandered out the end of his flute, accompanied by the sound of embarrassed throat clearing by a girl in the percussion section. There was a shuffling of feet and a mute dropped to the floor somewhere in the brass section. The boy looked like a cornered mouse. His terrified eyes lifted to the bandleader, the Hawk. The notes became shaky, the volume faded. Everyone watched, waiting for the Hawk to swoop in for the kill. They didn't have to wait long.

"Mr. Thibault!" he shouted. He walked across the room and stood over the kid's music stand.

"Do you suffer from asthma?"

The last quivering note faded, he lowered the flute, and held it protectively across his chest.

"Or bronchitis? Or perhaps you smoke excessively?"

Someone snickered in the back of the room. Thibault dropped his chin to his chest.

"The flute is a wind instrument. What does that mean, Mr. Thibault?" the Hawk continued.

Silence. Thibault hugged his flute. When Cory saw the red blotches bloom above his tightly buttoned collar, she looked away.

"It means you *blow* into it."

The Hawk emphasized the last three words with strokes from his baton on the kid's metal music stand.

Cory rubbed her palms down her thighs. Prickly sweat broke out under her arms, as she tried not to stare at Thibault. The red splotches spread to his face and neck, and it seemed as if his pale blue eyes glistened. The Hawk circled around behind him and stood with his arms folded across his chest.

"Again," he commanded, "and this time let's hear something."

The Hawk rocked back and forth on his heels as Thibault raised his flute and took a ragged breath. He blew across the mouthpiece, producing a quivering note. His fingers missed the correct keys, hitting sharps that made her wince. Cory looked away. Others looked at their feet.

The room was hot. Cory plucked at the front of her shirt, peeling it away from her skin. Thibault kept playing. Her stomach felt sick. She shifted in her chair and watched. The Hawk still stood over the kid from behind, glaring at the top of his head as he faltered measure after measure. Thibault's playing had become so soft it could barely be heard. The sound of blood pumping in Cory's ears crowded out the music. She jiggled her leg on the ball of her foot and looked over at the whisperer, sprawled out in his chair, his clarinet resting comfortably across his lap. He was tall and looked older. A senior. He watched the Hawk toy with his prey, too, but his face was passive, detached.

He turned back in her direction, and Cory felt her face flush, worried he had caught her staring. Leaning over, he whispered, "That poor slob. If there's one thing the bandleader can't stand, it's incompetence. Don't bother showing up if you're not prepared." He shook his head from side to side. "Schroeder's going to finish him off."

Something in her stomach roiled. Was she prepared? She thought so when she signed up for this, but now she wasn't so sure. What would this guy do to her? *I don't even want to be in the All-Star Band. Regular school band is good enough.* As if someone else had control of her body, Cory reached down and pulled the bell off her clarinet. She yanked the pieces apart and stuffed them into the case. The whisperer looked at her and a confused expression swept over his face. She snapped the case shut, grabbed the handle, and raced for the band room doors. As she threw her body against them, she heard the director's voice behind her.

"I guess we scared another one off. Or perhaps she just couldn't stand Mr. Thibault's playing!"

Nervous laughter leaked out of the band room as the doors swung shut behind Cory. Her clarinet case bumped against her shin as she ran down the corridor.

Chapter
Four

WHEN CORY ARRIVED home, Jessica was sitting on the living room floor with her legs spread wide in a V-shape. She leaned over one leg, grabbed an ankle, and pulled her torso flat against one thigh. A muffled groan escaped her folded-up posture.

"Why do you do that if it hurts?" Cory asked but didn't really care.

"I have to get a better turnout. So how was the band thing? When do you find out if you made it?"

Cory threw the clarinet case on the couch and went to the kitchen. "I didn't go," she called back, trying to sound casual. She opened a cabinet and stared inside. None of the boxes of cookies or chips appealed to her.

Jessica appeared at the entrance to the kitchen, leaning against the doorway.

"What happened?"

Cory turned her back and opened the refrigerator. Now that the immediate fear was past, she felt embarrassed. Embarrassed about being such a quitter—or rather, not even trying. What was she supposed to say? *I dived out of there before I even played a note? I left because I was afraid of the bandleader?*

Jessica was trying to be nice, for a change, which made Cory feel even meaner for some reason. "Nothing happened, okay?" She slammed the refrigerator door and brushed past Jessica as the front door opened.

Her mom walked in from work, tossed her purse on the nearest chair, and stared as Cory walked past and ran up the stairs.

Taking the steps two at a time, she blew into her room and flopped across the bed. She could hear her mom and Jess talking about her downstairs as she thumbed through Jess's discarded magazine.

"What's with her now?" Roni asked.

Jess replied, "Band tryouts today."

Cory could hear them from her room, through the open door. She missed some of the conversation, as they must have moved toward the kitchen. Then she heard her mother's voice, probably standing near the bottom of the stairs.

"She didn't even go? What's that girl's problem anyway?"

Cory heard what sounded like Roni rummaging in her purse and strained to catch her words.

"Why am I paying for lessons, so she can do nothing with them? Why can't she follow through with anything?"

She couldn't hear Jess's reply. Just an empty silence until her mother continued.

"That's no excuse. That's the end of it. I'm not throwing hard-earned money down the drain for lessons she doesn't even appreciate." A small thump sounded like her mother had thrown something.

Cory jumped up and stood next to the open door, listening. She wanted to run to the top of the stairs and yell down at them: *Shut up, just shut up. You don't even know what you're talking about!* Instead, she slammed the bedroom door. She didn't go downstairs for dinner, and no one came up looking for her.

September 23
My life sucks. I don't even want to talk about what happened today.

Chapter
Five

CORY AWOKE TO the sound of the downstairs phone ringing. She turned over, pulled the covers around her, and listened to see if someone would answer it. Nope. It kept ringing, forcing her consciousness from the soft tenderness of sleep to the sharp-edged memory of last night. The events flashed through her mind. Slamming the door, her mother's voice calling her a quitter . . . not worth the trouble, a waste of money on lessons. She had waited upstairs, waiting for the call to dinner that never came. Waiting for someone to find out if she was okay. She fell asleep waiting.

The phone stopped ringing. She flipped the covers back and rolled out of bed. Last night, she had resolved to get an afterschool job to pay for her lessons. Maybe some more lessons or a better teacher and she'd be able to move up to second chair, at least. Cory stood and stretched. The job idea seemed perfectly reasonable last night, but this morning, the prospect of a sixteen-year-old with no transportation finding a job here in Hicksville seemed far-fetched.

At least it was Saturday. The house would be empty with Jess at the ballet studio teaching the little kids and Roni doing her Saturday errands somewhere. Good. After getting dressed, she hopped downstairs to get some coffee and that's when she noticed the note on the counter, written in her mother's spidery handwriting.

Pick up Hershey at that farm. Woman called again this AM. Get him ASAP.

She couldn't believe it and had to read the note twice. How was Hershey getting out? Jess was probably just sticking him in the backyard in the morning and forgetting to bring him in. It was just like her—her head always in dance mode. Now, not only did she have to go back there to fetch him, she was sure to get a lecture from that woman this time.

Cory took a sip of coffee and poured the rest down the drain. She slipped into her sneakers without lacing them and trudged to the door.

When she turned down the driveway by the Safe Harbor Farm mailbox, a sweet scent wafted through the air. Someone cutting grass. It was the smell of summer, the essence of the whole season packed into each breath. Just before the entrance to the barn, a gray-striped tiger cat fell into step beside her.

Today the barn was empty except for one horse standing in the center aisle on cross ties. He was enormous, blocking the aisle. Cory stood in the doorway, called a timid *hello,* and waited. She peered inside. The woman she met yesterday appeared from the back of the barn accompanied by a man wearing coveralls.

"Take him off the cross ties," the woman ordered.

They seemed preoccupied. Cory figured she'd wait a minute and see if they noticed her.

The man reached up to unhook the cross ties and clipped a lead rope into a metal loop on the underside of the halter and stood, feet spread apart. He was tall but frail looking. Bits of white hair showed from under his billed cap. She figured he must be old—at least sixty. He glanced up and locked eyes with Cory, then lifted one finger as a sign to wait. Then he turned and nodded at the woman.

"He really gave me a fight this morning. Guess I shouldn't have tried to change the bandage by myself," she said, looking down the horse's front leg. She reached up and gave his neck a solid pat, then took a deep breath.

The horse had a front leg wrapped in a thick, white bandage from his hoof halfway up his leg. As soon as the woman squatted down alongside the bandaged leg, the horse immediately shot backwards a few steps, pulling the man off his stance.

"Here we go," she sighed.

She slowly stood up, walked back a few steps to where the horse now stood, and patted his shoulder.

Cory sucked in a deep breath, surprised she'd been holding it.

"Keep a firm hold of him, Jack, but if he really panics, don't fight him."

He winked and smiled at her, then addressed the horse. "We know our job, don't we, fella? Vee thinks she's the only one around here who can handle you."

Vee? A strange name.

Vee shot Jack a disgusted look and eased her way alongside the injured leg. She unwound the bandage, revealing a horrible cut. The ragged edges of the wound were gray and weeping.

"Looks bad," the man commented flatly. "Too bad. Will be an ugly scar."

Vee went over to a cabinet on the wall and removed an armload of stuff—jars and gauze and bottles. She set it down on a nearby hay bale and stood back to assess the wound, sliding her fingers into her back pockets, elbows sticking out like wings. She cocked her blond head.

"Yup," she sighed. "Every time I turn him outside, he tries to self-destruct."

They both stood in silence with their backs to Cory, staring at the leg like they were in no hurry.

Finally, Vee turned and grabbed a brown bottle, unscrewed the top, and poured the contents down the front of the horse's leg. The liquid bubbled and hissed as it slid into the wound, becoming a white foam, then puddled on the floor. The horse snorted and lifted the injured leg.

Vee patted his neck. "C'mon, c'mon," she said soothingly. "Hydrogen peroxide doesn't hurt. You're just mad I got the better of you."

She reached for another jar and sponge. An acrid odor permeated the air as Vee poured a bronze-colored liquid onto the sponge. She leaned over and wiped two strokes down the horse's leg. The horse froze, then shot backwards with his head up and eyes rolling. Jack was pulled along with him, taking giant steps to keep up. Cory stepped backward, even though she was well out of the way.

"There's a lot of dead tissue that should be removed," he said.

Vee moved deeper into the barn where the horse and man now stood. She leaned over once more, sponge poised above the leg. Suddenly, the horse exploded. He twisted and skittered backwards a few steps, but Jack stopped him with two sharp jerks on the lead rope. Instead, the horse stood up on his hind legs. He was huge. He tottered, as if he would fall over backwards. His hind legs slipped on the cement floor.

"Jack, let go of him!"

Jack let the rope slip through his fingers and stepped away. The horse crashed back onto the floor, causing sparks to fly from his front shoes. Vee stepped toward him, grabbing for the dangling rope.

"Ho, ho. Easy, you idiot. It's okay."

The horse went up again and hovered in the air. From where Cory stood, it looked as if his hooves were just above the woman's head. Every muscle in Cory's body was taut. She thought about rushing in, trying to help, but wasn't sure what she should do. The horse came down, but gathered himself and launched upwards again with tremendous force. He shot straight up, smashing his head into a light bulb and crashed back down in a shower of broken glass. He froze. Dark splotches of sweat stained his neck and flanks.

Vee, still clinging to the rope, pulled him forward and away from the broken glass. "Let's see if he learned anything," she said.

She bent over and dabbed at the wound. The horse danced from one foot to another but didn't try to rise on his hind legs. Vee managed to medicate the wound and wind a bandage around the leg again. She straightened up and brushed a stray hair back away from her forehead.

"Well, that's done until tonight," she said.

Jack appeared from the back end of the barn, tossed a blue plaid sheet over the horse's back, and buckled it into place while Vee slid an overturned bucket next to the horse and stepped up on it to inspect the top of his head.

"Good news—no cuts," she reported to Jack below.

She stepped down from the bucket and turned to face Cory.

"Ah, the dog girl. Thanks for waiting, c'mon." She nodded in the direction of the small office where Hershey was kept the last time he ran off.

Cory stood stupidly rooted to her spot in the doorway, surprised to realize the woman knew she was there all along. She stepped into the barn, avoiding the glass shards, and gingerly squeezed by the horse as Jack led him away.

Inside the office, Hershey jumped up to greet Cory. She snapped the lead onto his collar and murmured an apology for having bothered her again. Vee pushed up both sleeves on an oversized gray shirt that was torn on the elbow and sprouting wisps of hay. She removed a vial from the refrigerator and started filling syringes from it, lining them up on the desk and counting under her breath. Otherwise, the room was awkwardly silent. Cory wondered if she should leave and turned to the door.

"He's a nice dog . . . four, five, six . . . you really should keep an eye on where he goes . . . seven, eight, nine . . ." She looked up suddenly, directly into Cory's eyes. "Your phone number's on Hershey's collar, but not the address. You live around here?"

The lady had brown eyes, big and dark. Her face was tanned and deeply lined, though Cory figured she wasn't old. But not that young, either. She was that age that Cory could never pinpoint in adults— somewhere between thirty and fifty, maybe. Her hair, sun bleached and very blond, was tied back from her forehead, but small unruly strands had fallen out and hung like wisps of straw around her face. She unconsciously swept them away with the back of her hand as she worked filling and counting syringes.

"Larchdale Commons, the townhouses down the road." Cory nodded in the general direction of home.

"Used to be a field there. At least Hershey doesn't wander far before he stops." She turned to the dog. "Right, fella?"

Hershey thumped his tail against the floor. Cory made another move for the door, but before she could leave, Jack stepped into the office, which grew uncomfortably crowded.

"Jack!" Vee greeted him like they hadn't just been together two minutes ago. "Do you remember that old Larchdale place? The abandoned estate house and the two hundred acres?"

"Sure do, Vee. Was a great place to work the young horses on their open gallops."

Cory's thoughts wandered, since she was obviously no longer part of this conversation. *Wonder what Vee is short for: Vanessa, Victoria? Nah, she could never be a Victoria. Vampira? . . .* She realized that they were both looking at her. Did they want her to comment on the stupid Larchdale Commons development or something?

"An open field, huh? It's hard to imagine." In fact, she couldn't imagine the cluster of townhouses once having been an estate. Her words hung in the air, sounding dumb, but they didn't seem to notice.

"Guess we better get going. I got three horses to ride before it gets too hot." Vee reached up and rubbed the base of her neck.

Cory brightened. It looked like an opportunity for a graceful exit.

"You're doing too much, Vee. And that neck's acting up again, isn't it?" Jack asked.

Cory wondered . . . was Jack her father?

"Give it a rest."

"Now, I'm serious. You're not so young anymore."

Vee looked at him with an exaggerated expression of offense.

"I'm serious." He continued, "With old injuries acting up, you've got to get some help around here."

Cory skirted around Jack and stood at the door, her hand on the knob.

"Like this girl here."

She stiffened.

"You like horses?"

He *was* talking to her. Cory stammered, "Yeah, sure, but . . ."

"And she lives close by. She could come after school and help out. Do evening feedings."

Now Vee was looking at her, too. She cocked her head, sizing Cory up.

"Do you know anything about horses?" she challenged, as if Cory had come up with the idea. Although it was a good idea—she needed a job. And Cory did know horses. Back home, Dad used to drive her to take lessons. Well, until he left.

"I used to ride."

Jack patted her back. "So, we can teach her whatever she needs to know."

Silence. They both continued to stare at her.

"Did some eventing. Small stuff, though. Mostly hunters." Cory shrugged.

Vee softened, apparently considering the idea. Cory looked from one to the other. She should say something. She had wanted to find a job today, and this would be a chance to pay for her own clarinet lessons, or at least help out some. Not to mention the added benefit of being around horses again.

"I get out of school at two-thirty, but I don't get home till after three."

"Okay." Vee looked sort of surprised she was agreeing to this. She nodded, as if to convince herself. "Okay," she repeated. "Jack, you work it out with her. I've got to get on some horses." She turned and left the office.

Cory looked at Jack, who smiled at her.

"Now that I've roped you in, what's your name?"

"Cory Iverson."

"Can you start Sunday morning?"

"Tomorrow? I guess."

"You'll be a big help around here."

His eyes were almost clear blue, like a big husky dog she had once seen. He reached down and stroked the top of Hershey's head.

"She's not really sure she wants me, though." Cory nodded toward the door where Vee had exited. They heard the sound of a stall door sliding open and the clop of horse hooves retreating down the cement aisle.

Jack looked at the wall separating the office from the barn aisle as if he could see right through it. "Don't worry. Vee talks to everyone like that. I like to say she's direct. Treats me like excess baggage sometimes. Good thing I'm not the sensitive type." He chuckled.

Cory smiled. "What time should I be here?"

He moved his focus to the right corner of the room, as if the answer were painted on the wall.

"Oh, seven ought to be plenty of time. We'll have all the horses in by then."

Cory stifled a sigh. *Seven. On Sunday morning?*

Jack must have read something in her expression. He patted her shoulder. "Horses get hungry early." He gestured for her to precede him through the office door and escorted her to the entrance of the barn. "See you tomorrow."

Cory started down the driveway with Hershey in tow but turned to look back. Jack stood in the doorway of the barn and waved to her. Hershey strained at the leash, as the gray cat leapt onto a fence post.

Just what had she gotten herself into?

Chapter Six

CORY POURED SOME dog crunchies into Hershey's bowl, grabbed a bottle of Coke out of the refrigerator, and flopped down on the couch in the living room. A car pulled up outside. She propped up on one elbow to watch as Jess and Roni climbed out and reached into the backseat for armloads of pink and purple fluff. Roni's rapid step on the walkway announced her arrival at the front door and broadcast her mood. Quick, staccato. Not good. Keys fumbled in the lock, but Cory didn't open the door for her.

Jess squeezed through the partially opened door, obscured by a billowy cloud of ballet skirts, which were dumped into the nearest chair. Roni, behind Jess, glared at Cory, slammed her purse on the end table, and went upstairs.

"Guess what?" Jess asked. "I've been asked to try out for *Shakespeare's Glen!*"

"What's that?" Cory asked without interest, but swung her legs around and sat up. The name sounded dumb. It probably was dumb.

"It's the best preprofessional program in the country, that's all. And it's in *Massachusetts.*" Jess put particular emphasis on Massachusetts, probably figuring *that*, at least, would grab Cory's interest.

"Preprofessional program? Why don't they just call it overpriced ballet school? Why do ballet nerds always have to have some special name for everything?" She checked for a reaction from Jess, some sign she had hit a nerve. Jess didn't seem to have heard, preoccupied with hanging up the flouncy skirt of pink netting. "Sounds great, Jess, but how do you think you're going to commute to school in Massachusetts?" Cory snorted.

"It's a summer program," Jess continued, "and I could live with Dad up there." Jess glanced up at the ceiling, assessing whether Roni was within earshot. Evidently, Jess's idea was the reason for Roni's foul mood.

Cory pulled Jess into the kitchen. "Boy, you've got a lot of nerve, not only bringing up the forbidden subject, but actually suggesting you go *live* with him! I'm surprised you're still breathing."

Jess pulled a can of Diet Coke out of the refrigerator and leaned against the counter. "I don't care. I really want to go, and that's the only way we could afford it. I'm going if I get the scholarship—and it's a big if. It only pays tuition, not living expenses."

A door upstairs slammed.

"Yeah, but now you've really set her off," Cory said, sliding a ring up and down her finger. "She'll be ranting and raving about Dad now all the time."

"I don't care. Let her rant all she wants." Jess kept her voice low.

"Yeah, sure, you'll be gone dancing your toes off and I'll be home listening to her breaking dishes and screaming about all the rotten things he did to her."

Jess looked away. "I'm sorry about that part."

Cory felt somewhat badly that she had put such a damper on Jess's big news, but plowed on just the same. "So, how about Jeff? Have you told 'love bug' yet that you'll be out of reach all summer? Bet he won't like that."

Jess poured half the can of Coke down the drain and pitched the empty in the trash. "You really need to get something going in your own life, you know that?" She pulled the pins out of her bun, shook her head, and let her hair fall like yellow liquid over her shoulders.

"I do have stuff going on. I got a job today."

Jess's eyebrows shot up. "You're kidding. Where?"

Cory hoisted herself up on the counter and decided to drop the boyfriend thing with Jess.

"At the farm where Hershey runs off to. I'm going to help take care of the horses."

"That sounds like a cool job," Jess said as if Cory had told her she was going to be cleaning out hog troughs or something. "Especially for you. The horse thing and all." Jess made a face as if someone had opened the garbage pail.

"Yeah, well, I'll like it, and besides, I'll be able to pay some for music lessons so I won't have to listen to Mom complain about wasting money and all."

"That's cool. So, how much are they going to pay you?"

Cory hesitated. Her dangling feet swung back and forth.

"They haven't told me. I'm supposed to start tomorrow. At seven." Cory jumped down from the counter. "Speaking of lessons, guess I'd better go practice."

"Yeah, well, don't wake me when you leave tomorrow."

Upstairs, Cory pulled the clarinet case out from under her bed and stared at it. She'd had to beg for lessons. Her mom told her she'd just quit when it got hard and she wasn't wasting the money if Cory wasn't going to do something with it. Cory had shown her—she was still playing six years later and she was in marching band. But still . . . The fun had worn off and her music teacher was giving her harder stuff to learn. She really wasn't putting in enough practice time lately. She thought of quitting, but how could she now? Instead of playing, she stood up, collapsed onto her bed and flipped the end of the spread over her. She could hear her mother in the next room, slamming drawers and muttering to herself. Cory drew her knees up to her chest and shut her eyes. She knew how it would be if Jess went to live with Dad next summer. She felt her mother's complaints all around her, penetrating her skin like a thousand stinging needles. Something crashed into the sink and set her heart pounding.

The bathroom door slammed and muffled the words her mother shouted to no one but herself. It was the same conversation in an endless loop: *How can he get away with this? What does he think we are supposed to live on? How could he walk out on them and ruin her life?* Cory pulled the spread up over her head. It got quiet.

Cory's muscles relaxed a bit, though not completely. She'd been fooled before. Just when she thought it was over, her mother would start up again, sometimes even worse. Breaking stuff and hollering so the neighbors could hear her. Cory flipped off the bedspread and walked across the room to peer out into the hallway. The door to her mother's room across the hall was ajar. Roni lay spread on her back across the bed in the dim room, one arm flung over her eyes. She'd been going to bed earlier and earlier lately, and when she did, she often slept the rest of the night. Cory knew why—the pills—but if they kept Roni asleep all night, she didn't really care. Stepping quietly to Roni's door and pulling it shut, a voice in her head said, *Horses get hungry early.* Cory was glad she had somewhere to go tomorrow.

September 27

I have a job now! It'll be cool to be around horses again. The worst thing is Jess is probably skipping off to Mass next summer for some stupid ballet camp and leaving me here alone. Mom's getting worse. I found some of her pill bottles and they were empty already. She woke me up the other night and told me Dad was the one who put that scratch on her car. I told her Dad wasn't here and she just stared at me like she didn't understand. Then she said I was taking his side and left. I wish she'd just get over it.

Chapter
Seven

CORY STOOD IN the stall looking at her hands. Red welts were already forming at the base of each finger and she had a huge blister filled with some disgusting fluid in the crook of her thumb. She kept meaning to get some gloves, like Jack told her to do after the first day on the job, but it had already been a week and they hadn't paid her yet. How stupid it was to agree to a job without first negotiating the terms.

She plunged the pitchfork into the dirty bedding, drove it in deeper with a jab from her foot, and lofted another forkful of wet shavings and manure into the wheelbarrow. A band of muscles along her back tightened. Days had passed of doing not much else but stalls and cleaning tack. She had hoped she would be working more with the horses, like grooming and turnout. And the money thing. She *had* to say something.

She propped the fork against the back wall of the stall and stood on tiptoes to look out the little window. After hours spent in the dark barn, the brightness of the sunlight made her eyes water. It was still warm for late September, but it was getting dark earlier. The quality of the sunlight had changed from intense white to a softer gold. Colors drank up the golden light and reflected it back in the intense green grass, dazzling white fence rails, and glossy chestnut horses. Cory sighed and turned away from the window, temporarily blinded by the dimness inside.

"Something the matter?"

Vee stood in the open doorway of the stall holding a saddle balanced on her hip and a bridle slung over one shoulder.

Cory squinted, still not focusing. "Not really."

"But there is something," Vee insisted. She hefted the saddle higher up for a better grip.

"I was just, well, I was wondering about salary. I have some stuff I'm supposed to be paying for . . ."

"Ah, that." Vee looked relieved. "Didn't Jack take care of it?"

Cory shook her head.

"C'mon." She indicated the direction of the office with a nod and this time hiked the heavy saddle up with her knee. "Jack was supposed to write out the checks Friday, but like a lot of things around here, it fell through the cracks." She walked down the aisle and glanced over her shoulder. "But you have to speak up! Things get forgotten around here all the time."

Cory followed her into the office. Vee dumped the saddle on a rack, wrote out a check, and handed it to Cory. She stared at Vee's backward slanted handwriting on her first paycheck. The figure made her heart flutter. She folded it, slipped it into the front pocket of her jeans, and throughout the rest of the day dipped a finger inside to touch the corner, making sure it was still there. That would pay for some lessons. Maybe more.

It was getting dark and about time to leave, when Vee called her from the other end of the barn. After topping off a water bucket, Cory dragged the hose down the aisle to coil it up before checking to see what Vee wanted. She found Vee next to a dark bay horse, lifting a saddle up onto his back. She buckled the girth, led him down the aisle, and out into the waning sunlight. Cory dropped the hose and followed, not sure whether Vee even remembered calling her. That forgetting habit she claimed to have.

The sun was low, casting the outdoor arena in cool shadows. The bluestone footing made a soft shush-shush noise as Vee led the horse in and adjusted the tack one more time. She turned to Cory and handed her a helmet.

"This is Pressman. Want a leg up?" Vee laced her fingers and held them out like a sacred offering. "Part of your compensation package—free riding lessons." She smiled up at Cory from her crouched position.

Without a word, Cory shoved the helmet down onto her head and attached the chinstrap. She could smell the horse as she approached—so familiar, so comforting. Her heart started a tap dance against her breastbone as she bent her knee and placed her shin into Vee's laced fingers. In an instant, she was lofted up into the air and onto the back of the horse. Her feet easily found the stirrups as she lifted the reins. From the saddle, he seemed even taller, so different from the small, dullish horses she had ridden in her lessons back home. Her legs draped around his barrel as he stepped off with an enormous stride. Cory figured she must look like a grinning idiot, but it felt so good to be back on a horse.

Her clenched back muscles relaxed and she rolled her hips in the saddle to match the horse's big step. The warmth of his sides brushing against her calves and the scent carried on a breeze reminded her of the hours she used to spend hanging around the barn at her lesson stable at home, getting ready for shows, watching her trainer ride and helping out. She'd missed this, but until now, she hadn't allowed herself to think about it much.

"He likes you." Vee's voice suddenly grabbed her attention. "You said you've ridden hunters?"

Cory shrugged. "Yeah, mostly showed hunters." The kinds of horses she got to show back home were nothing like the ones in Vee's barn—jumpers. Cory had ridden whatever she could. After a while, the owners started putting her on the new school horses when they came in for evaluation. Nothing like getting on a strange horse and trying to figure out their buttons. Some were mechanical and safe horses you could point at a fence and forget it, while others were so sensitive and explosive you had to manage every step of the ride. Those horses didn't stick around in a lesson program for long, but Cory sure got an education riding them while they were there.

"I took lessons for a few years," she told Vee. "Did some schooling shows, nothing big really." She turned the horse to face Vee. "But that was in Massachusetts, before we came here a couple months ago."

Vee only nodded.

An image of her dad squeezing her tightly to his chest floated up before her eyes. She was only nine and she had just won her first ribbon. She remembered her dad smelling of a mix of cigarettes and that minty gum he always chewed to mask it. He promised to buy her a horse if she kept winning ribbons like that. It almost hurt, he hugged so hard.

"Okay then. We'll start slow until you get your legs back." Vee lowered a jump into a small cross rail. "Guess I should have gotten your mom to sign a release slip before we started the lesson." Vee pulled at the visor of her cap. "Oh, well, just promise me you won't fall off, okay?"

She didn't fall off. In fact, she rode well considering the time away. Afterwards, when she slid down from the horse, her knees buckled a bit upon meeting the ground. They felt spaghetti-like as she walked back inside the barn to untack. She must have done okay because Vee even mentioned the possibility of doing some exercise riding. Maybe. In the meantime, lessons in addition to a paycheck was a pretty good deal. After she cleaned the bridle and lifted the saddle onto its rack in the tackroom, Vee appeared behind her with some lunging equipment.

"You seemed to click with Pressman pretty well," she said. "Some horses you get comfortable with right away, others take time. Sort of like driving a strange car. You got to figure out how much gas to give it."

"And there're some you never want to get used to. But I really liked him."

Vee smiled. "He's a good guy. Was my jumper horse for years."

"So he's a horse you clicked with." Cory tried out Vee's expression.

"Sure. He wasn't too complicated a ride and has a generous nature." Vee stared at the halter in her hands like she was remembering something. Cory was about to leave when Vee continued, "But then there's that one horse you really click with. The once-in-a-lifetime horse." Her eyes moved away from Cory's face and scanned the row of saddles.

"So Pressman wasn't your once-in-a-lifetime horse?"

"No. He's a great guy—don't get me wrong—but not *the one*."

Cory stifled a snort. "Sounds like you're talking about a boyfriend instead of a horse."

One side of Vee's mouth turned upwards. "Yeah, it's kind of the same thing. You find that one you really love and everything goes great when you're together. The horse almost reads your mind. He forgives your mistakes and even saves your butt when you screw up. Only thing is, it's tough if he isn't your horse. It's as bad as falling in love with some-one else's husband."

"Someone else owned him?"

"Owned a piece of him."

"So what happened to him? Where's he now?"

Vee turned quickly to adjust the reins on a bridle hanging along the wall. "Dead now." She looked back, like she wanted to say something else, but instead gathered the tack she needed for her next ride.

Cory felt the air go out of the room. Vee didn't seem to want to look at her and was busy piling saddle pads and girths across her arm. Did she say something wrong?

"I'll head home now."

Vee nodded.

Chapter
Eight

CORY STUFFED HER dirt-encrusted jeans into the clothes hamper. Her back muscles complained as she leaned over to push them down to the bottom. And not just her back—other muscles, like where her legs attached to her hips and her calves, were all stiff. The stiffness unknotted when she stepped into the shower and let a cascade of warm water pour over her head and down her back. She started humming a song.

"Where did this dirt come from? Cory!" Her mother's voice pierced through the closed door and the rush of water.

Under the stream of water, her shoulder muscles clenched again at the sound of her name. She mentally scanned the situation downstairs, wondering what dirt was upsetting her mom.

"Cory, get out here!"

She shut off the water, wrapped a towel around her wet hair, and grabbed a robe off the hook. She opened the door and peered out.

"What's the matter, Mom?"

"What's the matter?" she repeated. "The matter is the stairs are covered in filth from that barn."

Cory had left her shoes outside the front door, as always, when she came home from the barn, but sawdust from the stalls had clung to her socks and in the creases of her jeans. She took a step out into the hall, looked down and saw the sprinkling on each step.

"Don't worry, Mom. I'll vacuum it."

Her mom turned from her post at the bottom of the stairs without a word and disappeared into the kitchen.

Cory ran downstairs. The ancient Electrolux was in the very back of the hall closet under a curtain of coats and ballet costumes, which Cory impatiently swept aside. The machine weighed a ton. Tugging on it made the muscles of her back burn. Just as she pulled it out, a waterfall of gossamer tutus and other ballet flotsam rained down on her head. She shoved and kicked them back inside the closet, plugged in the vacuum, and started pushing it toward the stairs. Suddenly, the machine's steady drone ceased, choked, and shut off. Cory turned over the nozzle and saw a pink pointe shoe in its maw, the ribbons hopelessly sucked in and wrapped around the beater brushes.

"Hey!" Jessica yelped from the front doorway. "What's going on?"

Jess dropped an enormous dance bag on a nearby chair and dashed across the living room to rescue the dangling shoe. The ribbons were torn and the whole thing was covered with some black, greasy stuff.

"What are you doing?" Jess pulled the shoe free. "These are my best pointe shoes and now they're ruined."

"Don't leave your junk all over the place then," Cory shot back.

Jessica snatched up the shoe's mate from the floor and slung her gym bag over her shoulder, the weight of it pulling her tiny frame to one side.

"Sor-ry," Cory said.

Jess looked down at the ruined toe shoe, flung it against the wall, and trudged upstairs.

Cory saw her mom heading back into the living room and switched on the vacuum. Its drone filled the emptiness in the room.

October 2

Vee let me ride her horse today. Not just ride him,

but she's giving me lessons. So I not only got a job so I can keep up clarinet, but also can start riding and maybe showing again. Her horse, Pressman, used to be a Grand Prix jumper, so he totally knew everything and I just had to think what I wanted and he'd do it. It was incredible. I don't know about Vee, though. I must have brought up a really bad memory about a horse she used to have, because she was way more than just sad when she talked about him. Actually, she wouldn't talk about him, that's just it. She acts weird when certain subjects come up, I've noticed. Also Jess is pissed off at me (again!) but what's new there?

Chapter Nine

CORY RIFFLED THROUGH her locker crammed with paper, books, gym clothes, and spare shoes, looking for her calculus book. Digging around in the bottom, her fingers hit upon the book under a pile of cast-off athletic socks and old lunch bags. She frowned when she pulled it out and spotted the folded paper sticking up from within its pages. Math homework she had started in study period Friday but forgot to finish. A bell rang down the hall. Five minutes until class—calculus class. Not her favorite. She opened the book enough to pull out the paper, sighed, and slammed it shut.

"Hey, clarinet girl!" a voice called from behind her back. "You've got the locker next to mine."

Cory turned to find the tall boy from All-Star Band tryouts standing beside her, spinning the combination of a locker just above and to the right of hers. She'd gotten in the habit of watching him at regular band practices, sitting in the first clarinet section, far away from her seat in the back row. She hoped he wouldn't bring up the tryouts now. She didn't want to be reminded of her humiliating bolt for the door, much less talk about it. "Oh, hi," she responded and turned to face the open lockers. His was nearly empty.

"Hey, whatever happened to you that day? You left band . . ."

Here it comes. Cory gave a noncommittal shrug.

"You get sick or something?"

It was weeks ago. "Oh, yeah." She closed her locker with more attention than necessary. "The whole thing made me sick, actually."

"Yeah?" He sounded intrigued. "You're right, it was pathetic."

Cory looked up at him. Auburn highlights tinted long brown hair that stuck out in every direction. It nearly masked his eyes, fringed with dark lashes and set in an angular face bisected by a long, straight nose. It was an unusual face, Cory decided, but altogether not bad to look at. A dark shadow of stubble covered his cheeks and chin. When she realized she was staring, she shifted her gaze down to the book in her hand.

Calculus!

"I have to get to class," she said and hurried down the hall. He fell in step beside her with an easy, loping stride.

"Calc?" He nodded toward her book.

"Yeah. I hate it. Didn't finish my homework, either."

Breathless and jogging down the hall, she dodged a teeming artery of human bodies entering and exiting classes. He strode along beside her as kids stepped aside to make way for him.

"Let me see." He held out a long-fingered hand, palm up.

"What?" Cory glanced at him but kept walking.

"Your homework. C'mon." His fingers beckoned.

Her face felt hot. "Nah, no big deal. It's okay."

"This it?" He pulled out the manila-colored paper extending from her book. Her hand reached out to grab it back but instead stopped and dropped to her side. He was already reading it. After a few minutes, he stopped and placed the paper against the wall to jot down some figures. When he handed it back to her, he snapped a smart salute.

"Mission accomplished."

Cory gazed down at the paper in her hands. His tight, bold writing had completed the remaining three calculus problems and corrected the answer of one she had already done. She looked up at him. "Thanks. I guess."

"Don't worry. They're right."

Cory flashed a tentative smile and rushed down the hall and into class.

"Homework. Pass it forward." Mr. Brown's eyes bored into her as she dropped the sheet on his desk and slipped into her seat.

Chapter Ten

THE SOUND OF tires crunching on the barn's gravel driveway propelled the pack of Jack Russell terriers to their feet. They ran out of the barn to investigate. Cory leaned her head out the doorway to see who was coming. A dark gray sedan pulled up right in front of the barn's opening. The car didn't belong to any of Vee's clients. After a month of watching everyone come and go, she pretty much recognized them all.

As Cory stood in the doorway, a dark cloud to the west passed over, casting a shadow over the barn. A gust of wind flowed down the aisle and around her legs. Maybe a storm was coming.

The woman inside the car set down her cell phone and leaned over to look in the rearview mirror. She formed her mouth into an "O" and applied a thick gloss of lipstick in two fluid strokes. The door opened and she emerged dressed in a peach linen suit. A pair of dark glasses perched on top of her head held her straight ash-blond hair away from her face. She passed by Cory as if she were invisible, leaving a cloud of spicy perfume in her wake. The hollow sound of high heels on the cement aisle and the delicate tinkle of bangle bracelets rang out as this stranger glanced briefly at each stall nameplate, then zeroed in on one. She stood in front of Prophet's stall, staring in at him.

"Sure hope you can do all they say you can, big guy," she said to the horse and reached out for the latch. The stall door slid open a foot and abruptly stopped. Vee appeared behind the woman, her foot propped against the door to keep it from sliding farther.

The blond's head snapped around.

"What are you doing here, Angela?" Vee's voice was scary, almost menacing. Cory had never heard her speak to anyone like that. Vee stared eye to eye with the woman—they were the same height in spite of the stranger's high heels.

Angela moved back a step. Regaining her composure, she whipped off the sunglasses, flipped her hair back with a toss of her head, and smiled. "I came to take a look at my new horse." A bangled arm reached out for the stall latch to slide the door open, but Vee's foot remained planted against it. Angela glared at the source of the problem as Vee gave the door a shove to slide it shut.

Angela's smile broadened. "Now, Vee, that's no way to treat a client."

So she was a client. Vee sure wasn't acting like it.

Vee stood, her foot against the door. "What are you talking about?"

"This is my horse now." The lady nodded toward the big bay, eyeing them both through the grill. "Aren't you, boy?" She turned to him. "We'll see if you're as good as they say."

Angela told Vee she now owned the horse and was here to arrange for his delivery.

Vee's foot dropped to the aisle with a thud. Angela gave a nod to her, slid the door open, and gingerly took one step toward the curious horse. She raised her arm to pet his neck, but the horse shied away from the jingling glitter on her arm.

Vee grinned. "Still have a way with horses, I see."

Angela stepped out of the stall, shaking the sawdust off her feet like a cat exiting a litter box. "The paperwork's been finalized with the previous owners. The vetting was clean—guess you didn't manage to do him any harm here in training—so I've arranged to take delivery at Washington."

"That's not my problem," Vee said.

"On the contrary, it is. I have a little note here . . ."

She dug into a small designer purse, extracted a piece of paper between long-nailed thumb and forefinger, and shook it open. She handed it to Vee. Angela swept a stray hair away from her eyes.

Cory turned back to her work. She didn't want to get yelled at for standing around. She couldn't see what was going on but tried to listen. She felt a prickly sensation all over her skin, as if the air were statically charged. She had a bad feeling about this Angela.

Vee and Angela moved to the office. All Cory managed to hear was a muffled shout, then nothing. Before long, the door banged open and Angela came marching down the aisle. She had a strange look—a look like she saw something far ahead in the future, which made her smile. A creepy smile.

Cory turned back to picking out the stall but felt Angela's presence behind her.

"Ah, young lady . . ." Her voice was pleasant.

Cory turned to face her.

"You a rider or just clean stalls?"

Cory shrugged. "I ride some."

"You any good?"

"I dunno."

Angela smiled, ran her hand along the stall's grillwork, and stepped closer. Framed in the doorway, her body blocked the light from shining in from the aisle. The spicy perfume oozed from her, competing with the acrid, damp bedding. Cory took a step back to avoid it.

"Well, you're either good or you're not." Angela looked down at her hands and adjusted the thick-banded diamond on one finger. Her hands were square, calloused, and heavily veined—out of character with her long polished nails and glittering rings. "I was told that once." She leaned back and glanced down the aisle at the office. "You're either good or not right from the start, and no amount of lessons or clinics is ever going to change that basic fact. So were you born with it?"

Cory shrugged. She felt like she was being set up, but for what?

Annoyed with this Angela woman, she blurted out, "Vee says so."

Angela shifted her weight and thrust out one bony hip. She chuckled. "Then it must be true! So, how much does she pay you here?" She glanced back toward the office again. "Can't be much."

This bony blond had a lot of nerve asking about her pay. "It's enough," Cory said, wishing she could get out of the stall, get by Angela who was blocking the door—where the heck was Vee, anyway?

"Enough?" Angela scoffed. "What's enough?"

The heat and perfume made her head swim. A dull ache began to play around the right side of her temple, causing that eye to water.

Roni had interrogated Cory about her pay when she started. "You were only taking a job to pay for lessons—music lessons," her mother said. "Now you're on to riding. That's your problem—you never stick with anything."

The memory made her wince.

"Fifty bucks an hour," Cory said and raised her chin. She knew this was ridiculous and unbelievable.

Angela straightened up.

"Fifty dollars." She pulled the sunglasses from where they were clipped to the front of her dress and nibbled on one end. "You must be good. I'm surprised that Vee wastes your time doing this." She nodded at the loaded wheelbarrow.

"Yeah, well, I'm mostly just helping out."

"How about you come work for me, then, if you're that good. I've got a bunch of green horses to get started and some showing." Angela's finely shaped eyebrows rose. Showing was the enticement most working students fell in line for.

Cory felt she was being toyed with.

"No thanks," she answered, then added, "I think I can learn more here."

Angela shrugged and left. Apparently it was nothing to her after all.

What the hell? What was that all about?

Angela's car roared to life and sped off down the drive. Cory stepped into the aisle to get a breath of fresh air. The dark clouds were rolling in overhead.

Vee emerged from her office and came up behind Cory to watch the dust trail subside. "What got rid of her so fast?"

Cory spun around. "I'm sorry. I don't know . . . I hope I didn't piss her off or anything."

"No, don't worry." Vee put her hand on Cory's shoulder. "I'm always happier to see the back of her head."

"She offered me a job at her barn, riding for her."

"Wow, that Angela's really something. She comes in my barn, steals my client's horse out from under me, then tries to steal my help while she's at it." Vee was trying to make a joke, Cory figured, but she sure wasn't smiling. "So, what did you tell her?"

"I said I could learn more here."

A smile flashed across Vee's face. "You told her that?" Cory felt two quick slaps on her shoulder, the same way Vee praised horses. "Good girl."

Cory waited for an explanation. There was none. "Who was she?"

"No one you want to know, believe me."

Cory looked over at her, but Vee was staring off in the distance. They stood as a dark cloud front hovered over the barn, darkening the entranceway. She turned, picked up the pitchfork, and stepped back into the stall.

"You've ruined me," Vee murmured.

Cory was pretty sure she wasn't supposed to have heard her. It was safer to pretend she hadn't.

Vee leaned in to the stall. "Hey, ever been to the Washington International Horse Show?"

Cory shook her head no.

"Well, looks like we're going this year."

But it didn't sound like it would be any fun.

October 14

Today was brought to you by weird people—good and

not so good ones. First, that tall, kind of geeky but cute guy who talked to me during the band tryouts (I don't even know his name!) shows up at my locker and asks me if I was sick that day. Guess he figured the only reason someone would bolt out of the room like that was if they were about to hurl. I told him I was sick, I don't know why. Yes, I do know why. Because I kind of would like him to think I'm not some loser kid who's afraid of the band director. Then at the barn this other weird person shows up. Some lady Vee used to know bought Prophet and we have to deliver him to the Washington International. The thing is, Vee didn't know anything about Prophet getting sold to Angela and she was pissed. There's definitely something weird between the two of them.

Chapter Eleven

ORY SPUN THE combination dial on her locker an extra few rotations as she peered down the corridor. Why hadn't she seen him again? It had been two weeks. Didn't he have to get books? Maybe not. She remembered how empty the inside of his locker looked last time. Well, she couldn't wait forever. She pulled out her calculus book and opened the front cover. The homework assignment he did was tucked inside, all correct, like he said. Cory slammed the locker shut and trudged down the hall toward the cafeteria. She had hoped for weeks now to run into him again. She'd planned what she would say this time. She was having a relatively good hair day despite the humidity and wore a nice sweater . . . Maybe he was sick? Expelled?

She entered the cafeteria, tiled in an institutional green. As Cory slid the tray past the day's lunch choices, she lobbed a cellophane-wrapped tuna sandwich on it with a bag of chips, then found her usual seat—in the far corner. She took a bite of the grayish tuna and looked up over the edge of her sandwich. The room swarmed with students getting up from their chairs, pushing each other, walking in roving packs. It made her think of a pile of writhing maggots in a garbage pail. She dropped the sandwich and stood to toss it out when she spotted him across the room, sitting among a group of guys she didn't know. She sat back down and fed chips into her mouth one after another. When she glanced up again, he was gone.

"Mind if I join you?"

Cory swiveled around. He was behind her left shoulder.

"Feel free." Her mouth sprayed a few chip crumbs.

He swung a long leg over the back of the bench and sat down opposite her in a way that looked as if he might spring up again at any moment. "Where you been?"

Cory had wanted to ask him the same question. "Me?" squeaked out instead.

"Yeah, you." He seemed to have lost interest in the conversation already and was looking around the cafeteria, over her head.

"I've been here. Where else? How 'bout you?" She thought that sounded casual.

His eyes stopped scanning and looked directly at her. "I can't eat here. You want to go?" he asked, getting to his feet.

Cory looked at her half-empty lunch tray.

He nodded at her food. "Bring it. We'll have a picnic."

She crammed the lid back on her drink, grabbed the chips, and jogged to catch up with him as he strode toward the exit. He walked fast, making her feel like a little terrier at his heel, scurrying to keep up. They were headed to a wing of the school she had never been to, the one that housed the metal and wood shops. He stopped at gray double doors marked with safety warnings and pushed one open. He held it for her so she would have to duck under his outstretched arm. With his other hand, he gestured like a maître d'.

"Your table awaits, madame."

A cavernous bay hung off the back of the school, lined with cinder block walls and storm fencing under a corrugated roof. The floor was a concrete pad, slanting toward a storm drain. It smelled of machine oil and rust.

Cory looked around. Against the wall stood a workbench, over which each tool hung in its outlined place. *Like a police crime scene for tools.* Cory smirked. A gutted truck carcass squatted in the center, painted a combination of plum purple and Bondo gray. It was missing windows on the driver's side. Tubes connecting to some sort of machinery ran out of its open hood like a patient in I.C.U.

He slapped the truck's frame as if it were a faithful dog. "Hop in. I'll take you for a spin."

Cory barked out a nervous laugh. It was ridiculous being here. And what was with him talking so weird, like her grandfather or something? But she climbed through the truck's doorless opening and sat down. He slid in behind the wheel, leaned over to open the glove box, and pulled out a wrapped sandwich, apple, and juice box. The juice box was tiny, like little kids bring to school, and didn't seem to fit in his large hands.

"Boston," he said, unwrapping his sandwich.

"What?"

"You asked where I was. Boston."

Cory's mind struggled to keep up. "Oh, right." She looked down at her almost empty bag of chips. "Why were you in Boston?"

"Because Harvard is there."

She fished out a chip from the bottom, deciding it was easier to chew and wait than ask questions he wasn't answering anyway.

He leaned back in his seat, staring forward. "My mom wants me to go to Harvard next year. Her dad went there and so did her brother."

"Next year?" Cory calculated . . . *He's a senior. He'll be applying for schools and leaving next year.* "That's great. Harvard's a great school," she said, thinking she was saying *great* too much.

His profile reminded her of the Greek statues she had seen in the Boston Museum of Fine Art—the same long nose and full lips. Cory looked around to see if anyone else was nearby, then turned in her seat, planting her back firmly against the side frame of the truck. From this vantage, she stole another glance at him. His hair was curly, long over the collar, and dark brown. A small bone along his jaw pulsed as he chewed a bite of his sandwich.

She twisted in her seat. "Is it okay being here?"

He turned to face her. "Huh?"

She gestured toward the empty bay. "Are we allowed to be here?"

"Yeah, I think we are supposed to be here," he said, looking around like he just realized where he was.

She wished someone else would come into the room, and then again, maybe not. He slumped down in the seat and propped a foot against the dashboard, forcing Cory deeper into her corner. She tried to regain the thread of "safe" conversation.

"Is your family from Boston? We used to live in Massachusetts, too."

"Oh yeah?" he said. "Did your family move here, or are you political refugees?"

Cory couldn't tell if he was making fun of her or not. She looked down into the chip bag, tipping it to see what was left in the bottom, but she no longer felt like eating. "My mom got a job here. We moved this past June."

"Just you and your mom? No dad?"

Wow, he's direct. "My sister, too. My parents got divorced." She paused. "Dad still lives in Mass, and Mom's best job offer was down here, plus she has a sister in northern Virginia. So, we had to move."

"Had to." He repeated her words. "That means you didn't want to. Is the 'had to' your mom's words or yours?"

"Definitely mine." Cory was surprised at the tone of her voice. "I hate it here," she added.

He stared at her for a while, then stuck out his hand.

"How do you do? My name is Kevyn. Kevyn with a Y. Everyone in my family is trying to send me to Massachusetts and you were ripped outta there by yours. I think that means we're cosmically linked."

Cory took his hand and shook it. The warmth radiated into the coolness of hers.

"So, clarinet girl, you have a name, too, I suppose?"

She dropped his hand and smiled. "Cory with a Y." His face wrinkled into a smirk. "So, Kevyn-with-a-Y, why don't you want to go to Harvard? That's what you mean by being dragged to Massachusetts, isn't it?"

"Very astute." Kevyn leaned toward her and dipped his hand into her bag to fish out the last of the broken chips. He talked out of the side of his mouth, chewing. "Don't want to go 'cuz everyone wants me to go so bad."

"Where do you want to go?"

"Nowhere," he said dully and sat up. "Besides, my mom's sick. I don't want to go off and leave her here on her own."

The charged, flirtatious atmosphere inside the truck went flat.

"Sorry," Cory murmured. *Change subjects.* "So, did you get into All-Star Band?"

"Nope. Got in trouble for quitting that, too, when I got home. You did the right thing, you know, leaving. I left, too."

"What do you mean?" Cory sat up straighter.

"Walking out. A protest. That guy is a sadist, picking on that pathetic kid. I tried to get the whole band to walk out behind you and me—a student protest—but no one had the guts. No one has conviction these days. So, they threatened me with suspension for trying to start a student uprising." Kevyn chuckled. "Uprising! That's what they called it. What a joke! Harvard will love *that* on my application."

Cory opened her mouth to deny that she walked out of tryouts as a protest but shut it again.

"Yeah, that would have been great," she agreed, crinkling up her chips bag. *Stop saying great!* "So, what's the deal with this truck?"

"It's mine. I'm fixing it up."

Before he could go on, the bell for the next class rang, echoing around the empty garage. Cory jumped in a Pavlovian-dog response, but Kevyn sat motionless. She had only seven minutes to get to her next class, French, on the other side of the building.

"What do you have next?" she asked, gathering up her trash and grabbing her purse.

"Oh, Navel Contemplation 101 or Advanced Shooting Hoops Techniques." He turned more toward her and hiked his knee up on the seat.

"No, seriously. I'm headed to the language department. AP French."

"I think I'll stay here and work on the truck." He sat up straight in his seat. "Hey, you can help."

Cory had never skipped a class and certainly not while actually on the school grounds. It was crazy. "Okay," she heard herself say.

"Right!" He jumped out and handed her a pair of dirty coveralls. "Don't worry about the class." He looked straight into her eyes as if he were reading her thoughts. "Hey, we'll speak French while we work, if that makes you feel any better . . . donnez-moi le wrench, s'il vous plait. Le carborator ne marche pas."

Cory laughed. A light and tingly sensation shot down her arms, to her fingers and toes, like the time she and her sister snuck a few beers one afternoon.

"You won't be missing much. Everything I've learned, I've learned from my 1990 Chevy truck." Kevyn patted the hood again and smiled at her.

She smiled back. In fact, she couldn't stop smiling.

Chapter Twelve

CORY FILLED THE horse's water bucket and pinched the hose in half to stop the flow. But it didn't stop. She gripped the thick black tube in two hands and pressed harder. The water still gushed out of the hose, overflowing the bucket, and onto the stall floor. She stared in horror as the water puddled at her feet. *Vee is gonna kill me.* She bent the hose double again for good measure, but the water kept pouring out, coming faster now, flooding the stall and spilling into the aisle . . .

She awoke to the sound of rushing water. The toilet flushed again. Cory opened her eyes and looked around her bedroom, struggling to make sense of what she could make out in the dim light. *Not in the barn, I'm home, in bed.* Her eyes adjusted. On the other side of the room Jessica's bed was empty. Light seeped in from the hallway. From the bathroom down the hall, she heard gagging, choking sounds. Another flush. Cory propped herself up on her elbows, thinking what to do, then scooted under the covers when the bathroom light went out. She watched as Jessica felt her way back to the bed and climbed in.

"You sick?" Cory asked.

"Oh! You're awake?"

"Am now. What's up?"

"Yeah, feel kinda sick." Jessica pulled the covers back over her. "Must be the pizza. Too greasy. Made me feel gross."

Cory had eaten four pieces of pizza to Jess's one small slice. And she felt okay.

"Hope it's not food poisoning," Cory said, "or I'll be worse than sick."

"Nah, I'm sure it's nothing." Jessica paused. "I'm worried about the Massachusetts thing, the dance scholarship auditions, I guess." Her voice sounded small in the dark room.

"What, you're worried about escaping this place and spending the summer doing what you want? Right."

"There's more to it than just doing what I want," Jess said. "I have to make the final cuts. I have to keep up once I'm there. This isn't like the local stuff I do at the studio—this is with real dancers who . . . well, you have to look right and be perfect all the time."

Cory couldn't imagine Jessica not looking right, not being perfect. She had long, straight blond hair. She had perfect skin and a tall, lean body. Everything seemed easier for Jess. She had made friends right away after moving here, and she had a boyfriend—even if he was a creep. She had landed in a dance studio where she was the star, and Mom was willing to cart her all over creation for her lessons and buy her ballet stuff.

"Oh, boo-hoo, Jess. You whine about how hard everything is and then you always end up being the best. This is no different."

Jess turned her back to Cory. "I hope so," she murmured to the wall.

Silence.

"Hey, I saw that guy again." Change of subject.

Jess turned her head. "Yeah?"

"Had lunch in his truck, and guess what?"

No response. Cory continued, "He thought I left band tryouts as a protest. He tried to form a mass walkout afterward and got in a lot of trouble."

"Oh great, a rebel without a clue."

Cory turned over but knew she wouldn't be able to go back to sleep.

"'Night, Jess."

There was no response from the small, blanketed lump facing the wall. After a while, Cory got up, grabbed an item from its hiding place in her desk, and slipped out of the room, quietly closing the door behind her.

October 29

Great, it's almost 2 in the morning. I have to get up at the butt crack of dawn to be over at the barn and I'm wide awake thanks to Jess. Really not looking forward to tomorrow. Vee has been in a pissy mood all week because she has to go Washington to deliver Prophet. I asked Jack what's up with her, and he wouldn't say anything except that she has bad memories of the place. Now Jess is being a super B, too, just because she has to try out for that dance school. What a shame they don't just take her for her incredible perfection, sight-unseen, like she probably expects. I think she's doing something to make herself sick. This is the second time I heard her vomit up her guts since she got picked to try out. And I don't buy her story that it's nerves. I could look around in the bathroom, in case she's using something. Mom's not home yet, either. Great, I'll be creeping around looking for pills for two headcases now. Oh, and skipped my first class ever today with Kevyn-with-a-Y. But so worth it.

Chapter Thirteen

THE PARKING LOT was filled with horse trailers—huge rigs pulled by monster-sized trucks, some as big as Cory's townhouse—all surrounded by scurrying people unloading hay, wheeling tack trunks, and yelling at each other. Horses wearing thick shipping wraps exited trailers and were led, prancing on the end of ropes, to a bank of temporary stalls. Jack slowed through the exhibitor parking area, surveying the scene for an easy parking spot. Cory craned her neck to take it all in. Vee stared straight ahead, unmoved. She had been in a vile mood all morning, her scowl darkening the closer they got to the Washington International's showgrounds.

Cory wanted to jump out, explore the shed row, and wander up and down the aisles to stare at the world-class horses she had only ever seen in magazines. Some horses had coats so shiny they looked as if they had been wrapped in cellophane. People milled around, smoked, and congregated in groups, clutching Styrofoam cups of coffee steaming in the early October morning air. *They must be the owners or trainers.* The only ones who could get away with standing around.

Vee told Jack to stop the truck in a spot on the farthest edge of the parking area, well away from any other vehicle. She slumped in her seat and took her first look around.

"Let's get this over with." She sighed and reached for the door handle but didn't open it.

Jack opened his door and stepped out. He leaned in the open window. "I'll find out where we're supposed to take him," he said to Vee. "You wait here. I'll be right back." He turned to leave, then called, "Cory, you want to come, too?"

Cory slid across the seat and jumped out like the truck was on fire. She jogged to keep up with Jack as he headed toward the massive stadium and down a dark passageway that led under the building. He entered a door marked "Press."

A woman with short steel-gray hair and a deeply lined face glanced up from her desk. She paused a moment, smiled, and rose to her feet. "Jack, right? It's been a while." She rounded the desk with her arms spread open. Much shorter than Jack, she wrapped him in a brief but polite hug. "Where have you been keeping yourself? We all thought you dropped off the face of the earth." She stepped back. "We heard a rumor you were working with—"

"Great to see you, Barb." Jack nodded to Cory. "Actually, my friend, here, and I are just delivering a horse for Angela Hamilton. You got her location?"

Barb's smile faded. "Angela Hamilton, sure, she's in shed row B, has a block of stalls down toward the end. You can't miss it. Barn colors are burgundy and silver. You know her—she has the whole place swathed in fancy curtains and director chairs with the farm's name on them. So, working for Angela Hamilton? No wonder she can't lose these days."

Cory wondered what that meant, but Jack didn't reply. He nodded and brushed past the desk to a door that led onto the main concourse of the arena, Cory on his heels. The area was jammed with every sort of horse-related vendor selling everything from saddles to oil portraits of horses and dogs to custom-made boots and jewelry. The air was a mixture of candied popcorn and saddle leather. She pushed through the crowd, trying not to lose sight of Jack's thin figure and white hair as he weaved across the concourse and headed down a steep set of stairs flanked on one side by the arena seating. At the bottom was a small warm-up area near the arena in-gate.

"This place is really something," Cory said to his back. Jack stopped and for the first time looked around at her.

"Yeah." His gazed moved past her to a spot in the arena. "I've spent some good times at this show."

"Vee hates it here, though."

Cory calculated whether she should say more. She studied Jack's face. Under the shadow of his cap, his pale eyes tracked a horse as it negotiated the jump course. His mouth was turned down with concentration.

Without glancing at her, he replied, "Vee hates all horse shows, not just this one."

"But she *used to* show, right? She showed here?" Cory hoped to hear something about why this place could send Vee into such a black spiral.

Jack turned toward her. "Sure, she showed lots, here and everywhere."

A matter-of-fact statement, not what she wanted to know.

"But she especially hates this show."

Silence.

Cory kept quiet, hoping he'd say more. But he didn't. Instead, he turned back to watch another horse enter the ring and jog a warm-up circle. A bored announcer called out the name of the rider on course and struggled with the horse's foreign-sounding name. Cory tried to imagine Vee at this show, riding in this ring with Pressman years ago. She really wished she were coming here to watch her ride, instead of just delivering a horse.

"So why especially this show?" Cory pressed.

Jack lifted off his cap to scratch the back of his head. "Something bad happened at this one. You'll have to ask her."

End of story. She got the message. Cory leaned against the rail to watch the class.

The next rider entering the arena was young, maybe Cory's age. The horse was a gray with a blindingly white tail, which he swished impatiently. They cleared each fence, and when the rider came down the last line, they jumped each in perfect rhythm, shifted to trot, and circled before exiting the gate. Cory stepped back as the girl rode past, patting her horse's neck with two sharp slaps.

"Nice trip." Jack's voice brought her back. "Hangs a little with his left front, though. And too flat over the fences."

Cory looked at him, surprised. "It looked perfect to me."

"It was nice, not brilliant. Rider needs to support more from her leg for brilliant."

For just being Vee's farm manager, Jack knew a lot more about training than she had thought.

"I'd like to be that good," she said, more to herself than to anyone else.

Jack turned to her, his face partially shaded under the brim of his cap. "Really?"

Unable to read his expression, Cory wondered if he was making fun of her and felt silly for saying it. She looked off to where the rider had disappeared. "But I guess that will never happen."

"Why's that?"

"Well, she . . ." Cory gestured to where the rider had been. "She probably started riding when she was like two years old or something."

"Vee started when she was fourteen and was long-listed for the Olympics nine years later."

Cory assumed Vee was from one of those Maryland horsey families and grew up on a big farm, riding and showing dozens of horses since she was able to crawl.

"And," Jack said, "she's teaching you." He poked an index finger into her right shoulder and smiled. He pulled off his cap and opened his eyes wide in mock horror. "Speaking of Vee, she'll have fogged up the whole truck fuming over where we've been. She's tense as a caged tiger, as it is." He slapped Cory on the shoulder with his cap and nodded toward the stairs.

After unloading Prophet and finding his assigned stall, Cory stood just outside, watching him wear a path by walking and spinning in circles. He lifted his head, twitched an ear, then let out a shrill whinny with such force it shook his sides. He cocked an ear to listen again. A whinny came from another distraught horse somewhere across the stabling area, but not the whinny Prophet was hoping for. He commenced circling again.

Jack peered in at him with a worried expression. "I don't like him getting all heated up like that. Let's get a cooler on him."

Jack grabbed a burgundy cooler hanging on the rack nearby with Angela's farm logo embroidered on the hip and slid the door open. Prophet stopped to study Jack, a familiar person. He ceased circling and lowered his head, nostrils quivering, and sniffed the blanket. Jack flung the woolen cooler over Prophet's broad, tall back in one fluid movement, then tied it in front.

"You're going to a new home, guy," Jack said. "Be good. Be good, be smart, and keep yourself out of trouble. Nothing we can do about it now. Angela's got your papers, and it's a done deal."

Prophet butted Jack with his head and rubbed it against his shoulder. Cory watched, expecting Jack to chastise him for this forbidden behavior, but instead he ran his hand up under Prophet's forelock and scratched him there. "Use the brain God gave you. Don't make trouble for that woman, okay?"

Vee appeared beside Jack and slid her hand down Prophet's neck, then into her never-empty pocket to extract a sugar cube.

"You're a great horse. One of the true greats. You don't deserve this," she whispered to him as he grabbed the sugar. Vee's voice dropped lower, inaudible.

Cory moved away from the stall, feeling as if she were intruding on a family farewell. Vee stepped out and slid the door shut, sighed, and turned to leave.

"Okay, let's get out of here," she announced to no one in particular.

Cory gathered up Prophet's shipping boots, sheet, and lead rope. She took a last look around to spot anything she might have forgotten, whispered a hurried "good-luck" to the big bay horse watching her, and ran after Vee. Jack was already out of sight, probably back at the trailer preparing for a swift departure.

Cory dashed after Vee, not wanting to get lost in the swelling crowd. More and more people poured into the main concourse, but Vee weaved her way against the incoming tide like a trout swimming upstream. Cory scuttled behind, tripping on the trailing end of the sheet, and dropping a shipping boot. With her arms laden, she could barely see where she was going, let alone keep track of Vee, who hadn't offered to carry a thing. She peered around her armload and noticed people turning and staring as Vee dodged through the crowd. A woman in her forties with a long blond braid leaned in close to her friend and whispered behind her hand.

Vee exited the shed row and started across the vast parking area toward the far corner where the truck and trailer were parked. A group gathered along the fence of the warm-up arena turned as one and followed Vee's progress as she wove in and around the various trailers. She walked faster with her eyes straight ahead, skirting around a huge six-horse rig pulled by a silver dually.

A tall, athletic woman with cropped dark hair and fancy-looking sunglasses jogged up beside her. "Vee! It *is* you." She made a show of catching her breath, her palm fluttering against her chest. "Had to run to catch up with you, and I don't exactly have my running shoes on!" She extended one leg and pointed to her tall, shiny black boot. "They're new, not broken in yet, and you know what torture that is." She smiled at Vee, but the smile wasn't returned.

Vee kept walking but slowed as the woman fell into step beside her. "Hello, Gretchen."

Cory closed the gap, following a few steps behind. She was the barn help, invisible to the woman in the riding boots, and Vee showed no interest in introducing her.

The woman continued smiling at Vee. "I wanted to let you know how pleased Cliff and I were with the job you did on Prophet."

Vee grunted.

"He was never an easy horse, as you know, but you really turned him into a solid jumper. He's in the Open class tomorrow if you're going to be around . . ."

Vee stopped and turned to her.

"All my work's a waste, now that you sold him to Angela."

Cory saw a flush spread from Vee's collar up along her jawline as her eyes bored into this Gretchen woman. Even Cory knew better than to stick Vee's nose in the fact that someone else would be riding the horse she fixed and trained for over a year.

Gretchen sighed and shook her head. "Vee, this thing with Angela, I don't know. You need to move past it. She's a very successful rider—"

"Because she rides horses other people have brought along and trained? She ruins them, or worse yet, she cripples them. Then what happens? She buys another one. Is that what you wanted for Prophet?"

"What I wanted for Prophet was to be *shown*."

Cory noted the emphasis on the word *shown* and the condescension in Gretchen's tone.

"And that wasn't going to happen with you in charge of him, was it, Vee? I was going to judge for myself, but like everyone says about you, you've lost—"

"No, you're right, Gretchen. I wouldn't have shown him. And that's the end goal of all of this, isn't it?" Vee swept her arm out and gestured to the arena, the trailers, the shed row. "That's what matters, to win at the Garden or at Washington or Tampa. It doesn't matter what you have to do to the horse to get there, does it? And, hey, if one horse's spirit is broken pushing him too fast and too soon to the big fences or you cripple him, why, just get another."

Vee's voice rose. People watching moved closer.

"Vee, you've lost it. So what if we want to have a horse that competes at the big shows? That *is* the point, and there's nothing wrong with it. Just because you lost your nerve, you turn on everyone else who's still out there competing."

Vee's fists clenched into tight balls, jammed into the pockets of her coat. Cory had seen her upset, but not like this. She held her breath, wondering what would happen, what she should do if Vee hit Gretchen. The two women stood staring at each other. Vee's nostrils flared as she took in a deep breath. "You own a one-of-a-kind talented horse. You handed him over to a butcher. *You* live with it."

Vee brushed by Gretchen and kept walking to the trailer. Her hand reached up to her eye and brushed something away.

Gretchen called after her, "A bit dramatic, aren't you, Vee? I guess *that* hasn't changed."

October 30

Super long day taking Prophet to Washington. Was sad stripping his empty stall when we got back. I'm going to miss him. Such a cool horse. When we got back, Vee just went up to her house. She hated being at Washington, but I loved it. I don't know what it was about that place, but I keep imagining being able to ride in that arena. Maybe I could do it, with Vee training me like Jack said. But really, who am I kidding? I like imagining a me that's not really me. Anyway, glad I ate at the show, no food in the house here. Mom's in bed already. Don't know where Jess is. Probably out with Jeff.

Chapter
Fourteen

CORY SAT ON the low retaining wall that surrounded the main entrance to the school, pulled her knees up close, and leaned back. The bricks were still warm from the afternoon sun. She ran her finger between them and thought about getting out her blue Sharpie to draw a line in the cement groove between the bricks in whichever direction she wanted it to go. Like that kid's book her mom used to read to them about the boy with the purple crayon. The bright blue line would meander crazily up the side of the school, outlining windows, back and forth until she had turned the whole front of the school into an Aztec-looking mosaic.

It was chilly just sitting and waiting for the bus. She remembered that jerk, David, the one who tossed her shoes up on the wire last month, telling her, "No juniors take the bus home, only freshman and druggies. Freshmen because they couldn't drive yet, and all the other losers who either can't get a license, or lost it already."

How about kids whose parents don't just give them a car? She raised her eyes to the wire where her sneakers still hung. She told her mom a kid stole them out of her gym locker.

The sun was low and shone with an anemic light. The trees were nearly bare, and what few leaves still clung on were dull and shriveled.

Her thoughts wandered back to Washington's arena. She could see the brightly colored jumps as she turned her horse to the first fence . . .

"Solving the problems of the universe?" Kevyn appeared and hiked himself up on the wall beside her.

"Yeah, and I got it all figured out."

"I thought you did. I can tell. So, really, what's going on?"

Cory sat for a while without answering. What she was really facing was going home to an empty house, starting supper, and hoping her mom was in a good mood tonight. She swung around to face Kevyn.

"This will sound weird . . ."

"Weird I like."

"Yeah, I guessed that about you." Cory laughed. "But listen. Have you ever thought about how your life would be totally different if, like, you had been born to some other family?" She hurried to add, "Or something?" Kevyn looked at her without responding. "Yeah, well, I guess not." Her gaze glided away from his face, back to the sun sinking behind the tree line.

"I might have been named Ruperto," he said, breaking the silence.

Cory's head snapped back to look at him, expecting to see a snide smile plastered on his face. Instead, he was looking out at the same bare tree line, expressionless.

"Seriously?"

"Seriously. My mom was engaged to a guy she met in college—Ruperto Enriquez the Fourth. She met him during her semester abroad. I could have been a Fifth—ha, ha!—and be living in Venezuela, and speaking Spanish, and—"

"Your mom told you about some guy she was supposed to marry? What happened?"

"She didn't marry him." Kevyn shrugged. This explained everything.

"I figured that, but what's the story?" Cory looked at Kevyn more intensely. Why would his mom tell him about boyfriends from college and adventures in South America? When she tried to imagine her and Roni having the same conversation, well, it didn't happen, or it turned into yelling.

"That's pretty much the whole story," he said. "I knew she did a se-mester in South America in college. She talked about it all the time. Part of the push to get me to go—to college, that is. It was the high point of her life, she said, after having me, of course." Kevyn made a formal bow toward her and smiled his half-smile. "Or so she says."

"So, *Ruperto*, have you ever been to South America? You know, to check out the dad you almost had, and maybe find out where he's now? Do you know whatever happened to him? Does your mom keep in touch?"

"No, but thanks for asking, *National Inquirer*. She never heard from him again. Guess a guy gets the point when you practically leave him at the altar."

"Wow!" Cory slipped down off the wall, turned, and slapped him playfully across his thigh. "C'mon with the details. Your mom sounds like she's hot."

Kevyn looked down, his expression hidden. "Yeah, I guess so. A lit-tle weird, especially for a guy, to think about whether his mom is hot or not." He ran a hand through his hair. "Hey, you can talk to her yourself if you're so interested."

The whine of an air brake diverted their attention to the buses as they lumbered into the parking lot. Cory shifted her weight from one foot to the other. She had to get on that stupid bus now but sensed that maybe Kevyn was going to ask her to go somewhere.

"Yeah, sure, I would love to ask her about college and stuff," she said, looking out the corner of her eye for bus number eighty-three. It hadn't arrived yet. The damp air carried the smell of diesel fumes from the idling buses. Kids stood, picked up their backpacks, and ambled to-ward them.

"I have to play a gig tomorrow night." Kevyn leaned back and drummed the back of his heels against the wall.

Cory tucked a strand of hair behind her ear. "Yeah? Where?"

"It's not much, just a few sets at a teen club. You know, one of those no-alcohol places. No big deal, but it's a good chance for us to get some public appearances, some exposure. You want to come?"

Cory spotted eighty-three turning into the parking lot. She shifted her weight to the other foot. *Was he asking her out? Like a date asked out?* "Where is it? I mean, what time and stuff?"

Her bus pulled in front of them. The ugly snub-nosed beast was belching black smoke, and the same driver—the acne-scarred skinny guy who kept staring back in his rearview mirror—was at the wheel. She took a step backward, toward the bus.

"Guess you have to go, huh?" He nodded his chin toward the buses. "If you want to come, it's at a community center near the Columbia Mall. Meet me here around six thirty, okay? We can go to my house, and you can meet my mom and have girl talk about Ruperto while I get my stuff." Kevyn stood up and handed Cory her backpack.

"Okay. Sounds great." Cory ran to board the bus. The driver's scowl made her smile back at him. She took a seat near the window and watched Kevyn wave as the bus pulled away. Gliding past the school's gray façade, she envisioned a neon pulsing heart on every single brick.

Cory settled into a seat and stared out the window. She thought about what Kevyn had said about his mom. It would be great to have a mom like that, one who told you funny things about herself. Cory tried to remember any scrap of an amusing tale from when her mom and dad were together or even dating.

She remembered seeing pictures and how they looked really great together—her mom so pretty with long hair then and her dad wearing a bright-colored shirt and smiling under a thick mustache. But there was one picture Cory had always liked, taken a long time ago at the beach. Her mom was seated on a lounge chair, wearing a gauzy cover-up with seahorses on it. Just as the picture was taken, a strand of hair had blown across her face. Her dad was kneeling beside her, his arm draped over her shoulders. In that instant, he turned and was reaching toward her face to brush away the strand. They were looking at each other, not posing for the camera like in all the other pictures of them.

Cory had slipped this photo from the album and kept it under the lining in her underwear drawer. She wasn't sure why.

The bus pulled up outside the entrance to her townhouse community. Cory stood, just as the driver glanced in the review mirror and slammed on the brakes.

Chapter
Fifteen

THE PACK OF Jack Russell terriers met her outside the barn, swarming like a school of canine piranha, as she led the last horse in from the fields. The sun was just above the horizon. Her hoodie, which was fine that morning, wasn't keeping her warm anymore. This time of year, the barn work was getting tougher. She had to walk out to the far fields after dark, wrestling with gate latches she couldn't see and struggling with impatient horses anxious to get to their dinners.

After every horse was fed, she stood at the back entrance looking out over the empty paddocks and watched the purple sky darken. One of the barn cats—a longhaired tiger—curled around her leg. Cory squatted to pet him, wondering if any of the horses in this barn were capable of showing at Washington.

"Cory, grab a cooler," Vee shouted. "I don't want his muscles to seize up." Vee had just gotten off a horse. She pulled the saddle off his back and started unbuckling his tendon boots.

Cory snapped to attention, pulled a woolen cooler off the rack, and flung it over the horse. Slipping her frozen fingers up underneath, she felt the damp, smooth muscles of the horse's shoulder. She leaned against him, breathing in his horsey smell. He pressed his body against her and tried to rub his head along her arm.

"Are you going to dance with him or walk him out?"

Cory led the horse to the indoor arena and trudged around the perimeter, dragging her feet in the cold sand, dreaming of a hot shower.

The light snapped on, bathing the cavernous indoor arena in light.

"Want to jump Pressman?" Vee called from somewhere inside the barn. She appeared with the big black gelding, all tacked up and ready to go. Strange thing is, Cory had ridden him but she had never really seen anyone jump Pressman, even Vee. She mostly took him for trail rides or taught lessons sitting on his back. Cory had ridden him for that first lesson, but mostly on the flat and little cross rails. Besides, now Cory was riding some of the more challenging horses. Last week she had ridden a young, green four-year-old and a couple jumpers that were in for a "tune-up." She was a little beyond an ancient, arthritic jumper.

Vee laughed. "What? You look horrified. He's not that bad."

Cory figured since Pressman was Vee's old jumper, he must be twenty-five years old at least. The office walls were covered with dusty photos of him at the Garden and at Washington. Old blurry photos, dotted with fly droppings, showed smiling people in formal dress handing a much younger Vee shining silver cups or bronze horse statues and ribbons. Pressman's eye in the photos was always showing the white part, rolled back in suspicion at the people on the ground around him. Cory looked at the same horse standing before her now. His eyes were sunken, rimmed with small gray hairs, and hooded by half-closed eyelids. Vee stood, waiting for an answer.

"Sure, okay. Let me put this guy away first."

"No, I'll take care of that. Get on." Vee grabbed the horse's lead and disappeared.

Cory dragged Pressman by his reins into the center of the arena. "So, Press, what's it gonna be? A couple cross rails and then go lie down?" She swung up onto him, her back muscles feeling like an unyielding rope. His head shot up when he eyed the jumps and pranced a few steps sideways. "Hey, guy, take it easy. Okay?"

She walked around the arena, weaving around the jumps. He was a different horse all of a sudden. He felt like a live wire under her, rippling with energy. Vee came back in and adjusted some jumps to a higher setting, clanging the metal cups and pins, sliding them up a good foot and a half from where they had been earlier. Cory wondered which horse Vee was going to ride later that night and asked her.

"No one. I'm done for the night." She slid another rail up higher, looked over her shoulder at Cory, and smiled at her again. "But you're not."

Chapter
Sixteen

THE HINGE ON Vee's pickup creaked open like the passenger door was going to break off. Cory picked up a bottle of liniment that rolled out onto her foot and tossed it back onto the bench seat, which was already covered with extra barn coats, dog leashes, papers, and mysterious bits of tack. She brushed the mess aside and placed some papers on the dashboard where more were stacked. When Vee got in and shut the door, the dome light went off and left them in the dark. It took a moment for Cory's eyes to adjust. Just as well, she didn't really want to see what she might be sitting on. She felt under her left thigh and extracted a hoof pick.

"You did a great job with him tonight." Vee's voice filled the darkness.

"Thanks." Cory shifted in her seat. It wasn't a long ride to her house, but in the confined space of the truck cab, she felt the need to keep the conversation going. "He was fun," she added.

And it was fun. She had never dared to jump so high—ever. The horse seemed to read her mind. He responded so quickly to everything she asked of him.

"Yes, isn't he fun?" Vee's voice was lighter than Cory had heard before. "That's how I would describe him exactly. Keep in mind, he isn't as elegant as Prophet, but in his day he would get you over anything you put in front of him. It might not be pretty, but if you could stay on top, he did his job and cleared it."

Cory glanced at Vee's face in profile. She looked younger in the dimness of the cab.

"Why don't you ever jump him anymore, then?"

"A horse only has so many jumps per lifetime in his legs. Pressman already knows how to jump. I don't need to do it just for fun. I'm saving him to teach someone else."

Cory didn't dare look over to see whether Vee was really saying what she thought she was saying. As the truck made a sharp turn, she reached forward to grab the stack of envelopes from sliding along the dashboard and onto the floor. Too late. They spilled in a paper waterfall at Cory's feet. Gathering them up, in the dim light she made out the return address of the vet, the feed store, breeding farms, and a few others she didn't recognize.

"I'd like to be a good enough rider to show. Like at Washington," Cory said.

For a half-mile or so, they both watched the lines in the road ahead of them without exchanging a word.

"My turn's up here on the right. The townhouses."

The heater in the truck was cranked up full blast. Cory unzipped her hoodie a few more inches.

She picked up the dog leash, played around with the snap end, clicking it open and shut. Vee turned onto her road.

"You really want to show?" Vee asked, as if Cory had proposed some repulsive plan, like wanting to become a stripper or something. "It's that big a deal for you?"

"I guess." She set the dog leash down on the floor. "It's just that when we were at Washington, I saw this girl riding there"—Cory glanced over to judge Vee's reaction—"and she was really good." The truck turned into the parking lot. Cory pointed toward the end of a row of townhouses.

Vee stopped and put the truck in park. "Why? And why

Washington?"

Cory wasn't prepared with a reason. There wasn't a reason. It was more like a feeling. She twisted in her seat and reached for the door handle. The truth was she felt good when she was riding. It was something she was good at. And like Jess told her once, but she never really believed, everyone has to be good at something. Lately her daydreams of entering the in-gate at Washington on a big, muscular jumper were becoming more real. A nice daydream, but still a daydream. She took a deep breath.

"It's just that—"

Vee laughed. "Why not the Garden or Badminton or—I know, Rolex?"

Cory's hand gripped the handle harder. Vee didn't have to be all sarcastic and everything. "It would be nice to be good at something. To ride in a big show. Well, maybe not Washington, exactly, but a show like that."

Vee turned and hiked her knee up on the seat between them. "To prove something? Because it never works out if you're using a horse to prove something to somebody, you know."

Cory looked out the passenger window. She was trying to prove something, but she wasn't doing it for other people. It was for herself. Vee's words made her inch farther away until she felt a hand lightly touch her knee.

"Sorry." The hand withdrew. "It's normal for a kid to want to show. I get it, I do." She brushed a stray hair away and sighed. "The thing is, I've just seen a lot of bad stuff at shows. Washington, in particular. People pushing horses for their own egos. Breaking them down and then tossing them away like they're disposable."

Cory let go of the door handle.

"Being there again brought it back. The good and the bad." Vee shut off the engine. "But some of the good, too." She smiled. "I admit I loved sitting on Pressman in the middle of the arena and having the ribbons handed to me." She fingered the stack of envelopes on the dash. "And it wouldn't hurt to have a junior rider there to bring in some more business."

Cory spun around to face her. "Not you?"

"Nah, I've had my day. Besides, it would be better for business if a junior rider made it. It's tougher for a professional to qualify."

It was as if a balloon deflated in her chest. "You have to qualify for Washington?"

"Takes a year of showing to build up the points. And you have to have a horse that can do it at that level, and there aren't too many of those."

"So, you're saying it's a pretty stupid idea, then. Okay, it was just something . . ." Cory cracked the passenger door open. The dome light illuminated the cab. "Uh, thanks for the ride."

Vee acted as if she wasn't listening. "We'd have to find just the right horse. Not much time, but I have a few ideas." She fished around the flotsam on the dash and extracted a thick zippered binder. Cory held the door ajar as Vee ran her finger down the page. "I'll make some calls. We'll see." She snapped the binder shut and gave Cory a quick smile. "We'll see. No promises."

Cory knew what "we'll see" usually meant, at least when her parents said it. It meant "forget it." She stepped out of the truck and raised a hand to wave as Vee pulled away. The headlights swept over the dark yard and walkway as she walked toward the house.

Chapter
Seventeen

I T LOOKED LIKE no one was home again, but when Cory approached the front door, voices floated from inside—a male voice and her mom's laughter. Must be that guy she'd been dating. Cory sighed. She had been looking forward to a night alone since Jessica was sleeping over at a friend's house. Now Cory had to put on a polite face and meet some strange guy in her living room. She pushed opened the door. Only a small lamp was on in the living room. Her mom's back was to her, sitting on the couch. She was reaching up to the man's face. His eyes met Cory's and he gently pushed her mother's hand aside. He sat back on the couch and smiled.

Her mom turned, her carefully penciled brows rising. "Oh, you're home?"

She had a glass of red wine in her hand, the rim smeared nearly all the way around with a matching shade of red lipstick. An empty bottle stood on the coffee table between them.

"Hey, Mom. Just got back. I got a ride home." Cory nodded toward the window where the truck's taillights shone at the end of the parking lot.

"From where?" her mom asked.

"The barn." *Where did you think I was until after nine?* She was starving.

The man inched to the edge of the couch and struggled to stand up. He stuck out his hand at her. "I'm Bucky. Your mom here's been telling me all about you. You're the ballet dancer, right?"

"No." Her mom snorted. "No, Bucky, I told you she's gone for the night." Her voice had a wheedling tone, as if she were reasoning with a small child. "This is Cory, the other one."

Cory grasped his outstretched hand. It was big and moist. She glanced at his face. His thin, dark moustache glistened and perspiration beaded along his receding temples. He dropped back down into his seat, causing the shirt's buttons to strain around his paunch.

"I'll just take Hershey out. Nice meeting you." Cory sped through the living room to the kitchen and out the back door with the dog at her heels. She sat down on the steps, waiting for Hershey to find his perfect pee spot. The sky was clear with a full moon, illuminating the whole backyard. But it was getting colder. Cory could see her breath. She called the Lab to hurry it up and stood to go inside.

In the kitchen, she grabbed a slice of lukewarm pizza from the open box on the counter and headed upstairs for a shower. As she passed through the living room, she raised a hand to wave and managed to mumble a goodnight around a mouthful of pizza crust. She thought about the hot water hitting her sore shoulders, warming her cold feet, as she took the stairs two at a time.

November 4

People sure are weird. Just when you think you got them figured out, they do stuff totally opposite. Like Kevyn. I thought he was just too into himself to notice me, let alone ask me out. Well, maybe not officially ask me out. And Vee. Total turn around about showing and not sure why. Think it had something to do with that stack of bills but also maybe she really does miss it in spite of what she says. Then I come home and Mom is sitting with some fat, smarmy-looking guy. Not the Roni type for sure and definitely a big step down from Dad. But, hey, maybe this guy keeps his word, unlike Dad, and if Mom's happy for a change, makes life easier for me. So who cares?

Chapter
Eighteen

CORY TUCKED THE journal between the mattress and box
spring, too tired to get up and put it away, snapped off the
light and wriggled farther under the covers. She pulled them
over her bare arms against the chill in the room and rolled on her side
to face the wall. She had no idea whether she had fallen asleep or not, or
whether it had been hours or minutes, when a wide shaft of light from
the hall played across her face, then narrowed. She flipped onto her
back, propping up on her elbows as her eyes adjusted to the dimness. A
figure stood inside the doorway. Jess? Not Jess, too big. Her mind struggled to make sense of it. The figure moved toward her bed, knocked
against the far edge of it, and grunted. A man's voice. Bucky!

"Hey, this is my room!" Cory pulled the blankets up to her chin,
suddenly aware of her bare breasts under the light t-shirt.

He rounded the corner of the bed and leaned toward her, falling on
one hand.

"I found you," he said playfully and groped in the dark, swinging
one arm out like a blind man trying to find her. She scooted toward the
wall, but his arm brushed against her. It wrapped around her shoulder
and down her arm.

"Get out of my room!" Cory shouted.

He pressed against her, crushing her against the pillow.

"I want you," he slurred. His breath stunk of garlic and wine. Her arms were pinned under his weight and tangled in the blanket. She rocked back and forth, struggling to free them, to push him off.

"Get off! Mom!"

No answer from the living room. No hurried footsteps on the stairs to rescue her. Cory screamed again, "Mom!"

Hershey pushed into the room, bumping the door against the wall. The hall light illuminated Bucky's face, flushed and greasy with sweat. At the sound, he turned toward the door and Cory managed to extract one arm. She pushed against his shoulder with all her strength. His body rolled away. She pulled her other arm out and with both hands braced against his chest, shoving him off. He slid to the floor on hands and knees and remained there, head down. Hershey sniffed the crown of his head and emitted a low rumbling growl deep in his throat. Cory threw back the blankets and leapt for the door as Bucky staggered to his feet.

In the hallway she called downstairs one more time, "Mom!" then dove into the bathroom and locked the door. She leaned against it and listened. Blood pounded in her ears, her breath ragged, but no other noises came from the other side of the door. She listened for the sound of her mother rushing up the stairs, the sound of her slamming the door behind Bucky's retreating, the sound of someone coming to help her. Silence. She listened as if her very skin and every cell were open and alive and waiting to sense that it was safe. Hershey scratched and whined at the door. There was an uneven tread along the hall. The sound of slow, careful steps down the stairs. Where was her mother? Had he hurt her?

Cory's skin was cold, but covered with a slimy film. She wanted to shower again, but she couldn't stay in the house. In the mirror over the sink, wide eyes, rimmed in red and smeared with mascara, stared back at her. She plucked the scanty t-shirt away from her chest where it was sticking to her. Hershey whined at the door.

"Find Mom," she whispered through the crack in the door. Turning, she scanned the small bathroom for a weapon. Nail trimmers, half-empty shampoo bottles, hairbrush . . . nothing. She grabbed the aerosol can of air-freshener from the shelf and resolved to spray it in Bucky's eyes if he got near her.

Hershey's toenails clicked along the hall, and she heard him slump down at a favorite spot at the top of the stairs. The room filled with the smell of sweat and horses as Cory pulled her dirty clothes out of the hamper and stepped into the crusted jeans. She had to get out of the house. The barn. The barn was safe. She quickly finished dressing and stood at the door with her hand on the lock, listening.

She could make out a muffled voice downstairs, the thud of something heavy—a bottle—hitting the carpet.

She cracked open the bathroom door and peered out. Hershey thumped his tail. Cory straightened her back and took one tentative step into the hall. The refrigerator hummed in the quiet. At the head of the stairs, she heard a sharp intake of breath, followed by the creak of the old couch's frame. She knelt down to pat Hershey and whispered, "Good boy. Bite him after I leave, okay? In the nuts." His tail thumped once.

She crept to the bottom of the stairs. The living room was dark and smelled of sweat and sour wine. Cory opened her mouth to call for her mother again, but clamped it shut when she spotted her lying on the couch with Bucky's large frame pressing over her. Roni turned, her eyes rested on Cory, but remained unfocused, expressionless. Her smeared lipstick rimmed her slack mouth. Cory stared back. Her jaw ached from clenching it. Roni didn't move, struggle, or jump up in embarrassment.

Forcing down the bile rising in her throat, she said, "I'm outta here."

Her mother's eyes followed her as she opened the door, slipped outside, and slammed it behind her.

The frigid air stung Cory's face. It must have dropped twenty degrees since she went to bed, and still all she had on was the stupid hoodie. She had no idea what time it was, but probably pretty late since all the lights in the neighboring houses were off. No cars moved along the street. The streetlights shone a halo of light onto the sidewalk. She jogged, heading to where the lights ended and the woods began, her footfalls strangely loud in the silence.

The edge of the woods and the dark gap in the trees loomed ahead. She ran for it, dragging the frigid air into her lungs. The cold was brittle, transforming everything around her into silent, glistening forms along the wooded path. The trees and bushes wore a fuzzy, soft coating of frost that sparkled in the moonlight as if embedded with a million tiny rhinestones. Her nose dripped and her bare fingers were red and numb. She ran down the path, flying over the unseen roots and rocks without tripping, as if she were being carried on a moving sidewalk of air.

She exploded from the woods into an open area near the farm's far paddock. Horses swathed in blankets dotted the field. When she appeared, one horse raised its head, sniffed the air, and nickered softly. Pressman. In the moonlight, she could make out the heart-shaped mark on his head. Cory climbed the fence, jumped down onto frozen feet, and cut across the pasture. Approaching the sliding doors of the barn, she prayed the Jack Pack was up in the house with Vee. She didn't need a bunch of dogs waking everyone at this hour. She held her breath and slid open the barn door wide enough to slip through, then closed it. All was dark and still, except for the sound of the horses stirring in their stalls. One nosed his bucket, banging it against the wall.

"Go back to sleep," she whispered. "I'm not here to feed you."

Cory didn't turn on any lights but felt her way down the aisle, gathered an armload of woolen coolers and turnout rugs, and mounted the stairs to the hayloft. The orange tabby was at the top of the stairs.

"Surprise," she said. "Didn't expect to see me again tonight, I bet."

She arranged some hay bales to form a bed, spread a cooler over it, and lay down. Her stiff fingers clawed at the pile of horse rugs and woolen coolers, struggling to pull them over her shivering torso. Her teeth chattered uncontrollably. When the orange cat padded over, she lifted a corner of the covers. He marched under them, curled up behind her knees, and purred. Cory was grateful for the warmth as well as the company. Scratching and scurrying noises came from the dark corners of the loft where the moonlight didn't reach.

Oh, dear God, please don't let it be rats.

Another cat appeared from the darkness—a silvery gray with fur that turned darker on his paws and the tips of his ears. He padded over to Cory and rubbed his head against her cheek. A shaft of moonlight sliced across his face, illuminating his pale eyes. He sat so close she could smell his damp breath. He stared at her with his blind-looking eyes, just like those of her mother that night. Looking but not seeing. Watching her without emotion, letting her leave the house without a word of protest. Cory squeezed hers shut to block out the memory. A wail, long held back and pressing on her chest, wound out like a long, thick snake into the frigid air. She gulped, sucking in the cold air, hurting her throat. Tears slid down her face but she didn't bother brushing them away. The silvery cat meowed once and licked her face with a raspy tongue.

More cats appeared from the corners of the loft, kneaded at the blankets, and surrounded her in a furry cocoon. They curled up against her body and sent a dozen small pools of warmth against her frozen limbs. The silver cat settled last beside her head. Cory finally slept.

Chapter
Nineteen

CORY AWOKE TO the sound of barn swallows skittering along the beams overhead. All the cats were gone, even the friendly orange tabby. She heard someone downstairs, probably Jack, dumping grain into buckets, running the hose, leading horses down the aisle for morning turnout. Could she slip out the front while he was out back with a horse? No, he'd probably spot her. Maybe she could tell him she got here really early. Sure. With no coat and in the same clothes she had on yesterday. Cory sat up on her elbows, thinking, but it was difficult to concentrate. All she could think about was how much she had to go to the bathroom.

Footsteps on the stairs sent her leaping from the bed, gathering up an armload of coolers. She wasn't ready. She didn't want anyone to find her up here, with this makeshift bed. Balling up the rugs and coolers, she stowed them behind a pile of hay. *Get them later.* She straightened her clothes and ran fingers through her hair.

"You living up here with the cats now?" Jack asked, stopping near the top of the stairs. He sized up the platform of hay bales and stared at her, waiting for an answer.

"I can explain."

"Don't have to. But if you needed a place to stay, why didn't you go on up to the house and knock?"

Cory didn't answer. She reached behind the hay for an armload of rugs to carry back downstairs. She knew she'd never have had the nerve to show up on Vee's doorstep in the middle of the night. She was thirsty, and a film of cotton had grown over the back of her tongue. She scraped it along her front teeth, sticking it out a few times as if she were a cat who had just tasted something nasty.

Jack turned to go back downstairs, so Cory followed. She really did want to tell him something, give him some explanation about what she was doing in the hayloft—God knows what he thought—and at the same time she wished she could jump out the window and fly away.

Downstairs, she ran to the bathroom. When she came out, Jack hoisted a large bale of hay off the pile, swung it down to the floor, and sliced it open with one fluid motion, the smell of summer invading the November cold. Staring at his back, she said, "It was a guy."

He didn't turn around but continued filling the hayracks along the aisle. "Yup. Guys usually figure in any sort of trouble."

"A guy attacked me." Words tumbled out.

Jack stopped working and faced her.

"He didn't rape me or anything," she hurried to add, "but I didn't want to stick around and let him."

"Makes sense." Jack nodded. His voice was calm, but his lips formed a hard line.

"I had to get out of there. I couldn't think of anywhere else to go." Cory heard her voice rise in pitch and felt her throat closing around the top. *Stupid, stupid, don't cry now.*

"What about some breakfast?" Jack suggested, laying a hand between Cory's shoulders. "I got a taste for some Bob Evans sausage gravy myself."

Cory smiled. "Yeah. Sounds good." She wrapped her arms around herself and rubbed up and down. "And lots of coffee."

Jack led them to a corner booth and ordered without even opening the menu. Cory couldn't imagine anyone who could eat the whole Farmer's Breakfast at Bob Evans, but Jack was making a good stab at it. He seemed to know all of the waitresses on the early shift, and they were giving her some strange looks. After getting cleaned up in the bathroom, she'd ordered a tall stack and plowed into them like she hadn't eaten in days. It felt comfortable to sit in the brightly lit room and just eat, not talk. When they did talk, it was about the horses—about Vee's favorite broodmare that was finally pregnant after many tries and who was riding what horses on the circuit this year. Safe topics.

Cory pushed her sticky, empty plate aside and wrapped her hands around the porcelain mug, topped off for the fourth time with scalding hot coffee. She slumped in the booth as a wave of fatigue swept over her. She looked at Jack through hooded eyes. He must have been a good-looking guy as a young man. He still had a chiseled face, a straight aristocratic nose, and those intensely blue eyes. His hair was thick and pure white. His arms and hands, resting on the table, were muscular, but his fingers were long and tapered.

"Do I have some food on my face or what?" Jack smiled.

Cory sat up, realizing she had been staring. "No!" Embarrassed. "I was just wondering . . ."

"About?"

"Well . . ." She fiddled with the saltshaker and groped for a topic. "How long have you worked for Vee?"

Jack sat back. "There was a time Vee worked for me."

Cory looked up but said nothing. Jack had a way of dispensing little tidbits of information and then clamming up. She decided she would use his game against him for a change until he decided to spill the details.

They sat at the little table with the sun pouring in as the day grew toward midmorning. The waitress came by with the coffeepot but saw their cups were still full. Cory peeled the paper off a soda straw the waitress had left with her water. Jack's hands were wrapped around the coffee mug as he stared out the window at the parking lot.

"Okay, so tell me!" Cory burst out, opening her hands in a gesture of frustration.

"Tell you what?" His face was blank.

"Really? What you just said, how Vee used to work for you. How come?"

Jack sighed. "It's a long story and not a very pretty one."

"Then you don't have to tell if you don't want." She looked around to see if the waitress was nearby for some more water.

"No, you're part of the barn now." He set his cup down. "It's okay."

And then Jack proceeded to tell her a story of a man born with money, living on a farm with a fortune in racehorses, who pissed it all away drinking until the day came when the young woman working for him breaking and training horses had to take him in as her groom.

Chapter
Twenty

"WHERE WERE YOU?" Jess ran down the stairs. Cory glanced up from the couch. Jess's face was pale against the dark blue sweater. The straight-legged black jeans she wore clung like Saran wrap around her skinny legs. Her legs were two long, thin lines from her feet to her hips—no curves—a perfect dancer's body.

"Breakfast with Jack," Cory said.

"Jack, huh?" Jess teased in a singsong voice. "Is he cute? It's just that Mom's been asking where you were."

"I bet she has." Cory didn't explain who Jack was. "Look, Jess, where is Mom?" she asked in a lowered voice.

"Out with a client looking at some property, probably all day. "Why?"

Cory slumped back against the couch. Now that she was finally warm and fed, she was so exhausted. She wanted to sleep, but the thought of going back to her room, to her bed where he had been, repulsed her.

"Why?" Jess asked again, standing over her. "You look like hell, by the way."

Cory raised her eyes. Up close, she noticed that Jess's "skinny" jeans were gapping around her waist.

"So do you," she said.

Jess shrugged and smiled. "Trying to get back at me, huh? A little sensitive this morning, maybe?" She punched Cory in the forearm. "Seriously. Did something happen or what?"

Cory's brain felt like it was stuffed with cotton and there was no way to explain last night. "Ask Mom." She lifted herself off the couch to get in the shower. She had to get some sleep before going to meet Kevyn that night.

The steam in the bathroom was so laden with the berry scent of Cory's body lotion it was nearly edible. She slathered it on her freshly shaved calves and up her thighs. Her legs were rock hard from all the riding, and the loose layer of fat on the outside of her hips was gone. She hadn't noticed, except for the fact that her pants weren't so tight any longer.

She wiped the mirror off and looked critically at her bare face. The longer she stared, the more the person who looked back seemed like a stranger. Tonight her face did look different somehow. It wasn't her imagination. She saw features she never noticed before—how her right eye was a slightly different shape from her left, how the fine blond hair on her cheeks swirled backward toward her ears. Cory reached for her make-up and started the process of transforming that face into something even less familiar, but hopefully more desirable.

She carefully selected her clothes, pulling on a black camisole with laced edging; straight, slim jeans that hugged her hips; and a jean jacket. She chose a necklace that hung provocatively low, nestled in the valley of her breasts, leading the eye down toward a hint of cleavage. The dangling earrings accentuated her long neck—exposed when she swept her heavy hair up into a high, loose knot. She could see hints of auburn in it now, probably from spending so much time outdoors this fall. Lastly, she pulled on an old pair of cowboy boots over her jeans and clomped downstairs. She was in a hurry to meet Kevyn, to start the night, to turn everything around that had all gone so wrong lately. She wanted to let the night bring on whatever it had in store for her. When she flung open the front door, Roni was coming up the walkway.

Cory stood with her hand on the door. Her mother wore a woolen suit in royal blue and stylish pumps with a modest kitten heel. She was a businesswoman again, carrying an oversized portfolio and looking like any working mom, any normal mother coming home after work. Cory remembered a long time ago when her mom *was* the normal working mom when they lived in Massachusetts. She used to come home and start dinner and ask about homework. Normal mother things. Cory squeezed her eyes shut and opened them, trying to reconcile the two women—the one she saw last night on the couch and this one, digging through her portfolio and talking on her cell phone. For a second, just the briefest moment, Cory questioned if what she had seen last night was really true, if it really happened. Her mother ended the call and tucked the phone away in her purse. When she glanced up, she gave Cory a hard look up and down.

"Where are you going?"

"Out. Meeting a friend."

"What friend?" Her heels clicked along the sidewalk. The blood-shot eyes told Cory it was true—it did all happen last night.

"A friend from band. Kevyn. You don't know him. I'm meeting him at the teen center." She hated herself for explaining. She wanted to brush by her mother and give her the finger as she walked away.

"And what are you dressed as, a cowboy?"

Cory stepped out and pulled the door shut behind her.

"I don't know that I should let you go meet a boy I don't even know. What kind of place is it, anyway?"

Cory opened her mouth to explain, to describe Kevyn as a good guy, to justify going out with him and being safe . . . safe! She wasn't safe last night. No one cared that she was out all night. Cory recalled her mother's dead-looking eyes, that watched her walk out of the house in the middle of the night and registered no concern whatsoever. She looked into the same eyes now, a mascara shadow beneath them. Despite the cool evening, a flush of heat burned like a flash fire up her neck and over her face. In the distance were the normal sounds of the neighborhood: kids riding their Big Wheels, the bounce of a basketball, a trash can lid being replaced. She noticed the thread of silver in the part of her mom's hair where the color was growing out. She could smell the acrid scent of the boxwood shrubs lining the walk. Everything seemed sharper, minute details she'd never noticed, seemed all in slow motion somehow.

"You want to know where I'm going now? How about last night?" Her voice grew louder. "Did you care at all where I went last night?"

Roni grabbed her by the elbow to steer her back into the house. "Don't you dare talk to me in that tone!"

Cory shook her off. "And you are never to have that man back in our house again, ever!" A huge band around her chest tightened. "He attacked me, and you didn't do anything!" The neighborhood sounds stilled.

"What are you talking about?" Her mom's arm dropped to her side.

"He came in my room. He attacked me."

"Oh, go on. That's crazy." Roni stomped on her words. "He didn't attack you. He was upstairs to use the bathroom and went in the wrong room, that's all." She pulled the bottom of her suit sleeve to straighten it and headed down the sidewalk where the kid was riding his bike.

Clickety-click. Clickety-click. The sound faded as he rode away from them. They stood facing each other, staring.

Cory drew a deep breath. "No, Mom, he was drunk. I pushed him off, but he knew what he was doing, and you didn't help me. You've never helped *me*."

Her mother took a step back. Cory brushed past her and turned. Roni stood with her mouth parted, but silent. She looked smaller somehow. Cory turned her back, walked to the end of the sidewalk, then broke into a run.

Chapter Twenty-One

THE TEEN CENTER, a stupid name, was really the fellowship hall of an interfaith center near the mall. It possessed all the charm of a school cafeteria: cinder block walls, cracked linoleum floors, and garish neon lighting. The fall pumpkins and dried cornstalk decorations helped some. Keeping the lights low helped more. Kevyn had sent her a text asking her to meet at the center since he was running late, and promised she could meet his mom another time. Luckily, Cory managed to snag a ride with Jess and her boyfriend, Jeff, before they took off for a movie.

Cory walked in as the band was setting up. Kevyn waved hello, then leaned down to adjust the amp. As she moved toward him in the overly bright room, she worried that maybe she had applied too much make-up, and second-guessed the decisions about her clothes.

"Hey, glad you got my message," Kevyn called over to her. "I'll just be a second here." He turned back to the tangle of cords at his feet.

Cory drifted to a table pushed against a wall, deposited her purse, and perched on its edge in the dimmer light. The Teen Center administrator, a guy probably in his forties, walked around adjusting the drink set-up and talking with the cop posted by the door. His black rock band t-shirt was probably from the eighties and a small rhinestone glittered in one ear. Whenever he spoke with someone, he stroked a thin soul patch that ran in a dark line down his chin.

Mr. Soulpatch stood over Kevyn and told him to dial down the amps. Yeah, *he* likes it loud, but the community center regulates that sort of thing.

She didn't know the other guys in Kevyn's band, and it didn't seem like he was going to introduce her. Soulpatch turned to her. She averted her eyes, but no good.

"So, what type of stuff does your boyfriend's band play?"

Not my boyfriend, she thought, but said, "'Billie's Blues,' 'Ornithology,' that sort of thing but more progressive, more updated, you know?" Cory had listened carefully to Kevyn's description of his band's music and used his words. She had even played some of the music with him after band practice, just to try it out. Turns out, she and Kevyn were the only upper classmen in the regular band's clarinet section who were not selected for the All-Star because of the "walk-out incident." Outlaw clarinetists, Kevyn called them.

"Never heard of 'Billie's Blues'—is that a Skynard song? Think it rings a bell."

The guy's voice brought her back to the conversation.

"No, Charlie Parker, like the band's name . . . *The New Yardbirds*," Cory explained.

He fingered his soul patch in a thoughtful gesture. "Parker, humm . . . Played backup for CCR?"

"Nope, sorry, Mr. Burke." It was Kevyn. He came up behind them and slung an arm around Cory's shoulders. "We renegade clarinetists aren't satisfied by rock alone."

Cory turned toward him and was warmed by the idea of being included, as if she were one of the guys in the band, too.

"We're a jazz band. The New Yardbirds." Kevyn's words were short bursts of enthusiasm. His eyes gleamed in the backdrop of the neon lighting. His hair had grown long over the fall and was now curling over the back of his collar.

"Jazz!" the guy said, his eyes growing large. "I thought you were a

Southern rock band. Yardbirds, that's slang for chickens, isn't it? What the hell! Kids don't care about jazz!" Sweat formed on his brow.

Cory moved closer to Kevyn to protect him from the storm of disapproval. She was a little worried now, too. She had secretly thought to herself that maybe this was a mistake, that maybe the band would be a flop playing for high school kids. She saw them now filtering into the club in groups and wondered how many would just leave, how many would turn on Kevyn and the band and make fun of them. Energy radiated from Kevyn's body. She brushed her hand against his and he grasped it as he explained the sets to Mr. Burke. Kevyn didn't care if no one got his music. Cory leaned against him, lingering inside his safe and confident aura.

"Not to worry, Mr. Burke," Kevyn said. His hand slipped out of Cory's as he strode off to the bandstand. Mr. Burke shrugged and walked off.

The band warmed up, emitting a cacophony of sounds and rhythms all in their own stream. The din of the instruments mixing with shouts and the clatter of dishware reverberated against the cinder block walls. Kevyn grabbed his clarinet and blew a column of air down its body without a sound as he lightly touched each key. Cory, drawn by the action, was mesmerized by his fingers playing up and down the black body of the instrument. He turned his back on the crowded room. His shoulders lifted as he drew in a tremendous breath. The sound of the clarinet, deep and resonating, vibrated out its bell and over the noise. The notes glided up the scale to the top of the register until they reached the sound there that was almost piercing, a deliciously painful squeal. When the ear could stand it no longer, he slid back down the scale again to the deep, woody tones at the bottom. Kevyn spun around. All heads turned to look. He signaled the rest of the band with two snaps of his fingers, then a sound of primal rhythm and energy erupted, underpinned by drums, bass guitar, and punctuated by trumpet blasts. The throb of the beat echoed deep in Cory's chest as her foot tapped the beat. Heads bobbed in time, heads attached to confused and stunned faces. Her shoulders relaxed. It was all so unexpected. So

Kevyn.

A kid dressed in black with greasy hair and pale skin stood directly in front of the band, legs spread apart, and inserted his iPod earbuds. When he slumped over to the drink bar he drew a like-dressed crowd in his wake. He gathered them around him and with a smirk made an obscene gesture to the band. Laughter erupted from the black circle. Cory's heart hiccupped as she saw how others watched the group, pulled in by the negative energy. No one wanted to choose the wrong side, to be branded a loser.

The band kept up the energy with a bass guitar riff filling the air. A couple girls broke from the crowd to dance right in front of the band, glancing over their shoulders to smile at the guys as they writhed to the beat. One girl in a jean miniskirt and wearing big hoop earrings tossed her fringe of black hair back and forth across her face as she danced. Strands of it caught on her lacquered red lips. Eyes turned from the circle near the drink table to watch her instead. Other girls mimicked her, dressed almost exactly alike but without the exotic black hair and catlike movement. They watched her, but she watched no one. She's the kind of girl who sets the standard for everything, Cory decided. Sure enough, in a few minutes the dance floor swelled with bodies, bumping into each other, laughing, and trying out new moves.

The song ended and more lights were dimmed until only one bright spot shone directly over the band. From Cory's vantage point in the darkened room, Kevyn was luminescent in a white oxford shirt, the sleeves rolled back on his forearms. He dragged a stool to the front of the stage, perched on the edge of it, and casually examined the clarinet in his hand. He put it to his lips and began a tune so mournful, so deep, it caused a hush to fall over the room. Cory moved closer to the stage and watched his fingers play over the holes, touching them firmly with confidence, familiarity, and tenderness. An intense longing felt like a stab deep below her navel. He cradled the instrument, playing the most deliciously sad song.

She hadn't realized she was staring at him until he looked straight back at her. Her eyes darted away, grateful for the darkened room.

But when she glanced back, their eyes met again and she didn't turn away. And yes, he smiled a little, she thought. Feeling overheated in the crowded room, she slipped out of her jean jacket, revealing the thin, lacy camisole underneath.

Kevyn took a deep breath and closed his lips around the mouthpiece, his eyes closed. He arched back, reaching for the high notes, a plaintive wail, then tipped forward to lock his eyes on Cory again. Could she be falling in love by watching a guy play a clarinet? It was as if there was no space between them, no other people in the room. Couples, swaying to the music, glided in and out of her field of vision, but an unbroken channel remained between them. His hands move deftly along the instrument and felt as if they were moving along her own body. Her skin inside her clothes was electrified, imagining the lightest touch. She wanted to go on stage and stand behind him in the spotlight, rest her head against his shoulders, and slide her hands up under his shirt and play the same notes on his muscled abdomen. As she imagined the scene, her eye caught a look from the drummer. He was softly backing Kevyn's solo on snare, but she realized, he was watching her watching Kevyn.

She dropped her gaze to the floor. A flush of heat spread over her face. When she headed across the room for a drink, she saw that Kevyn was following her movements, but so was the drummer.

When the music stopped, couples on the dance floor stood frozen in their spots, embracing, as if it would start up again soon. A smatter of clapping started in a dark corner and swelled around the room in a chain reaction, followed by shouts and whistles.

Kevyn hopped down from the stage and headed toward her. The dance floor was choked with couples moving to the recorded music. Kevyn started weaving his way to her when a blond girl hooked him around his waist. He spun toward her, and she pulled him back into the crowd. Cory sprung to her tiptoes to see over the heads into the crowd. She caught glimpses of the girl with Kevyn, her enormous white teeth all in a perfect row, smiling. The toothy girl cocked her head and leaned in to catch what he was saying to her.

A light touch pressed her elbow. Startled, she turned to see the drummer standing beside her, his face shaded by a fedora. An unlit cigarette hung from his bottom lip.

"Hi." Her gaze slid away, back to the dance floor.

"Hi, yourself." His voice was low, like a man's voice, an older guy. He followed her eye. "Cute couple, huh?" He nodded, indicating Kevyn and the toothy blond.

"What do you mean?"

"Well, just that they look good together. Cute girl."

Cory took a deep breath. *Right.* What was she getting upset over, anyway? "Yeah," she said, then added under her breath, "she sure is." The girl was still smiling—smiling with glimmering blue eyes that only looked at Kevyn. She rubbed her hand up and down his arm. Cory's muscles tensed. "Who is she, anyway?"

The drummer looked at her with mock surprise. "You don't know? That's Briana . . . Kevyn's girlfriend."

Chapter
Twenty-Two

CORY THREW HER full weight at the exit door, almost at a run, and spilled outside into the parking lot. She sucked in the cold air in huge gulps, walking up and down the length of the building, playing back in her head everything Kevyn had said to her. Did he mention a *girlfriend*? How could she have gotten it all so wrong? Was she just his "stand mate"—someone he shared jokes with in band?

God, she was freezing. She had left her jacket inside, and she wasn't about to go back in to get it. Who could she call? She pulled out her phone and looked at the contact list. Someone who could come to get her and not ask questions. Jess and her boyfriend were probably still at the movies. Jack. She was cold, and before thinking about it another minute, she punched in the barn's number and listened to it ring. It was late. There was probably no one in the office at this hour . . . five, six rings . . .

"Hello . . . help you?" It was a bad connection.

"Jack. I'm glad it's you. Can you come get me? Remember the place I told you I was going tonight? I hate to ask, but something happened and I need a ride." Cory tried to sound casual.

"Cory . . . you 'right? . . . 't happened?" She only heard pieces of words, but Jack sounded worried.

"Listen, I can barely hear you, but I'm good. Don't worry. I just need a ride home, okay? I want to go home now."

"Is it him, that guy? Is he there? I'll be right there . . ."

The call dropped. Cory tried calling back, but there was no answer. She slipped the phone into her pocket and looked up and down the empty street. She rubbed her arms and jumped up and down to keep warm. The back door to the club opened again, casting a shaft of light into the parking lot. A dark figure walked toward her.

"You forgot this."

The drummer, with her jacket in hand. She grabbed it and slipped it on.

"You left kinda quick. What's the story?"

She wanted to be alone, but then again she didn't. Not out here in the dark.

"I just didn't want to stay. I have to go home."

"Oh, yeah? I can give you a ride if you want."

"Don't you have to stay and play another set? Besides, I've got a ride."

He leaned his back against the wall and put one foot up against it. "Sure, well that's good. Hey, you look cold. Do you want to wait in my car?"

Cory shook her head. She stood beside him and slumped against the brick wall.

"Okay, hey, I think I know what the problem is."

Cory turned her face to him as he pushed off from the wall and stood over her, a hand placed on either side of her head. Cory shrunk lower, but there was nowhere to go. His breath smelled strongly of mints in the cold air.

"See, I've been in this band with Kevyn for a long time. A lot of girls really like him, and he's a cool guy. Don't get me wrong, but Kevyn doesn't exactly discourage them from getting certain ideas about things, you know. Girls think they've got something exclusive with him."

Cory sucked in her breath, a sound like a quiet sob. Her hands covered her face. This was so stupid. It's not like they were dating or anything.

"Hey, it's okay. I'm sorry to tell you."

The drummer's arms wrapped around her. He gently pulled her closer as her face grazed his leather jacket. He was sympathetic. He was trying to be nice. And, he was honest, unlike Kevyn. He stroked the back of her head, cupping it in his hand. She looked up to tell him she was okay now. Up close, she saw he was much older. Fine lines spread from the outer edges of his eyes and he hadn't shaved. He tilted his head, paused, then pressed his lips against hers. She shifted back, but was trapped. Her arms hung at her side. His hands slid down her back. Too low. She swiveled and leaned away, but his arms drew her in tighter, boxed in, trapped. Like being pinned under the covers again. When he leaned in, she turned her head aside. She smelled beer as he pushed his lips onto hers.

Her hands flew up between them, against his chest, and shoved him away. She heard screaming. She was screaming. Her throat burned, but she couldn't stop. He moved a few steps away, a look of confusion on his face.

"What the hell? I thought—"

A figure came out of the darkness and flung him to the pavement. Jack leaned over to haul him back to his feet. The other arm pulled back, ready to let fly with a dead-on punch to his face. Cory ran to Jack's side and grabbed his arm.

"No, Jack, stop!"

His face turned toward her in the dim light. His eyes were ablaze in a way she had never seen before.

"I'm going to show that son-of-a-bitch what it means when a lady says no."

"Let's just go, okay?" Cory hung on his cocked arm, the muscle hard under the thick jacket. He dropped it to his side and nodded to the truck waiting at the curb. Jack gave the drummer a hard look, took Cory's elbow and guided her to the passenger door. Vee was driving. Cory climbed in the cab and slumped down in the seat. Jack hopped in and had barely shut the door before Vee peeled off from the curb.

The truck cab smelled familiar—horse liniment from a bottle that spilled months ago and stale French fries. "Thanks for getting me," she mumbled.

The dashboard lights illuminated Vee's face, lined and tired looking.

"Jack says you had trouble last night and there you are in a dark parking lot with a guy. Is that smart?"

Cory sat up straighter. "That's not the same guy." She looked from Vee to Jack. He must have told her everything. She drew a deep breath. "The guy who attacked me the other night was a friend of my mom's, when I was home. And not the guy I came here with." An ice pick jabbed her just under the heart when she pictured Kevyn. "I came here tonight because I thought this guy really liked me, and instead I got it all wrong because he has a girlfriend. I got upset, so this other guy came out to talk to me and it started out okay but then he got, I don't know, and kissed me. I panicked. He was, I don't know, and it was all too fast and I guess I way overreacted."

Jack snorted. "So, I beat the snot out of some poor kid who just wanted to steal a kiss from you? Mother of God! What if he presses charges? Maybe I should go back and apologize?" He turned in his seat, looking backward. By this time, they were blocks away and the drummer was probably back inside the club, telling Kevyn what a bat-shit crazy friend he had.

"How old are you, Cory?" Vee asked.

"Sixteen."

"How old you figure that boy was?"

"Maybe twenty-four, probably older."

"Two words. Statutory rape. Don't worry, Jack."

"Easy for you to say, Vee. You gonna come bail me out when they send me to jail?" Jack laughed.

Vee's laugh filled the cab of the dark truck.

"Hell no! I won't be bailing you out, my friend, because whatever trouble you get into, I'll be sitting there right beside you."

She reached over Cory to pat Jack's knee, but whispered to Cory, "Your *mother's* friend?"

Cory made a tiny nod but stared straight ahead. When she shut her eyes, all she could see was the image of Kevyn in the spotlight.

November 8

Men suck. They are either big, fat liars who say things and just disappoint you, or they are creeps who only want to get down your pants. I don't need them. And I'm not going to be like those weak women (no names, Roni) who will date anyone just to have a guy around to make them feel like they're someone. I'd rather be by myself than settle for a smarmy loser. I'm going to Washington. If I have to live at the barn to get good enough, I'm going to do it. Screw all that other stuff.

Chapter
Twenty-Three

CORY QUIT BAND. She didn't want to run into Kevyn, let alone sit near him. Her clarinet sat in its case under her bed, keeping company with a discarded tennis racket, a wood burning kit she used only once, and a collection of dust bunnies. She thought about it under there each night when she crawled into bed, feeling guilty that she had quit, but she couldn't face it right now.

It was weird to think she took the barn job to help pay for clarinet lessons. Now, instead of playing, she spent all her free time at the barn working or poring over horse ads with Jack and Vee. They were trying to find the perfect horse for her to ride in the jumper shows. They'd gone without her to look at some "prospects" but always returned with stories of how the horse was unsound, how it was totally crazy, or how a horse advertised as a solid four-foot jumper couldn't get over a cross rail. Cory hadn't gone on any of the shopping trips yet. Vee said she didn't want her falling in love with something she knew would never work out.

By now the grass was dormant, the fields had turned brown, and the area underneath each gate was churned up mud. Overnight, frost had glazed the ground and turned it into a slick sheet of frozen mud. According to Vee, this was the best time of year to get a deal on a horse, what with the holidays coming up and people wanting to dump their excess stock before winter. Hay prices were high this year, too, because of the drought. A lot of farms had no margin to carry one more young horse over the winter that wasn't going to earn its way anytime soon.

Cory conducted her own horse search. Sitting at the old computer on her desk, she scanned the internet classified ads for horses and logged into several horse search engines. Her dream horse, as she envisioned him, was a tall dappled gray with a shockingly white tail that would float behind him like a flag as they flew over the jumps. She even saw the horse's perfect head with an alert expression, pricked ears, and big, dark eyes. She was getting carried away creating *National Velvet* stories, as Vee called them. As she reminded Cory on more than one occasion: "There are no perfect horses."

One day during a lesson, when Vee was lecturing about her favorite riding philosophy, Cory had questioned the notion of a perfect horse and rider combination. "What about the horse of a lifetime everyone talks about?" she asked. "The *one perfect horse* out there for each rider, the one that you just sync with?"

"If that horse exists," Vee said, snorting, "he's keeping company with the *one perfect man* out there."

Cory never believed Vee was quite as cynical as she let on. She kept Pressman, after all, and had practically built a shrine to him in her office. She also had Allegra, and Vee called her "the damn near perfect horse" except for the fact that she would never stay sound. Vee bred her to a stallion in California, after searching for an ideal match for over a year, but Allegra didn't get pregnant. Vee kept pouring money into vets, breeding fees, and fertility drugs. When she finally came in foal this spring, Vee had the ultrasound print of the fourteen-day-old fertilized egg copied and mounted on her office wall.

Cory turned back to the horse classifieds and typed in her requirements:

Age: 5 to 10 years
Height: 16 hands minimum
Breed preference: Hanoverian, Oldenburg, Thoroughbred

Experience: jumper
That was a no-brainer.
Color: gray
What the heck, might as well go for her true dream horse. She punched in the last key and hit the search button.

For a hundred-mile radius from her house, the results showed only eight horses. She dismissed five candidates immediately based on their lack of experience or past injuries. Another was a cribber. The last two were promising, especially one that was a stunning dappled gray. She clicked on the picture to read more.

EPIPHANY
Nine-year-old Hanoverian mare, seasoned jumper, in the ribbons at Washington, The Garden, Vermont, and Wellington. Perfect Amateur Owner/ Children's Jumper horse, uncomplicated and kind. Always sound, easy temperament, not mareish. Owner's poor health forces sale.

Cory drank in the picture. It was her dream horse. It was exactly like she had imagined. When she scanned down to the tiny box marked "price," she slumped in her chair. Forty-five thousand dollars! *Well, forget about that one.*

Jess came in wearing her usual baggy sweatpants and oversized sweater. She tossed her dance bag on the bed, lifted the sweater over her head, stepped out of the sweats, and kicked them across the floor. She then shimmied out of the leotard with her characteristic fluid movement. As she turned to pick up the discarded clothing, Cory looked at her more closely. Jess's stomach was actually concave below her ribs, which stood out prominently along her side. Her spine looked like a string of pearls along her slender back.

"So, how's *The Buttcracker* rehearsals coming along?" Cory asked.

"Ha. Hilarious, Cory. I never get tired of that joke." Jess sounded peeved. "*The Nutcracker* rehearsals are going well, thanks, as if you care."

"Oh, lighten up. Just kidding."

Actually, she wasn't kidding. She hated *The Nutcracker*, hated being dragged to see it every year because Jess was in it. She was five when she landed her first role as a mouse in the chorus, up until last year when she was selected for the starring role as Clara. Cory swiveled around in her chair to face Jess.

"So, are you at least a human again this year, like that Clara girl, or some flower or fairy or something?"

Jess struggled into a t-shirt so tiny it looked like a five-year-old owned it.

"I'm too *big* to be Clara this year. She's supposed to be a kid." Jess pulled another baggy sweater over her head, an almost exact match for the one she tossed in the hamper. "Actually, I'm the Snow Queen."

"Not the head Sugar Plum Fairy?" Cory knew that was a coveted role. A poisonous delight touched her smile when she asked Jess such a seemingly innocent question.

"No, they always get a pro for that, for the principal dancer roles." Jess dropped onto the bed and became absorbed in unwinding the tape thickly wrapped around each toe.

God, she had such ugly feet from dancing—the toes were all calloused and raw looking all the time. Cory felt particularly irritated with her skinny body, gnarled toes, and baggy sweaters.

Scooting her chair closer to Jess's bed, she asked, "So, you aren't a human this year? A snow queen? Is that like an ice princess, only more bitchy? Do you ever wonder what exactly it is about this ballet that makes it a Christmas tradition? A creepy old pedophile uncle gives a young girl an ugly nutcracker that turns into a prince who, of course, she falls in love with. Then he fights off the Rat King to protect her because, of course being a *girl*, she can't fight for herself. Then all these weird characters dance for her like she's some kind of princess or something. And she falls for the prince because all girls should have a prince, when actually it is the *rat* that should have turned into the prince to make it much more true to life." Cory took a deep breath.

Jess stopped working on her toes and stared at Cory. "What's up with you? Does this have something to do with that guy who ditched you?"

Zingo. Jess had good aim, too. Last week, Cory had told her about that night at the Teen Center in a rare moment of openness. After all, Cory owed her for the ride there. She'd gotten her boyfriend, Jeff the Jerk, to go out of his way for once and do her a favor. He was a creep, but a creep with a driver's license. She also had told Jess about the attack, and how she had to spend the night in the barn. Since then, neither one of them had actually seen Bucky back in the house, but Cory saw evidence of his having been there—his brand of cigarette butts in an ashtray, bottles of beer in the trash. It was an uneasy truce with her mom. Cory avoided ever mentioning the incident again, and apparently her mom was making some effort to only entertain him when no one was home.

At that time, Jess, in turn, had told Cory that she really wasn't a shoo-in for the scholarship to the summer dance program in Massachusetts because the final selection criteria stipulated she be judged again on her performance once she got there. But she neglected to mention that fact to Roni. Cory suggested she ask if Dad would pay.

"Did you at least call him, you know, in case?" Cory had asked while they were making dinner.

Jess lobbed an empty can at the trash and missed. "Yup."

"Well? Let me guess, hmmm. The answer was no?"

"Bingo! Seems Ashley needs her teeth fixed now." Jess sat up and mimicked their dad's tone. "Too many expenses at the moment to be paying for luxuries like summer camp. Sorry, kid!" Jess hopped on the counter and curled into a small, bony ball.

"Sucks. Second family trumps first every time."

Dad had a new wife who was very pretty, but in a sort of scary way. Too tanned and lots of make-up. She came with a daughter, a little nine-year-old dweeb who seemed to need more than her share of everything.

"Don't worry, you'll get the scholarship. Who's going to be better than you?" Cory smiled and had meant it.

Now in the quiet of their bedroom, Cory spun back to her computer. *Note to self: don't tell Jess anything or she'll use it against you.* After a few minutes she heard Jess pad across the room and stand over her shoulder.

"Sorry I've been a creep lately. I guess it still bugs me. The thing with Dad. And I'm worried . . ."

Cory shrugged without turning around.

"So, what are you working on?" Jess leaned closer. "A horse that costs forty-five thousand dollars! That's as much as a sports car." She stuck her face inches from the screen. "Pretty, but I'd rather have a nice car."

"I'm looking at horses for sale. Something to train and show at Washington next year—but obviously not this one." Cory looked longingly at the gray mare, then turned to Jess. "Vee's looking for something I can train up and show, you know, local stuff."

"If she's such a big-time trainer, how come she doesn't want to show it?"

This was a natural question coming from Jess, who always wanted to be out in front on the stage. Cory figured she would never understand anyone willing to give up the spotlight to someone else.

"Vee doesn't show anymore," Cory explained.

"She get hurt or something?"

"I don't think so. She still rides and trains horses. She just doesn't show."

"That's weird. You know why?"

Cory had wondered why. She had tried to find out from Jack, but everyone went mute whenever the subject came up. She eventually accepted that Vee had her reasons. Jess pulled a chair over by the desk and shoved Cory aside so she could have access to the keyboard.

"Let's Google her. So, she was a big-time rider. Was she in the Olympics or anything? What's her name?"

Cory felt a little uncomfortable. She hesitantly gave up her name. "Vee Stewart."

Jess's fingers paused over the keyboard.

"Vee? What kind of name is that? What's her real name?"

"I dunno. I've asked, and she says Vee is what people call her, and Jack won't tell me, either."

Jess jiggled her leg, bouncing it impatiently on the ball of her foot.

"Hmmm. Vee. Short for Vicky, Victoria, Vivian? Does her farm have a website?"

Cory snorted. "I don't think she even has a computer."

Jess stroked her chin in thought. "Okay, let's link her name up with some horse association or show or something. Just because *she* doesn't use the internet doesn't mean that other people haven't written about her."

Cory rattled off the names of some famous shows and all of the usual horse associations. "Gee, Jess, if dancing doesn't work out, you have a future with the FBI."

Jess gave Cory a hard look. "Dancing has to work out." Then she turned back to the screen. "Okay, none of these names are working. Even searching with the names of shows she must have been at and horse associations . . . She just doesn't exist!"

"Let's try Jack's name and hers," Cory suggested, remembering the story Jack told her about Vee working for him at one time.

Nothing came up that remotely resembled a Stewart who rode with a Jack McCaughlin.

Jess stood up from the desk and stretched. "She's a mystery woman. I gotta go, but if you can find out her real name, maybe we can get some answers." Jess grabbed her cell phone off the bureau and left.

Cory stared at the screen. She saw Jack's name in some search lines, but none that included a Stewart. She clicked on the first one and read. It turns out Jack used to own a Thoroughbred breeding farm called McCaughlin's Choice. She linked his name with the farm and got eighty-five hits. There were newspaper articles with pictures of a much younger Jack, standing in the winner's circle next to a pretty, stylish blond woman and a racehorse. There was another of him in a tweed jacket handing a trophy cup up to a jumper rider at some show.

The articles talked about the successful racehorse trainer Jack McCaughlin sponsoring jumper classes at Washington and Culpepper. He moved from training racehorses to show jumpers on his farm in Virginia. Some of this Cory had learned at breakfast that day, about how he owned a horse farm and lost it and his family because of drinking. When he told her the story, she had pictured a small farm. Nothing like this. He had been rich, really rich, it looked like. A big deal in the racing world and in the horse show circuit. No wonder people recognized him at Washington. And when *did* he meet Vee? He said that Vee at one time had worked for him—Cory figured showing one of his jumper horses, yet she couldn't find a single reference to Vee in any of the numerous articles about Jack or in the list of show results for his horses. Cory shut off the computer and started to wonder just exactly what was Vee's story.

November 16

I feel bad about quitting band, but there's no way I'm going to sit in the same room with him and pretend like nothing happened. Too bad, makes taking those extra lessons kind of a waste. So, I guess I'll have a lot more time to work at the barn now—and find out the story behind Vee's real name. Weird. And speaking of weird, Jess plans on going on up to that expensive "enrichment program" this summer even though she might not get the scholarship after all. Ballsy move. Hey, maybe I should just call about that horse, Epiphany, and worry about how I'm going to pay for her later, like maybe something magical will work out. Ha, ha, like maybe even ask Dad to buy her for me. I'm sure he would, maybe if my name was Ashley.

Chapter
Twenty-Four

I T WAS FOUR in the afternoon. Cory had been sitting on the hard bleachers in the auction barn, staring out the large double doors, since two. They were there to buy hay since Jack was in a panic over the fact that it was late fall and the hayloft was only partially filled. It had been a bad summer and hay was scarce. He said if the loft wasn't full by Christmas, they weren't going to get through the winter.

At least it was a break from horse hunting. When Vee finally allowed Cory to come along, she was excited. It was fun at first, but then it wasn't anymore. There was the horse that ran off with her. Then there was the one they drove five hours to see based on a video of him jumping a four-foot course. It turned out the video was about a million years old and the horse was stiff and lame.

On the longer horse shopping trips, Cory amused herself by calling Vee by different names to see if she would react. So far, her test of the obvious "V" names had failed to elicit any reaction other than a confused-looking scowl. In her free time at the barn, Cory had scrounged around in the office, peering into files and riffling through vet bills to see if she could find Vee's full name, but everything seemed to be billed or addressed to the farm or to Mrs. Stewart. She was failing as a secret agent.

Now at the auction barn she sat shivering, a little discouraged that fall was dragging its heavy feet toward winter. They had been there all afternoon while Jack wandered around inspecting pallet loads of hay, pulling out snatches, sniffing it, and commenting on the maturity of the seed heads. Cold radiated through the concrete floors as the auctioneer droned endlessly over a microphone, calling out to bidders. Cory tugged her coat tightly around her and stuffed her hands under her armpits. The air was a swirl of scents—summery new-mown grass from the tons of hay and burnt coffee from the food stand, all mixed up with damp wool and mud.

"I'm gonna walk around. My feet are cold," Cory told Vee as she scooted past her out of the row of bleachers. She headed to the storage section where the hay piled on pallets was a sweet maze of narrow aisles and stacks. People were still milling around, pulling out stems, and sniffing for mold. A ruddy-faced man in coveralls was particularly interested in the same lot that Jack had decided to bid on. Cory wondered if she should run back and report that they might have some competition when the hiss of air brakes caught her attention. A huge tractor-trailer pulled up to a partially open bay in the back of the storage barn.

Men shouted and the screech of metal rang out as a ramp slid over rusted tracks and slammed to the ground. She stepped outside, wondering if another hay dealer was late bringing in a load.

Just outside behind the building, a group of horses milled around in a pen. More horses were being shoved into the same pen by men shouting and flailing arms at them. The horses started to run in a clockwise motion around the muddy enclosure, eyes wild, kicking out at ones that got too close. More horses were walked down the truck ramp into the pen. Some were sore, barely able to negotiate the steep incline, while the men inside the trailer whipped at their legs and shouted, "Go on. Get outta here."

The horses formed a dark storm cloud of muddy color, spinning in a circle that threatened to burst out of control. Cory held her breath.

Drawing closer, but staying next to the building's shadowy wall, she watched as the men lifted the ramp back into the trailer and shut the doors. They were going to leave all of those horses in there together. Some looked like babies, maybe no more than yearlings. Some were clearly old, with ribby sides and sunken eyes, standing placidly in the eye of the storm.

Cory hushed and cooed at the circling horses, with no effect, as she slowly approached the pen. A horse broke out of the swirling storm and lunged at her, yellow teeth bared and ears pinned flat against his head. Seconds later, the horse was knocked aside. Cory fell backwards, out of range. When she looked up, a mare, which had been standing in the eye of the storm, lunged again at the attacking horse, driving him farther away. He swung his head around to bite her, but backed off instead and retreated to the far corner of the pen. The mare lifted her chin in sharp nodding motions at the spinning horses. She showed them the angle of her eye until they slowed and backed away.

Cory let out the breath she hadn't realized she'd been holding. Quieter now, the horses nosed at bits of hay imbedded in the muddy ground. The mare came to the fence where Cory stood and looked at her. Cory reached up to touch the side of her neck. "Hey, thanks. I owe you one."

The mare was taller than most of the others, with a much larger build. She wasn't especially attractive, since it looked like she had been partially clipped for the winter and her coat was a strange mousy gray. Her tail was completely covered in mud, hanging in stringy clumps, and her mane was matted, uneven, and rubbed out in some sections. She had nicks and cuts on her legs, her hooves were overly long and cracked, and there were two open sores on either side of her withers. Her black eyes, though, watched everything around her. Her head was large but not unattractive, except for her enormous ears, and it was perched on the end of a long, arched neck. The others in the pen kept a watchful eye on this mare. When she turned sideways, Cory noticed the marker on her hip. All the horses wore an oval sticker with a number on their flanks. Cory brushed the mud off the mare's sticker and felt a little jolt when she read 537. It was the number of the house she grew up in back in Massachusetts.

"You seem to be the boss, here, huh?" She reached up to stroke her. The mare lowered her head and rubbed it against Cory's hand. "You like that, huh? The only other horse I know that is so crazy about having her ears rubbed is Vee's Allegra. Don't guess you guys could be related, no way."

The mare stood still, breathing quietly, and waited.

"Who are you, I wonder." Cory looked around her. No one was outside or around anywhere. She knew the auction office had lists of items for sale and consignment. They probably know something about the horses.

"I'll be back. Don't worry." She fished in her pocket and pulled out a wad of Kleenex, a dog biscuit, and a couple of lumps of sugar. She held her palm out to the mare, who devoured the sugar with one delicate swipe of her lips.

Cory ran back to the office. She stepped in a long line behind a fellow wearing a shiny blue baseball jacket, boots, and a cowboy hat. She tapped the cowboy's shoulder. "What's up? Everyone come late for the hay auction?"

The cowboy turned around. He was young, probably only a few years older than she was. He had wispy blond stubble on his chin and was dipping dirty fingers into a paper carton of French fries. He licked the ketchup off a finger and looked at her.

"Not hay, horses." He nodded toward the depths of the auction barn, in the other direction from the hay storage.

"The horses in the back you mean?" Cory asked.

"No," he said. "Our farm don't use horses like them. We don't buy from the kill pen." He turned his back on Cory as the line moved forward.

Cory stood still. She didn't understand. *The kill pen?* "What's the kill pen?" she asked under her breath, almost afraid to hear the answer.

The cowboy turned around and looked at her hard. After drawing a deep breath, he answered in a softer voice. "See those guys over there, coming in to the arena?"

Cory looked back into the bleachers area where Vee and Jack were bidding on hay.

"Yeah," she answered tentatively.

"Well, those guys are the meat men." His blues eyes narrowed, looking over to a group of men taking seats in a back section of the bleachers. "They come to this auction and buy the horses going for meat."

"What?"

"The horses in the kill pen usually don't sell for any more than meat prices. These guys buy them, truck them over the border to slaughter. For people in France who eat Trigger burgers."

Cory started sweating inside her down coat. "But some of them are young. They're all going to be killed? They can't be saved, any of them?"

The cowboy hitched one shoulder and took a step away.

Cory heard the hysterical edge to her words. She lowered her voice, trying to make it even and calm. "But anyone can bid on them, right? If someone else buys them, then they don't go for meat, right?"

"Yeah, sure, I guess. They're mostly broken-down racehorses and such. People dump them 'cuz they're crazy or crippled or something. Otherwise, they usually don't end up there."

"But they could be okay. It could be that a horse is there by mistake . . ."

The cowboy's shoulders slumped and he glanced away. "Yeah, could be a mistake, but not likely. Not likely."

He turned away and started a conversation with an older man. Cory moved when the line moved, but had no idea what she was going to say when she got to the office registrar. How could all of those horses be sent off to be slaughtered? Some of them were babies. The mare appeared sound. Cory saw her trotting around the pen, and she seemed fine. The line moved forward. She'd tried out horses that weren't much better and people wanted twelve thousand dollars for them.

Cory found herself in front of the office registrar. A woman in a dirty canvas vest, her head bent, studied the paperwork in front of her. An inch of dark roots showed along her part. Cory cleared her throat.

"Ah, I'm here with Safe Habor Farm, ah, with Jack McCaughlin and

Vee Stewart . . ."

The head snapped up, and there was a smile on the face that met hers.

"Jack. Yes, he registered earlier. You need more numbers for bidding?" She pushed some bidding paddles toward Cory. "And you'll need the sales catalog if you're looking at the horses." A glossy brochure appeared before Cory. She grabbed it and the bidding numbers and headed back to the pen to check on the mare.

Tearing off her gloves, she furiously thumbed through the pages, down the columns of numbers. All the horses for sale at the auction were listed by their assigned number. Most of the sale horses had names, owners' names, and some breed information listed. She scanned the column of numbers. Some horses only had a number listed and were described as grade horse or quarter horse type, age unknown. These were the horses in the kill pen. Cory found number 537. When she looked up, the mare was standing by the fence, as if waiting for her. The sales brochure provided a little additional information.

Hip number: 537
Mare, approximately 16.2 hands
Gray
Foaled: 1998
Epiphany by Eisenhartzen out of Dancing Shoes
Consigner: Equestrian Liquidators

Cory looked at the mare and at the name again. *Epiphany!* The same name as the horse advertised in the online classifieds. They were both gray mares, the same age, but there was *no way* a mare in a kill pen could be the same horse that was advertised for forty-five thousand dollars.

Cory walked up to the mare and rubbed her enormous ears.

"Epiphany?"

The mare nickered softly.

"Holy shit. I've got to save you."

Chapter
Twenty-Five

A GUST OF WIND carrying the bite of ice pellets blew across the outdoor yard, picked up Styrofoam cups from the overflowing trash cans. It sent them scuttling across the empty lot. The horses in the pen snorted at papers sailing up on the draft. The ones strong enough to bully others were gathered against the only shelter from the wind. A young-looking horse wandered from group to group, after being chased off from the shelter, from the hay, from the dregs in the bottom of the water bucket. He finally came to stand next to the gray mare.

Cory's breath came in short, quick gasps, expelling puffs of condensate. The weather was turning. She fingered the auction number in her pocket. She could bid on the horse in the farm's name, but with Vee and Jack sitting right there? And then what? Cory reached up to scratch the inside of the mare's huge ear, rhythmically stroking it as she thought. She had to convince Vee and Jack to at least look at her. Then she had to convince them to buy her. The magnitude of the task, stacked up side by side with the stupidity of it, glued her feet to the spot. What was the use? Vee had rejected the horses they had tried out so far, and they, at least, looked a whole lot better.

The loudspeaker announced the horse sales were to begin in

twenty minutes. Cory, shocked out of her lethargy, spun around to run back to the arena and find Vee. Instead, she ran smack into a man who must have been standing right behind her in the dark.

"Whoa, there!" he grabbed her forearms and settled her back on her feet at arm's length.

He was no taller than she was, but broad in the chest with a short, thick neck. He had a thin dark mustache that made her think of Bucky and wore a John Deere baseball cap, the bill of which was black with greasy fingerprints. She resisted the urge to wipe off the spot on her coat where he had touched her. The man nodded over at the mare, standing by the fence.

"You looking at that one?" He stared at Cory in the dim light. "She's the best of the bunch."

"Yes," Cory said quickly, then bit off the word. She thought better of her answer. *Don't call someone else's attention to Epiphany.* "No, the other one," she added, waving her arm in a vague direction toward the back of the pen. "I think that one,"—she nodded her head to indicate Epiphany—"is lame, actually." *Darn it, why doesn't she go off somewhere?*

"Do tell."

He sauntered over to where the mare was standing, watching, and raised one hand to stroke her head. The mare wheeled on her hind legs and ran to the darkened end of the pen.

"Looks sound enough to me. But a bit flighty," he added.

"None of them are broke," Cory said. "That's what I heard, anyway." She was making it up as fast as it came into her head.

"Do tell."

He turned his gaze away from the horses and took a step toward her. "Who'd you hear that from?" he asked, cocking his small head. He looked like some kind of bug.

"The guys who brought them here."

"Commercial shippers? They don't know shit. They're just a bunch of screw-ups who can't hold a real job working with horses."

His words hit her like a jab. Why was she out here in the dark with this creepy guy?

"Yeah, well, that's all I heard. I gotta go."

She spun on her heel and walked purposefully back to the arena, trying not to break into a run. She felt his eyes on her back. Or maybe it wasn't exactly her back.

Inside, Jack and Vee were in the same seats. A cup of lukewarm cocoa sat on the bleachers in Cory's spot. Jack smiled at her when she reappeared but turned his attention back to the bidding. Opening her mouth to tell him about the mare, she shut it again. What should she say? It wasn't her money or her place to tell them which horse to buy. It was all a waste of time. An unlikely *National Velvet* story, as Vee liked to say.

She took a sip of the watery cocoa and stared over the rim of the cup at the crowd. More people had filtered in and were filling the empty seats, wrapped in down parkas, faces hidden under the visors of ball caps pulled down low. They looked like rows of dull-colored birds sitting on a telephone wire, fluffed up in an effort to stay warm.

A tall woman in black breeches and a black and gold parka slipped by and settled at the end of a row in front of Vee. A heavily ringed hand reached up behind her to adjust a ponytail of white-blond hair, releasing a draft of spicy perfume. Cory spotted the creepy guy from outside. He came in and joined a group in the last row on the opposite side, struggling to slide past people, nearly losing his balance on the risers.

Vee sat up straighter, her eyes focused in the same direction. Cory heard her mumble *vultures*. Jack glanced up at the group. They were sitting in the last row, high above the crowd, legs spread wide and big, rough hands resting on their rounded bellies, talking and laughing.

"Who are those guys?" Cory asked.

"Nobody." Jack sighed. "They're here for the horses. None of our business. We'll get our hay and get out of here."

"I know they're here for the horses," Cory said. "I saw that guy outside looking at them."

Vee leaned forward to look past Jack. "Which guy?"

"The one in the last row, wearing the John Deere ball cap."

Vee sat back and crossed her arms over her chest, frowning at the back row. She leaned forward again. "And what were you doing outside alone?"

Jack gently put his hand on Vee's knee.

He turned to face Cory. "Those guys, especially the one you saw outside, are known for cruising the sales to buy cheap horses and try to turn a buck on them." Jack glanced around behind him to see who might be listening, then continued. "They buy cheap horses they might be able to fix up to sell them to hack stables or riding schools, but mostly they buy horses by the pound to ship them to slaughter."

"I know," Cory whispered back. "Some guy in a cowboy hat told me."

Vee's eyebrows raised in mock surprise. "Well, you certainly have gotten around, talking to everyone here tonight."

Cory fiddled with the zipper on her pocket, opening and shutting it, and thought about the mare outside. *There was a chance Vee would bid against the meat buyers just to screw with them.* She fingered the sale brochure rolled up inside her pocket and remembered the advertisement she'd found on Dream Horse for Epiphany, emphasizing the breeding. Vee had researched every Hanoverian stallion in the United States and Europe when she was picking a sire for Allegra. Maybe she would know something about this mare's sire. Maybe she could get Vee interested that way.

"Have you guys ever heard of a stallion called Eisenhartzen? Probably a Hanoverian?"

Vee set down her empty cup. "Sounds familiar, but I've never heard of the E line at all. Maybe it's just not big in this country." She pulled her purse onto her lap and started digging through it.

Cory pulled out the program listing and scanned Ephiphany's entry. Maybe Vee knew something about the dam, but less likely. "How about Dancing Shoes? Ever hear of that horse?"

"Sure, I know her." Vee uncrossed her legs and leaned forward. "In fact, Deb Harty owned her for a long time. Had her at a farm near where I was training." Vee's voice got softer as she recalled the horse. "She was a gorgeous mare, super jumper before she got hurt and went into the broodmare barn." She gave Cory a skeptical glance. "Why do you ask?"

Cory inhaled a ragged breath. "Well, because one of her daughters is outside in the kill pen."

Chapter
Twenty-Six

VEE DUCKED BETWEEN the bars of the pen and quietly approached the mare. Cory eyed the *Only Authorized Personnel Allowed* sign posted overhead and hung back. Vee ran her hands softly, lovingly over the mare and spoke in a low singsong voice. The other horses stepped from the shadows, curious but wary of a person among them. Their ears flipped back and forth, picking up signals, quickly assessing the situation. The gray mare stood near a pool of light cast by the halogen lamps by the doorway. In the dimness, she didn't look so dirty and pathetic. Clouds of condensation sparkled in the frigid air. The young horse hovered behind the mare.

"Cory, please run and get my clippers from the truck," Vee said lightly rubbing a spot on the mare's haunch.

Clippers? What did Vee think she was going to do now? Cory eyed Vee's dirty, down parka, with rips repaired with duct tape. What would anyone think if they caught her in the pen messing with the horses and clippers? They might all get thrown out.

"What do you need clippers for, Vee?" Cory asked, not wanting to get into trouble.

She approached the fence where Cory was standing. Her brown eyes looked almost black in the weird half-light. "Get them, and I'll show you."

Cory flew through the auction hall, out into the parking lot, and yanked open the door to the truck, which was never locked. Inside, she swept her arm behind the seat to find the clippers just as the announcer started the bidding on the first horse. Through the gap in the arena's doors, she caught a glimpse of a muddy pony being led into the ring. Finally, in desperation, she pulled at a box behind the seat, bringing it up along with half-empty bottles and some cast-off bridle pieces like flotsam from the ocean bed. Inside were the small, battery-operated clippers Vee had asked for.

The lining of her nose burned from the cold as she ran back to the auction yard with the whole box in tow. Jack was inside the pen, jogging the mare back and forth while Vee stood off and examined her. He came to a skidding stop, exhaling clouds of breath and doubled over with the effort.

"Sure has the big donkey ears of a Hanoverian," Jack teased, "but how likely is it a horse with her breeding would end up in this place?"

"It happens. I heard the other day a Thoroughbred was turned over to Days End Rescue who had sold for over a million as a yearling in Kentucky. Remember that Derby winner, what's his name? Ferdinand . . . he was Horse of the Year but ended up as pet food." Vee spotted Cory and grabbed the box through the fence. "Good girl."

She checked that the clippers were working, then took a surreptitious look around the empty lot. "Good. Seems you didn't attract any curious followers." She shaved a patch on the mare's flank not much bigger than an index card, stepped back, and smiled. "Look," she said.

"What?" Cory stepped closer.

"Branded. Hanoverian. See the top of the H here? How it swoops inward like two backward facing C's to form the letter? I thought I felt it through her coat, but I wanted to be sure."

All three jumped back when a shadow crossed in front of the light. Vee stopped talking and stepped away from the mare to pat the youngster lurking nearby. A tall man wearing Carhart overalls strode over to them. Cory's heart knocked against her ribcage.

"Hey! What are you doing in there?"

Vee turned around and pretended to notice the sign for the first time.

"Get out," he said, "right now!"

A jolt commanded Cory's feet to start running, but she stood her ground. Vee and Jack were interested in the horse now, and this man was going to ruin everything. The loudspeaker announced the next horse. They might be coming out here any moment to take these horses in to be auctioned, to take Epiphany, and she hadn't asked Vee yet what they planned to do.

Vee slowly slipped out of the pen, followed by Jack, and walked up to the man.

"Are you an auction official?"

"Who wants to know?"

"I want to know who to speak to about getting these horses some water. Their buckets are empty or frozen, and there's no shelter out here. It's starting to rain, if you haven't noticed."

"I got nothing to do with that." He frowned and waved a dismissive hand at the horses. "All I know is none of you are allowed out here in the pen."

Vee opened her mouth, but Jack stepped forward holding an empty bucket. "Get this guy to show you where to fill a bucket. You and Cory come back with some extra ones and I'll help you tie them up so the horses don't knock them over again. Then we all get out of here, okay?"

The man in the dirty overalls grunted and walked away. Jack winked at Vee, handed her the bucket, and flapped his hands at her to go on. Cory and Vee jogged after the tall man.

He entered the barn, turned down one of the long aisles of empty pens, and stopped beside a water hydrant. Cory looked around the empty, frozen darkness. Back here she could barely make out the auctioneer's droning voice. She wanted to ditch this guy and talk to Vee before it was too late.

Vee hung the bucket under the spigot. The sound of water splashing hard against the plastic bottom echoed around the tininess of the empty pens. Rain, coming down harder now, pounded against the corrugated metal roof, making conversation almost impossible. A shrill whinny punctuated the noise. Cory spotted the outline of a pony tied to a post in the corner and thought it was probably the one who was auctioned off earlier. The pony whinnied again and strained to turn its head toward the sound of the water. Vee stopped the spigot and offered the pony the half-full bucket, which he drained to the bottom without taking a breath. Vee turned to give the man a hard look, but he had left.

Cory filled another bucket, but went rigid when she looked up. Epiphany was being led into the ring, followed by the youngster right behind her, pulling and rearing at the end of her lead rope. The man walking the young filly jerked down hard on the lead and yelled at her to stop acting stupid. Vee dropped the bucket to the ground, grabbed Cory's sleeve, and dragged her toward the procession. The workers brought in a large group from the pen and housed them in makeshift stalls. The quieter ones were tied to posts. Jack walked in behind the last horse and hustled them to their seats.

Cory blinked, entering the brightly lit arena. The auction seating was now filled and their seats had been taken, so they squeezed in the end of the back row. Cory silently hoped the auctioneer would be able to see their bids. *If* they bid. She still didn't know what Vee and Jack had in mind. The auctioneer held one hand over the mic while he consulted with a man standing over his shoulder, pointing at a sheaf of papers in front of them. A worker spread a fresh layer of wood shavings onto the floor of the arena. All around her, the buzz of voices, laughter, and movement in and out of seats added to the tension in the air. The thrum of the rain on the roof matched the throb that had started on the side of Cory's head. She leaned over to Jack, seated next to her, and was about to ask what they intended to do about the gray mare when the horse was led into the arena.

A reverb squeal from the PA system silenced the room. After some apologies, the auctioneer announced, "Hip number 537, nice-looking gray mare, good breeding by . . ." He squinted at the sales brochure and stumbled over the German name of the sire. "Let's start the bidding at five hundred, do I hear five?"

Cory tugged on Jack's sleeve, but his only response was a subtle *easy girl* gesture. A small woman led the horse around the ring. The filly called to the mare with a panicked whinny. The bidding was already up to six hundred and fifty dollars and Cory couldn't tell who was bidding. She peered into the audience, spotted the meat men, and watched for any signs. The guy in the John Deere cap raised an index finger. Seven hundred! *No! She can't go with him.* Then she spotted another bidder, the fancy black breeches and jewelry lady. She waved her paddle and nodded as the auctioneer acknowledged her. Seven-fifty. It was happening too fast, it would be all over and Jack and Vee hadn't done anything yet. Cory turned again to Jack,

"Can't you at least make a bid on her? Can we at least try to get her?"

Jack smiled. *He smiled.* It was so infuriating she wanted to scream. He leaned closer and whispered in her ear, "We only have about twenty-five hundred that we can realistically spend on her, including our hay money."

Cory moved to object, but he shook his head. "We let the posers run the bidding up in the beginning. We wait until the bidding slows down, the casual bidders and the faint of heart drop out, then we take our chances going head-to-head with whoever is left in the game. Let's just hope they aren't as serious as we are."

Cory sat back, but her eyes moved over the crowd like a cat tracking prey. The meat man was still bidding, up to eight fifty, and Jewelry Lady quickly matched him after each bid. They were running up the stakes.

The auctioneer droned in a barely intelligible babble, "Nine-and-nine-and-nine-and-a-nine-do-I hear-nine?" The bidding slowed. He called for eight seventy-five, and a new bidder from a group in the front row on the opposite side held up his hand. Jewelry Lady matched quickly, and they battled the price up to a thousand dollars in a few minutes.

The man in the front row stood and stared in the direction of the woman, and called out before the auctioneer's call, "I bid twelve fifty!"

"Crap, what's he doing?" Vee leaned forward to get a better look. "What an ass."

Jack slapped his forehead. "He's a fool. He's letting some pride get in the way of business sense."

Jack shook his head in disgust. The man had sat down again.

"Poser," Vee sneered.

Epiphany started to trot on the end of the lead, sensing the excitement building in the crowd around her. She lifted her head and showed off a beautifully arched neck set high on her shoulder. Jewelry Lady sat up and raised the bidding.

"How much do we have?" Cory asked. "I could work for just lessons, and, you know, I've saved about three hundred already. You could have that."

Vee scooted past Jack and took a seat next to Cory. She leaned close so she wouldn't be overheard. "Thanks, kiddo. That's generous, but we wouldn't take your money. Besides, we don't know anything about this mare except for her breeding. And this is cash and carry. We have to pay before taking the horse."

Vee dug around in one of her many bulging pockets of her barn coat and extracted a checkbook. She flipped it open and frowned at the writing scrawled there. Cory tried to look over at the figures, but they were illegible. "We have the money we were going to use to get hay, about twelve hundred. I also have some money in the barn account here that I put away for a rainy day. We have the money we earmarked for your junior jumper horse, but if we spend any of that . . ."

Cory's eyes cut to Epiphany in the ring and she stopped listening. The meat man's hand was up. "I don't care about a jumper. We should save her!"

The bidding was up to seventeen hundred—more than the hay money already. Cory knew what the cost of buying Epiphany would mean. They wouldn't be able to buy a show jumper prospect as well. Too little money, too many horses. So, there'd be no Washington International Horse Show, no riding on the show circuit this year. There might not be enough to buy more hay to get through the winter. Cory had never considered how much money Vee needed to run the barn. But she had seen how much vet bills were, how much it was to shoe the horses every other month.

Jack leaned in. "I was going to come in late with a bid, after things cooled off, but these hotheads are running up the price so high I'm not sure my strategy's going to work."

The auctioneer called for the next bid.

"Then what do we do?" she whispered back, her eyes locked on Jack's.

"Do I hear nineteen hundred . . ."

A new hand rose briefly and signaled the auctioneer with a curt, confident snap of the wrist. It was a woman with a group of young redheaded girls who all looked alike—pale-skinned with ruddy cheeks. Her bid set off a new cascade of bidding from the outspoken man in the front row, Jewelry Lady, and the meat man. The auctioneer took his cue, and the increments rose steeply. He was now jumping figures in the hundreds, his voice growing louder to be heard over the rain pelting the sheet-metal roof.

Cory slumped against the back wall in the shadows. This was hopeless. Epiphany circled and circled before the crowd.

Out of the corner of her eye, she saw Jack raise an index finger and nod. She sat up. The bidding jumped, twenty-five hundred . . . twenty-seven hundred . . . The figure went up again. He was bidding! The crowd stirred and necks craned around to see who had joined in the game. The escalating amount electrified the crowd, which watching like a thousand-eyed beast. Sitting just under the roof, the noise was deafening. Cory strained to hear how high the price was now.

"We can't go higher than four thousand. Orders from the boss." Jack nodded in Vee's direction. Cory knew even that figure was a lot for a horse they knew nothing about.

Jack raised his hand at thirty-two hundred. Vee watched the horse circling below and scowled. The bidding had slowed, but the auctioneer was calling for the next raise. Jack sat still.

Vee whispered, "Does she look a little short on the left hind to you all of a sudden?"

Jack shrugged. The man in the front row and the lady in black were still in contention for the bidding.

"I really think she's lame behind," Vee said louder.

Oh, God, Vee and her imaginary lameness again.

Jack held a hand to his ear. "Can't hear you over all the noise."

Vee exhaled in frustration. "Jack, she looks short on that left hind, do you see it?"

Jewelry Lady heard and turned around to see who had made the comment, then spun back to watch the horse. She didn't raise her hand for the next bid.

The meat man took the bid, followed by the lady with the red-haired girls. The horse was up to thirty-seven hundred now. Cory shifted in her seat. *I saw her first. How could these people end up with her?*

The auctioneer called the next bid and pointed to the meat man. He shook his head no and waved him off. The auctioneer then scanned the crowd for Jewelry Lady. She hesitated, shifted to look at Vee, then nodded acceptance. It was up to thirty-eight hundred. The man in the front row watched the mare, and nodded. The auctioneer called for thirty-nine. Cory shot Jack a pleading look, and he raised his hand at four thousand. She held her breath. *Oh, please, oh please, everyone just give up.* The freezing rain pelted the roof for several minutes. The auctioneer called for forty-one. No takers. He looked at the bidders. They averted their eyes. The man in the front row scanned the sale catalog; Jewelry Lady spun a cuff bracelet and didn't look up.

"Going once." The auctioneer raised his gavel. "Going twice for four. Nice mare, four thousand . . ." He looked around one last time.

The redhead stood up. One of her kids pushed her from behind. She stepped forward and shouted, "Forty-one!"

Cory sank into her seat. Jewelry Lady stopped digging in her purse, noticed the bid, and raised it again. The price went up and up until the bidding stopped at forty-five hundred. Kids surrounding the redhead woman jumped and cheered. Cory hated them all—the startled woman who looked as if she only now realized what she had done and the gaggle of red-haired girls orbiting around her. Epiphany was led out of the ring and a small bay horse was brought in. It was over.

Chapter
Twenty-Seven

CORY STOOD AND jumped off the bleachers. She wanted to reach the dark of the parking lot and get out of there, but Jack turned the other way and motioned for them to follow. He strode past the horses that had been sold, waiting to be loaded, toward the auction's business office. Cory searched for Epiphany and spotted her with the new owners who were jogging the mare back and forth down the aisle.

"She's lame!" the woman wailed. "I paid forty-five hundred dollars for a lame horse."

Vee shot Jack an *I told you so* look.

The woman dragged Epiphany to the window of the business office.

"This horse is lame," she repeated.

The heavyset woman with the graying hair leaned out and checked Epiphany's hip number, then consulted the sales roster.

"Says here she was run through an 'as is' sale. You bought her, you take her. As is." She went back to sorting a stack of checks.

The woman threw the lead rope to one of the girls standing nearby.

"What about the three-day soundness guarantee? She isn't sound."

The office manager didn't raise her eyes from counting the checks.

"Doesn't apply to an 'as is' sale."

The woman's face bloomed red. "I'm not taking her. I'm not paying for her."

The office manager nodded to a security guard standing outside the screened window. "You are under contract to pay, says so in the agreement you signed when you registered. You can bring her back and run her through the next sale if you want, for a consignment fee."

"I'm leaving her here. *You* can sell her in the next auction."

"No, ma'am. Next auction's not until after the holidays." She turned her back on the woman and walked to the dark interior of the office.

Jack walked up to the red-haired woman, who was fumbling with the lead, trying to slip it through a ring to tie Epiphany up to a post. Maybe she really was going to leave her.

"Excuse me, but I overheard you saying you didn't want the horse after all."

The woman spun around. "No, I don't. Who would want a lame horse for that kind of money? They have my credit card info, so I can't even refuse to pay. And now I'm stuck with a dead lame horse, the cheaters. Cheats!" She tossed this last comment to the empty office.

"Well, ma'am, if you don't want the horse, I may be able to help you out." Jack's voice was like honey, and Cory thought she detected a hint of a Virginia accent she'd never noticed.

"You see," he continued, "the poor gal's always been off and on lame. Never know when she's going to show up sore on that leg . . . ever since she had a bad fall over a fence at Difficult Run in the Prelim a few years back."

"You know this horse?" The woman's eyes widened.

"That's the only reason we were bidding on her. We just wanted to take her home again." Jack lowered his head and shook it gently back and forth. "She was sold to a big-time event rider, and when she didn't hold up during the competition, well, she dumped her at the auction. We got wind of it and hurried down here to buy her back so she would have the retirement she deserves."

Cory opened her mouth then shut it again. *What was Jack going on about?* She glanced at Vee and saw the hint of a smile playing over her lips.

"My last bid was four thousand, that's all we got that we can spend to retire her."

"But I spent forty-five on her," she whined.

"Well, the 'as is' sale is risky business, risky indeed. I'd say learning that lesson for only five hundred is relatively cheap." Jack smiled and fixed his intense blue eyes on her, no doubt waiting for the answer he was sure he would get.

She hesitated, then pushed the kids out of the way, untied Epiphany, and tossed the lead to Jack. "Take her."

Cory grabbed the rope before she could change her mind. Jack pulled a dog-eared envelope out of his vest pocket, counted out the money, and laid it in her outstretched hand. Vee ripped off a check and placed it on top of the stack of bills. Cory was in a hurry to get Epiphany out of there and headed as quickly as she could to the lot where the truck and trailer were parked, but the mare, lurching beside her, was moving with a more pronounced lameness. *Oh God, we really did spend all that money on a lame horse. And it's my fault.* Cory patted her neck, assuring her they would figure out what was wrong.

Vee jogged up beside her with an old rain sheet she managed to find and threw it over the horse before heading outside. She bent to fasten it as Jack joined them. "So now we are the proud owners of a lame, albeit well-bred, horse." Vee stood up and stretched.

"So quick to judge," Jack teased and smiled at Vee. He quickly bent over and lifted Epiphany's left hind hoof, then held out his hand, palm up. A small stud screw rolled around in the hollow of his hand.

Vee's eyes widened. "How did you know it was there?" Then she looked at him suspiciously. "What did you do?"

Jack urged them toward the trailer to load the mare. When they got inside the truck, he started the engine and turned the heat up to full blast.

"I found the stud in the box with the clippers. I wedged it in between her heel bulbs when I sent you both off to get the water, figuring the stud would make her go sore when she went through the auction and it would keep the bidding down. Tough little mare didn't start showing sore until it was nearly over."

Jack pulled the gearshift into reverse and turned to pull out when the office manager ran up to the driver's side. Cory felt her stomach clench. *What now?*

He rolled down the window. The woman caught her breath.

She smiled at Jack as the rain rolled down her face. "You did a nice thing in there, taking a broken-down horse. I see a lot working here, and there are not enough people anymore like you, Jack." She slipped him a folded-up piece of paper and winked. "One good deed deserves another."

Jack unfolded the paper. It had a name and phone number on it. He looked at her, puzzled.

"I know you came here for hay and got shut out. All the hay here tonight was crap anyway. That there is the name of a good hay farmer who holds some aside for his special customers. You call him, he'll fix you up. I told him so."

She started to leave, then turned back again. "Oh, and you may want to know, that young filly that was attached to your horse, she got bought by a nice family, too. She's gonna be just fine. All in all not a bad night." She waved and jogged back into the building.

Cory's feet and face tingled as the heat in the truck brought her circulation back to life. The cold rain had turned to snow, quiet and mesmerizing in the headlights as they drove through the night toward home. The woman's final words echoed in her ears, *not a bad night.*

November 22

Wicked tired so can't write too much. Such a weird day. We bought a horse, one just like the Dream Horse, with the same name and everything. Is that too strange or what? I feel guilty because they spent all their money on her, and she could be a disaster. Vee warned me all the way home that the mare could be lame, or unbroken, or a total psycho, so not to fall in love. Too late.

Chapter
Twenty-Eight

THERE WERE ONLY two seats in the narrow corridor of the guidance office suite, the one-piece chair and desk kind. Cory slid into one with a swivel of her hips as if shimmying into a pair of tight jeans. The bookshelves were filled with SAT prep books, college guides, and technical career manuals. She pulled down the *Guide to America's Top Colleges* and thumbed through it. She had no idea what she wanted to study, let alone where, or if, she wanted to go to school. And no one ever asked her. It was like the future didn't exist. Maybe a little bit like she didn't exist.

The guide was filled with pictures of grassy quads spilling out in front of ivy-covered brick buildings, groups of students in lab coats peering at a test tube, or in the college's colors cheering the home team. She tried to see herself in any one of those pictures and couldn't. The tuition prices were another grim stab of reality. In another picture, the students were crimson-clad all-Americans—Harvard University. It made her think of Kevyn, and she had been successful the past two weeks not thinking about him. She shut the book with a satisfying slap and looked up.

Kevyn stood in front of her.

"Hey," he said.

Cory's eye darted toward the exit. No escape.

He folded his long body into the other desk next to her and placed a large manila folder in front of him, taking pains to line it up precisely along the edge of the desk. He crossed his arms and turned away.

Great. Awkward. Cory squirmed in her desk.

With his eyes on the closed office door, Kevyn asked, "Looking at colleges?"

"Huh?" Cory looked down at the book in her hands. "No, not really." She flipped the catalog face down on the desk. "Just killing time."

"You *do* have a problem with waiting, don't you?"

"What's that supposed to mean?"

He twisted around to face her. "I thought something happened to you. I texted you, but no answer. Then I figured I'd see you at school. And you weren't even in school, or in band, the whole next week. You just disappeared."

Cory scowled at him. *What was he mad about?*

"Half the band was out looking for you that night, until one guy said you took off in a white truck at intermission. Not cool." He went back to staring at the closed door.

All the words she wanted to say jammed up in her mind and got stuck just behind her teeth. Finally, she seized on the one thought that had been eating at her, and the words exploded at his face. "Why did you invite me, anyway, if your girlfriend was going to be there?"

"What girlfriend? What are you talking about?" A furrow between his brows deepened.

"The girl you were dancing with—blond, pretty, big teeth? Ring a bell, or is she passé now, too?"

Kevyn uncrossed his arms. "What made you think Briana was my girlfriend?" He stared at Cory. "And what kind of a jerk do you think I am?"

"The kind who plays women against each other. Your drummer told me, that's who."

"My drummer?" Kevyn shook his head, then smiled. "That bastard." He stretched his long legs out in front of him and leaned back,

hands cupping the back of his head. "That drummer was a contract mu-
sician for one night, a hired professional. He didn't know any of us, just
came to play because our regular guy was out of town. So that's the
story, huh? That SOB was just making trouble . . . who knows why?"

"I think I know why," Cory said. "He followed me outside." She
thumbed the pages of the book like a deck of cards. "Kevyn, I'm sorry."

"So, what happened? I know you didn't take off with him, 'cuz he
came in to play the next set. Said you took off. What was I supposed to
think?"

Kevyn reached over, grabbed the catalog, and popped her on the
top of her head with it. "Sorry? Sorry's not enough."

She covered her head with one hand and grabbed for the book with
the other. Kevyn encircled her wrist with long fingers and before she
knew it, had pulled her and her whole stupid desk over inches from his.
With one finger he turned her face toward him and kissed her lightly
on the lips. He whispered, "You will have to pay for your crimes," and
wiggled one eyebrow menacingly.

His face was so close. The shadow of his kiss lingered on her lips.
She had to resist the urge to raise her fingers to her lips, like some dopey heroine in a romance novel.

"What's the punishment?" she whispered back but failed in her attempt to wiggle one eyebrow.

The office door swung open and Mrs. Haggerty, the guidance secretary, stood in the doorway.

"Miss Iverson? You had an appointment?"

Mrs. Haggerty made every statement into a question. Cory
struggled out of her desk, which was essentially locked together with
Kevyn's, and stood up. The secretary held the door as she slipped by
into the inner offices.

"Don't worry, darling, I'll wait for you no matter how long, no
matter what they do to you!" Kevyn called after her, pounding his fist
against his heart. Mrs. Haggerty gave him an *I'll deal with you later* look
and pulled the door shut.

Cory entered a small office. The half-drawn blinds blocked out the glaring afternoon sun and cast the room in a golden light with swirling dust motes. The delicate scent of flowers and furniture polish covered a much deeper smell of old books and dusty carpeting. Ms. Jankowski, the guidance counselor, closed the door, shutting out the sounds of the school—the bells, the lockers slamming, the constant voices. It became surprisingly quiet. Cory glanced down at the Oriental carpet beneath her feet and felt bad that she was wearing her dirty barn shoes.

"Take a seat." Ms. Jankowski gestured to an armchair in front of her desk.

She was a tall woman, dressed in a drab, dark blue dress that tugged at her waistline. She looked stuffed into it, Cory thought, like a giant blue bratwurst. Ms. J—that's what everyone called her, at least to her face—took a seat behind her desk, pushing aside some of the dozens of flowerpots covering its surface. There were bigger versions of the same type of strange flowers all along the window ledge and bookshelves. They looked like something from outer space—plants on long stalks with red mouths, surrounded by pink petals. Although they were kind of disgusting, she couldn't look away. Ms. J typed something into the computer, then folded her hands on the surface of the desk.

Cory twisted in her seat. "I like your plants," she lied.

"Thank you. I do, too." She looked at a small one fondly, like it was a child.

A little deformed-looking child, Cory thought. She looked past Ms. J to the shelves of books. She couldn't guess what they were about by their strange titles: *Surprised by Joy, Long Journey Home.* No pictures of people anywhere. No family, she figured. Ms. J sat at her desk, looking like one of those dull brown female birds amidst her brilliantly colored office surroundings. Her face was plain, no make-up, but her eyes were really pretty—large and dark and outlined by thick black lashes, like a woman in an old Italian painting.

Cory cleared her throat. "Ah, you called me in. I mean, I got a note to report to my guidance counselor . . ."

Ms. J checked her computer screen. "Yes, Cory, I wanted to see you about your schedule. And another matter."

Ugh. Another matter. That didn't sound good, Cory thought.

"I see you dropped band about a week ago." Ms. J turned her eyes from the computer screen to look directly at her. "Any particular reason why?"

Her face got hot. What could she say? "No, not really." She thought of Kevyn, sitting outside.

"You know that will leave you short three credits this semester? Do you have plans to pick up an extra load next semester to make up for the drop?"

Cory didn't have any plans. She had wanted to quit, so she did. Now everything was different, but too late.

"Not really." She picked at a jagged fingernail. The brown eyes held her in their grip. "I guess I can pick up another course next semester."

"Or you could go back to band. You only missed a week, and I'm sure Mr. Schroeder would welcome you back."

Cory let out a snort.

"Something the matter? Was there a problem I should know about?"

"Ms. J," Cory said, "even if he did take me back, he would spend the rest of the year making me miserable for dropping his course." Cory slammed her mouth shut. She waited to hear Ms. J tell her that wasn't so, and Mr. Schroeder was a dedicated teacher who only wanted the best out of his students, and other clueless crap like that.

"I understand. Mr. Schroeder can be a difficult personality at times."

Cory stopped picking at her nail. Did Ms. J just admit he was diffi-cult? She added, "Besides, it wasn't because of him. Because of some-one else. But it's okay now."

Ms. Jankowski stood and walked to the closed door to the outer of-fice. She paused there, listening. So was she just imagining it, or did Ms. J know something about her and Kevyn?

"So it's okay to go back now?" Ms. J didn't wait for a response. "Good. I can fix it in the record as an excused absence, not a drop. I'll speak to Mr. Schroeder if I have to. Now,"—she nodded her head in agreement with herself and took the armchair next to Cory—"let's get down to some more important matters."

The flood of relief Cory felt over the whole band mix-up was short lived, as a new surge of anxiety stiffened her muscles. Maybe Ms. J had heard something from her teachers about her work falling off. She had really tanked a few tests lately with all the stuff going on. Ms. J crossed her legs at the ankles, folded her hands across her straining midriff, and told her she wanted to talk about something so ludicrous that Cory laughed.

"You want to talk about my *calling*? You mean like people who become priests and stuff?"

Ms. J laughed, too. "No. I like to meet with juniors and start them thinking about what I term their *calling*. What I mean by one's calling is the journey everyone must take to find what it is in life that they're meant to do, what brings them joy, what's fulfilling in their lives."

Cory thought of the pictures in the college guide, the ones of kids not like her, who were headed toward their "calling."

"I don't think I have one. I'm not good at anything special."

"You don't have to be. Calling is not just about doing what you're good at. I'm sure you know of people who are really quite exceptional at something, yet they don't seem to be especially happy doing it or always feel that they're not doing it well enough."

Cory frowned. She thought of Jess, how she danced all the time now but seemed to enjoy it less and less.

"If it were a matter of just finding what you are good at," Ms. J continued, "it would be so much simpler. It's true, people usually derive a great deal more joy or satisfaction from doing something they're good at as opposed to something they really have to work on, at least in the beginning, but it doesn't always give them joy for the long term."

"There's one thing I'd really like to be good at. But, what if you never do find something you're good at, and what if not everyone even has a calling? I don't know if I believe that people are destined for one thing and you have to find it. What if you never find it, or what if you spend your whole life doing the wrong thing?"

The older woman smiled. "All good questions. That's why I like to start these conversations with juniors, so we can explore those ideas before you are faced with a lot of big decisions next year."

"Like college."

"Like college and a lot of other ones." Ms. J shifted in her chair and took a deep breath. "Cory, in my experience I've observed that it's the nature of human beings to want things. Money. Success. But problems arise when we stop wanting anything beyond ourselves, our own needs, and we think that fame, riches, beauty, wisdom, or even love from another person will satisfy and fulfill us. Even great artists have lived unhappy lives because they missed this essential truth."

Cory glanced at the clock over the door. She was afraid Ms. J caught her because she laughed and glanced at her wristwatch.

"I'll tell you a quick story about someone famous, then I'll let you go. Leonardo DaVinci. He was excellent at everything he did. At the end of his life, however, despite everything he had achieved, he spent his last days feeling as if he had missed the point of life. How do we know? Not long before he died, he wrote in his notebook in tiny handwriting, almost as if he were ashamed: 'We should not desire the impossible.'"

Ms. J sat back as if to signal that all was clear now. Cory wasn't sure she understood the point of the DaVinci story, aside from the fact that he was a guy who was really good at everything he did but was still miserable. *Great.*

"O-kaaaay, but what if you think you know your calling but you're wrong? What if—"

"You begin again. You quit and start over."

All Cory heard was the word quit, the word that had dogged her all of her life, the name she had been called—quitter. She had so often been accused of being someone who didn't work hard enough, long enough, or wasn't dedicated.

"You can quit?" she asked. "What if you've spent a lot of money on school already, or you spent a lot of time learning about something you'll never use again?"

"You have to quit. It doesn't matter how costly. You stop what you are doing and you replace it with something else. A nicer way of saying quitting." Ms. J looked down at her hands, still folded in her lap.

The room was quiet. Cory had nearly forgotten she was in school.

"Well, my dear." Ms. J slapped her thighs and struggled out of the armchair. "It's time to get you off to your next class, I imagine."

Cory stood and stepped through the door, shocked to see Kevyn still waiting for her. They merged into the throng of students streaming along the main corridor.

"You look deep in thought," Kevyn said.

"Yeah, I guess."

"Ms. J pick you out as one of her special ones?"

Cory slowed and turned to look at him. "What do you mean?"

Kevyn nodded toward the guidance office. "It seems she picks a few kids every year to come to her office to talk about stuff. Philosophy and life and stuff."

"Why?"

"I don't know why. I just heard about it. Maybe it's because she was a nun and she needs to feel like she's helping people."

"What? How do you know she was a nun?"

Kevyn pulled Cory by the arm and started walking. "I just heard she was. But she's okay. Everyone likes her."

Cory looked down at her feet, at her dirty barn shoes dropping dried mud along the linoleum corridor. "Hey, Kevyn, can I ask you something? Do you think you have a calling?"

November 24

Ms. J fixed it so I could go back to band, and Schroeder never said anything about it. Who knows what she told him. I can't believe it's almost Thanksgiving, which makes me kind of sad. Makes me think of home. And Mom seems to get worse around the holidays for some reason. This year Aunt Livia's coming with

Douglas. I never know what to call him. It's not like he's her husband or anything, and I'm not calling him Uncle 'cuz that's just creepy. Maybe I'll ask Kevyn to come over to help dilute the family drama.

Chapter
Twenty-Nine

T HE TIP OF the knife pierced the crispy brown skin, then plunged deeper into the flesh. A stream of buttery juice ran from the incision, down onto the platter, as a slice of pale meat rolled away from the breast. Aunt Livia's "partner," Douglas, shrugged back his French cuffs with a roll of his shoulders, then stood for a moment, knife poised once more over the turkey, examining it with a wrinkled brow. The surgical precision of each slice caused the turkey to fall on the platter, piling up like magazines evenly fanned out on a coffee table. Aunt Livia, sitting at Douglas's right elbow, beamed at his deft carving skills. Cory wanted to grab the knife from his hand, hack off some thick slices, and eat. She had been smelling turkey for five hours now and was starving. Cory never understood her mom's thing about always having a man carve the turkey. Most guys she knew couldn't tell the turkey's neck from its butt end.

Everyone crowded around the small table. Aunt Livia's eyes were locked on Douglas. Her mom fussed with her hair and straightened some offending object on the table setting. Jess seemed to be drifting off, uninterested in the other people at the table or the food. Her focus was over Cory's head, staring to the darkness outside the sliding door. Cory knew she had called Dad again. She also knew that Jess told him she had to stay with him over the summer or she wouldn't be able to go to that dance camp thing. Judging by her zombie imitation, that must have gone well.

Wow, another cheery family holiday.

She looked at Kevyn out of the corner of her eye. He caught her and slipped his hand in hers under the table. She had been afraid to ask him to her family's Thanksgiving dinner, and when he said yes, her fear turned to dread of a different kind. Would her mom embarrass her? She felt as if she had been holding her breath all week, hoping everything would go well. Hoping everyone would just act normal for a change. Cory took another sip of the one glass of Beaujolais that she and Jess were allowed on holidays. Its rawness slid down her throat. Probably not the best stuff. She placed the glass down with exaggerated care. It wasn't a great idea to have snuck one earlier on an empty stomach.

Aunt Livia—actually Olivia—was Mom's younger sister. She moved to Washington, D.C. after college, years ago, and worked for some political lobbyist or something. Cory didn't understand her job, but it paid a lot of money, according to her mom. Also according to her mom, it cost Aunt Livia a chance to get married and have kids. Roni had told Cory the story of Aunt Livia packing her VW Squareback—one their grandmother had bought for her when she got the job—with her books, a place setting for one, and a good winter coat before taking off alone for D.C. Aunt Livia now lived in a townhouse in Georgetown. Cory examined the small woman in the Prada suit and thought how different she was from her mom.

Aunt Livia grasped Cory's wrist. "Oh, get the camera out of my handbag and take a picture of Douglas carving the turkey. It's just over there, on the coffee table." She flapped a manicured hand toward the other room. Cory figured she might as well, since Douglas was taking so darn long about it. She struggled out of her chair, careful not to step on Hershey, who was wedged in his usual spot under her feet. Aunt Livia's handbag, not unlike Livia herself, was a small stiff box sitting pertly on the end table by the door. Her mom's bag was deposited there, too. It was an overly large, soft bag with an open zipper, collapsed across the surface of the table. Cory opened Olivia's bag, spotted the camera among the sparse contents, and snapped it shut again. When she moved her mom's slouching purse aside, the opening gaped wider. Among the receipts, tissues, and make-up in a side pocket, there were several opaque brown bottles with white labels. Cory looked over her shoulder, then removed one. The name of a local pharmacy and a doctor she had never heard of were printed on the label. A bunch of warning stickers covered the rest of the label, but she could still read "Vicodin." She opened the bottle. About ten blue and white pills rolled around in the bottom. Cory fingered the other bottles in the bag to bring their labels into view. All of them were empty. The dates on the bottles were within the last four weeks and all from different doctors.

The oven had been on all day heating up the house and making the air heavy with the scent of roasted meat. Cory blew a strand of hair away from her face and pulled at the collar of her sweater. She hadn't eaten much and the two glasses of wine on an empty stomach made her head spin. Before replacing the bottle, she shook out two pills and jammed them down into a side pocket of her jeans, then returned to the dining room.

"Want me to take the pics, Aunt Livia? Why don't you stand next to Doug and I'll take both of you?"

Douglas scowled. He hated to be called Doug and Cory knew it. She also knew Aunt Livia rarely allowed her picture to be taken. Livia waved in a dismissive gesture and suggested that Roni should be in the photo. The two sisters were arguing over who should pose when Kevyn jumped up and took the camera.

"I'll take the picture. All you guys stand around Mister . . ."

"Carver," Douglas replied.

Kevyn lowered the camera. "Really? Your name's Carver? That's awesome!"

Roni and Aunt Livia took their places on either side of Douglas, who stood stiffly in the middle. Jess didn't get up. Cory nudged her chair. "Come on, Jess, family photo op."

"I don't feel like it, okay?" She slouched lower.

"Okay, just the sisters then."

Cory stepped aside. "Kevyn, take a picture of my mom and her sister with Doug the Carver."

The two women posing on either side of Douglas were opposites of each other. Her mother's skin was dull under her carefully applied make-up. Livia smiled with her chin tilted up in a studied manner. They stood, arms linked about each other's waists and smiled for the camera, but they were like magnets, exerting a force repelling each other.

Satisfied with the picture, Aunt Livia sat and smoothed the top of her skirt. "The table looks gorgeous, Roni," she remarked.

A borrowed card table was pushed up alongside the regular dining room table to enlarge it. The few silver serving dishes stood out amidst the cheap furnishings and bare walls of the townhouse, like dressed-up prom-goers lost among the aisles and garish lights of Walmart.

Before everyone arrived, her mom had spent all day clearing things out of the living room and scrubbing grime off every surface. She brought up long-forgotten things from boxes in the basement. Little dishes of nuts appeared on tables, sachets of soap and guest towels were placed in the bathroom. Jess, tired of the orders to clean up, had made some remark about it only being Aunt Livia, not Queen Elizabeth.

"I'd prefer Queen Elizabeth," Roni had answered, snapping the tablecloth over the card table extension and tugging at it to fit. "Do you know she sends Christmas cards to family members embossed with *Olivia Kennedy Parker* like she was one of *the* Kennedys?"

Now Roni sat at the table, smiling at her sister. "Well, thank you, Liv. I do try hard to make things look nice."

"You always were the artistic one. I could never even draw a stick figure, and there you were, winning a full scholarship to MCA."

Douglas had finally given up carving and passed around the platter of sliced turkey. Cory had a mound of potato with a shimmering pool of gravy at its center. Wondering what the holdup was with the stuffing, she looked up to see the smile freeze on Roni's face. She knew her mom went to college for a few years and took art. She also remembered when she and Jess were small kids, Roni used to paint in the sunroom of the house in Massachusetts. And she had always helped design the scenery at Jess's ballet performances.

"What's MCA?" Jess asked, snapping out of her stupor.

Cory watched her mom's focused concentration on her plate as she cut up the turkey slice into ridiculously tiny pieces. She didn't answer.

"It's Massachusetts College of Art, in Boston. A very good school," Livia answered for her, then turned to her sister. "Roni, I'm surprised you haven't encouraged the girls to pursue art, since you *were* so good."

"I still am, Liv. I'm not dead yet."

Aunt Livia laughed. "Of course, that's not what I meant. It's just that you didn't keep up with it. You know, you quit school and let the scholarship go, and then you married Robert . . ." Livia's voice trailed away as if to say, well that explains it all and I don't need to say more on that topic.

Roni reached for an overly full wine glass, nearly slopping it onto the white tablecloth. She held the glass aloft in a shaky hand. "Here's to lives carefully planned and executed with no messy detours along the way." She took an enormous swallow, leaving a crescent of lipstick on the rim, and turned back to pushing food around her plate.

Douglas shifted his long legs under his chair and cleared his throat. "Yes, what is it Woody Allen always quipped? Something like, 'Life is mostly plan B.'" He smiled at Roni and Livia for approval. His peace offering.

Kevyn complimented the food and asked for more of something—Cory wasn't really paying attention but was grateful for his efforts. Another larger sip of wine. She still was hearing the word *quit* as it dripped off Olivia's carefully outlined lips, past her bleached white teeth. She watched it fly through the air like a carving knife to lodge in the middle of her mother's chest. She knew how that quitter word hurt. She also figured her mom must have been saving up all of those knives thrown at her, pulled from her own heart, only so she could toss them back at Cory. Roni said nothing to Aunt Livia but reached across the table to slide the wine carafe closer.

Chapter
Thirty

KEVYN'S HOME WAS a townhouse like hers, but in an older section of town. It was all brick, surrounded by a parking lot, and not in a gated community with a fake country club sounding name like Fox Chase or The Paddocks. Kevyn's mom was seated at the table in the dining area along with an elderly lady in a dark suit. His mom was a lot smaller than Cory had imagined and a lot younger looking. She had chin-length dark hair with tiny threads of silver running through it. When she turned to greet them, Cory saw a familiar profile of high cheekbones and sweeping eyebrows that were similar to Kevyn's, but in a more feminine face. Kevyn's mom, who insisted Cory call her Ginny, stood and made her way over to them with some difficulty. A decorative cane was propped beside her place at the head of the table.

"Mom," Kevyn stepped forward quickly to meet her, "you don't have to get up." He glanced nervously toward Cory. "This is Cory, Mom. Just had my second dinner at her house but thought we would come back here for dessert." Kevyn rubbed his hand over his stomach.

"Glad you did, sweetheart. Cory, come in. Have a seat." She gestured to the table covered with a bright orange plastic tablecloth and littered with turkey-themed paper plates. "This is our neighbor, Mrs.

Welty."

Mrs. Welty smiled and reached up to fiddle with a hearing aid.

Cory took a seat next to Kevyn, sitting up very straight. Kevyn's mom settled in at the head of the table and pushed some pies down toward them. A carton of melting ice cream with a scoop stuck in the top sat in the center of the table.

"Help yourselves, kids," his mom said. "I'm exhausted from standing in the kitchen and cooking all day, otherwise I'd be a better hostess." A small dimple appeared when she smiled, giving her an almost elfish look. "Mrs. Welty, you were telling me about your grandson who is in college." She gave Kevyn a pointed look. "Remind me again where he's going to school?"

Mrs. Welty visibly brightened at the topic. She described her grandson, the future Nobel Prize winner at some school in the South working on his premed degree, while Kevyn carved out hefty chunks of pie and deposited them on two plates. He nodded and grunted at the appropriate times during Mrs. Welty's story. Cory devoted more attention than necessary to getting the forkfuls of pie up to her mouth without dropping any. His mom sat, chin in hand, watching Kevyn.

"So, you see," Mrs. Welty continued in a paper-thin voice, "he will have the grades to get into Harvard Medical where he wants to go next year."

Kevyn's fork stopped halfway to his mouth, then he replaced it on the plate. "Harvard. Good school. The best, I hear."

"Oh, yes, indeed." Mrs. Welty beamed. "He's smart enough, that boy is. He'll be a wonderful doctor, and when he is, I'll take all my business to him."

"Great school," Kevyn repeated, "but cold as hell and really far away." He shot a look at his mom.

Ginny sighed and turned to Cory. Her blue eyes under the dark eyebrows were intense. "I'm sure you've heard that I want Kevyn to go to Harvard? He doesn't want to entertain the idea. What do you think?"

Cory's mouth opened but her mind didn't come up with any words to fill it.

"Mom!" Kevyn said. "Way to make her really uncomfortable."

Ginny slid her hand along the table and grasped one of Cory's. Cory started at this sudden, too-familiar gesture. Ginny's hand was warm and dry. She gave a squeeze and quickly released it.

"Of course, I'm sorry for putting you on the spot, Cory. But did Kevyn tell you that he's now ninth in his class standings, and that most of the men in his family went to Harvard? He's a legacy." Her dark eyebrows rose. "And he has been recruited already for the music program."

"And right after we finish dessert, I'll take her upstairs to see the shrine to Harvard in our study, okay, Mom?" Kevyn's voice had a new edge to it.

They sat around the melting ice cream and abandoned pie plates. Mrs. Welty sat quietly, smoothing the paper napkin on her lap. Cory fidgeted in her seat.

Finally, Ginny leaned back in her chair and laughed. "I'm a pushy mom, Cory, and I drive Kevyn crazy, you can see." She grabbed his arm, pulled him toward her, and planted a kiss on his cheek.

Kevyn gave her a small smirk and an eye roll. "It's like you always said, Mom. Pursue what you're good at . . . and you excel at being a pain."

Cory stiffened, expecting Kevyn's mom to rise from her chair and demand he show her more respect or to storm off to another room in a fury. Instead, she pulled the ice cream carton toward her, leaving a white smear across the orange tablecloth in its wake, and dipped into it with her spoon.

She smiled at him through a mouthful of ice cream. "Yup, I'm a real ballbuster when I set my mind to something."

Cory almost choked.

Ginny caught her reaction. "I'm sorry, Cory, you must think we are a bunch of foul-mouthed rednecks. And I never asked you anything about your plans. Do you know where you want to go to school and what you want to do?"

Ginny tilted the carton to scoop along the bottom edges, then looked up, waiting for an answer. Cory didn't have one. No one had ever asked her what her plans were, not since she was a little kid and people would ask what she wanted to be when she grew up. Now here it was again, that same question about what to do with her life. Like Ms. Jankowski and her "calling." It seemed everyone else around her had definite ideas about what they did or didn't want to do. She blurted out, "I have no idea."

"An excellent answer," Ginny said, pointing the dripping spoon at her. "Kids your age shouldn't have any idea what they want to do. They need to go to school with an open mind, try out everything, and discover what their path in life should be." She grabbed Kevyn's hand. "As long as you go to the *right* school, that is."

Kevyn dropped his forehead to the table and groaned, "I give up."

Chapter
Thirty-One

CORY SAT IN Kevyn's truck and watched the figures of Bucky and her mom drinking coffee at the dining room table through the front window of her townhouse. So he did make it over for Thanksgiving, after all.

"Hey, Kevyn, I don't want to go in there now. Want to go somewhere else?"

He shifted the truck into reverse. "Where to?"

"I want you to meet someone." Cory pointed in the direction of the farm. "I'll tell you where to turn."

In the truck's headlights, the gravel driveway to the barn sparkled with frost. Cory felt a little weird bringing Kevyn here. Usually she kept the separate worlds of home, school, and the barn apart and liked it that way, but today it seemed like they were getting mixed up together like chocolate and vanilla ice cream stirred up in a bowl. When they stopped in front of the barn, she hopped out and slid the barn doors open wide enough to slip through. Kevyn followed her. The night had turned cold, making everything feel brittle and sharp. Kevyn wore only a light leather jacket. Cory shivered in her thin woolen dress coat. Her legs, covered only in thin pantyhose, felt naked, exposed. Their breath comingled in the air.

A deep-throated nicker came from the darker end of the barn. Cory smiled, snapping on lights as she advanced down the aisle.

"That's Epi. The one I want you to meet. She must have heard us."

Cory hoped she didn't sound like a dopey little girl in love with horses. But right now, she didn't care. She grabbed Kevyn's hand and pulled him to where Epiphany was stalled. Vee still had her in isolation, in case she had picked up anything contagious from her time at the auction. In the weeks since they had brought her home, she'd put on weight and looked more like the other horses and less like a rescue. She was still confined to her own paddock outside, which she didn't like one bit. She spent her time in the stall banging the door with her hoof and outside walking the fence lines and calling to the other horses.

Epiphany nickered again and tossed her head. She walked circles in her stall. Cory grabbed a handful of horse treats from a bin on the shelf.

"It's okay, girl. It's just me," she cooed. "And I brought someone to meet you."

She slid open the stall door and stepped inside, beckoning Kevyn to follow her. He lingered in the doorway. The mare ignored Cory and walked up to Kevyn, towering over his head.

"God, she's big. Are you sure she's okay?" he whispered.

Cory laughed. "She's just checking you out. She's a boss mare, protecting me, she thinks."

Epiphany smelled the top of Kevyn's head as he stepped farther into the stall. Her breath tussled his hair. The mare moved to stand behind him, sniffing along his neck and shoulders, then took a tentative lick of his jacket.

"This is creepy. She isn't going to bite me, is she?"

Cory watched the mare with increasing interest. The horse was definitely evaluating Kevyn. Epiphany slid her massive head down along his back and rubbed her forehead. He laughed and glanced behind him. In one effortless toss of her head, she sent him flying across the stall into Cory, both slamming into the wall. Epiphany went back to pulling snatches of hay from her rack. Kevyn caught his balance, asked if Cory was okay, and gingerly stepped around the piles of droppings as he slipped out of the stall.

Cory patted Epiphany's neck and leaned close to breathe in her sharp horsey smell, a mixture of raw earthiness and sweet hay. She looked out of the corner of her eye to see that Kevyn wasn't watching and whispered to the horse, "Yeah, I really like him, too."

Cory introduced Kevyn to the other horses. She showed him Allegra, who was now visibly pregnant, and Pressman, explaining she was to ride him in a show next month to get some experience. She threw more hay in to horses that had eaten theirs and dropped treats in their buckets with the ease of someone familiar with a task. Kevyn brushed the stray wisps of hay off her coat and picked a strand out of her hair.

"You really like it here, don't you?" he said, more like a statement than a question.

Cory shrugged. She really did, but it was difficult to explain why. When she was at the barn it felt as if nothing else existed. She loved the feeling of sitting down after the work was done and listening to a barn full of horses munching on hay. She especially liked it when it was raining outside and everyone was inside and warm and . . ."It makes me feel safe."

Kevyn's brows slid together. "From what?"

Cory looked away. "I don't know. Safe."

She envisioned her mom sitting at the table with Bucky. Even if he weren't there, she knew the atmosphere in the house would be dictated by her mom's mood. Every time Cory opened the door at home, she sent out invisible feelers to sniff for danger or a volatile situation brewing. Every time she could feel the tension in her shoulders and every nerve standing ready to fire at the sound of a cabinet door banging or an angry shout upstairs.

Cory gave what she hoped was a reassuring smile. "It's just quiet here. Safe's probably not the right word."

Kevyn didn't say a word, but placed his hands inside her coat, his long fingers nearly encircling her waist. It made Cory feel delicate, cherished. An odd and new feeling.

He drew her against his chest and whispered in her hair, "I can see why you like it." He stroked the back of her head. Cory inhaled his scent and leaned her head on his shoulder. The heat from his body radiated into hers and loosened taut muscles. She turned her face and placed her lips lightly along his neck. She thought of running her tongue along the ropey muscle there, tracing it up to behind his ear. She shifted closer, hoping to blend into him.

The image of her mom with Bucky popped into her head. For the first time in her life, Cory tried to imagine Roni as someone her own age. She must have had a boyfriend, maybe a dream to become an artist. Instead she got married and never finished school. Cory knew she was born soon after that. Maybe she was part of the reason. A warm tear slipped out of the corner of her eye. Her nose was leaking now, too. *Stupid.* She pulled away from Kevyn and dabbed at her nose with her sleeve.

"Hey, you're not crying, are you?" Kevyn held her at arm's length, searching her face. She turned away.

"No, it's just freezing in here. C'mon."

Cory led him into the heated office. As she turned to close the door, Kevyn reached up from behind her, under her coat and sweater, and placed both hands palm down against her bare belly. The sensation was like two planks of frozen fish resting against her bare skin. She spun and leapt aside but stumbled against a loveseat near the door. Her flailing arms knocked several pictures off the wall as she tried to keep her balance. When she fell across the loveseat, Kevyn dove on top of her.

"C'mon, Cory, I've got to warm them up some more," he teased, batting away her defensive hands.

"You idiot, look what you did." Cory laughed. "I'm going to get fired if Vee sees this."

Picture frames were scattered on the floor. A few had slid down behind the loveseat and dust floated through the air. One frame had lost its backing and was lying upside down. Cory pushed Kevyn off her and lifted the black backing. Luckily the glass hadn't broken. She flipped the picture over to reveal a photo of Pressman in his younger days with Vee sailing over a huge jump at The Garden. Vee's favorite horse. Yup, she would be killed if the picture were damaged. The black-and-white ultrasound photo of Allegra's baby, which had been tucked in the outside corner of the frame, was gone. Cory got down on her hands and knees to sweep an arm under the couch.

"Oh, gross. God knows what's under here." She ducked down to peer underneath.

Kevyn was at her side, sitting cross-legged with the frame in his lap. "Who are these people?"

Cory located the ultrasound picture and spun around to sit next to him. She peered over his shoulder to see what he had in his hand. "Where did you find that?"

It was a picture of a bride and groom standing outside on a lush green lawn. People dressed in tuxedoes and gem-colored gowns surrounded them. In the distant background, Cory made out a dark fence and the figures of several horses grazing in a field. The groom was a tall, dark-haired man with classic good looks—like the kind of guy who modeled for men's outdoor wear magazines. He had his arm loosely draped around the waist of a blond who was turning toward him, her profile to the camera. She wore a strapless, flowing white gown and clutched a small bunch of flowers held in one hand behind her back. She looked as if she was about to stand on tiptoe to kiss him when the picture was taken. It was Vee.

Kevyn pulled the picture closer so he could see what had interested Cory so much. "It was behind the picture of that horse. The whole thing fell apart when it fell off the wall. Someone you know?"

"Yeah, my trainer. The lady I work for. I told you about her. I didn't know she was married." Cory scanned the picture again. Vee looked so happy. She was young. Her skin was bronzed but smooth and her hair was a lustrous golden color. She flipped the photo over to find a short, yellowed clipping from a Virginia newspaper taped to the back.

Genevieve Marie Sullard, originally of Ontario, Canada, marries Reginald Lee Stewart in a June wedding. Reginald is a huntsman for the local Lexington County Hunt and is employed in the family Thoroughbred breeding business at their Stone Church Farm. Miss Sullard is an accomplished horse-woman, employed as a rider with racehorse training legend Jack McCoughlin. The couple also plan to make their home in Lexington.

Cory stared at Vee's name, her real name, and tried to memorize the spelling. She fit the picture carefully against the black backing and placed the picture of Pressman over it, then slid the glass into the frame. She propped the ultrasound image back into the outside corner, as it had been before, and hung it back on its hook.

"Photographic archeology," Kevyn mused.

"What?"

"Makes you wonder what's behind the rest of these pictures, doesn't it?"

They stood side by side staring at the wall of pictures restored to their original positions.

"If she had a wedding picture behind a photo of a horse, maybe she's got all kinds of other things stashed behind the rest, like long-lost deeds to properties and birth certificates of abandoned children," Kevyn said.

Cory swatted him with the back of her hand. "I don't think she exactly hid the picture. I think the other things were more important at the time and were layered on top. Like the ultrasound of the foal tucked in the corner. Oh my God, Vee is nuts over that baby. But I never knew she was married," she mused. "I wonder what happened to him."

"Probably buried him under the riding arena. She's a pretty suspicious character, if you ask me. Goes by a false name, hides evidence behind pictures. I think we should investigate further," Kevyn joked, lifting a few of the other pictures away from the wall and peering behind them.

"It's her nickname, you dullard, like mine. She probably didn't like Genevieve." Cory stood with one hand on her hip.

"Yours? You have a nickname I don't know about?" Kevyn acted shocked. "What is it? C'mon, give it up."

"It's Cory. That's my nickname."

"Cory's not your real name?"

"Nope, it's Coraline. Horrible, huh? I guess everyone has *something* to hide." Cory looked up at Kevyn under a fringe of dark lashes and he brushed a stray hair away from her face. "So what's *your* big secret?"

"Maybe you need to work harder to uncover it."

He pulled her close and placed his lips gently against hers. His mouth was so warm, so inviting as he sucked gently on her bottom lip. His arms wrapped tightly around her, pressing her into his hardened flesh. She ran her hands along his arms and slid them behind to the small of his back and pulled him closer so she could feel his hipbones against her. He drew back a moment to look at her, his face so close, then pulled her head toward his lips again. Cory felt she was drowning, melting, disappearing. Her atoms had spun off their orbits, reformed, and were now mixing totally with his body. A knife-like sweet pain rose up through her middle, followed by a sense of something opening up like a budding flower. A flow of thick, warm desire melted down along her insides. She heard Kevyn murmur "Coraline," and for the first time in her life, she adored the sound of her name.

November 27

I flushed them down the toilet. I don't know why I took them in the first place. Maybe I thought I would get back at her by using them, too. I don't know. It was just stupid. I don't want to be like her. I think maybe we're alike enough already, and I don't want to end up like her. Maybe she had a perfect sister who made her look like a quitter and she just started believing it. But I'm different. I have Kevyn, and I'm going to ride at Washington. And Genevieve Marie Sullard Stewart, whoever she is, is going to help me get there.

PART II
Winter

Silver light on snow,
Intensifies the glare.
Pure white that blinds the eye,
And cannot see what's there.

~ From the journal of Cory Iverson

Chapter
Thirty-Two

AS SOON AS Pressman landed over the brick wall jump on the outside line, Cory snapped her head around, searching out the last combination of fences on the show course—the triple. Three huge oxers loomed across the entire diagonal length of the indoor arena. She'd practiced this type of combination at home, and she knew *he* could do it, but now they looked so much bigger. Show nerves. Everyone was watching. But like Vee had told her, galloping around a course of big fences on top a thousand pounds of horse thrust is no time to be grappling with a case of nerves.

Three huge jumps across the diagonal, a change of lead, one small vertical, and she'd be through the course. She'd gone clear so far—no faults. Pressman was jumping like a machine.

She held her breath as she turned the corner and the jumps loomed in front of her. They were impossibly huge, and coming up fast.

Breathe!

Cory blew out and sucked in another lungful of cold air. In spite of the frigid temperatures, she was sweating under her show coat. The three-beat rhythm of Pressman's canter around the turn stilled her panic. She counted in her head: one-two-three, one-two-three . . . His ears flipped back toward her as she steered him onto the diagonal line, then shot forward. His muscles gathered under her as he shortened his stride just before the first enormous jump. As the thrust of his hindquarters lifted both of them, Cory bent low over his body, precariously suspended by sheer balance and the shifting center of gravity to match his movement. Landed. One stride, then the thrust and the lift came again. She was ready, in balance. His massive head and shoulders rose in front of her as she bent so close to him she could see the stitching in the tiny braids along his mane and smell the earthy scent of his sweat. His hooves touched down again.

Her weight shifted slightly to the right on landing, and she scrambled to center herself. No time, no time. Pressman was gathering for the last jump. Out of balance and left behind the motion, he took off before she was ready. She grabbed for a piece of mane to steady herself, but the little button-sized braids offered nothing to grasp. A tug on the reins. She jerked his mouth. He landed. But the triple combo was behind them, they had made it. Cory hardly noticed the ankle blister rubbed raw by her ill-fitting boots as she righted her seat to get balanced in the saddle. Pressman shook his head in annoyance.

She steered him to the last jump, the little vertical rail, the one she hadn't worried about. They had too much speed coming into it. Her shoulders ached and her legs didn't seem to respond to what her brain was telling them as she tried to slow Pressman. She grabbed at the reins. As soon as he turned the corner and spotted the jump, he started a flat-out run. Her heart beat a wild tattoo against her chest and droplets of sweat rolled down her side. She shortened the reins again, pulling, knowing it was the exact opposite thing she should be doing but couldn't stop herself.

Not good, not good, she thought, trying to sit up and take charge. The horse wasn't listening. Annoyed at her, he ripped the reins through her fingers and ran faster. The jump was right in front of them. Cory folded forward over his neck, released her grip on the reins, shut her eyes, and prayed. Pressman took off from a spot a good distance from the jump at a high-speed run. A loud thunk, like someone throwing a baseball bat against a wall, and her stomach squeezed up something nasty into the back of her throat. They landed. Pressman threw his head down between his front legs and bucked, pulling the reins through her fingers. As he slowed, she looked behind her. The rail on the last jump was rocking in the shallow cups that held it, but it was still up. Her mind struggled to process what her eyes were seeing. *How could that be? She heard him hit the rail.*

They had gone clean. They were in first place. The faces of the crowd in the seats and those gathered around the in-gate came into focus. They were applauding. A bubble of joy and sheer relief rose up through her tired body, and a smile broke out across her face. She reached down and patted Pressman's sweating neck through the ghostly columns of steam rising off his body in the frigid air. When she looked up again, she spotted Jack and Vee by the in-gate. When she saw Vee's expression, Cory stopped smiling.

In the trailering area, Cory dismounted, loosened the girth, and walked Pressman in slow circles by her side, hoping he would cool off soon so she could put him away. Vee had not let her stop to take off her boots, which she was sure had rubbed her ankle bloody by now. She barely had time to grab her down vest to throw on over the lightweight show coat. It didn't help because she was already chilled from the sweat-drenched shirt frozen to her back.

Vee was really mad.

She chewed her out for fifteen whole minutes without a break while Cory untacked Pressman, ranting about how she should never, ever, *ever* pull on his face coming into a jump. Cory said nothing. She quickly wiped down the tack and stored it away, with Vee dogging her steps, recounting each minute mistake she had made on the course. Eventually Vee ran out of steam. She sighed and pulled Cory into a violent embrace. She released her just as quickly.

"And worst of all, you could have been hurt. My heart was in my throat watching you two galloping out of control into a jump!"

Cory adjusted Pressman's cooler, which had slipped to one side, as she walked him out. The shadow of Vee's hug still warmed her. Replaying the scene of the last fence in her mind, she knew she had overreacted. And, to top it all off, she hadn't won the class after all, as she thought, but had come in second to a rider who went clean with a faster time.

"I guess second place is better than nothing," she mumbled.

"What's that?" A girl walking a big gray gelding in the opposite direction around the same circle looked at her.

Cory hadn't realized she had spoken out loud. "Nothing, just talking to myself," she called back to the girl, making the universal gesture for crazy person in the air around the side of her head.

The girl's musical laugh rang out in the frigid air. She was about her age, Cory figured, and her size, but definitely better dressed for the job of walking out a hot horse. Her red, curly hair spilled out from under a woolen cap pulled down almost to the top of her eyes. She had on fleecy, heavy boots and an oversized down parka. She passed Cory going in the other direction once more.

"Saw you in the Open Jumper class, right?"

Cory slumped. *Yeah, that was me. The one who almost got run away with.* "Right. I'm the one who really screwed up through the combination and nearly bought it over that last fence."

"Hey, happens to everyone. You've been showing a lot this year? I don't think I remember seeing your horse on the circuit."

"This is my first rated show—for jumpers, that is. I started this fall, and I'm trying to get over the show nerves."

"Just started this fall and you're showing in the Winter Series? That's incredible!"

Cory swiveled around to catch the girl's expression, to make sure she wasn't making fun of her. "Actually, I started riding this horse with a trainer this summer"—she nodded at Pressman—"and really hope to qualify for Washington next year."

The girl stopped and cut across the circle toward Cory. She cocked her head to one side and smiled, revealing a deep dimple on one cheek. "You didn't mean you just started *showing* this summer, did you? No way!"

Cory slowed her pace. "Well, not really. I took lessons and showed some before but on hunters. Nothing like this with a trainer at the bigger shows and all."

The girl let out a piercing squeal that caused her horse to startle and back up a few steps. "No way!" she shouted. "Man, I'm going to quit right now." She spun around and addressed an invisible audience. "To everyone assembled here, let it be known on this day . . . ah, what's the date?" She turned back to Cory. "Okay, on December eleventh, I, Regina Hamilton, do hereby quit riding henceforth because it is clear that I will never be as good as—" She gestured at Cory. "What's your name?"

"Cory Iverson."

"—I'll never be as good as Cory Iverson, who has only been riding jumper horses for a freaking five months." She bowed to Pressman and to Cory. She then turned serious. "Really. I've been riding all my life, and I'm not as good as you."

"I'm sure *you* are much better," Cory said. "And my horse . . . well, he's not my horse but my trainer's, and he's awesome and makes it look easy." She liked this strange girl. She didn't know why. A bit dramatic, but that intrigued her even more.

"Nope, I'm not better. You can ask my mom. I'm sure she'd agree." Regina's small mouth turned down at the corners. "That's why I'm playing groom today instead of riding." She gave her horse a few friendly slaps on the neck. "Come on. Let's dump these high-maintenance parasites and go get something hot to drink and warm up." Regina didn't wait for an answer but started dragging her horse toward the temporary stabling area.

Cory was so glad to be out of her boots and sitting down. She wrapped her hands around the Styrofoam cup of hot chocolate and listened to Regina talk—nonstop. But that made it easier to relax and not have to try to be friendly; Regina was friendly enough for both of them. It turned out she was nearly Cory's age, but she had grown up in this area on a horse farm and had ridden all her life.

"Before my life, actually," she explained. "My mom rode when she was pregnant, so does that count?" Regina whipped off the knit cap and ruffled up her flattened curls. She told Cory how she had always shown, ever since she could sit up in a saddle, but confessed she was still terrified every time before entering the ring. "You wouldn't believe it. I'm still so messed up before a show. I don't sleep the night before *at all*. And the morning of the show I have to go to the bathroom like a million times. I'm not kidding. And do you know how hard it is to pull down those skin-tight white breeches in a porta-john in one-hundred degree weather during the summer? And without touching anything in there? Eww!" Regina sat back and roared with laughter. "It's so disgusting, I usually just pee in the stall and pray he doesn't freak out and trample me. That would be quite a sight—finding me lying in the horse's stall with my pants down around my ankles. I can imagine what people would think, especially horse people."

Cory's face hurt from laughing and from the long hours out in the cold. It felt so great to talk to someone who was like her, someone who had been showing for years and could admit she still got the jitters. Vee never got nervous, or so she said.

"Oh, that's not like my mom—she's my trainer," Regina said. "She loses it, all right, but not like she's afraid of them."

Cory was going to ask what Regina meant but thought it was better left alone. She steered the conversation in another direction. "I gotta tell you about this new horse we got . . . well, we kind of bought her at a sales auction, and when we came home one night she was in a different pasture than the one she's supposed to be in. My trainer was furious because she thought someone had screwed up and put her out in the wrong place, but it turns out she was lonely and jumped the fence. We didn't know that until we put her out the next day, and she walked, yeah, *walked* right up to the five-foot fence and sailed over it right in front of us."

Regina's eyes widened. "You're kidding! Are you going to show her?"

"I hope so, maybe, some day. Right now my trainer is riding her, getting her tuned up. At least we know she can clear the fences."

Regina tossed down the last of her hot chocolate and pulled out a show schedule. They decided to compare notes on which shows they would be going to over the upcoming months and try to meet up and stable the horses near one another.

"That is, of course, if my mother lets me ride. Seems she had a little issue with my grades last semester." Regina rolled her eyes. "I have a tutor now, for calculus. I just don't get why I have to take calculus—it's so boring. Oh, but the tutor is pretty hot, so that makes up for it." She smiled wickedly.

Regina jumped up and crammed the woolen hat back on her head. "Better go." She slapped ten dollars on the table and told Cory in a fake gangster accent, "Hey, you take a dive the next show we're in together, and I'll double that."

Chapter
Thirty-Three

CORY TRUDGED ACROSS the showgrounds under a bruised-purple mass of thickening clouds. The sky looked a lot like the muddy watercolor paintings she did as a kid. The parking lot, previously crammed with trailers, had thinned out. Jack and Vee, off conducting some horse training business, had told her to be back at the stabling area by four to leave for home. Cory hugged herself, glanced at the watery winter light and thought maybe she would head back to the stabling area and see if they could get on the road earlier.

Cutting through the deserted parking lot near the maintenance building, she turned the corner and heard an angry voice hiss, "Now! Lift it now."

Something told her to stop and wait. What were people doing back here when it was almost dark? She inched closer and hid behind a huge tractor parked behind the building. The familiar sound of a horse cantering on the hard bluestone footing was all she heard. Then nothing. A woman's voice called out, "Now, hit him now!" Then the staccato sound of hoofbeats.

"Figure that one learned him something," a man's voice said.

"We'll do it again to make sure," the woman said.

Cory bent down and peered between the tractor body and its giant wheel. Two people stood near a dark bay horse ridden by a small man. A jump was set up, made out of a few poles resting on hay bales. The rider cantered the horse in a tight circle, then pointed him toward the jump. As the horse approached it, he raised his head and shortened his stride. The rider slapped his flanks with a short, thick crop and gunned him at the jump. As soon as the horse lifted off the ground to jump, the woman yelled, "Now!" Together with the other man, she lifted the jump pole quickly so the horse smacked his front legs against it with the sound of a limb breaking off a tree. The bay horse landed and took a few sore steps from the stinging blow, then slowed to a trot.

"That ought to do it. If he doesn't snap his legs up quicker after this, I don't know what else to do with him," the skinny blond woman said.

"Sell his ass for dog food," her partner replied.

The woman turned to roll the poles back up against the machine shed. It was Angela! The woman who took away Prophet. The bay horse was tense and jumping in horrible form. His flanks were sweating despite the frigid cold. The rider jumped off and consulted with Angela as the other guy threw a cooler over the horse and started walking him in the direction where Cory was crouched behind the trailer. The horse's ears pricked up as he walked nearer. He raised his head and whinnied. *Oh, please, don't look over here. Don't rat me out.*

The man slapped the horse with the end of the reins and growled, "Shut up, you cow, or you'll get us all in trouble."

Angela jogged to catch up with the man and told him to have the horse ready because she was riding in the next class. He walked the bay closer.

Cory gasped. It was Prophet. She was sure of it, even though he wasn't acting like the horse she knew.

"Oh, poor guy," Cory whispered. She remembered how much Vee loved that horse and how hard they had worked to restore his confidence, and now . . .

She curled into as small a ball as she could and wedged herself behind a large tractor wheel as the man walked Prophet by her. She waited until everyone had left, flattened against the mud-caked wheels and surrounded by the smell of damp earth and diesel oil. The still air carried the sound of Prophet's hooves receding into the distance, with Angela's voice threatening him that he'd better be good for her. A discarded show program scuttled along the ground in a breeze and stopped at her feet. Cory slid down, her back against the jagged tread of the tractor wheel, and wrapped her arms around her knees. Dropping her head, she started to shake.

December 11

Didn't get home 'til super late, much later than I ever imagined. Scared I did something that's going to cause a whole lot of trouble.

Chapter Thirty-Four

"CORALINE." MS. JANKOWSKI'S voice was soft, but insistent. "Mrs. Thurber sent you here because she's concerned about you. Your performance has gone from a solid A to a nearly failing grade. Today she wrote me to say you fell asleep in her class, and now I see for myself that you can hardly keep your eyes open."

Ms. Jankowski's office was overheated, and the hum of the humidifier in the corner was lulling Cory to sleep. If only she could close her eyes for a minute.

Ms. J stared at her. Cory pushed herself up in the chair and tried to shake off the fuzziness enveloping her brain.

"I was out late last night. Really late, and I'm just a little tired, I guess."

More staring, more silence.

Images of what happened late last night ran through her head: the horrible scene in the show steward's office between Vee and Angela. Cory winced when she recalled the look on Regina's face. She'd had no idea Regina was Angela's daughter.

Cory struggled to focus. "I have a job, after school and on weekends. Sometimes it's late when I get home," she explained to Ms. J's expressionless face. She didn't really want to get into the whole explanation, how Angela got suspended for mistreating a horse. And it had to be Prophet, no less. Vee went ballistic when Cory told her what she had seen, then dragged her along to the steward's office. Angela would probably get a year's suspension. When they were leaving, she tried to catch Regina's eye, to somehow convey to her she was sorry, but Regina kept her eyes glued to the floor.

Cory blinked, trying to snap out of it. Just over Ms. J's right shoulder, a small crèche sat on the window ledge. Almost Christmas, she thought. Her mind leapt from one thing to another. She didn't want to discuss why she gladly stayed late at night at the barn to avoid going home—there were about a dozen reasons why. Reasons any guidance counselor would love to get her hooks into. The image of her sister disappearing in her clothes came to mind, and how she knew Jess must be throwing up what little bit of food anyone ever convinced her to eat. Mostly, though, she worried about the little brown pill bottles she'd found in her mom's purse at Thanksgiving. Now she was finding them all over the house, hidden behind the good china in the cupboard, in the bottom of the bathroom drawers under discarded make-up, and in the laundry room among the boxes of detergent. When she found a new hiding place, she'd carefully pull the bottle from its secret nest to examine the label, check the dates, and find out where her mom was getting the stuff and how often—all the while glancing over her shoulder like a sneak. Then she would carefully slip them back where she'd found them, vowing to check back later to see if they were still there. She kept a mental tally of how much Roni was taking but had no idea what to do with the information.

Wow, she was having such a hard time focusing her thoughts. Now, sitting in Ms. J's office, struggling to stay awake, she didn't have the strength to think up plausible answers for why her grades were tanking. Part of her really wanted to unload it all on Ms. J, but she was afraid of what would happen. Would they investigate her mother? Would someone take her and Jess away or make them go back and live with their dad? She didn't want to leave now and go back to Massachusetts, and from what she gleaned from Jess's phone calls to their dad, he didn't exactly want them back, either.

"I don't think it's just a job that's wearing you out, Cory." Ms. J's voice broke into her stream of consciousness. "I think you have something else on your plate."

On your plate. What a weird expression. She imagined a big steaming pile of horse crap served up to her on decorative china. "Yeah, you could say so."

Ms. J scribbled something on a notepad. *Oh, great, here we go. Detention? Note home to parent?*

Getting up from her desk, Ms. J came around to hand Cory the paper. "Cory, sometimes you have to ask for help. You have to ask for it and then take it when it's offered. Bring this to the school nurse after we finish here—unless we are finished already?" Ms. J gestured, palms up. "It's up to you. Give this to her and go sleep for a few hours in the back room of her office. I've sent word that you're excused from your next class."

Cory took the note held out to her and stood up. She looked briefly at the bulk of Ms. J standing so close to her and suddenly wanted to reach her arms around the woman's vast middle and rest her head on her chest. She imagined the older woman gently stroking the back of her head. Instead, she murmured, "Thanks," and headed to the door.

"Sometimes the world looks a whole lot different after a good sleep. You open your eyes and see things differently." She paused as if she had made some amazingly insightful comment. "Oh, but there's a price for your ticket to slumberland." Ms. J indicated the note in Cory's hand.

She looked down at the slip of paper. "Of course there is."

"I want you to write me an essay."

Cory stepped forward. "I don't have time to do my regular school assignments . . ."

Ms. J held up her hand to silence her. "An essay, which only I will read, in strictest confidence."

Maybe she'd hand the note back and call it quits.

"And ungraded, of course." Ms. J smiled and patted Cory on the shoulder, the warmth of her hand penetrating to the skin. "I'll give you a theme, and I want you to think about it all week, how it impacts the people you meet, the things you choose to do or not do."

"Okay, so what's this theme going to be?" she asked, fearing the worst—something about her inner self or her goal in life. She felt silly saying the word *theme*, like Ralphie's teacher in the movie *A Christmas Story*. What an outdated word.

Backlit by the office window, Cory couldn't make out Ms. J's expression when she said one word: "Desire."

"Desire!" Cory wailed, desperately thinking, what can you say about *desire* to an ex-nun? "What kind of desire?"

"That's up to you."

The nurse's office was in the far corner of the school on a floor partially below ground level. It looked like a prison holding cell. Cory had never seen the school nurse who greeted her, but then again, why would she? It wasn't like she went there ever. When she handed her the paper, Cory noticed how the woman's skin was almost the same shade as her brilliantly white uniform. Her pale eyes scanned the note, then she smiled as if some secret message were printed there.

"Ms. Jankowski sent me," Cory explained.

Without a word, the nurse led her into a darkened room and pointed to a cot in the corner. Despite feeling weird about sleeping in the nurse's room, Cory removed her shoes and crawled under the covers. The nurse seemed to cast a glow standing in the doorway of the darkened room. Maybe it was her white uniform, Cory thought, just before the woman switched off the light and gently pulled the door closed.

It seemed she had just fallen asleep when she heard a bell ringing and ringing. Cory opened her eyes and sat up. When she realized what time it was and that she had slept through lunch and two of her afternoon classes, she flipped the covers off and swept an arm across the floor to locate her shoes. The nurse was nowhere around, so Cory gathered her things and raced down the hall to her last class of the day. Band. And she was late.

"Good of you to find time to join us, Miss Iverson," Mr. Schroeder said as she slid into her seat behind Kevyn. "Since you obviously don't feel the need to warm up with the rest of the band, I assume you wouldn't mind playing the melody line from the Overture in D Minor for us, so we can hear how it's done."

Cory sighed. Kevyn spun around and shot her a sympathetic smile. This was her punishment for being late. Public humiliation. Mr. Schroeder's specialty, the sadistic bastard. She extracted the reed from her mouth, fit it against the mouthpiece, and cranked it down into place. She blew a column of air down the body of the clarinet to warm it, then sat up taller in her chair. Another deep breath. She knew this piece of music—they had been practicing it all term—but she had never played it alone and in front of everyone. She reached forward and adjusted the sheet music with a steady hand and started to play. A warm, rich tone filled the band room as the notes communicated directly from the page to her fingers, which were flying over the clarinet's keys. She heard the music as if it weren't coming from her but from another source. The other people in the room disappeared. Mr. Schroeder and his sneer disappeared. There was only the music swirling around her, reaching a crescendo in an empty white room. The melody wove around, enveloping her in a safe cocoon. When she stopped playing, total silence. She glanced around her as if waking up from a trance. A room full of faces stared at her, then they all started to clap. Cory smiled, especially when she saw Schroeder's open mouth. He slammed his baton against the director's stand. Something inside her had burst free and for some strange reason she wasn't afraid of Mr. Schroeder anymore.

Kevyn was waiting for her outside the doorway when she left the band room. "Where did you disappear to all day? I was looking for you."

"I was asleep," Cory replied without much explanation. "But I'm awake now."

Chapter
Thirty-Five

THE BARN WAS eerily quiet for the late afternoon. Usually when she arrived, the pack of terriers met Cory at the door and Vee was always around somewhere. Today, however, Jack was leaving the office, pulling the door shut behind him.

"Vee's done for the day—had an appointment or something—and I've got to drop the tractor off for servicing. You're on your own."

Jack backed the truck down the driveway with the tractor loaded on a flatbed. Cory had to get the horses in to feed them so she could get home at a reasonable hour and do some homework for a change. The silver cat with the strange eyes appeared at her feet, wrapping itself around her legs. He meowed plaintively as she reached down to meet his arching back.

"Where have you been? You appear at the strangest times."

After she'd gotten the horses in from the fields, changed their blankets, and made sure their hay and water were full, she headed down the aisle to leave. A deep-throated nicker stopped her. Epiphany. Cory turned back, grabbed a handful of horse cookies, and walked to her stall. Epiphany gobbled up the treats and tossed her head. She looked so different now. Her coat was a dark, dappled gray with a thick silvery white mane and tail. Her wide-set black eyes watched Cory as she slid open the stall door. The silver cat sat in the aisle with his eyes squeezed shut, purring.

"Want to go for a ride?"

The mare blinked. As if she were watching a movie of herself, Cory went to the tack room and got the saddle. She'd never ridden Epiphany. She didn't have permission. But when she watched Vee's training sessions with her, Epiphany didn't look too hard to handle. *What the hell?* She didn't think she could play that piece in front of everyone in band today, either, and she did. She was great, in fact.

After tacking up, she led the mare into the arena. A few swallows skittered along the rafters. It was also against the rules to ride when no one was around. Cory swung her leg over the mare's back and dropped gently into the saddle. She let out a long-held breath. "Let's get to know each other, okay, girl?"

As she reached forward to pat Epiphany's neck, the mare leapt into a canter around the arena, crossed the middle, then started in the other direction. Cory swallowed her panic, grabbed a fistful of mane, and struggled to gain some control. With her head high, scanning the arena, Epiphany headed toward an opening in the sliding doors to the outside and stopped in front of them.

"What was that about?" Cory said, catching her breath. "You want to go outside?" She knew that would be upping the ante in the risky game she was playing. "What the hell."

Cory leaned over, and from the mare's back, grabbed the door and slid it open wider. A waft of cool air blew across her face. Hesitating in the doorway only a moment, they headed outside down the long pathway between the now empty paddocks toward the woods. A bubble of giddy laughter formed deep inside her, swelled, and flowed upward until it erupted into the evening air. She was light, as if a heavy backpack had been lifted off her shoulders. The sun hovered above the tree line, paired with the outline of the moon against a leaden sky. It would probably be another hour before sunset.

Entering the woods, she realized it was considerably darker there than in the open pastures. Epiphany walked purposefully along the narrow path as if she had a goal in mind. The trees were bare and black against the fading light. A carpet of brown leaves swished and whispered as they made their way deeper into the woods. Cory knew the paths pretty well. She'd been down most of them either on foot from her house or while riding out on one of the training horses.

At a fork, Cory steered Epiphany to the left in order to make a big loop and head back to the barn. The mare stopped and resolutely pulled her head in the other direction. The path to the right went on much farther into the woods until it ended in a broad field. Sometimes Cory and Vee would take the horses there to gallop, but she didn't know what lay beyond that point. And she sure didn't want to get lost tonight, especially on a horse she wasn't supposed to be riding in the first place.

"C'mon, we have to go back." She nudged the mare to the left, but Epiphany stood in one spot. Cory tilted her head up and sighed. The sky was turning gray with fingers of pink streaking through. It couldn't hurt to go a little farther.

The horse moved to the right and trotted, stirring the invisible forest creatures with the crunch and crackle of dried leaves along the path. Out of the corner of her eye, Cory caught the sudden flash of a white-tail as it bounded out of sight. Epiphany snorted and broke into a canter. Cory leaned closer to her neck, breathing in the horse's heated body, avoiding the low hanging branches. When they broke from the woods into the clearing, they surprised an entire family of whitetails browsing in the field. Their heads, on delicate long necks, snapped up. A dozen dark eyes stared, but the deer remained rooted to the spot, like dark topiary statues, until the horse passed. The rough-edged limbs of the bare trees rimming the field looked like black broomsticks against the fading light.

On the far side of the field, Epiphany turned into an opening that led back into the woods. They followed along a dark tunnel of trees until the soothing swish of dried leaves was broken by the sound of hoofbeats—hoofbeats running fast on packed ground. Cory strained to look down the path, into the shadows. The dimming light was making it harder to see. Everything was rimmed in gray. They needed to turn back, though Epiphany seemed more resolved than ever to move into the darkness. There was a loose horse somewhere, or they had somehow wandered onto someone's property because Cory could hear the hoofbeats more clearly now. The strange horse must be closer, and that would be trouble.

Epiphany gathered herself, every muscle taut, and moved faster toward the sound until they broke from the dark woodland path out to a large grassy expanse. The light was so dim, Cory could just make out the silhouette of a horse about twenty feet away, his breath billowing clouds of steam into the damp night air. He was huge. His dark form ran toward them—he was less than five feet away—when he threw up his head and emitted a high-pitched whinny. Cory tried desperately to turn Epiphany's head, to kick her, and get her to turn back down the path, but she was made of stone. The dark horse moved closer.

Epiphany stood still, tossing her head left and right. As Cory's eyes adjusted to the dim light, she saw the outline of a fence separating them from the dark horse and breathed a small sigh of relief. The outline of a barn, the roofline trimmed in tiny white Christmas lights, squatted in the distance. Epiphany took a step toward the horse as Cory grabbed at the reins. The dark horse snorted loudly and stomped his front hoof. Epiphany rolled her head again, acknowledging him. It was a him— Cory was sure. A real him, a stallion. He sniffed the air, catching the drifting scent of Epiphany, and raised his lip. Cory had heard terrible stories about how dangerous a stallion could be when he had his mind on getting to a mare, and a rider would make no difference. She turned Epiphany away again, and this time she complied. With one last toss of her head, she turned and left the dark horse without a backward glance.

As they moved farther away from the stallion, Cory's legs were shaking. "What was that about? Is this where you were sneaking off to when you used to jump out of your paddock?" She ran her hand down the mare's neck. "So, you just wanted to show him to me?" she whispered. The mare's ear swiveled back to catch the sound of her voice.

The moon was nearly full, surrounded by a shimmering veil of light. The warm dampness from the earth rising in a mist hovered in swirling wisps a few feet over the field in the cold night air. Cory and Epiphany rode past the glen where the deer had been, now empty, and trotted back down the path to the barn. She was glad she had left the lights on. She hurried to untack Epiphany, rub her down, and leave absolutely no trace of her having been ridden tonight. The wind was picking up. It rattled the barn doors in their tracks and sent wisps of hay and leaves scuttling down the aisle. Some of the horses stirred and circled in their stalls. Before she left for the night, Cory tossed another flake of hay in to Epiphany and slid her stall door shut.

She leaned in and whispered to the mare, "Tonight was our secret. I won't tell about the stallion you've been visiting, if you don't let on to Vee that I rode you."

December 12

I'm not sure what changed today, but something's sure different. Things are just working out, and it's not like that's ever happened before, especially for me. It all started when I was so wicked tired that Ms. J sent me to the nurse, but when I woke up, I felt different. I guess I was different. Like she put a spell on me, or something. Then, wow, the whole thing in band. For the first time, I really think stuff's going to work out somehow. And riding Epiphany. Why I did that, when I knew it was dangerous, I don't know, but I just felt it was all going to be okay. Like magic or something. It feels like I've been locked in a cage, but not really, because I just didn't realize the door's been open the whole time.

Chapter
Thirty-Six

"HEY, CORY, WHY did you tell that security guard that we were with the lighting guys?" Kevyn hurried to catch up, pushing through a gaggle of ballet dancers.

"Years of experience sneaking backstage at places like this. Security's always real jerks about letting people back here. Upsets the performers." Eye roll.

Cory grabbed Kevyn's hand and pulled him through a swirling sea of costumed dancers stretching or marking their dances in the narrow passageways behind the stage area at the Rouse Theater. She wanted to see Jess before the performance began, to wish her luck, and this time she really meant it. She'd teased Jess a lot in the past about taking the "Buttcracker" performances so seriously, but tonight was different. They brushed past more performers, bumping into a few who turned their made-up doll faces to them and frowned. A dancer in a yellow tutu studded with colorful flowers lifted one leg toward the ceiling like a marionette without the strings. Another group of performers dressed in velvety Victorian coats and dresses stood in the wings beyond the stage, talking and sneaking sips from Starbucks paper cups.

"I didn't know they made so much noise," Kevyn said, indicating the dancers' feet.

"The end of their pointe shoes are as solid as wood," Cory explained. "You don't usually hear the clunk-clunk in the audience, unless you're in the front rows. Ruins the illusion of fairy princesses and enchanted flowers when you hear them go clomp, clomp, clomp all over the place." Cory tugged Kevyn along, dodging around a costume rack of exploding pink and yellow netting that threatened to engulf them.

"You know a lot about dancing. Does Jess know as much about horses?"

"She came to a few of my shows early on, when it was warmer. But, no. Horses involve three things Jess doesn't do—cold, dirt, and outdoors. Besides, when they start rehearsals, neither Jess nor my mom has time for anything else."

When they reached the dressing room door, Cory opened it a crack and peered in. Spotting Jess seated at a bank of lighted mirrors, Cory called, "Hey, Queenie! Yo, Snow Princess, we're here."

Jess jumped from her seat and hurried to the door, slipped outside, and shut it behind her. "Nice, Cory. There are professional dancers here tonight."

"So, when you go pro you have your sense of humor removed?" Cory was annoyed. How could anyone take dancing as a fairy this seriously?

Jess glanced at Kevyn standing quietly behind Cory.

"He can't come in with you, you know." Jess quickly added, "Sorry, Kevyn."

He seemed to welcome the excuse to leave and promised to go find their seats and wait there. He disappeared down the crowded passageway. Cory turned to Jess, wanting to say something to get back at her for being rude to Kevyn but bit off the words.

"Sorry!" Jess called after Kevyn's retreating back, then looked down at the floor.

Her face was beautiful in spite of the heavy theater make-up, as if it were porcelain, not at all like the clownish girls in the hallway. Her eyes were darkly outlined and rimmed with sparkles, slanting upward under each eyebrow. Her pale hair was swept back in a low chignon, crowned with a silver band, studded with shimmering snowflakes. It made her look unworldly, magical, and somehow more breakable. But not serene, like an ice queen. Waves of energy coming off Jess threatened to make Cory just as jittery—they were so palpable. She ran her hand down Jess's forearm and noticed it was freezing to the touch.

"Jess, you look gorgeous. You're going to just *kill* tonight."

Jess returned a weak smile and led Cory into the dressing room. The small room was crammed with women and girls helping each other into costumes and pinning up hair. An elderly woman was in the corner frantically sewing a ribbon onto a pointe shoe. The air was thick with hairspray. Jess sat down on a low bench near the bank of mirrors amidst the frenetic running back and forth, struggling into leotards, and constant chatter. She looked like an island in the middle of a violent storm beating at her shores. Jess glanced down at her hands and started to say something, then bit her bottom lip and stared off into the far corner of the room. Cory quickly sat down next to her to catch what she was saying.

"I don't think I can do this. I'm not hitting my turns. My footwork's sloppy." Jess lifted her eyes to Cory. They were shining with tears, threatening to brim over and ruin the silvery make-up.

Cory's first thought was to rush to invalidate everything Jess was saying. *Of course, you can do it. You're always nervous before a performance. You'll be great*—and all the usual niceties. Instead, she reached over and took her hand. Show nerves.

"Cory, I'm afraid of making a mess of this. It's a big deal this time. They've hired all these pros, and if I mess up in the partnering, I make them look bad, too." Jess's voice faltered. "I'm just so tired." She raised her hand to brush away an imaginary stray hair.

A million thoughts rushed into Cory's head, but the words seemed wrong. She rubbed Jess's hand between hers. Her face looked pale beneath the silvery glow.

"Jess, you are the best dancer I have ever seen. You always have been. I know I make fun of ballet, but tonight you really are the Snow Queen—you look so magical." Cory swallowed, thinking, desperate to say something that would make a difference. "You're made for this. You've always wanted to be a dancer, and look—it's perfect. It's—" Cory struggled for the right word "—it's your calling."

"Haallooooo!" a voice sang out, followed by Aunt Livia's head poking around the dressing room door. She entered, partially hidden by an enormous bouquet of snowy white roses. Cory's mom slipped in behind Livia with carnations wrapped in cellophane from the supermarket. She tossed them on a low table at the entrance, as if she had no idea how they had come to be in her hands.

Aunt Livia swept Jess up in her arms, crushing her against the bouquet, then held her at arm's length.

"Oh, so exciting! A major role. When we saw the Bolshoi perform in Moscow . . ."

Aunt Liv was off and running. Cory shut out her name-dropping aunt's prattle and decided to go find her seat. A final glance in the dressing room told her Jess was animated again and at least acting the part of prima ballerina as her mom and Aunt Liv buzzed around her like a pair of honeybees.

Cory spotted Kevyn in the auditorium foyer, along with Douglas and Bucky, standing in line at the bar. They made a strange trio: Kevyn in his best outfit, his black jeans with white oxford shirt untucked, of course. Douglas wearing his customary uniform of French cuffs, subtle-patterned jacket, and pressed flannel slacks. Bucky who had donned what Cory surmised was his "dress-up" belt buckle—a large silver-plated monstrosity, paired with a leather vest and pointy snakeskin boots. His hair was slicked back so you could see the comb marks in it. Kevyn turned to hand Cory a plastic cup of soda. Bucky had a beer in one hand and wine in the other. Cory couldn't avoid him entirely, but she'd at least gotten pretty good at ignoring him.

"A double for your mother," he explained. "She says she needs to load up before the show."

Cory turned her back without response. *Great.*

She followed the men to their seats. Not long afterwards, Aunt Liv and her mom squeezed past their sideways-tilted knees to their seats as the lights dimmed and the orchestra started up. In spite of the stupid ballet story, Cory felt a small thrill as the curtain opened on a Victorian Christmas scene.

Kevyn leaned over and slipped his warm, rough hand into hers. It fit like a love letter tucked into a scented envelope. Cory leaned closer to him and let herself be lifted out of the here and now by the kaleidoscope of colors and movement on the stage. In the darkness of the theater, she saw Aunt Livia, in her proper Chanel black dress, press her leg against Douglas's creased trousers. She smiled. It was Christmas, after all.

A moment later the scene on stage changed. All of the color disappeared, replaced by shimmering white. The little girl playing Clara wandered into a blank landscape of shadowy trees. Jess appeared and dominated the stage. She was silvery, tall, and so achingly delicate she made you want to protect her and at the same time stand back and revere her as a magical spirit or royalty. She moved in front of a corps of dancers dressed as snowflakes, but Cory couldn't take her eyes off her sister. Jess leapt as if there were no gravity and floated across the stage. Her legs and arms were inhumanly long, agile, and capable of moving with grace in any direction she commanded.

A male dancer entered the stage. He, too, was entirely in white, dressed in a military-looking top with epaulettes. Cory sat forward. Jess had been especially worried about the partnering, the lifts, and hitting her turns just right. As they came together, the Snow Queen was lifted up as if she weighed nothing into a pose with her back arched and arms flung backwards, then swooped down facing the floor in a pose like a swan. The partner then placed her so gently back on her tiny pointed foot where she spun and spun until she was a blindingly white sparkling whirl. From the skywalk above, a dusting of fake snow started to fall. Soapflakes. Cory relaxed. Jess was wonderful. She was more than wonderful. She was fulfilling her calling.

After the performance, the wind had picked up. Trash flew down the sidewalk, hitting Cory on her legs before she brushed it aside and watched it flutter along the ground. The back of her coat was plastered against her legs as she pulled the front closer around her.

"Hurry up, I'm freezing," she called to Kevyn over the howling wind.

Kevyn struggled with the keys in the lock, then pulled the door open for Cory. It nearly ripped out of his hands as it ground against its hinges. She jumped into the truck, and the two of them pushed and pulled the door shut. She leaned over and unlocked his door, the freezing air swirling around her legs before he slammed it shut.

"Let's get the heater going." Kevyn started the truck and leaned over, fiddling with the dials. "Unfortunately, it takes a little while to warm up."

"That's okay," Cory said. "I have you to keep me warm."

Kevyn smiled and pulled her across the bench seat. The motor hummed, and the vent blew cool air in their faces.

"That was really something tonight," he said. "Your sister's really good."

Cory nodded. She recalled the snowy scene of the silvery queen and her snowflakes. It reminded her of something—the deer in the glen, their delicate gracefulness and how they moved on long, thin legs.

Kevyn leaned over her and grabbed a small box out of the glove compartment.

"I wanted to wait until Christmas, but I thought maybe tonight would be a better time. Besides, I want you to have it for your next show." He held the gift-wrapped box out to her.

Cory inched closer. It felt like a small bird was trapped inside her chest, beating its wings to get out. The box was bigger than a ring box. *Okay, not that.* She tugged at the ribbon, tore the paper off, and lifted the lid. Inside on a white satin cushion sat a perfect replica of a miniature gold horseshoe on a chain, a small diamond at the base of the shoe. She didn't know what to say.

"I thought it would bring you luck," Kevyn said, studying her face.

"It has already." Cory pulled him to her and kissed his lips. They felt cold and chapped. She ran her tongue across, then separated them. The heater was starting to work.

Kevyn's arms wrapped around her more tightly as the wind rocked the truck. Cory had always thought the stories in ballets were dull—princesses, love, and enchantment—but now she wasn't so sure they were that dumb after all.

Chapter
Thirty-Seven

CORY THREW THE covers back and rolled out of bed. The clock glowed one thirty. It seemed like she had just fallen into bed, barely able to keep her eyes open to brush her teeth. Now she was thirsty. The wind was blowing so hard it rattled the screens. When her feet hit the floor, Hershey stirred, groaned, and rose to follow her. Sweeping the afghan off the end of her bed, she wrapped it over her shoulders. The house was freezing because her mom always turned the thermostat way down at night to save money. In the light from the single electric candle in her window, she could make out a small lump in the other bed. Jess. It was hard to believe the floating, magical creature on stage tonight was the same person, now wrapped in an old quilt, making snorting noises in her sleep.

Downstairs, the Christmas tree in the corner of the small living room was still lit, casting a warm glow. Jess and her mom must have left it on for some reason when they got home. A few shimmering packages were already stashed underneath. Seeing the presents, she fingered the small horseshoe dangling around her neck. It was the perfect present from the perfect guy. She smiled in the dark and walked over to the tree to shut off the lights.

"Leave it on."

Cory stopped on the spot. The shadowy outline of her mom sitting in the armchair was partially obscured by the tree. Cory waited and said nothing.

"I like the light. I like to look at it. Looks good, don't you think?" Her mom turned her face toward Cory.

"Yeah, Mom, it looks great."

Roni's eyes glistened in the electric light. She turned her attention back to the tree.

"When you were kids, we used to wait till Christmas Eve to light up the tree. Do you remember that?"

Cory took a breath, realizing she'd been holding it. She nodded in the dark.

"Robert wanted it that way. He said that was what his family did when they were kids."

Cory stared at her mom's profile, studying it for the telltale mouth droop or slur of difficult words. Instead, tonight her voice was calm, and her words came out clear and precise. She edged toward the sofa to perch on its arm. Ice cubes shifted in the glass in her mom's hand.

"Why are you up, Mom?" Her voice sounded small in the silence of the house.

"Just licking my wounds. Again."

Cory sat still. She heard a deep sigh. Glancing toward the kitchen, she debated the wisdom of getting her glass of water and disappearing upstairs. She didn't want to hear any more about her mother's wounds. It was the first Christmas since Dad left. But there was something different about her mother tonight. Her stillness. The constant anger that surrounded her like a cloud, radiating off her skin, was not there. Instead, she looked like a marble statue of a woman—still and white, staring out at the night. Cory imagined the face illuminated by the window candle would be cold and smooth to the touch. A bead of water ran down the forgotten glass in her hand. Cory slid from the arm of the couch down to the seat and wrapped the afghan around her.

"Aren't you freezing, Mom?" She noted her mother's open robe and thin nightgown underneath. Her mother made no indication she heard

Cory.

"She was beautiful tonight, wasn't she? Just like one of those snow-flakes falling out there." She nodded to the window.

Cory shifted and thought she would go back to bed after all. Jess again, always about Jess.

"Yeah, Mom. She was beautiful and great, as usual." She felt some mental nudge, something that made the image of Jess's cold skin and anguished face swim up before her eyes. "I just wish *she* could enjoy it more." She wanted to say something else that would make Jess appear more damaged, less perfect, in her mom's eyes.

Roni turned from her fixated stare out the window. She asked quietly, "What do you mean, Cory?"

She was on the verge of a betrayal. She couldn't tell her mom that Jess seemed so miserable and desperate lately that she was afraid for her. She was afraid Jess was starving herself.

Before she could respond, her mom turned back to the window and spoke to the blackened panes. "I wish she would enjoy it more, too. She's driven to get into a dance academy, but her desire is killing her."

Cory heard *killing*. The room was silent except for the sound of the wind outside knocking the string of Christmas lights against the gutters. Knocking against the closed-up house full of all the secrets it harbored. The little hidden things she had to carry every day, scurrying around in the dark.

She also heard the word *desire*—a word she had been thinking about obsessively ever since Ms. J gave her that stupid essay assignment. Earlier tonight with Kevyn she had thought about desire—another meaning of the word—when they were alone in his truck.

Now her mom spoke about desire that kills. Killing Jess. And Cory knew, even if her mom didn't realize it, that she might be right. The treacherous word *bulimic* formed in her mouth and she tasted it there. She weighed its strength against her teeth, which were holding it back. If it were spoken out loud, in this dark, quiet room tonight, what chain of events would it ignite? The word started to dissolve on the warmth of her tongue and slipped back down her throat. She might be wrong.

What good would it do to panic her mom and piss Jess off at her forever?

"She really is driven, isn't she?" Cory said lightly, laughing, to have some words in the empty space. "I really don't get it."

Her mom's eyes looked smoky gray, but her face seemed younger in the soft light, bare and scrubbed of her usual vivid make-up. Now she looked pale, younger, and somehow more vulnerable.

"No, I don't get it, either," she told Cory and shook her head. "I think you're probably more like me on that score."

Cory's mind leapt in defense. *I'm nothing like you.* But she didn't voice her thoughts. She envisioned the tiny brown bottles hidden in her mom's purse and throughout the house, like secretive nesting mice burrowed in for the winter.

"Why do you think that, Mom? I always thought you were more like Jess—you two had that ballet thing going together and all."

"Jess is like your Aunt Liv. They both had a plan for their lives from an early age and have never deviated from it. I look at you, and I can see more of myself."

"How so?" Cory asked. She wasn't sure she wanted to hear the answer but was starting to see a truth unfold that had always been living with her. A truth that kept to the shadows. She saw glimpses of it out of the corner of her eye, or snatches of it as it left a room she had just entered. Now it was standing before her, not evading her, prepared to reveal itself. Her mom smiled a pressed-lip, no-teeth smile and hugged her thin robe more tightly.

"It's that I see you go from one thing to another, like I did, and when something gets too competitive or too hard, you move on, just like I did."

Cory opened her mouth to protest, but her mom raised her hand to stop her.

"Just wait. I don't mean this as criticism. Honey, my life is half over and I've got the time now to think about a few things. Regret a few." She shook the glass, rattling the ice cubes. "But people are all different. Jess and Liv will roll over anyone who gets in the way of their goal, even to the extent of making themselves miserable. But me, I was different. I ran away from anything resembling a challenge and I think you're the same way. I was always afraid I wouldn't be good enough, so . . . well . . . if you don't try, you don't have to deal with failure or disappointment."

Cory saw herself at All-Star Band tryouts fleeing through the doors. "Just because I like to try new things doesn't mean I can't stick with something when I like it."

"I know, I know." Roni took a small sip. The ice tinkled. "It just means you haven't discovered your heart's desire yet. But when you do, I don't want you to run from it if it gets hard."

Cory frowned in the dark. She saw the pattern her mom was outlining, one where Jess and Liv succeed, and the alternative. She didn't like it.

"So what was your heart's desire, Mom?" Her tone sounded challenging. She tried to soften it. "Was there ever something that really got you excited . . . like something you had to have or do?"

"There was." Roni nodded.

"Art school?" Cory asked, remembering rooms full of stretched canvases in the old house in Massachusetts and the comforting smell of linseed oil when she came home from school. That would mean her mom was upstairs in the sunniest room of the house happily painting.

"No, I loved art, but that wasn't it."

Cory thought she would tell her, but instead, she looked down and again fussed with her ratty old robe, pulling off cotton pills.

"Then *what?*"

"What?" Roni looked at Cory as if she hadn't heard.

Cory sighed and leaned forward.

"What was your desire? What was the one thing that 'defined your life'?" Cory gestured with finger quotes.

Roni looked up. A half-smile transformed her face; it didn't match the sadness around her eyes. "Robert."

"Dad?" Cory sat up straighter. "You hate Dad."

Her mom stood and turned toward the tree so Cory couldn't see her face.

"You're wrong there." Her voice was small. "I loved your

father—still love Robert," she corrected herself. She reached out and cradled an ornament in her palm to examine it. "Maybe that's why he could make me so angry. I cared what he thought, cared too much . . ."

Cory sat on the couch, dumbstruck, staring at a woman she had never really seen before. She knew her dad wasn't dependable. She remembered his big promises and no follow-through. He was enormously fun to be around but could turn without warning like a summer day into a violent thunderstorm.

Her mom tinkered with the ornaments, redistributing a few. Cory was on the verge of commanding her to sit down and stop screwing with the tree—she had a million questions now—when Roni picked up her glass and headed into the kitchen. Cory heard the ice being dumped into the sink and the sound of the dishwasher's broken spring as the door opened. Then her mom walked through the living room past Cory and called over her shoulder, "I'm going to bed, I'm really tired. See you in the morning."

She had one foot on the stairs when Cory roused herself from her thoughts. A gust of wind blew around the corner of the house, seeping under the crack beneath the front door, and spit ice against the windowpanes. Hershey moaned in his sleep.

"Mom, you can't go now!"

Roni hesitated on the stairs. She turned with slumped shoulders, but her face wore an expression of calm.

Cory patted the cushion beside her in the dark room that smelled of pine and wax candles. She looked at her mother and said, "Come back. Tell me more about you and Dad."

Chapter
Thirty-Eight

CORY SAT WRAPPED in her afghan in her darkened bedroom, the light of the computer screen casting long shadows across Jess's sleeping body. She still couldn't sleep, especially now. The sleet was falling heavier, hitting the window like someone drumming fingernails against the glass. The heat pump outside hummed constantly, struggling to warm the house. It was nearly three a.m. She'd sat up talking with her mom and learned Roni had been her age when she met her dad, and left school soon afterward to marry him. Maybe, Cory thought, she had more to do with that than she knew.

The email pop-up flashed across her screen. When it loaded, Cory laughed. Kevyn had sent her a message.

Pawned my gift yet? LOL Luv, Kevyn

She stared at the signature. *Love* spelled with a *U*. She wondered, did that make it less serious than love with an *O* and *E*? But, still, those glowing letters on the screen made her feel a bit warmer. Jess turned over in her bed and sighed. Cory angled the monitor away and sat the keyboard on her lap.

Tonight, her mom had pulled out an ancient picture of herself with Dad before they had gotten married. It showed a young woman with long, dark hair to her shoulder, her chin lifted, looking into the camera. The man behind her had his arms wrapped protectively around her slender frame. His hair was very blond, and his eyes were so intensely blue they matched the cloudless sky in the background.

Her mom, gazing at the picture, had said, "Just because you love someone doesn't mean you can live with them."

The pose reminded Cory of another similar picture—the wedding photo she accidentally discovered of Vee and her husband. She wondered what had happened to him. Vee never spoke of him. Maybe he was also someone she couldn't live with.

Cory diminished her email screen and brought up a search engine. She was no good at this—looking things up about people—like cyber investigative genius Jess. She had poked around on Google when she found out Vee's real name but never discovered any information she didn't already know. Cory glanced around at Jess's sleeping form and for a moment debated waking her up. Instead, she turned back to the screen to type in a name, some full names now, and some other stuff to help limit the search. She started with Vee's husband's name—Reginald Stewart and New Hope Farm. She was surprised at the number of hits. It turned out "Reggie" Stewart had been a successful amateur steeplechase jockey and the manager of his family's racehorse breeding farm. He was, by profession, a patent lawyer who had attended UVA Law School.

Impressive.

She opened a society page article, and an image of Vee and Reggie, much like the wedding photo, appeared with an article about the wedding, describing in excruciating detail, the attendants, her gown, and the flowers. She then scanned through some dry articles he published on patent law and more interesting ones on bloodstock selection for racehorses. She yawned and thought about calling it a night when she clicked on the last search result on the screen.

Reginald Lee Stewart died at home this week surrounded by loving family members and his devoted wife, Genevieve.

She sat forward and read the obituary. Vee's husband died at age thirty-eight after a prolonged battle with cancer, it said. Poor Vee. Cory cleared the screen and searched on Genevieve Stewart, wanting to find out what Vee did after her husband died. Did she ever marry again? And how did she end up at her farm in Maryland? Hershey stirred at the sound of the keyboard.

Starting with her maiden name, Cory discovered that Vee had been long-listed for the Canadian Olympic team. It looked like she was a pretty successful trainer before she married Reggie. Cory knew that Vee had worked at Jack's farm starting young horses for the track and retraining others for a show career. She also knew that Jack lost the farm and everything—he had told her all about it that the morning they went out to breakfast—but there was a big gap of time in between that no one would talk about. Now she'd fill in some of the holes. Why did Vee refuse to show anymore and why did it seem she had enemies around every corner?

The wind pelted ice against the house as Cory typed in *Genevieve Sullard Stewart* and *New Hope Farm*. She pushed *enter*. The screen filled with entries—articles from horse magazines and horse show results. Cory clicked on one that looked intriguing, with a portion of text stating . . . *winner of Grand Prix Special, Genevieve Sullard-Stewart, celebrates with New Hope Farm partner . . .*

She opened the page and saw a picture of the young Vee dressed in a formal black hunt coat, holding aloft a huge silver trophy and smiling. Her other arm was wrapped around the waist of a blond whose arm was likewise raised to support the giant trophy. Cory sat up and squinted at the screen. She enlarged the photo and gasped. The caption in its entirety read: *This year's winner of the Grand Prix Special, Genevieve Sullard-Stewart, celebrates with New Hope Farm partner, Angela Hamilton, after a jump-off win on her horse, Pressman.*

Angela? Her partner?

Cory stared at the picture of Vee with her arm wrapped around Angela, looking at the camera, smiling. She read the story of their success in the Grand Prix showing Pressman and their partnership at New Hope Farm, their goals for the future and the shining promise of their combined skills as trainers and seasoned horse show campaigners.

Cory glanced at the date on the photo and tried to calculate how long it would have been after the death of Vee's husband. No more than five years, she figured. Cory couldn't believe they had ever been business partners and co-trainers at New Hope, let alone friends.

She did a chronological search and read on through the night, uncovering the truth about Vee.

December 30

It's been weeks and I never said anything to Vee about what I found out. Never asked her because the next day she put me on Epiphany to train and that's what I really wanted. I didn't want to screw that up. But I wonder. What if what happened to her, happens to me?

Chapter
Thirty-Nine

CORY TIGHTENED EPIPHANY'S girth with a particularly savage tug. The mare swung her head around and knocked Cory aside in protest for the rough treatment. Pushing the massive head away, she mumbled an apology. Vee had been criticizing her every second of every lesson ever since she started riding Epiphany. She was either too late to the jump or too rough with her hands or too forward in her position. If the horse made a bad jump, it was always Cory's fault.

The image of yesterday's bad training session and the words they exchanged afterwards buzzed around in her head like a swarm of blood-thirsty mosquitoes. *Get off. I'll have to fix her. She'll never trust a rider who buries her into a fence like that.* Cory handed over the reins to Vee without looking at her. As she turned her back to place her foot in the stirrup, Vee added, "You'll never make it to Washington riding like that."

Cory shook her head. Had she heard right? At the time, Cory thought of a million smart-mouthed responses. *Why don't you show her instead? Oh, yeah, I forgot, you don't show anymore.* Instead, she had un-snapped the strap on her helmet and left.

Now she was supposed to go back in with Epiphany and act like nothing happened. Right. She was going to pretend she didn't know Vee was a big fraud after all—like she didn't know Vee was too afraid to ever show again and she lost her whole business because of it. Sure, Vee could talk big, but when it came down to it, she was just as uncomfortable riding those big combinations. Now Cory had to go in the arena for a lesson and attempt that combination jump again. With Vee's coaching. Vee, who crashed over that same kind of jump and quit. She was a quitter, worse than Cory.

She'd spent more than a few nights thinking about the internet articles she'd read about Vee. They were filled with descriptions of her and Angela as partners in the New Hope Farm training and sales business. They had been successful, but then the tone of the articles changed. Not long after the picture of them raising the cup, Cory clicked on an image that shocked and then sickened her. It showed a large chestnut horse nearly vertical as if she were being drilled into the ground head-first. The rider was airborne over the horse's head, cartwheeling in mid-air. Cory's eyes sought out the caption: *Sullard-Stewart Loses Grand Prix Bid at Combination—Ends Winning Streak at Washington.*

After discovering that picture, she had hungrily scanned the article for more information. It said Vee cracked vertebrae in her neck and was taken to the hospital. They quoted Angela as saying Vee had been under tremendous pressure to qualify several horses for the Winter Circuit and alluded to Vee's exhaustion. Cory clicked down the search retrievals in chronological order—more on the accident, then sympathy for Vee, then speculation on why she had not returned to the show circuit. Months later, articles about her "loss of nerve" and her "unwillingness to take chances any longer" dominated the reviews. Cory wondered who was reporting on Vee's reluctance to return to showing when she clicked on a picture of Angela holding the reins of a muscular chestnut horse. Behind her, sweeping green pastures and miles of white fences faded into the distance. The article announced Angela as the proud owner of New Hope Farm. Further down in the article Angela sadly recounted how her partner had been devastated by a riding accident and as a result couldn't return to the show jumping circuit. She hinted at a nervous condition. Because of this, the business had suffered and

Angela was compelled to buy her out.

Cory stood in the arena, which was bitterly cold today, and watched a cloud of breath swirl around Vee's head as she struggled to drag a jump standard into place. She had set a double combination down the diagonal line—a tricky line to ride. Why couldn't she cut her some slack and make it a little easier for a change? Cory crammed the helmet down more, slipped on a glove, and led Epiphany around to look at the jumps.

"Let's start with the vertical, then down to the small roll top," Vee called, interrupting Cory's thoughts. "Just sit quietly and wait for the jump to come to you."

Vee took up a position across the arena. Her head was slightly tilted to one side, feet apart, and each hand slipped into a back pocket with her elbows sticking out like wings. *Her concentration pose, studying every tiny move I make.*

Cory sat taller and resisted the urge to grab up more of the reins. The scenery swam by in her peripheral vision as she stared with target lock-on at the fence galloping toward her. Airborne. Epiphany's front hooves touched down, making a soft whisper in the slushy, shifting arena sand.

"Okay, let's try something a little more challenging." Vee adjusted the ground lines on the large oxer.

Cory noticed the top poles, garishly painted with red and blue stripes, were about even with Vee's chin. The fence was at least five feet and the spread . . . She circled around the jump and stole a sideways glance. *You could drive a car between the front and back rails.*

"Helloooo? Did you hear me?" Vee asked.

"Huh?"

"Cory, she doesn't need to see it. Come down the long side and don't mess with her during the approach. If you start pulling or adjusting her, she gets worried. Sit quietly, and lots of leg off the ground."

Cory turned Epiphany, and with the lightest leg aid, she leapt into the canter. She sat deep, molding her legs around the mare's belly. Turning the corner, the fence was now dead ahead. Epiphany's head lifted slightly as she caught sight of it. Her ears faced forward to the jump, then flipped backward, listening for Cory's signals. Almost at the base of the jump, Epiphany compressed herself onto her hind legs, then catapulted forward and up. They flew through the air forever. Cory peeked out over the side, past the mane flying in her face, in time to see the top rail of the jump passing under her left foot.

Just as suddenly they landed. Cory's head snapped forward with the jolt just as Epiphany threw in a little buck. A sharp sting of cold rushed into her lungs as she gulped for air. She realized she'd been holding her breath again over the fence. A bubble of laughter worked its way up from her gut and escaped out cracked, frozen lips.

"Fun, isn't it?" Vee's mouth curled into a half-smile. "Congrats, now you're a member of the five-foot club."

Cory was warm despite the biting cold around her. She reached forward to give Epiphany a friendly slap, then sat back as the steam rose off the mare's neck and surrounded them.

"You're doing great!" Vee called, resetting another fence.

Cory shook her head to dislodge the words from the article when they invaded her thoughts. *Loss of nerve for a Grand Prix rider means the end of a career . . . accident at Washington over the triple combination . . .*

Vee pointed at the triple along the diagonal with a sweep of her hand. Cory took a deep breath and asked Epiphany to trot, picking up the pace. She squeezed to move the mare on, but it was as if her legs were overcooked spaghetti. The cold stung the inside of her nose as she sucked in great gulps of it, trying to hold back a lump that was rising in her throat. Gusts of wind rattled the large doors in their tracks and swept small eddies of sand across the arena, causing her eyes to water. Vee was explaining the approach to the triple, detailing every move, every step. She pointed at the jump, gesturing with her arms spread wide. Something about getting to the base correctly for the first element. Her words were being carried away by the wind rattling the doors and drowned out by voices in Cory's head.

Vee must have taken Epiphany through a triple, or she wouldn't have asked me to do it . . . would she? The voices prattled on.

Vee stood near the approach to the triple, feet wide apart. *The same combination that got her neck broken.*

The triple combination—three elements with only a stride in between each—was spread across the arena like an endless forest of garishly painted poles and panels waiting to pull a horse and rider under. Cory shook her head to dislodge the image of a crash.

She leaned down to whisper in Epiphany's ear, "Let's go," and picked up the canter along the outside line. She gathered up a few inches of rein. They were tacky from the dark patch of sweat on Epiphany's neck and had stiffened in the cold. Epiphany's head rose up. The mare spotted the fence and Cory became a projectile hurtling toward the monstrous jump. She tried to shorten Epiphany's stride, but it was no use. Vee was yelling something over and over. *What was it?*

Cory tried to sit up straighter, but it was like a strong hand was pushing her forward from behind. She grabbed more rein, but Epiphany lunged forward. *Please, dear God, just jump it!* She gritted her teeth with the effort of squeezing with her legs. At the last minute, two strides from the jump, she looped a few fingers around a lock of mane and bent forward in anticipation of the enormous thrust of the jump. But it never came.

For a split second, all forward motion stopped under her. Epiphany hesitated before the jump, sending a spray of blue-gray stone dust in front of her like a smokescreen. Cory catapulted out of the saddle like from a slingshot onto Epi's neck. Her face brushed the rough hair of the mane as she desperately wrapped her arms around the mare's muscular sweat-soaked neck. Epiphany lifted her head in an upward jerk, smashing into Cory's cheek and causing pinpoints of light to dance before her eyes. The sharp smell of horse sweat wafted in a cloud as Cory sniffed in a combination of dust and blood.

With one eye buried in Epiphany's mane, the other watched the blurred image of Vee running toward them. Then Cory felt the second thrust, upward and back, which flung her upright into a sitting position. She noticed the reins hanging in a loop by Epi's ears and watched in horror as those ears, head, then neck and shoulders rose in front of her as the mare attempted to half-climb, half-jump the fence. Images her brain could scarcely make sense of flashed before her eyes—the mare's neck up close again, the faint white line of hair that ran along her underbelly, a hoof studded with evenly-spaced nails, but cracking at the outer edge. Then only the blue-gray expanse of stone dust stretching across the arena at ground level. Vee's jodhpur boots appeared. The stitching had come undone along one seam and Cory wondered if Vee's feet were wet. She heard a bird call in the distance. The arena sand scratched the side of her face, and something wet spread in an ever-widening circle under her hip and thigh.

Chapter
Forty

CORY DRAGGED THE end of a soggy French fry back and forth through a ketchup blob until the end broke off. She tilted her head and dropped the unbroken part into her mouth, fished out the other end, and stuffed it in, too. Licking her fingers, she reached past Kevyn for more ketchup. Jess sat across the table, watching in silence. The Double T diner buzzed from the noise of several kids at other tables, out of school on Friday afternoon.

Cory winced when she rolled onto that hurt side of her hip to reach for the red plastic squeeze bottle. It was still sore from the fall, but the enormous bruise that had blossomed over her hip and down her thigh, had turned from an angry eggplant color to yellowy green, more like a rotting daylily. The first week afterward she walked with a distinct limp. Then, it was only sore in the morning. Now, three weeks later, she was reminded of the fall only when she leaned on the hip or when reaching up with her sore shoulder.

"Do you want to see a movie?" Kevyn asked.

"I don't care." Cory stared out the window to the parking lot at nothing in particular. It was a sunny day and warm for a change. A perfect day for riding. Except not.

Kevyn took a sip from his chocolate shake. "We could all go over to

Bradley's and see who's there and—"

"I said I don't care. Whatever." Cory didn't turn from the window. A carload of kids arrived, spilled out, and sauntered up to the entrance. One of the boys ran and jumped onto the back of the guy in front of him. She heard the second guy's muffled curse through the glass window. Turning back to the table, her eyes adjusted to the relative darkness. She noticed Kevyn's sideways glance at Jess but ignored it and reached for another fry from the untouched pile on Jess's plate. The diner was hot and smelled of grease mixed with a sweet, syrupy scent. Cory struggled out of her hoodie, annoyed that she was hot and annoyed that she couldn't get her arm free and doubly annoyed that she knew she was being a pain and Kevyn didn't say anything about it but just looked at Jess for sympathy.

"Or," Jess spoke up, "you could just stop being such a bitch to everyone and go back to riding."

Cory's head snapped up. She opened her mouth to tell Jess to shut up, that she didn't know what she was talking about, but instead slumped in the red plastic booth. She felt trapped by Kevyn next to her, the edge of the table, and Jess's accusing stare. She couldn't do what she wanted, which was to bolt through the dining room, past the dessert counter, the cashier, the long line of people waiting to be seated, and get out of there. And she didn't want to have to explain later, or ever. Out of habit, her hand reached up to her throat to touch the gold horseshoe charm that normally hung there. But she had stopped wearing the necklace when she stopped riding. What was the point? She was never going to show again, much less ride at Washington. Not now, not after what she had said to Vee. And what Vee said back.

"I can't," Cory mumbled and looked away.

Jess pushed her plate aside and reached up to slide her long hair out of its ponytail. In practiced, swift motions, she smoothed, twisted, and coiled it into a knot on the back of her head, binding it with the elastic band again. "Why not?" she demanded. "It's been weeks and you haven't said what happened. You've been hanging around, miserable, and making everyone else miserable, too. Why'd you quit?"

"I didn't quit!" Cory snapped.

"Then what?"

Kevyn slid closer. The warmth of his thigh radiated against her sore hip. He put a hand on the back of her neck and lightly stroked it with his thumb.

Cory squirmed. How could she explain? She repeated, more calmly, "I didn't quit." Her eyes welled up and a ring tightened around the top of her throat. She turned away to grab a couple of napkins from the dispenser.

Kevyn removed his hand, lifted his hamburger, and took an enormous bite. He shrugged his shoulders as if to signal he didn't care whether Cory told him or not. Jess swirled the straw around in her soda glass, spinning the slush of ice.

A busboy knocked over a stand containing an entire dishpan of dirty plates. They crashed to the floor in front of a group of kids being led to their table. A short muscular guy in the front of the group stepped over the mess, looked down at the busboy, and kicked a coffee cup back in his direction. They were the same guys from the parking lot.

"Hey, Jess," Cory lowered her voice, "isn't that Jeff? The guy you used to date?"

Jess shrunk farther into the booth but stared in his direction. "Yeah, that's him." She shuddered. "The jerk."

A waitress stopped by the table and dropped off the check. "Can I get you anything else?"

Three heads shook no to her retreating back.

The guy who kicked the coffee cup—the jerk—was wearing long denim shorts despite it being January. A long reptilian tattoo wound up the outside of one calf. A baseball cap, planted backward on his head, covered closely shaved hair. He pulled a chair out for a dark-haired girl. After she was seated, he slid his arms down her sides and nuzzled her neck before he sat down. He turned, looking over his shoulder at Jess, and smirked.

"Want to go?" Kevyn asked to no one in particular.

"No!" Jess shrunk back. "We don't have to. You guys aren't done yet, and Cory was going to tell us what happened."

"No I wasn't."

Kevyn got the waitress's attention waving the paper bill, and ordered a brownie sundae with three spoons. When it came, Cory ran her spoon along the edge, scraping up the overflowing hot fudge. Jess stared at the tabletop like she was memorizing the pattern.

At the next table, a burst of laughter broke over the din of voices and rattling dishware. Five pairs of eyes cut over to Jess. The dark-haired girl turned around in her chair and pointedly stared in her direction with black-rimmed eyes. Then her hand, each finger tipped with black polish, reached out toward Jeff the Jerk and wrapped around his thick neck to pull him closer. She turned her face away from Cory's table and pressed her lips against his in a deep kiss. Jess focused on making an accordion out of the paper sleeve of her soda straw.

Cory scooped ice cream into her mouth, the spoon scraping the dish in a tap-tap rhythm. Snatches of conversations rode the waves of the noisy dining room and drifted by their booth. A large crowd had gathered in the foyer around the hostess stand, ogling the dessert case, filled with layered cakes and marbled cheesecake slices, sitting on lace doily thrones.

"She told me to get out," Cory said between swallows. "I can't go back after that."

Jess looked up. "Who told you? What happened?"

Cory had been walking around for three weeks hoping to figure that out. What *had* happened? She tried to recount what she remembered. She'd fallen off—or more precisely, she remembered lying in the wet arena sand gasping for breath with the wind knocked out of her. She remembered Vee's warm hands touching her, telling her to be still until she was sure nothing was broken as the wet seeped through her breeches. Cory recalled getting a shaky leg back up on Epiphany. Vee told her to take the small vertical in order to get the horse's confidence back. Cory jumped it, with her palms sweating and an electrical current running down her back and legs, making them weak and shaky. Fear. It was the first time she had felt this kind of fear. Epiphany jumped okay, but then after some more warm-up jumps, Vee lowered the combination and adjusted the back rails. She told Cory to come through it again.

Cory circled. She picked up a canter and glanced at the grid of vertical, hard wooden poles before her. She heard Vee's voice, the steady metronome of instructions, but as she approached the first jump, she pulled the mare's head to the side and turned her away from it.

"What are you doing?" Vee yelled, annoyed at the maneuver.

"I—I just wasn't ready," Cory stammered.

"Well, get yourself together and be ready. And don't pull a last-minute stunt on her like that again."

Cory remembered how she felt her face go flush, her mouth dry. She came down the long side of the arena again, staring at the jumps. This time she pulled the mare up long before the jump.

"I can't do it!" The words exploded from deep within her chest. Her fingers shook on the reins. She knew the mare didn't trust her; Epiphany was getting tense through her back and taking short, mincing steps.

Vee had been patient. That was the worst of it, Cory recalled. She came over, put her hand on her thigh, and said to take some deep breaths.

"It's hard to go on after a fall and act like you still have it all together—but you have to for the horse. She's looking to you for direction." Vee patted Epiphany's neck. "And if you don't believe in yourself, then you'll make mistakes. The horse will lose all trust in you, and you'll be riding for a fall."

"Riding for a fall?" Cory gasped at the words. Images of riders crashing spectacularly over huge fences filled her mind.

"Meaning if you fear you might fall, you make the mistakes that guarantee you will."

Cory blinked to clear the image. It made sense. She had to do it. She turned Epiphany, took her back to the rail, and asked for the canter. She rode down the long side again and turned the corner to the combination. The vertical rails looked impossibly high.

"And then I pulled the mare out of the jump again, at the last minute," Cory explained to Jess and Kevyn, who had not said a word. Their blank faces stared back at her. "That's very bad. Teaches the horse bad, bad habits, like diving out of a jump at the last minute, dumping the rider. It's dangerous." Cory looked down at her lap.

"So," Jess pushed her drink away, "she told you to get out because you were afraid and messed up the horse some? That's a little extreme, don't you think?"

"Vee was mad, all right. Said I would ruin the horse and if I wanted to show at places like Washington I had better get it together, or something like that." Cory looked up and fixed her gaze on a distant corner of the noisy restaurant. "Then I said it."

"Said what?" Jess asked, her eyes locked on Cory.

"I said something like 'sure, you can talk, you quit jumping when you fell. And you never went back. Lost your whole farm and everything!' I called her a big hypocrite—that she never show jumped again so how could she tell me to suck it up?"

Kevyn drew in his breath. "Wow. What did she say then?"

Cory tore her napkin in strips, tossing the pieces on the table. "Nothing. For a long time she didn't say anything. It was scary. I just sat there on Epiphany. I almost wondered if I had really said the words out loud." Cory took a sip from the dregs of her soda glass. "Then she told me to get out."

Kevyn pulled her closer to him, his warm breath on her neck. He whispered in her ear and kissed her just under the lobe, but she didn't hear his words—only Vee's voice in her head ordering her to leave.

"So you came home?" Jess asked.

Cory looked into Jess's eyes, fixed on her. "Yeah. I can't remember even walking home."

Laughter erupted from the Jerk's table, followed by a falsetto voice stuttering, "Je-Je-Je-Jessica." Jess turned in his direction. The cartoon voice came again, "Je-Je-Je-Jessica. Pleeease! We could go to my den and breed like rabbits." The howls of laughter erupted again. Jeff the Jerk stood up and made gyrating motions against the table, accompanied by more laughter and pointed looks in Jess's direction.

"Let's go." Kevyn tossed his spoon into the empty ice cream bowl and stood up. He grabbed the bill and shot a deadly look at the Jerk.

Jeff's lips curled into a sneer. "She's probably not interested in breeding like rabbits 'cuz she's too busy tossing cookies." He stuck an index finger in his mouth and leaned over the table. The group jumped back in mock horror of being splashed by vomit.

Jess sat frozen, her face ashen. Cory pulled her from the booth and followed Kevyn to the cashier. As she rang up the bill, the hostess asked them if everything had been satisfactory in a manner that suggested she really didn't care. Kevyn handed Cory his keys and told her to start the truck—he had forgotten to leave a tip. He turned back toward the dining room.

Cory and Jess stepped into the brilliant winter sunshine. The cool air caressed her overheated face. She wanted to tell Jess not to pay attention to those guys—they were all jerks—but one glance at Jess told her any words would be useless. Jess had collapsed in on herself. She had become even smaller, like some delicate origami tissue paper folded up into an impossibly small, tight design. Cory hiked up into Kevyn's truck and turned the ignition. They sat, staring out the windshield toward the entrance of the Double T.

Kevyn emerged and jogged toward the truck. The restaurant door banged open and the Jerk appeared. He ran at Kevyn, bellowing like an injured bull.

"You asshole!"

The front of Jeff's shirt was covered in blood and dripped from his face.

"Oh, my God." Cory's hand grabbed for the door handle.

"Don't go out there." Jess seized her elbow and hauled her back.

"Are you crazy?" Cory shook her off. Fear shone in Jess's eyes. "What did that guy do to you?" Jess turned her face away. Just as Cory reached for the handle again, Kevyn jerked the door open.

"Scoot over!" He shoved his body against hers, pulled the door shut, and locked it.

The Jerk tried the door, then pounded on the hood with his fists. His eyes were wild, staring at them through the windshield.

"Kevyn, what did you do? He's covered in blood!"

"Hollywood blood, maybe." Kevyn laughed.

"Ketchup?"

"It's really amazing how far those bottles will squirt." Kevyn sat back and smiled at Jeff through the windshield. Cory laughed. Even Jess smiled a bit now.

"It's a shame, really. I like the Double T, but I guess we won't be welcome back anytime soon." Kevyn leaned forward and reached for the gearshift when a rock hit the windshield in the area in front of his face, transforming it into a spider web of tiny cracks.

"Your fag boyfriend thinks that's funny, Jess? Do you all three do it together or something?" Jeff shouted.

"That's it." Kevyn's mouth formed a tight, straight line. He opened the door, jumped out, and threw himself at Jeff. They both fell to the ground, disappearing beyond the front bumper of the truck.

Cory couldn't see anything. She was afraid Jeff might have a knife. Desperately, she rummaged in the glove box—just papers—and ran her arm behind the bench seat. She felt something heavy and metallic and wrenched it out. A tire iron. She turned to Jess. "Lock the door. Call the cops, if no one has already."

She jumped out and ran around the front of the truck. Jeff was on top of Kevyn with one knee pressed into his chest. He turned his bullet-shaped head in her direction.

"The emo's sister! Maybe I'll fix this guy so he doesn't think he's so funny anymore." He started to reach into his jeans pocket.

The tire iron hung loosely at the end of Cory's arm, hidden behind her leg. Now it seemed to take on a life of its own as it swung through the still, winter air in a glistening arc. Cory watched it, firmly clasped in her hand, as it struck Jeff's right arm with a thud just below the shoulder. Jeff slid sideways and dropped to the pavement. Cory, reeling from the effort of the blow, nearly tripped over his prone body. Kevyn leapt to her side, grabbed her arm, and pulled her backward toward the curb and away from Jeff, who rose and staggered, cradling his right arm.

Out of the corner of her eye, Cory saw the truck move toward them. Against the glare of the sun on the windshield, she could make out Jess behind the wheel, barely taller than the dashboard. She was coming at them. No. She was aiming toward Jeff, who noticed at the same time and took a few steps backward. Kevyn roughly pulled Cory to the side and started running. The truck kept coming. Jeff, supporting his injured arm, turned and started jogging, but the truck sped up, chasing him across the lot. He glanced over his shoulder, turned, and ran headlong back toward the restaurant entrance where a large crowd had gathered.

"She's going to kill him!" Cory said.

Jeff dodged between two parked cars, cut back, and ran to the curb outside the entrance where the rest of his group stood, watching. He hopped on the curb and called out, "Crazy bitch!" as Jess sped by.

At the far end of the parking lot Jess stopped the truck and slumped over the wheel. Kevyn grabbed Cory, ran over, and slid behind the wheel. Peeling out of the parking lot, he pointed the truck down Route 40 toward home. Leaving the highway, they rode along some back roads until they came to a cornfield. Kevyn craned his neck, scanning the area, then veered the truck into the field.

"What are you doing?" Cory asked.

The truck bucked and rolled over the frozen cornrows, tossing Cory back and forth, knocking her into Kevyn and Jess.

"After that Thelma and Louise act you two put on"—Kevyn struggled to keep control of the wheel—"I thought I should keep to the back roads. I'm going to take the fire trail back to behind the school. Pop out there, avoid the cops stopping me with a cracked windshield."

"Who's Thelma and Louise?" Jess scrunched her brow.

"Never mind. Just some women who drove off a cliff," Cory said. Jess looked worried. "In a movie." Cory was more concerned about Kevyn's skinned knuckles gripping the wheel and the bruise that was blooming under his right eye. His pants were wet from rolling in the parking lot slush. She sat in silence, rocking around inside the cab like a bobblehead. She was worried about the police now, too.

When they hit the dirt track access road and leveled out, Kevyn turned to her. "Does insanity run in your whole family, or is it just you two?"

Cory thought about what had just happened. She'd attacked a guy with a tire iron. Then she remembered the image of Jess behind the wheel of the truck. Jess, who had just gotten her learner's permit, bearing down on Jeff the Jerk. Jeff, running for his life. It was funny.

Instead of answering, she laughed. "Hey, Jess, you should have seen your face behind the wheel. You looked like a demented little kid. And going after Jeff, that was great." The heavy weight she'd been dragging around with her lifted. Someone might have called the cops, but she was sure Jeff the Jerk would never admit that one girl beat him up and another chased him away.

The laughter erupted in waves, convulsing her chest. Tears streamed down her face.

Jess punched Cory in her sore shoulder and laughed, too. "Yeah, and you looked like that crazy sheriff in—what was that movie? The one where the guy goes after everyone with a baseball bat?"

"*Walking Tall?*" Kevyn chimed in. He was smiling. "Massachusetts rednecks, who would have thought?" His eyes cut over to take in Cory and Jess, who could hardly breathe from laughing so hard. He lowered the window, letting in a rush of swirling, cold air. Cory pushed in the CD and a ZZ Top guitar riff filled the cab and blared out the open window, sending birds fleeing from the trees. Kevyn turned it up more.

Jess and Cory sang-shouted the lyrics and laughed.

Cory rested her head against the seat and let the wind swirl her long hair in all crazy directions and across her face as the truck careened through a tunnel of evergreens along a forbidden path. She closed her eyes and let the music's throbbing metal tones fill her skull. She felt Kevyn's hand on her thigh and turned to him.

"The girl's all right." He smiled a lopsided smile at her, his one eye nearly swollen shut.

Chapter
Forty-One

CORY RAN THE tip of her pen along the groove carved into the top of the library table, tracing the letters pressed into it years ago. She mindlessly followed the curves and lines that spelled out *Jake '98* and wondered who Jake was and why he felt the need to carve his name in the table. Probably boredom, she guessed. She could understand that.

She was trying to write that stupid essay for Ms. Jankowski. The one she promised her. She'd tried before, more than a few times, but the page remained stubbornly blank. She had no clue what to write about *desire*. What kind of a topic was that, anyway? Sighing, she pulled a heavy dictionary toward her and looked up what it had to say.

DESIRE:
to hope or long for; express a wish for, request; impulse toward something that promises enjoyment or satisfaction; longing.

That was little to no help. She looked up synonyms for desire.
wish sometimes implies a general or transient longing, especially for the unattainable; want specifies a felt need or lack; crave stresses the force of physical appetite or emotional need; covet implies strong envious desire.

Cory copied and underlined *longing, especially for the unattainable* in her notebook. That spoke to her. The black ink of that phrase seemed to grow bolder on the dictionary's yellowing page as she continued to stare at it. *That's you*, the words told her. *That's desire.* Longing for the unattainable.

She was familiar with unattainable desire. The monster who eats a raw hole just under the sternum. And when you no longer live with the desire, you're stuck with its unwelcome twin: unattainable. Unattainable was nothing but a fat, lazy slug that moves into the hole burned in your heart by desire—the desire that's abandoned you. Unattainable sits down in a ratty La-Z-Boy and stuffs his face with sour cream chips, chugs beer, and says to you, "Well, that's it—no sense trying now."

Cory felt Unattainable sitting on her heart. She felt him whenever she passed a horse trailer on the road, whenever she saw her show coat hanging in the cellophane cleaner's bag in her closet, and especially when she trolled through the internet horse sale pages, trying to find that advertisement she saw for Epiphany or any hint of her original owner. She never did find that ad again and wondered if she'd misremembered or maybe even imagined it. The whole thing was evaporating—becoming less and less real. Vee turned out to be a fraud, the horse was probably just an unlucky nag that ended up in the sales, and now the crazy dream of going to the International was, well, unattainable.

Cory looked across the table at her study partner, Noreen, as she twiddled a strand of her hair in the same annoying manner as Jess. Twiddling hair and flipping pages, Noreen had already answered the twenty study questions on the industrialization of Europe. Cory read the first question:

What characterized the change in women's roles most after the Industrial Revolution, and why?

Ugh.

"Hey, Thelma." Kevyn slid into the empty chair beside her.

Noreen looked up with a confused look on her face. "Your name's really Thelma?"

Cory shook her head. "It's a joke."

Confusion furrowed Noreen's brow. She gathered her papers and books, gave Cory strict instructions to finish her half of the assignment, and ran off to a tutoring session. She was helping a senior get through calculus, she explained.

Cory studied Kevyn's face. She never got tired of looking at his profile. In the week since the attack, his face still had a few abrasions, the worst one over his right eye. His hands looked healed, except for a few scabs along the knuckles.

"You don't mind if I sit here, do you, Thelma? You're not packing a baseball bat under the table there or anything?" Kevyn nudged her with his shoulder.

"Don't remind me," Cory whispered. "I jumped every time the phone rang for days."

"Why?"

"I was afraid the police would call, and maybe come get me for assault."

"*Aggravated* assault, maybe." Kevyn smiled.

"Not funny. I'm so relieved the Jerk doesn't go here. I sure didn't want to run into him in the halls."

Kevyn chucked her on the chin with a balled-up fist. "You could take him. He's probably more afraid of you now."

Cory frowned. "Not funny." She had relived that moment of the sickening thud of the tire iron hitting his forearm. She didn't want to think about the whole horrible day—or the past few weeks, either.

Kevyn scooted his chair alongside her and whispered in her ear, "I think tough girls turn me on. C'mon, baby, hurt me!"

Cory turned and swung a blow to his shoulder.

"That's it," he panted. "Harder."

Heads turned. A librarian shot them the warning look.

"Shut up!" Cory hissed. "You moron." But she was laughing, too. She gathered up her books. "Let's get out of here."

Kevyn fell into step beside her, then ran ahead to hold the door. He blew a kiss to the librarian as Cory ducked under his arm.

"Unbelievable." She rolled her eyes.

They wandered to the school's fine arts wing and sat down on a decorated bench, pushing aside the tented sign that read in capital letters: DO NOT SIT! THIS IS ART!

Cory turned to Kevyn, who was drawing a moustache on one of the art deco-like faces that covered the bench.

"Speaking of which . . ."

"Speaking of what?" Kevyn looked up under his brows like a big, innocent kid.

"Speaking of *that day,* how did you get your windshield fixed? Did you make Jeff the Jerk pay for it? You should have."

Kevyn stopped defacing the bench and sat still with his hands resting loosely on his knees. His head was bowed so Cory couldn't see his face.

"I got a friend to fix it, considering . . ."

"Considering what? He threw a rock at you."

"Considering I didn't exactly want to have another discussion"—he used finger quotes—"with Jeff the Jerk."

Cory dropped it. She didn't blame him. When he turned to her, he asked how Jess was doing. *Jess?* Kevyn mimicked Jeff's finger pointing down his throat gesture.

"Is it true?" he asked.

"I don't know." Cory had wanted to talk to Jess about it, to ask her if what she suspected was true. And how the hell Jeff knew anything about it. But she didn't want to bring it up right afterward, and then later, well, she didn't know how to ask her sister, *are you hurling on purpose to stay thin?* She looked at Kevyn and knew in an instant that he thought it was true.

"You should tell someone, you know."

"Oh, yeah, like who?" What could she do? She couldn't exactly tell her mom. Dad was totally out of the picture. She'd just have to talk to Jess about it.

Kevyn didn't say anything as he stood and pulled her to her feet. "C'mon. I've got something to show you."

Chapter
Forty-Two

I T WAS NEARLY four in the afternoon. The sun was still high in the sky but shone like a milky disk through a thin cloud cover. Kevyn parked the truck in front of a closed real estate office in a large strip mall, grabbed his camera, and slid out. Cory followed him down an alleyway between the buildings. A blue Dumpster, overflowing with trash, stood at the end of the alley.

"Where are we going?" Cory asked. She eyed the "No Trespassing" signs posted on the fence.

Kevyn didn't answer. He gestured for her to follow and to be quiet. Skirting the edge of the building, he descended down into a gully. "It's farther down," he called over his shoulder.

There is no way we can explain being back here. Around the corner, she caught up with him. He held a section of a chain-link fence aside, like a theater curtain, and indicated Cory should duck through.

"Come away, O human child! To the waters and the wild . . ." His voice resonated in the strange quiet.

Cory ducked through the small opening in the fence and grabbed the chain link. "Yeats. From *The Stolen Child*."

"Very good. Now tell me the rest."

He slipped through the fence behind her, took her hand, and the two of them skidded down a small slope into a wooded area. When they got to the bottom, Cory theatrically recited the rest of the poem, or as much as she remembered, and bowed.

"I'm impressed." He slung his arm loosely over her shoulder and led her farther into the gully of pine trees that formed a strange oasis between the backs of the strip mall on one side and a rickety stockade fence and warehouses on the other. They followed an overgrown path of cracked asphalt. The damp smell of rotting leaves they kicked up mixed in the air with the exotic spiciness of the Chinese restaurant at the end of the shopping mall.

"What is this place?" Cory asked, startled to see a pastel pink structure with a roof like a circus tent.

"It's the Enchanted Forest—or used to be."

The little house's color was faded, like an old Pepto Bismol bottle, with green mold creeping up its sides. It was buried deep in the undergrowth of brambles, its roof half-covered with fallen pine needles.

Kevyn walked by without much of a glance. He headed toward a brown structure in the distance, explaining to Cory in a lowered voice, "My mom used to come here all the time as a kid. It's an old theme park from the fifties. All fairytale stuff. It closed like a hundred years ago, and everything's been sitting back here ever since. They built the stores and parking lot over part of it"—he waved in the direction they had come—"and called it the Enchanted Forest Shopping Center. Did you ever wonder why there was a castle and dragon at the entrance?"

Cory had, but she thought it was somebody's bad idea for a marketing gimmick.

He walked faster, past a string of brown gingerbread men holding hands and eerily grinning, pushing stray branches out of their way. Kevyn swung his bag around, dug through it, and pulled out a camera. He raised it to his eye and spun the lens.

"The light's perfect—makes everything look more creepy." He sounded so pleased.

"More? I imagine it looks just as bad on a sunny day." Cory heard the whir of the film advance as Kevyn snapped off a few pictures. "Isn't there something here that's not creepy?"

"Yeah, c'mon. We have to find Cinderella's Castle before it gets too dark."

Cory tripped over a tree root that had erupted through the path. They passed another tiny house with a crooked chimney, like something Dr. Seuss would draw. All the windows, doorways, and walls were off-kilter.

"There was a crooked man . . ." Kevyn turned and smiled at Cory. Her blank face must have indicated she had no idea what he was talking about. "You know," he continued to recite in a singsong voice, "who had a crooked house, and . . . Not a nursery rhyme kid, huh?"

"No, not really. And, Kevyn, why are we here, anyway?"

They walked along a broken half-wall of faux stone blocks. A leering egg-shaped man sat atop it, looking down at them. The bushes growing up almost to the top of the wall would certainly break his fall now, Cory thought.

"I'm going to take some shots in here," Kevyn said. "For my senior English project, I'm illustrating Yeat's work with my own pictures—scenes of abandonment, loss, ruin—like the themes of lost youth and regret in a lot of his poetry."

He was breathless, talking fast to explain and hurrying ahead through the park. "We've got about a twenty-minute window to get the shot I want of Cinderella's Castle. I think it's this way."

They passed an oversized dinner plate with a face painted in the middle of it, lying broken against an old fence. It looked like an object from a Dali painting come to life. The paint was faded, except for the plate's red lips.

"And the dish ran away with the spoon," Cory murmured. "But where's the spoon?"

"Hooked up with someone else later and took off, leaving poor, desolate plate here to regret his decision to trust that sexy spoon." Kevyn looked back at Cory and smirked.

"How do you know the plate's a guy?" Cory asked coyly.

They stopped in front of the cracked plate, half-covered with

Virginia creeper vines. Its paint was chipped, especially around the decorative edges, but the face still carried an expression of naughty boy excitement.

"Look at him." Kevyn nodded in its direction. "The spoon was shapely and hot. Couldn't help himself."

Cory laughed. "Yeah, and he probably abandoned a loving salad plate and three tiny saucers."

Kevyn swung his camera around and up to his eye to take a few shots of the broken plate.

"Serves him right." Her tone changed.

Kevyn glanced up from his camera.

They continued along the crumbling path, which widened and was now edged by a low stone wall. The tall pine trees blocked out the sun, casting the whole area in deep shade. Some trees had fallen on the wall, others had dropped heavy limbs across the pathway.

Kevyn brushed away dead leaves with the toe of his boot. "Look, this is the old track. We're close." He broke into a sprint along the path and disappeared down a winding set of crumbling stairs. The sun sunk lower, touching the tree line. As Cory followed, she made a quick calculation of how long it took them to get here and how long it would take to get back to the hole in the fence. If they could find it again in the dark, that is. At the bottom of the stairs, Kevyn ran ahead and called for her to hurry up.

"What are those?" Cory moved closer to get a better look at the round, large structures sitting in a row. "They look like teacups."

Kevyn raised his camera, twisting the lens to find the exact light. "Get in one. I'll take a shot."

Cory walked up to the second enormous teacup sitting in a row with its chipped twins. The sides of the cup came up to about her middle, and each one sat on a thick disk—its own saucer. On the opposite side of the handle was a small opening to allow people to step inside. Cory heard the whir of the film advance, the only sound interrupting the silence of the woods. The floor of the cup was littered with a thick layer of pine needles.

"It was a ride," Kevyn explained. "Pulled by a tea kettle. There, it's still there!" He pointed to a spouted kettle at the head of the row. "It took you underground to Alice in Wonderland's tunnel."

Cory prodded at the pine needles with the toe of her boot to reveal a small red shoe. A doll's shoe, dropped by some kid years ago. The teacups and kettle stood in a line, stretching into the deep shade of the pine trees. A bird called overhead.

"It's so sad. It's like they stopped for the last time, everyone got off, and they've been waiting here ever since for the next load of people to come for a ride. Like the whole place has been put under a spell—waiting for people to come back. And they never will." Her words were rushed. "And everything is getting old and rotting and swallowed up by vines." She glanced around, searching for one thing that would prove her wrong.

"Like parents," Kevyn said.

"What?"

His hand, holding the camera, dropped to his side. "Like parents. The kid grows up and goes away and the parent keeps everything the same, waiting for the kid to return. Which he won't."

Cory looked at his face, trying to decide if he was kidding. He peeled a strip of paint off the teacup's side. His face was blank, like the spirit that was Kevyn had vacated his body. She reached out to touch him—to shake off the spell.

"What's going on, Kev?"

"Nothing." He swung the camera across his body and out of the way. "Really. Nothing."

She leaned against him over the lip of the cup, pulled him close, and put her head on his shoulder. They stood in the silence of the pine grove. His heartbeat thumped lightly against her breastbone. When Kevyn drew her closer, she scrambled to keep her footing in the slippery pine needles. The stubble of his chin scraped her cheek as she turned to look up at him. *Not nothing. But he doesn't want to tell me.* She wriggled from his arms and stepped back. Kevyn flashed a half-smile and planted a quick kiss on her forehead. The cloud passed.

"Let's go find Cinderella and kick some stepsister butt."

January 21

Snuck into the old Enchanted Forest with Kevyn. Such a creepy place now it should be called the Haunted Forest. When we were there, Kevyn said something weird about parents waiting for kids who don't come back, and it made me really wonder what's going on with him. He won't say anything. And as usual he totally dodged the questions about what colleges he's heard from or where he's going next year. But the place got me thinking. I felt like it was full of something like childhood hopes and promises and stuff that had all been broken and abandoned. One good thing. I've been trying and trying to write that stupid essay about desire and at least now I've got a few ideas.

Chapter
Forty-Three

THE ROAD WOUND through the countryside. Kevyn drove with the radio off for a change. Although he looked over at Cory occasionally, he remained quiet. She craned her neck as the small farms, neatly fenced paddocks, and grazing horses sped out of view. That familiar feeling tugged under her breastbone again. She missed Epiphany, she missed riding, and somewhere deep inside she even missed Vee. Or she missed the person she thought was Vee.

Around the next turn in the distance, she spotted the telltale sign of a horse show. The pasture was jammed with trailers, horses crowded the warm-up ring, and brightly colored tents dotted the area surrounding a large barn and indoor arena.

"Stop. Turn here," Cory shouted at Kevyn.

She had been quiet for so long, slumped down in the passenger seat, she probably startled him.

"Here? Why?" He obediently turned in, just the same.

As soon as he parked the truck, Cory jumped out without a word and walked toward the indoor arena. She wanted to see horses, to smell them again, to listen to the sound of their feet hitting the sand after a jump—to be around other riders. Once inside she propped up her elbows on the top rail and stared at the horse on course. Kevyn came up beside her.

"Are you going to tell me what this is all about?"

She dropped her forehead onto her arms. He didn't deserve the treatment he had been getting from her lately. Tilting her head, she peered up at him with one eye.

"I suck. I'm sorry." She turned her back to the ring. "It's just that I feel like I put all my hopes in something that wasn't real."

Kevyn's brows knit together.

She tried again. "Like that whole Enchanted Forest place . . . It's all one big adventure, a beautiful place full of magic and fun until something happens and you find out it's all just a story, an illusion, and when there's no one left to keep the story alive and pretty anymore, it all falls apart and gets creepy."

Kevyn looked at her but didn't say anything. He pulled up the collar on his jacket.

Cory went on. "I think I know people. I think I know what they're all about, and it turns out, over and over again, I'm wrong."

He watched the rider in the ring. "Cory, maybe you're still wrong." He took a quick look at her, then continued. "Maybe there's an explanation, maybe there's more to Vee's story than what you know right now."

Her whole body seemed to collapse as she sighed. "Maybe. I doubt it, but maybe." She turned around and faced the ring again. "You know, I miss this. I really wanted to go to Washington, but more than that, I just miss riding." She stamped her feet to warm them up.

Kevyn draped an arm over her shoulder.

"Cory!" The high-pitched squeal caused them both to spin around at the same time. Regina ran toward her, arms outstretched. "I didn't know you were going to be here, too." She threw herself at Cory and wrapped her in a huge hug.

Cory glanced at Kevyn over Regina's shoulder and raised her palms—her arms still pinned to her sides.

"I didn't know I'd be here, we just stopped in," she explained.

Regina stepped back and looked at Cory. "Where's your stuff? You're not riding?" She turned to Kevyn. "What's up with that?"

"If you find out, let me know, okay?" Kevyn gave Cory a pointed look.

"Hey, Regina, this is Kevyn. Kevyn, this is Regina. She rides jumpers, same as I used to. We'd hang out together at the shows." She glanced at Regina. "When we could."

"Used to?" Regina asked. "You're not riding? What is going *on*?"

Cory explained the whole story of her breakup with Vee as Regina led them to the snack bar area.

"We can talk here," Regina said, "because Mommie Dearest refuses to set foot in any showground's snack bar. Too many vermin, she says, and I don't think she meant mice." Regina's laugh was infectious. It rang like a musical chime over the din of the crowd and the show announcer, but when Cory asked how things were going with Prophet, she turned serious.

"Not so good. He's getting stronger to the fences, and I'm having trouble controlling him. He's really sensitive." Regina looked down into her paper coffee cup and spoke the words into it. "I think she's drugging him to calm him down some for the shows."

Cory's first thought was to ask Vee what to do to help Regina. Then she remembered . . . She wished for the hundredth time that day she could go back to the farm. Now she could only offer Regina some advice she had heard Vee tell her time and time again. "Just don't clench up on him. It makes sensitive horses claustrophobic, and they run." The thought of riding a drugged horse in a jumper competition chilled her. Not only illegal but extremely dangerous.

"So now she's going to dump him. She's decided Prophet is too complicated a horse for an amateur or junior to ride, and none of the professionals will buy a horse from my mom." Regina shrugged and smiled, trying to make light of it. "But he isn't selling. People come and try him, but they can't ride him. And what with her banned from showing and no one coming in for training . . ."

She left the thought unspoken, but Cory knew it meant they really needed the money. The income from the sale of a horse like Prophet could potentially be huge.

"She's trying to put together a deal, but the pressure is on to get him qualified for Washington. If he makes it there, more people will be interested."

The word Washington was a hit to the gut. Cory wanted to be there, too.

Regina glanced at her watch and leapt up, nearly spilling everyone's drinks. "Cripes, I've got to go!"

She came around the table to hug Cory. She also hugged Kevyn for good measure. Cory hated to see her go, knowing she probably wouldn't be running into her at shows anymore.

"Hey, Regina, before you go, how can I keep in touch, you know, without Mommie Dearest finding out? I know she was never too fond of me." Cory smirked.

Regina hesitated a moment before devising a plan for the two of them to communicate without anyone knowing.

"You'll hear from me. Soon!" Regina called back as she bolted through the exit.

Cory swallowed down the cold dregs of her coffee and stood to leave. As she and Kevyn headed to the door, Jack stepped in. He stamped some mud off his boots and looked up to see them. Cory scanned the small café for another exit, but it was no use. She stood still as he approached, then introduced Kevyn.

Jack pulled off a thick work glove to shake hands and faced her. "It's great to see you, Cory. It's been a while. We sure miss you."

Cory heard the word *we* and worried that Vee would be right behind him.

"Is Vee here, too?"

Jack smiled and shook his head. "Not a chance. I'm dropping off a horse for a client." His blue eyes peered into hers, and he lowered his voice. "Vee told me what happened. What you read, don't believe it. That's all I can say. Come talk to her, please. Think about coming back."

Cory opened her mouth but said nothing.

Jack pulled the wool cap off his head and looked around the café. "Well," he said, his voice louder, "I've got to get myself something hot to drink. You two take care." He touched Cory lightly on the shoulder, winked, and approached the counter.

Cory and Kevyn headed to the exit. She took another look at Jack, standing with his back to them. Kevyn pulled open the door and held it. She sighed and stepped out into the cold.

January 24

So glad to run into Regina today. She was cool with the fact that we (mostly me) were the ones who essentially got her mom thrown out of showing and all. Funny thing is she said the stewards needed someone to corroborate the story and someone else, she wouldn't say who, backed us up. I was really worried that Regina would hate me for telling, but it turns out she's not pissed like I expected. Of course, she can never be caught talking with me. Ever. I get that, knowing her mom. But we have a way to keep in touch without her mom knowing. But what's even wilder is what Jack said. That what I read about Vee isn't true. And to just come talk to her. I can't see me walking over there and asking her to tell me the real story. What if it's just as bad? What if she won't talk to me at all? I don't think I can. But I miss them. I miss Epiphany and I miss the me that used to be a rider.

Chapter Forty-Four

J ACK'S WORDS ROLLED around in Cory's head for days. She analyzed them over and over, sorted them like specimen slides, peering at each one under a microscope. What exactly did he mean, don't believe what she had read? She started taking the car and driving by the farm at night after her mom went to bed. A few times was tempted to stop, but she never did. Tonight, from the road, she could see the barn lights on and before she knew what she was doing, turned in.

Halfway down the driveway, she shut off her headlights and steered the car toward a puddle of light illuminating the entrance. She pulled over in the shadows, got out, and approached the barn. Still not sure what she should say, she stopped just outside the entrance, leaned against the wall, and listened.

"The vet's on his way. He's tied up with another emergency." Jack's voice.

"Another emergency." Vee's voice, with a biting edge, grew distant, then loud again. "I'd damn well classify this as a *major* emergency." Her voice faded, like she was walking away and coming back again.

Cory visualized it; Vee must be walking a horse. Colic. A colicky horse, bad enough to call the vet out. Jack said *emergency*. But who was it? She shivered from the cold. She would have grabbed a warmer jacket, but she had never intended to stop. Not really. She tilted her watch face toward the light—ten o'clock.

She stepped closer, rolling her foot from heel to toe to avoid making a crunching noise in the gravel. The barn dogs ran out to greet her, nosing her pocketed hands for a pat.

"It's my fault this happened. I should have been here," Vee said. "I'll be damned if I have to watch another horse die."

Which horse was it?

"She's not going to die," Jack said, his tone steady. "And it's not your fault. You can't be at the barn twenty-four hours a day."

Jack said *she,* meaning a mare. Epiphany. What if it was Epiphany who was sick?

The horse groaned—a deep, rumbling sound—followed by a silence more terrible than the groan. Then a thud.

"God, she's down. When's that vet coming?" Vee's voice sounded from deep within the barn.

Cory's legs went weak. She should run in, offer to help. Instead, she leaned her back against the barn wall and slowly sunk down to a squatting position. It was Epiphany that was sick, she knew it must be her. Cory's hands covered her eyes; they felt cold against her burning face. She had to go in to see her horse, but what could she say to Vee? What would Vee do when she saw her? Her mind leapt back to retrieve the painful memory of that afternoon—to replay the scene when she said those terrible things—like a tongue probing a sore tooth over and over. Cory still couldn't believe that she had told Vee she was a coward and a fraud. She hugged her knees to her body and wished she could block everything out.

The horse huffed and snorted.

Cory tilted her head back to look up at the stars. It was a clear night. She imagined how she must look, huddled on the ground in the dark, alone. Who was the pathetic coward now? A tear slid down her face and settled in the corner of her mouth, tasting salty. The dogs lost interest and wandered back into the barn.

A sweep of headlights coming up the driveway propelled Cory to her feet. The vet got out of his truck and grabbed vials, syringes, and a small metal pail from the side compartment. Under the floodlight, his bloodstained coveralls cast an eerie, greenish haze. As he rushed by without a glance, she fell into step beside him, to the brightly lit stall at the end of the barn.

Cory hesitated when she heard Epiphany's familiar deep, throaty nicker. She glanced into the darkened stall. Epiphany stood, pulling hay from her rack. The horse casually walked to the front of the stall.

"You're okay!" Cory whispered, breathlessly. The sense of relief flooded her so quickly she had to grab hold of the stall's bars to steady herself. There were only a few mares in the barn . . . which one?

She looked down the aisle to where the vet had disappeared. A stall door was slid back and Jack stood in the opening, but Vee was nowhere in sight. She could just make out the vet moving around inside the stall, stooping out of sight, then standing. *Allegra's* stall. Cory ran down the aisle, stopping behind Jack, and peered inside. Jack glanced behind him, then stepped back to let her move in front. He didn't say anything, but she felt the weight of his hand on her shoulder.

Allegra looked strange stretched out across the stall floor under a glaring light clamped to the stall bars. Its beam pointed to her sweat-darkened neck and illuminated the white of her eye, wide and fearful. Huge and helpless, she looked like a great whale washed up on the beach. Vee knelt beside Allegra's swollen belly, which rose and fell with her labored breathing. Vee looked up at the vet with dark eyes rimmed in red. She begged him to give the mare something to stop the labor. It wasn't colic. Allegra was foaling, but too early! The vet told her there was nothing he could do, the foal was probably dead, and Allegra was aborting it.

A jolt of electricity coursed through her body when Vee spotted her.

"Cory!" Vee's voice set her heart racing. "Thank God you're here! Run and get another bucket of hot water, and all my clean cotton wraps out of the tack room . . . hurry!"

Vee hadn't finished her orders before Cory took off, flying down the aisle. She returned as fast as she could manage, lugging the requested items. Jack met her in the aisle and took the bucket from her, shaking his head.

Inside the stall, Allegra hadn't moved. A dark mass the size of a cantaloupe, covered in a glistening coating like wet shrink-wrap, had appeared under her tail. The mare turned to look and dropped her head as a muscle spasm racked her body. Under the intense lights, the air in the stall was heavy, permeated with the scents of blood and manure. The mare strained and the cantaloupe spread and grew. With a wet sucking sound, the now enormous mass was expelled from her body in a rush, sliding onto the bedding in a pool of red-tinged fluid. Allegra let out a sigh and raised her head to look at it. The shining sack contained two small foals the size of collie dogs—dark, formed, and curled against each other like a yin and yang symbol. Their legs entwined, their tiny noses tucked against chests—chests that never drew a breath.

"Twins." The vet pulled back the protective bubble membrane to reveal their tiny bodies. "How did this happen? We checked her three times. Vee, I'm so sorry."

The mare struggled to her feet. Vee jumped up and stood beside her.

"Jack, she's seen them. Take them out of here before . . ." She pointed at the steaming mass containing the foals.

Vee's coat had a dark, wet stain across the front. She wiped a sleeve across her reddened nose.

"I guess they'll be a meal for the foxes tonight." Vee took hold of Allegra's halter and turned the mare's head away.

Another violent shudder expelled a silvery membrane sack, and the ropey umbilical cord dropped over the foals. Jack slid a shovel under the bodies as he and the vet steadied the slippery load into a wheelbarrow. He pushed it swiftly down the barn aisle and out the back door toward the woods. Allegra threw her head up, and a shrieking whinny exploded from her throat. Cory's ears rang when the mare circled and screamed again for the missing babies. Vee grabbed the back of Cory's jacket and pulled her away from the thrashing horse, but not before Allegra spotted her. The mare rushed toward her, mouth open. Cory steeled herself for the pain of blunt horse teeth tearing into her shoulder, or worse. Instead, the mare licked Cory's neck with her thick, muscular tongue.

"Cory, stand still," Vee said, holding up a hand. "She's picked you to be the surrogate foal. Her instincts are telling her to clean the baby. If it makes her feel better, let her."

Allegra licked Cory's neck and face and started down the sleeve of her thin jacket. Her tongue was smooth and nearly dry. Cory moved away but Allegra pinned her into the corner and continued methodical strokes along her chest and down her legs. The mare had calmed and stopped screaming for the foals but occasionally looked down the aisle to where they'd disappeared. The vet dropped several bottles of antibiotic on the tack trunk before he headed out to his truck. There was nothing more he could do tonight. A spray of gravel hit the aluminum siding of the barn as he pulled down the driveway.

"How long is she going to do this?" Cory whispered.

"As long as it takes." Vee slung her arm over the mare's broad back and rested her forehead against Allegra's shoulder. Cory couldn't see Vee's face. Allegra's foal had been her dream. Now that dream was being dumped in the woods behind the barn.

Vee slowly rubbed Allegra's still swollen but empty belly. Her hand was raw from being wet and exposed in the bitter cold.

Cory fixed her gaze on Vee's swollen knuckles as she tried to unknot the lump blocking her throat. "I'm sorry."

Vee stopped stroking the mare, but didn't look up. Maybe she hadn't heard.

Vee's voice was muffled against the mare's side. "I've lost everything now. Everything."

Cory shifted. The mare pulled her closer and continued licking. One sleeve was wet through to her skin. The smell of blood and mucus rose within the circle of the heat lamp.

"I'm sorry," Cory repeated. "I'm really sorry." She rushed to add, "I know how much you counted on Allegra's baby, but you can breed her again this spring."

"She's done." Vee turned away. Her hand dropped from the mare's side. "She's done, I'm done." She sighed but gave Cory a half-smile. "We're both too old for this."

Cory opened her mouth to protest but shut it. She knew Vee had spent a fortune on this mare and that Allegra was getting older and harder to catch in foal. But just giving up? The mare stepped away and Cory plucked at the wet sleeve sticking to her skin.

"Not just about Allegra. I'm sorry about what I said that time."

Vee didn't move, her back to Cory. "You may have been right, Cory. I probably didn't have what it takes to compete in the Grand Prix . . . after that."

Cory heard herself babbling some words about how that just wasn't so until Vee turned and touched her on the arm.

"Thanks. Thanks for coming back." The mare pulled snatches of hay from her rack. "She seems to have settled down. She'll be okay after a while." Vee nodded and stepped out of the stall. "Let's go into the office and warm up for a minute."

Vee left the office door slightly ajar, something she never did, complaining about "heating the whole damn outdoors." But tonight she cocked an ear toward the opening, satisfied she could hear Allegra should something happen, then plugged in the electric teakettle and sat down behind her desk. Cory perched on the arm of the musty sofa, just inside the door.

Vee dug around in the bottom drawer of her desk and extracted a dirty manila folder. She pulled out a photo, looked at it, then held it out for Cory. It was old, shot in black and white, and showed a jumper horse head-on, arcing over a huge oxer. Vee was riding, bent forward to stay with his enormous effort over the jump, her hands nearly up to his ears. Under the visor of her hunt cap, her eyes were straight ahead and focused on the next jump. She wore a smile that said, *We've got this blue ribbon in the bag.* The gold embossed letters in the bottom right of the photo advertised the photographer and gave the name of the horse: Northern Lights, '98.

"That was the horse I was riding when we had the accident. It was at that show when I supposedly broke my neck."

Cory's eyes snapped up from the picture. *Supposedly?*

"It happened at Washington," Vee continued. "Part of what you read was true. Angela and I were partners and the business included a training facility at New Hope Farm. But that's about it."

The steam from the boiling kettle filled the office with a warm mist. Cory shrugged out of her jacket, still clutching the photo, and slipped down onto the sofa cushions. Vee poured hot water into two mugs and the room became diffused with the smell of warm chocolate.

"Cory"—she came around the desk and handed her a mug—"there are only four people in this world who know the truth about what happened that day at Washington—Angela, her vet, Jack, and me. I made a deal with the devil afterward, and part of that deal was to never tell the true story."

She looked down into her cup, then set it on the desk untouched. "But now I think it's time I told you."

Chapter
Forty-Five

VEE PERCHED ON the edge of the desk. She pointed to the photo in Cory's hand. "He was a remarkable color. Can't tell in that picture, but he was the lightest color chestnut a Thoroughbred could be without being considered a Palomino. He had flecks of gold all through his coat. Made him almost glimmer under the lights in the arena." She reached behind her for the mug and wrapped both hands around it. "He was the best jumper someone starting out on the Grand Prix level could hope for. He never questioned, just flew over anything you pointed him at. He really saved my butt more times than I care to recall." Vee smiled with a faraway look. She blew on her hot chocolate and took a tentative sip. "He didn't deserve what he got."

Cory glanced down at the photo, at his face. He looked so eager, so ready to tear across the arena to the next jump.

"We were in the finals at Washington. Like I said, Angela and I were partners. We both owned Northern Lights—we called him Norton—and a few other up-and-coming jumpers. We also had clients who sent in horses for training. I had known Angela for a long time. We saw each other at shows, rode in the same classes, had the same goals . . . and she was always so much fun."

Cory thought of Regina.

"The business was really taking off. We had a couple good horses going up the ranks, but we really needed to make a name at the Grand Prix level. We needed some wins, and Northern Lights was our best chance. We pushed him to the higher fences, and he jumped anything we asked. He qualified for Washington, and all the cards were falling into place for us. We had clients in the wings, waiting to see how our horses did in the competition, and then they would send their horses to us to train and show. Nice horses, big money horses. That's how it works. You have to prove yourself."

Vee looked around at the pictures of numerous horses hanging on the walls of the office. Her eyes fell on the one with the ultrasound of the foal—foals—tucked into the corner. She stood and walked toward it. Cory held her breath. Vee brushed the image with the tips of her fingers and whispered, "Goodbye" as she dropped the photo in the trash can.

Perched on the edge of the desk, Vee continued her story. "I was tied in the first round and was schooling him for the jump-off. I got the sense that he wasn't quite right—nothing I could say for sure—but he didn't feel like himself. I asked Angela if he looked lame. She said I was always seeing ghosts and said he looked great. Still . . ." Vee tapped her lips and stared off, as if watching the horse again in her mind. "I went into the jump-off determined to get the fastest winning time. That would mean cutting every corner I could, taking the jumps at crazy sharp angles, and generally chasing him like a bat out of hell through a series of jumps already at the top end of his abilities. He was still a young horse . . ."

Cory waited silently. The old foxhound nosed open the door. Her toenails clicked over the floor as she headed to the braided rug on the other side of the room where she circled and collapsed with a satisfied grunt. The silver-gray cat leapt onto the couch and curled up against Cory.

"We didn't make it through the course, needless to say," Vee continued. "I remember coming into the double combination on the last line. We jumped long into the first fence and that ruined the approach to the second. The last thing I remember thinking is *too fast, too fast!* He threw himself up and over the second jump, and, that was all I remembered, until afterward. I was told he came straight down onto his right foreleg, which crumpled on impact. I flew over his head. Well, you saw the pictures."

Cory recalled the horrific picture of the horse nearly perpendicular to the ground. She nodded to Vee.

"I was knocked out. When I came to, I was in a small room they used as an emergency clinic. Head injuries aren't terribly exciting stuff at a horse show—it happens a lot—so the medical staff had left me with Angela along with a list of instructions. Of course, I wanted to see Norton right away, but she pushed me back down on the cot. Then Wade came in. He was the vet we were using at the time, but I was beginning to suspect even back then that he was treating more than just the horses. He was married, but that didn't slow Angela down any. He walked right up to me and told me Norton would have to be put down, that night, no questions."

Cory shifted uncomfortably on the couch. Her eyes glanced down again at the forgotten photo in her hand. The silver cat rose to stretch, circled, and settled down again beside her.

"I don't imagine you've ever seen a horse put down, have you?" Vee asked, looking directly at Cory. "No, of course not. Well, it isn't pleasant, even for an old horse whose life was well spent, let alone a young, talented horse." Vee sighed. "It's horrible when you are doing it for the animal's good, but when you know it's all your fault he's going to die—" Vee stopped short. Her breath caught. She impatiently tucked a strand of hair behind her ear. "You have to hold him still, even though he's really hurting, long enough for the vet to inject about thirty ccs of the tranquilizer—it's bright pink. Then you've got to jump back quick because he'll usually thrash and fight the stuff hitting his system before he can't stand up any longer. Then he hits the ground. Sometimes the horse will lie there paddling his feet, trying to fight whatever is flowing through his organs, stopping his breathing, his heart, and like a horse, he tries to run away from it."

The corners of Vee's mouth turned down as her voice broke off. She took a sharp breath, sniffed, and went on. Her voice was softer, so Cory had to move closer to catch all the words.

"When they told me about Norton, I ran, no, limped—I was pretty messed up still—to his stall. His leg was bandaged from just under his chest all the way down and over his hoof. He was standing with his head down, facing the corner in obvious pain. I slid the door open, and he nickered when he saw me. *Me!* The person who destroyed his leg. He tried his best to turn around and face me, hobbling on three legs. Wade was standing behind me and touched me on the shoulder.

"'He has to be put down, Genevieve,' he said. 'His leg is shattered. He'll never be rideable again.'

"I heard the words, but it didn't register. I was trying to find some shred of hope in a terrible situation. Then I heard it, the word Wade used—*rideable*. He'll never be *rideable*. So what? I thought. He might still *live*. I turned to Wade. I asked, 'Would he be pasture sound? Could you fix him so he could get around okay?'

"All the time, Angela was standing outside the stall. She jumps in with, 'Genevieve, he's a hundred-thousand-dollar show jumper. He's insured for twice that.'

"'What are you saying?' I demanded. 'We kill him just so we get our money out of him?'

"'Don't be naïve,' she told me. 'I don't want to see him dead any more than you do, but we can't sustain a hundred-thousand-dollar loss to our business.'

"Norton leaned his head on my shoulder to help take the weight off his useless foreleg. I looked into his eye, inches from my face, and I saw the depths of a soul reflected there that before this day I didn't know existed. That's when I made the agreement."

Vee stopped. She took a sip of what must have been cold hot chocolate and pushed it aside. She glanced around the room, her focus stopping at the picture of each horse that graced the walls around the office. She looked small, perched on top of the desk with her legs dangling down. Vee's eyes lingered on the photo of Pressman, the one that still concealed her wedding photo, the one Cory had carefully reassembled and hung back in its place. Cory listened to the rhythmic chomp of the horses pulling hay from their racks. Vee sat very still. Her eyes didn't leave the photo.

"I saved them."

Cory held her breath. *Who? Who did you save?*

Vee looked down into the depths of her cold cup and took a breath. Cory stroked the gray cat's head and his rumbling purr filled the silence of the room.

"I destroyed a beautiful animal with my arrogance . . . it was only right." She swallowed hard and glanced at the ceiling. "I bought Northern Lights so he could live. He was insured for over one hundred thousand. I had nothing but the farm and the business, so I signed it over to Angela." The words were rushing out of Vee like water from a burst dam. "She told me if I could match the insurance I could have him, and Wade could fix him up enough to get by. But I thought about the fate of Pressman, too. He was just as vulnerable to her bad business sense if he should get hurt. That night, my head pounding from my concussion, I signed over the farm and half the business to take possession of a ruined horse and to save Pressman. The condition was I could never tell what happened. I was never to contradict anything that Angela said about it, and I could quietly leave with the horses—that and the money was the ransom she exacted from me." Vee ran a dirty sleeve under her nose.

"Northern Lights recovered enough to enjoy going out to pasture, eating, doing horse things. He remained a cripple and eventually had to be put down a few years later. But he went with dignity, and we buried him under the crab apple tree out back. Probably where Jack's bringing the twins right now, I suppose." Vee got up to unplug the electric kettle, then resumed her seat on the desk. "At the time, I accepted the deal. I swallowed what was said about me—that I had lost my nerve and refused to show jump ever again. Figured it was a price I paid for my earlier pride. But Angela's blood price didn't end there. She saw to it by the things she said that I would be ruined as a trainer, as well. A few clients hung on, but when I didn't show their horses, they drifted away. Jack was going through hard times then and offered me the use of his farm to work horses. I made a living fixing other people's problem horses and would hand them back only to watch the problems creep back. I didn't show again—not with the burden of what I knew. You see, it wasn't enough for Angela that I had paid the insurance price for Norton. She saw an opportunity for more."

Vee hopped off the desk and listened at the open door for any sign of distress from Allegra. Satisfied, she leaned against the doorframe.

"I still had friends on the circuit who followed her and told me what was going on in the show world I had disappeared from. I learned the horrible depths of depravity that Angela had sunk to—that I'd unleashed—by not challenging her or stopping her."

"There's more?" Cory asked.

"Much more." Vee pushed back the sleeves of her bulky sweater and hung her head. A fringe of hair escaped the loose ponytail and hid her face.

"Another horse—an innocent horse whose only crime was that he was born with the same chromosomes that made him almost palomino like Norton—died, and I didn't do anything about it. That's the secret crime—the one I feel the most shame over." Vee poked at the edge of the braided rug with the toe of her boot. "I later learned that Angela found a horse at the auction—his name was Sandy Point, like the beach here—that looked just like Norton. Who knows why he was at the auction that night. Maybe he was a racehorse with a case of the slows or some kid's show horse who had lost interest in riding. All I know is he came through the sale and was a dead ringer for Norton. Maybe Angela planned it, maybe it just occurred to her when she saw the similarity, but his fate was to become Norton's stand-in for the death certificate."

Cory's head snapped up to look at Vee when it sunk in what she was talking about. "Angela killed Sandy Point for no reason?"

Vee smirked. "No, she killed Sandy Point for one hundred thousand reasons. She got Wade to sign the death certificate for the insurance, so she collected twice on a horse that, at the time, was still alive.

All I can imagine is they bashed his leg to simulate the injuries Norton had and claimed he had to be humanely destroyed, despite heroic efforts to save his life. I read it in the *Show Horse Magazine*—"Memorial to Northern Lights," the article was called. I thought about exposing her, turning them in, telling someone, but when I took Norton, a worthless, broken horse, I didn't get his papers. Why would I ask for his papers? He was never going to show again. There was no way I could prove I had the real Norton. Later, Wade sent me a note. It didn't say anything an outsider would recognize, but I knew it was a letter threatening me to keep quiet. He wrote how he hoped Pressman and my 'Golden Boy'— no name mentioned, of course—were safe and happy at my new farm and that they would continue to stay that way."

Tears left a trail down Vee's face through a hard day's accumulation of grime. Cory's muscles ached from sitting so still, so tense, but she dared not move an inch. She felt the whole world outside had shrunk away to a small and blurry place and only she and Vee were encircled in some capsule. But inside the capsule every detail was painfully clear— the dirt in the deep creases of Vee's face, a tiny hole in the elbow of her sweater, and a bluish vein that ran up the back of her hand clutching the mug. All the details stood out as if she were seeing Vee for the first time. Cory rose, walked over to where Vee was standing, and watched her hand as it moved through the space between them and lighted on Vee's back. Her shoulder blades felt like bony wings. Vee dropped her head.

"Cory, I just couldn't have *you* thinking I was a fraud, a failure. But you see, I've been thinking that about myself all this time."

Cory warmed at the sound of Vee speaking her name. "I don't think that. I think you were brave."

Vee looked up sheepishly. "Quite a story, huh? More than you bargained for, I bet." She stood straighter. It was as if the old Vee, the one who always showed a brave face, was shaking off the story and struggling to take charge again. "C'mon, let's go check on Allegra."

Chapter Forty-Six

ORY THREW OFF the covers and got out of bed. The glowing orange numbers on the bedside clock didn't immediately make sense to her brain—3:47 a.m.? She couldn't recall what had awakened her at this hour. The room was still dark. Jess's bed stood flat, neat, and empty against the wall. She remembered Jess was going to be gone the whole weekend to a dance camp—some seminar to get her ready for the big ballet competition. But in the semi-dark, the empty bed made Cory feel alone. She wished she could shake Jess's shoulder and tell her about what she had learned.

She padded over to the door and opened it, listening. A rhythmic snore came from behind the last bedroom door down the hallway, meaning her mom was home from her date with Bucky. Downstairs, the hum of the refrigerator was interrupted by the soft cascade of the icemaker dumping a load of cubes into the bin. Hershey scrabbled his feet against the carpet in his sleep.

Cory considered crawling back into the rumpled heap of blankets on her bed but snapped on the desk lamp instead. Wrapped in an extra blanket, she pulled the keyboard closer and switched on the computer. As soon as the monitor glowed into life, she typed in an email address and started to write.

Dear Ms. Jankowski,

I bet you never thought you'd actually ever see that "Desire" essay from me, but—surprise!

She sat back and stared at what she had written on the screen. The lamp cast a small circle of light on the desk. Within the intimate circle, she considered what to write as the rest of the house, the rest of the world, and even time became a reality somewhere beyond her. She leaned in closer to the glowing monitor, like a small confessional window, as her fingers returned to the keyboard.

At first I didn't know what to say about desire, so I just avoided writing anything at all. But that changed yesterday. I've been thinking about it, and I guess when most people think about desire, they imagine a force that's hot or burning, like the saying "burning desire," that drives people together or makes them run after some goal. But I've seen that desire is something much different. Desire doesn't burn after all, but instead it's a cold, bottomless well.

Cory sat back to read over what she had written, then hunched over the keyboard again. Her fingers pounded the keys, as if she were taking dictation.

No, not really bottomless because you find out when you fall into desire and hit bottom, it breaks your spirit. It's full of cold water that extinguishes any last bit of warmth within your body and leaves you down there, alone, unable to call for help.

I met a lady who had a desire to make things right and all it did was ruin her life. She made a mistake and her horse got hurt, so she wanted to take care of him. Instead, she got screwed over. She had a desire—a desire to do the right thing and a desire for justice, and that desire rewarded her with losing her business and her reputation and everything. And what about desire and love? That may be even worse. What if you desire a person and that person doesn't love you back as much, or at all? Desire is a horrible pain that hangs around you, wanting a person you can't have for the rest of your life until you start going out with any old creep just to make some of that desire go away. But it never does. Maybe being with someone else dulls it a bit. But maybe that drive to be with any guy at all is what makes you feel like crap about yourself. Any way it goes, it was desire for someone you can't have that ruins your life.

She looked at the blank wall in front of her, as if she could see through its thickness to the sleeping woman in the next room, then turned, her eyes resting for a moment on Jess's empty bed.

And not just desire for some one but also desire for some thing. I'm watching as a girl I know is killing herself, literally, over a desire for something. She wants to be the best dancer so bad, everything else in her life is shrinking away, including her body. Just to make the goal of getting into a big-time dance company someday. Her desire is not making her happy. Just the opposite. It seems to make her miserable. The more successful she is at dancing, the more driven and obsessed she gets, and the more she thinks she's fat and ugly.

I wanted to qualify to ride in the Washington International Horse Show, but I'm also afraid of not making it. Sometimes I'm so afraid that I think I'm only in love with the idea of being a good rider, but don't have what it takes to get there. I don't want to want something so bad and not get it. It would be easier to just not try.

Cory didn't go back and read over what had flown out from her fingertips. She pushed the key to send the email, snapped off the light, and climbed into bed, pulling the heavy comforter up to her ears. All the anger, frustration, outrage, and fear had spilled out of her like water shooting from a hose, at first with a force under great pressure, then to a steady stream until the last drop dripped out over the metal rim.

The next morning an email message sat in her inbox, flashing, waiting impatiently. Ms. Jankowski had responded.

You quit out of fear. You change course out of self-knowledge and wisdom.

PART III
Spring

I hate the color yellow;
It makes me think of cinder block hospital walls.
Purple's the true color of spring,
Lilacs to be sure. Tiny, clustered florets
If gently brushed when passing
Perfume the clear, white air.
I want to take the lilac and capture its scent,
Snap off the stem, bind it in a vase.
But by morning it's wilted,
Lavender shriveled to gray,
The stems refuse to draw the water, they exude no perfume.
A lilac cannot perform on demand.
~ From the journal of Cory Iverson

Chapter
Forty-Seven

CORY HATED MARCH. It wasn't winter any longer, but it sure wasn't spring. On the way to the showgrounds, she studied the fields through the early morning mist, trying to detect that luminescent green in the grass that signaled the return of warmer weather. The truck cab was cold, since Jack would never turn on the heat. Cory sat huddled in the middle next to Vee, who was studying the directions on the back of the show's prize list.

"I think we have to take eighty-three." She looked, scanning the road ahead.

"I know a back way," Jack replied.

"But the directions say we have to take eighty-three. We can't be late." Vee rolled and unrolled the program in her hand and stared out the passenger window. "This doesn't look familiar to me."

Jack gave Cory a sly smile. She guessed he was used to this. In fact, Cory was getting used to it, too. She'd been afraid that her month away from the barn would have changed things, but when she climbed back on Epiphany, she felt as comfortable as settling into her favorite chair. But they had lost a lot of time, and like Vee said, if they hoped to qualify for Washington, every show counted.

Showing again also meant a risk of running into Angela. Whenever they pulled into a showground, Cory's stomach would flip if she spotted her big blue gooseneck trailer.

The truck turned onto a gravel drive and rolled over some deep ruts, then passed the pillared gate of the Baltimore Equestrian Center. Jack beamed a "told you so" smile at Vee, who ignored him.

"I checked on the Washington International website last night and we're in thirty-second place." Cory checked Vee's reaction out of the corner of her eye. Vee knew darned well what place they were in because she checked the website after each show, as well.

"You have to be in the top twenty-five to be assured of a spot. They usually take the top thirty but not always."

Cory had heard this before. She also knew that she and Regina were battling for the top spot at every show.

As Jack pulled the truck closer to the main area of the showgrounds, Cory exclaimed, "Wow. This place is really amazing."

A small, finely lettered sign directed them to parking in one of the expansive pastures, each enclosed with a dazzling white four-board fence. The showgrounds were alive with grooms leading horses swathed in luxurious velvet coolers. Cory spun in her seat to look in the other direction. The parking area was already filling up with trailers, some looking larger and fancier than her townhouse.

Vee snorted. "The snowbirds have migrated, I see."

"Snowbirds?" Cory asked.

"The people who show in Florida all winter, then come back when the weather warms up. They've got the advantage in the early spring shows because they've been at it all winter while we've been under a foot of snow."

It had been a terrible winter. Most of the local winter shows had been canceled. As soon as Jack parked, Cory jumped out and opened Epi's door. She noticed for the first time how the trailer's paint had faded and there was rust along the fender.

"Get her out, let her stretch her legs and look around," Jack ordered. "We'll pick up your number and take care of everything here."

As Cory led Epiphany around the grounds, the mare held her head up high, taking in all the new sights and sounds riding on the cool air. At the huge oval show ring, a slicing breeze swept across the open area, setting the flags snapping and clanging against their staffs. Epi jumped. To soothe her, Cory ran a hand down her muscular neck and spoke softly into her cocked ear, "You'll be great, just like always. Don't worry." She zipped up her Old Navy hoodie and moved out of the wind.

A flatbed tractor-trailer rumbled past them into the arena, depositing a jump crew, which immediately got busy throwing down heavy poles and setting the fences. A small village of vendor tents, selling every kind of horse equipment or horse-themed décor or upscale clothing, stretched along one side of the show ring past the grandstands. Among them was a hunter green tent, its awning emblazoned with the name of the most popular horse show magazine in the country: *The Equestrian Journal*. Cory devoured *The Journal's* glossy pictures each month. Inside the magazine's tent, the walls were hung with photos of their famous covers going back several years. People strolled through the display, clutching steaming coffee cups and pointing at the familiar ones.

A group formed around the magazine cover of the latest Olympic Silver Medal team standing on the podium, waving their bouquets and extending their medals to the crowd. One man in this crowd, wearing a lopsided smile, matched one of the famous faces in the picture.

My God, Cory realized, *that's really him, in person.*

He was dressed in jeans and a worn baseball jacket and had an arm slung over the shoulders of a dark-haired girl Cory's age. A slender woman—a photographer—disengaged herself from a group of richly attired people and approached the Olympian with her camera raised. *The Journal's* photographers were here, and probably the reporters, too. Cory stepped forward for a closer look when Epi backed up so fast she nearly ripped the lead rope out of her hands.

"What's wrong with you?" she scolded.

Epi stood, feet planted as if she were ready to bolt. Cory turned her, trying to disrupt her fixated attention, but Epi was fixated on something. When Cory looked up, she spotted her, too.

Angela stood outside *The Journal's* tent wearing soft gray breeches, even though she was still banned from riding at Maryland horse shows. Cory tried to pull Epi away when Angela spotted them and strode over.

"This is the famous Epiphany, is it not?" Smiling, she looked up at the horse, shading her eyes against the glare.

"Yeah." Cory looked off toward the secretary's tent, hoping Jack or Vee would appear.

"Good-looking mare." Angela ran her hand along Epi's side, causing the horse's skin to flinch as if a big bug were crawling along it. "She's doing well this year, I hear."

Cory nodded. Over Angela's shoulder, she saw a group in *The Journal's* tent look over her way. Their heads came together momentarily. Nods. Sly smiles.

Angela noticed, too. Her voice rose a bit louder. "So, it's even more impressive what you've done with the mare considering where she came from." Angela's eyes darted to the crowd, checking to be sure she had their attention. "Not too many horses go from the kill pen to the Grand Prix circuit, after all." She gave Epi a resounding slap, smiled toward the crowd outside the tent, and walked off in the opposite direction. She turned back with a little three-finger wave. "Good luck today, hon." She smiled.

A chill ran down the back of Cory's arms. Epi lifted her tail and deposited a steaming pile of manure.

"Hey! Get that horse outta here." A man from the show staff waved at her, his face red. "Horses aren't allowed in this area." He pointed at a sign. "Pedestrians only."

Cory tugged on Epi's lead and pulled the mare away with her at a run. A dark-haired woman stepped out of the tent and pushed her way through the crowd after her.

"Wait!" she called breathlessly, holding up her press card. "Moriah Hennisey, from *The Journal . . .*"

Cory looked behind her. The woman, closely followed by a photographer, was headed in her direction. She didn't want anyone else asking a lot of questions about where they got Epi, and she didn't need everyone on the show circuit, especially *these* people, laughing at her and Vee because she was riding a horse that came from a cheap auction. She dived into a dense crowd, which opened up to allow the girl and the big, silver horse to pass, then miraculously closed behind her like the Red Sea, shutting them off from "Moriah of *The Journal*" and her nosy questions.

At the trailer, Jack lent a hand and soon they had Epi tacked up. Cory mounted and rode into the warm-up area. She tugged at the bottom of her dark gray show coat. It was snug across her chest, but it had never seemed to bother her before. She considered it her lucky coat because it was the one Vee had always worn on the Grand Prix circuit. Besides feeling tight, she now wondered if it was out of style.

"Cory? Hellloooo? Are you listening to me?" Vee called her back to attention.

"Have you noticed I'm the only one wearing a gray show coat?" Cory leaned down from where she sat on Epi and gestured for Vee to look at the other riders.

"Yes," Vee kept walking. "And you're also the only one riding a gray horse. The coat matches the horse. Let's get back to work here, okay?"

The warm-up area was as busy as the Washington beltway at rush hour. Horses jumped the practice fences from both directions, threatening a head-on collision. Shouts of "heads up!" filled the air so that no one paid much attention any longer. Trainers on the ground reset fences as another rider came sailing across. Coaches glared at each other, exchanged veiled threats. The air was damp, charged with nerves and the scent of horse sweat.

"We have to get you through the triple combo," Vee whispered by her side. "Your weakness," she added.

Don't have to remind me.

Vee didn't believe in yelling commands at her student at a show but coached in soft, discreet instructions. She explained once that you must not upset the rider before a competition—all the things that need fixing are to be done at home, and the day of the show you warm up and ride. If the training is there, it shows.

Cory wondered if the training was there today.

She started off riding along the long side of the arena, dodging riders, trying to stay out of everyone's way. A woman on a dark bay rushed up on her inside, turned her reddened face to Cory and shouted, "Heads up left, I said!" She sneered as she passed.

Cory jerked Epi off the track, out of the way. She glanced at the plain white triple combo set up along the opposite line and called out in a timid voice, "Heads up, combination."

No one noticed her.

As she made her approach to the three fences, that girl—the one the Olympic rider had his arm around in *The Journal* tent—came at it from the other end. Cory pulled Epi's head and circled her at the last minute. Out of the corner of her eye she saw Vee storming over to the girl's coach. It was that guy. *Her* coach was Jim Stedman, the Olympic rider.

Stedman, smiling in a charming way, walked up to meet Vee with his hands outstretched in a gesture of supplication. "Don't kill me. The girl has no sense of direction." He beamed a smile at his rider, sitting on a hugely tall black horse. She shrugged and called, "Sorry."

Vee walked up to Cory and touched her knee. "You have to get Epi through the combo once. Can't pull her out like that."

Cory opened her mouth to object.

"I know. Wasn't your fault, but the horse doesn't know that. Get her through, then we have to go." Vee grabbed Cory's boot and gave it little shake.

Cory gathered the reins and headed to the combo. She heard Vee holler above the din, "Heads up! Combo!"

She rushed into the first fence, but Epi obeyed and took off from a long spot. The mare dived at the second fence and pulled the top rail down. Cory looked behind her, just for a second, and Epi hesitated at the third fence, jumped, and cleared it only from sheer effort. Vee's face clouded over. Cory hated herself for screwing up. She wanted to get off and just go home.

"Let me try again," she started to say.

"No time. You're up."

Chapter
Forty-Eight

WAITING AT THE in-gate, Cory jumped when she heard the loudspeaker announce, "Number 157, Coraline Iverson riding Epiphany." It sounded like a voice from a distant planet.

Her cue to enter. She nudged Epi into the arena. A blur of faces lined the rails and grandstands. In her head, Vee's voice whispered, "Take your time."

Cory's face was hot, despite the spray of light rain. A dark cloud passed overhead, blotting out the light, and casting some of the jumps into shadow. The wind picked up again, setting the flag ropes clanging against their metal staffs. Cory startled, but Epi felt solid beneath her. A furry ear cocked backwards, as if to say, *Awaiting take-off.*

At the signal for canter, Epi lifted her head and searched for the first fence. Navigating smoothly over the line, Cory's shoulder muscles relaxed, but when she turned the corner for their approach down the diagonal, she spotted the Moriah woman next to a guy pointing a huge camera lens at them. She stared at *The Journal* reporter a fraction of a second too long and missed the spot for the first fence on the diagonal, causing Epi to scramble to get over it. It was followed by another huge fence. Cory grabbed at the reins and drove the mare at it. Epi rushed, pulling the top rail on the backside. *Four faults.* She rounded the turn and struggled to get Epi collected and back under her. *Don't rush,* she remembered. *Too late.*

Cory quickly calculated the faults. *I won't earn the points I need.*

The next jump was in front of them before she knew it.

Clunk. She heard the sickening thud of another rail down. *Four more faults.*

The fences came up fast, and the triple combo loomed ahead. Cory sat deep, put her leg against Epi's side. The corner of the mare's eye flashed back to look at her.

Another gust of wind whipped up the flags, sending them snapping in the air. The triple was straight ahead. Cory resisted the urge to grab up more of the reins. The first fence of the combo was a large vertical, flanked with monstrously sized sports drink cans in garish colors. Cory was afraid Epi would back off, but instead she tore forward, eating up the ground under them. She flew over the fence with what felt like two feet to spare, barely touched the ground on landing, and was in the air again over the second element. They were flying. Cory leaned close to the mare's neck and breathed in the scent. Epi touched down lightly. The third fence, the one she always screwed up, was next. Cory sat, waited, and asked with a touch from her leg. Epi responded as if their minds were linked, lifted at the exact right moment, and flew over the top. When they landed, Cory spun around to spot the last fence on course—a small oxer. When she cleared that, it was just a matter of riding through the flags and they'd be done.

Out of the corner of her eye, Cory saw a woman standing by the rail in a plaid coat. One just like her mom's.

Pay attention! She told herself, *Get through this. You've messed up enough already.*

As Epiphany blasted through the finish line flags, Cory heard the loudspeaker announce, "Epiphany with eight jumping and two time faults for a total of ten."

She slumped in the saddle, knowing she wouldn't be in the ribbons with that performance. Vee waited at the exit gate.

Cory held up her hand in a stop sign as she rode past. "I know, I know," she called over her shoulder.

She rode Epiphany to the outer edge of the showgrounds to cool her off and to hide out from having to face anyone. At the top of a rise, she watched a rider enter the ring and negotiate the course with clock-like precision. At the end of the round, the loudspeaker announced, "A clean round for Regina Hamilton, riding Prophet."

"Good job, Regina," Cory murmured to herself. She gathered the reins and headed back to the trailering area.

Jack forked dirty bedding out of the trailer into a muck bucket, looked up but said nothing as Cory approached.

She slipped down off Epi and silently set about running up the stirrups and untacking her. "Where's Vee?" she asked, looking around.

"Down at the ring, checking out the course for the next class."

"I'm not riding in the next class," Cory suddenly decided. She felt a surge of relief. "I'm not feeling too good. Can we just go home?"

Jack propped the fork up against the trailer, a look of concern in his eyes. "Sure, kiddo. You think you're coming down with something?"

Cory's gaze dropped to the ground. She was coming down with something all right. Cold feet. She hurried to put the tack away and wash down Epi so they could leave. On her way out of the trailer's small dressing room, she saw Vee standing by the truck, talking to a tall, impossibly thin woman in buff-colored breeches and a down vest.

The woman's hands were jammed into the pockets as she stood huddled against the cold wind. She reached out, clutched Vee's upper arm, and smiled. "*So* great to see you again, Vee. Your daughter's doing so well this year."

Vee stepped forward and wrapped the woman in a quick hug. "Thanks, Jane. Yes, Cory's doing great. She has a talented horse, but she's a great little rider herself."

Cory ducked back into the dressing room. *Why hadn't she told the woman I'm not her daughter?* Vee seemed happy, not at all mad that she'd messed up the ride.

Vee appeared at the entrance of the dressing room. "There you are.

Better get ready for the next class."

Cory started to object when Jack appeared by Vee's side. "Cory says she's sick. We'd better load up and get home."

Vee turned and reached a hand up to feel Cory's forehead. "Really? Do you suppose you picked up that awful twenty-four-hour bug that's going around?"

Cory ducked past her to where Epi was tied by the trailer. She began rubbing her down with a damp rag.

"If you're sick, we'll leave, of course. It's just that you finally nailed that triple combination thing. I figured you were on a roll."

Cory wheeled around. "But I totally screwed up the first part of the course."

Vee shrugged. "You weren't concentrating, and you made some mistakes. But the important thing is you learned how to ride the combo. So, this show's a success."

Cory rubbed harder. "I'm not really that sick. It's just that I don't feel comfortable with these people around, watching and stuff."

"People are always at shows watching." Vee's brows bunched together. She stepped closer. "What people?"

"Those Florida circuit people."

She made a dismissive gesture. "They're nobody special."

Epi took a step away from the brisk rubbing.

"Here." Vee gestured for the rag. "Give me that before you rub a hole in the girl's side." She tossed the rag into the brush box. "Now, what exactly happened?"

Cory looked at the sky.

Vee brushed a hair away with the back of her hand, but it immediately flew back across her face in the breeze. She stared at Cory.

"It's just that I don't feel we belong here." Cory took a deep breath and rushed to add, "These people have been showing all winter, and they have Olympic trainers, for God's sake, and their horses are like million-dollar jumpers . . ." Her voice trailed off when Vee's eyes narrowed.

"So, Cory, are you ashamed to be here with me and Jack?" Her voice was low.

"No! God, no, not at all."

"Then you think your horse is no good. Not as nice as any of the others here?"

Epiphany swung her big head around to look at Cory.

"No, of course not. I love Epiphany, she's awesome. It's just, well, what Angela said."

"Angela!" Vee spit out the name. "Where did you see Angela?"

"At the Merchants Village. I was outside *The Journal's* tent, and she came out and I couldn't get away."

Vee sucked in a deep breath, then asked, as if speaking to a toddler, "So, did she speak to you? What did she say?"

Jack put his hand on Vee's shoulder.

"She said nice things about Epiphany, how she's doing so well this year." Cory kicked at one of the trailer tires. "But then she said real loud how it's great Epi's gotten so far considering she came from a slaughter pen." She looked up into Vee's eyes. "And she said it right in front of all those reporters and people hanging around."

Vee's mouth formed a tight, straight line. "Okay, we'll go home." She grabbed the handle of the muck bucket near her feet. "But I have to dump this first."

Cory and Jack stood watching as Vee stormed off, dragging the unwieldy bucket, brimming with manure.

Jack stood for a while, then said, "Better load up Epi quick, kiddo. We may have to skedaddle out of here soon."

Cory was startled. "Why?"

"That crazy woman is *not* headed in the direction of the showground's manure-dumping pit." He reached into the truck, grabbed a small pair of binoculars off the dashboard, and raised them to his eyes. Cory led Epiphany up the ramp and into the trailer.

"Oh, sweet Jesus," he moaned, as Cory appeared beside him. He lowered the glasses, handed them to her, and pointed. She jumped up on the bumper for a better vantage point and peered through the binoculars. A resolute Vee, dragging the bucket, marched up to Angela's big blue gooseneck trailer. She yanked open the truck's driver side door, hauled that heavy bucket up to the seat, and tipped the entire contents inside, then slammed the door shut. Cory thought she detected a satisfied smile on her lips.

March 20

It's been so long since I've written; I almost forgot where I'd stashed this thing. I've been really busy training and getting Epi ready for all the shows. It's funny that Vee put me on her to train right after that time I snuck out on her at night. I never told her about that, but for some weird reason I always get the feeling she knows anyway. She seems to know a lot of stuff without being told. Anyway, Epi is super great, and I always feel like she's got my back even when I'm not helping her out much. Like today. A total disaster. I rode like crap but we (meaning she) pulled it out for the triple combo, which makes me feel bad about leaving before the last class. I don't know what happened, but some of that quitter came back as soon as I thought we were outclassed. We need the points for Washington. Regina is doing great, though. She'll get there. Sure hope she didn't have to sit on any horse poop on the way home. I feel sorry for her because her mom's such a psycho. Moms are weird, and they can really mess you up. Now it looks like Vee's my extra one. Horse show mom. She's got my back, too.

Chapter
Forty-Nine

A HEAVY HAND LANDED on Cory's shoulder, its warmth seeping through her brushed cotton shirt. She turned. Ms. J's face was backlit by the large cafeteria window.

"Come by my office, if you would." She added, "After school."

Cory grappled for an excuse—she wasn't up to facing whatever Ms. J had to say about her essay—but nothing came to her. She nodded.

After school, the empty corridors seemed wider without the constant flow of students rushing along it like a stream of ants. The guidance suite was dark, except for a light at the end of the hall in Ms. J's office. *Crap. She hasn't forgotten.* Cory didn't want to discuss the content of an "essay" of random thoughts she threw together in the middle of the night. What possessed her to send it, anyway? She poked her head around the corner into the office.

"Hi, Ms. J. You wanted to see me?" All innocence.

"Come in."

Cory ducked inside the doorway. Ms. J gathered up folders, sliding them into the desk drawers.

"Perfect timing. I thought I would close up and enjoy some of this nice weather."

She drew a clunky purse from a bottom drawer, snapped off the lights, and ushered Cory back into the hallway. When she pulled the door to the guidance offices shut behind them, Cory asked where they were going.

"The Glen Hills Garden Center. My little piece of heaven on Earth."

Ms. J's car smelled like mulch and pine. Affixed to the dashboard over the radio was a scary-looking medallion depicting Jesus with a blood-red heart with rays of gold shooting out of it. Maybe she shouldn't have gotten in the car with her—the whole teacher/student thing. Driving along some country roads, Cory stared out the window as the older woman chatted about the school's champion lacrosse team and the new chorus director. It started to drizzle.

The car's tires crunched along a gravel drive before coming to a halt in front of a row of several large greenhouses. The windows were fogged, giving their panes a milky-opaque look.

"C'mon." Ms. J opened her door. "I want to show you this place."

Cory surveyed the desolate surroundings—broken terra cotta pots in a pile, black plastic tarp over rotting plant beds, no one in sight. Ms. J pulled out her key ring, opened the door of the nearest building, and disappeared inside.

As Cory stepped over the threshold, she was stunned by the transition from the gray world outside to the kaleidoscope of colors inside. It was as if she had stepped into another realm. The heavily scented air was moist as a warm kiss against her face. Long, low tables as far as she could see were covered with orchids of every color. Tall sweeping ones on tender stalks, brilliant orange and pink ones with thick foliage. All with velvety petals open, their mouths revealing their fuzzy yellow stamens.

Ms. J was already shedding her coat. A fine mist of perspiration beaded her hairline. She went to an old refrigerator and pulled out two Dr. Peppers.

"Hope you like DPs. That's all I've got here." She smiled shyly. "It's my guilty pleasure."

Cory accepted the can, already beaded with moisture, and slipped out of her coat. "It's like the Amazon in here."

"It is. I like to come here when I need to think"—she gestured to the rows of nodding orchids—"and visit my children."

"Is this your garden center?" What Cory was really wondering was whether Ms. J might be a little crazy and they would get in trouble for being there.

She chuckled. "No. I work here. Part time, of course. But the owners needed a horticulturist who was an expert in the exotics. That's me." She grabbed a spritzer bottle and started spraying a pink spotted orchid that looked like some jungle toad. She raised her eyes to look at Cory. "It was my *calling*, you could say. But I didn't always know that."

Cory tagged along behind as the older woman went down the rows of orchids, pinching off dead leaves or spritzing God knows what onto them. It was quiet except for the hum of the compressors and the occasional hiss of water sprayed from the overhead sprinkler system.

"Which makes me think about your essay on desire."

Oh, here it comes. "You know, Ms. J, I didn't really mean all those things I wrote in that. I was up really late, and I had a really bad day." Cory took a sip to stop her mouth long enough to collect her thoughts. Ms. J stopped poking at the orchids and looked at her. "I mean, the things I said about those people . . ." Cory was afraid she would ask for details, demand to know who they were and try to help them. And that would only get Cory in trouble. Thoughts ran through her head so fast the words got jumbled up somewhere in her mouth and refused to come out in any sensible order.

Ms. J handed her a small black bucket and a pair of gloves. "See if these fit. Just pull the little weeds coming up in the bottom of the pots and any yellow leaves on the plants. You work down this row, and I'll start on the other side."

Cory pulled on the pair of stiff gloves decorated with bumblebees. *This is weird.* She picked some weeds and tossed them in the bucket. She could see the top of Ms. J's dark hair on the opposite side, bent over the flowerpots, moving along the row. The rhythmic drip of water from the overhead pipes punctuated her work pulling up tiny shoots. Thoughts about what she had written about Vee and her mom and Jess in that essay circled around her head like an annoying fly. Why had she said those things? She tugged a shoot and nearly uprooted the flower. Why was she here? Thousands of orchids, their bright tongues gaping out of open mouths, stood in an endless row before her.

"Why did you make me write that essay on desire, anyway?" Cory pulled harder at a stubborn withered leaf.

Ms. J pushed aside the plants. "You remember the story of da Vinci, don't you?"

"Of course." A sigh. "Quote, 'We should not desire the impossible.'" Cory frowned. This didn't explain anything.

Ms. J took a deep breath. "How to explain . . ." She pulled off her gloves. "Much of human spirit is spent in a quest for knowledge, justice, truth, beauty, perfection—even love. All worthy pursuits, higher ideals, wouldn't you agree?"

Cory kept plucking at the potted orchids and shrugged. "Sure."

"These pursuits, driven by desire . . ." She looked off toward the corner of the ceiling for a moment and seemed to change course. "A very wise man once said, 'By all means love, by all means desire, but think carefully about what you love and what you desire.' I wanted to make you think about *what* you desire."

"But it wasn't about me."

"But it was about what you've observed in people around you. Desire and how it operates on the human heart and spirit." Ms. J came around to Cory's side of the row. "We desire whatever we think will complete us. And we assume achieving that desire will lead to happiness. But the sad thing is, the objects of our desires, too, can become disappointing." Ms. J's face was flushed and glistening.

"Really, I'm not like them—the people I wrote about—and I don't think that way."

"Cory." She said her name in a forceful way that made Cory look up with alarm. "I think you do, that's the point. I'll tell you something from my own experience that I haven't shared with too many people." Her dark head bowed. "Before I came to the school as a counselor, I used to be a Sister of Notre Dame. I was a nun."

"Yeah, I heard. I didn't know you could quit." Cory tried picturing her in a long black habit with a string of beads hanging down the front.

"It's not the Mafia." Ms. J laughed and took a swig from her can. "I came to realize after several years that I wasn't a nun because I loved God and wanted to serve Him—even though I do love God—but I was a nun because I wanted to fill a hole in my life and thought being a servant of the Lord and learning and seeking knowledge would reward me with meaning in my life and fill that void. That was my desire—the fulfillment of myself, knowledge, the attainment of spiritual peace. It sounds like a noble desire, right?"

"I guess, yeah." Cory pulled off her bumblebee gloves and set them aside. God talk always made her uneasy. She plucked at a few yellowed leaves.

"Wrong." Ms. J wandered down the row to an area of the table devoid of any plants. Brushing some dirt away, she hiked her bulk up onto the table with a clumsy effort and patted the empty spot beside her. Cory hoisted herself onto the table next to her but placed the sweating soda can down between them.

"Cory, I'll give you the Cliffs Notes version—you kids still use Cliffs Notes?"

"Sometimes."

"Okay, here it is. Short version. Humans and their desires go wrong when they buy into the concept that we're sufficient unto ourselves—when we stop seeking anything outside of our own lives. We spend time, money, and energy running after something only to find we've become enslaved to our desires. The point is this, Cory. Desire's potential to bring you happiness depends on the legitimacy of the object desired. Something more than merely human input is needed if the search for fulfillment is to be satisfied." Ms. J fanned her face with her gloves. "When I left the order and started my new career in juvenile counseling, I felt the hole in my spirit start to close, and I actually felt closer to God than ever before. I was doing work according to my calling—the work I was meant to do."

Ms. J sighed. She lightly touched Cory's hand but quickly took it away. "I can see I've lost you. Let's put it this way." She took a gulp of soda and continued, "You tell yourself everything would be different if you could just lose weight. Or, if you had more friends at school . . ."

Cory felt her mouth turn down into a scowl.

"Okay, wait now. Then you get older and the desires become more important—that promotion at work, the money to buy a bigger house. Then I'll be happy, you say."

"Ms. J, I know those things don't count in life. I mean, they're important—"

She held up her hand. "But that sets up a pattern for your life. Then it's something more complex. You want to be, say, the best actress and though you've gotten starring roles, you haven't won the Oscar. So you're miserable. Or, you think the perfect partner will complete your life and you find out there's no such thing. But you keep searching. Or, you find a way to pull some honor out of the ashes of a disaster only to become consumed with guilt and dream of revenge."

"My essay."

"Your essay. You see the people you love chasing after things that give them no peace or pleasure. They're worshipping false gods."

"And I'm like that, too? That's why you wanted to talk with me?"

"Cory, I saw something in you when we first met. You were a seeker, who was looking around for something special in the world that would fill the empty hole. I was afraid you might look in the wrong direction." She hurried to add, "Or waste time trying to figure it out, like I did."

Cory wasn't sure about all the other stuff but she was sure she had felt the void—one which had widened when her dad left and her mom retreated into her own world, a void that was growing between her and Jess the longer she kept quiet, and a void that flattened and spread over everything. She'd wanted to talk to someone about that stuff and maybe that's why she wrote some of it in that stupid essay. "And those people? The ones in the essay. I don't know how to help. I don't know what to do anymore . . ."

Cory looked at the rows of open-mouthed orchids, blurring from tears that threatened to spill over.

"Tell me about them."

A cloud passed, casting the greenhouse into dapples of gray. Soon the sound of raindrops on the glass roof grew to a crescendo and nearly drowned out the words that poured out of Cory, the words that dripped down the glass walls, ran along the damp hoses, and circled the drain in the cement floor. The words that lightened her with their release.

Chapter
Fifty

CORY FLIPPED ON the kitchen light. Jess stood at the counter with a brownie halfway to her mouth. She blinked, shielding her eyes with her other hand.

"What are you doing?" Jess demanded.

"What are *you* doing?" Cory stepped into the galley kitchen and leaned past Jess to check out the half-empty pan of brownies. "It's midnight." When everyone went to bed, the pan had only two missing. Jess stuffed the end of the brownie into her mouth and hurried to cover the pan with foil.

"Nothing. I woke up starving. Is that a crime?" She spun around and stared at Cory.

"I guess not. It's just that you never want to eat at dinner."

"I don't feel hungry at dinner. At dinnertime I've just finished four hours of practice and I'm too damn tired to eat, okay?"

Cory took a step back. "Okay, okay. Don't bite my head off. I don't give a crap when you eat." *As long as you eat.* She eyed Jess's hips protruding like a prison camp victim's over the top of her low-slung sweatpants. Her arms lacked any shape, attached to her bony shoulder blades like a stick person drawing. Jess's eyes had become hollow with dark circles, and her hair lacked the shiny blond sheen it used to have. And the weirdest thing was that Jess's teeth looked older somehow—yellowed and surrounded by puffy red gums. Cory had been increasingly alarmed by her sister's appearance—she was starting to look like a heroin addict—and Cory was pretty sure she knew why. But what to say to her about it? Whenever she'd asked Jess about her meager meals, not daring to mention hearing her vomit in the toilet at night, Jess's only reply was that she had to maintain a certain look in order to make it through the Maryland Youth Ballet competition to be considered, let alone selected. She told Cory she'd eat a steak dinner with mashed potatoes and a giant sundae the night she won the competition. Cory had let it go then.

"Jess, I wonder . . ." she began.

Jess turned savage eyes in her direction. "What?"

"If maybe you're taking this whole looking thin thing for the competition too far?"

Jess had opened the refrigerator to survey the contents. Now she slammed it. "This *thin* thing?" She made air quotes. Cory hated air quotes. "This *thin* thing means the difference between getting into the Academy, and, by the way, determines my whole future career. This *thin* thing is not just 'I need to look good to get *boys.*'" She placed a nasty emphasis on boys. "It means how I will spend the rest of my life. Or not."

"I know. I know it's not just a thing—that it's important to you. I get that. It's just that when you make it your whole life . . . I don't know." Cory looked down and shook her head. The words weren't coming out right. She could feel rage emanating off Jess in waves. She tried to frame her thoughts, the ideas she had rolling around in her head like a bag of spilled marbles. "Ms. J says that desire can turn against you when—"

"What? You talked to someone else about me?" The vein in Jess's thin neck bulged. "How dare you talk about me to anyone!" Jess brushed Cory aside with the back of her arm and stalked into the living room. She pulled open the closet and grabbed a jacket.

"What are you doing?"

Jess flung open the front door. "Going for a walk." She turned to Cory. "That is, if you don't mind. You may want to report what I do to someone first." The door slammed.

Cory stood behind it, frozen to the spot. "At midnight?"

March 24

I told her about everything, and now I'm not so sure that was the right thing to do. She promised she wouldn't say anything or do anything without talking about it with me first. It felt right at the time and everything she said made sense, but now I'm not so sure. What if she has to say something to some authorities and Mom gets in a lot of trouble or Jess misses her big chance and it would all be because of me. She said I have to do something. That's the scary part. So, I try to and now Jess isn't speaking to me at all. She came home about ten minutes ago and is watching movies downstairs. At least she's back.

Chapter
Fifty-One

CORY STOOD OUTSIDE the men's dressing room, staring at the mannequins dressed in casual beachwear. She shivered, thinking of the cold rain falling outside the mall. The male mannequins were shirtless, displaying rippling abs, bulging biceps, and, most intriguing, a v-line cut of muscle just above the loose, low waistband of their swim trunks. She cocked her head, letting her eye wander down the male abdominal musculature to the top of the pants.

"I wonder . . ." Stepping forward, she hooked one finger inside the waistband, pulled it, and peeked down into the dark spaces between the plastic man's skin and his gaping pants.

"Bet mine's bigger." Kevyn emerged from the dressing room with an armload of jeans.

Cory jumped back and released the waistband. It snapped against the plastic with a loud smack. Her face burned.

"I was just wondering how anatomically correct they'd be." She laughed. "They're as disappointing as my old Ken doll, actually."

"Disappointed?" Kevyn smirked.

"Yeah, but not unexpected."

"You want to check out Barbie's equipment, too?" Kevyn nodded at the female mannequin.

Cory struck a pose, looking like she was considering it. "Nah. Let's just go, if you're done. I can complete my mannequin research at some other stores."

Kevyn tossed the pile of jeans on a returns rack and slipped his arm through Cory's. "Let me escort you. First some lunch, then we go to my place to really complete your investigation." He gave Cory a lurid stare, wrapped his arm low around her hips, and pulled her close.

In the noisy food court, they spotted an empty table and headed toward it with their trays. Kevyn immediately launched into his foot-long sub.

"When do you hear from Harvard?" When he didn't respond, Cory nudged his foot under the table. "Well?"

"You and my mom, God, what is it with freaking Harvard, anyway?"

Cory reared back in her seat, struck by the uncharacteristic vehemence in Kevyn's voice.

He shifted and continued with a calculated nonchalance, "I've heard from lots of great places. I got accepted to Swarthmore, St. Mary's, Hopkins, but all anyone ever asks me about is Harvard." He reached across the table and grabbed Cory's drink, but avoided looking at her.

"So sor-ry." She was getting pretty tired of people biting her head off for no reason.

Swiveling sideways in her plastic seat, she watched the shoppers passing by their table. The Columbia Mall was crowded, as usual. The food court smelled of warm chocolate chip cookies and overused deep fat fryers. Ketchup-stained wrappers from their lunch littered the tiny table between them, and something sticky on the floor pulled at her shoe, annoying her a lot more than it should have.

Kevyn had been aloof lately. Maybe he was getting tired of her. He also turned in his seat and thrust his long legs into the path of passersby, who had to step around him. Sucking noisily on the straw and poking at the slush at the bottom of the cup, he didn't notice or didn't care. He caught Cory's eye and gestured to a shop opposite them, displaying a row of mannequins in jewel-toned sparkling gowns.

"You got your dress for the prom yet?" he asked. One corner of his mouth turned up.

Cory swung around toward him but thought better of showing too much interest. She made a show of pulling out her cell phone to check the time. "You asking me?"

"Unless some other guy beat me to it, yeah."

"Very romantic." She tried for sullen, but a hint of amusement crept into her voice.

Kevyn unfolded himself from behind the tiny table, knelt down in front of her, and grabbed one of her hands. She looked around at the crowd turning to stare at them and knew her face was probably flaming red.

Clutching her hand to his chest and in a loud, terrible Irish accent, he asked, "Cory Iverson, m'love. Would yah be doin' me the honor of escorting this poor sod to the promenade? Aye, t'would make me the happiest man on Earth if ya would, to be sure."

Cory pushed him away and stood up. "You idiot!" She laughed. "Yes, I'll go, but, no, I don't have a dress."

Kevyn jumped to his feet. "We'll fix that right now. So, want one that's low in front or low in the back?"

She grabbed his hand and dragged him toward the store she had in mind and cocked her head slightly. "How about both?"

Chapter
Fifty-Two

VEE HELD THE screen door open as Cory stepped into the farmhouse kitchen. A troop of Jack Russells ran from the other room to greet her, barking furiously, their red tongues dangling.

"Shut up, you monsters. You know her," Vee scolded, and they ran off to another part of the house. "C'mon in and sit down." She gestured to a round oak table partially covered with piles of mail and show entry forms. In the center was a wooden bowl containing a thick key ring, a pair of sunglasses with an arm missing, and a few dog biscuits. Cory pulled out a chair, sat down at the only area free of debris, and glanced over at a small yellow notepad with a bold underlined heading: *To Do*. It was blank.

"We have to have our strategy meeting as soon as Jack gets here," Vee said, rinsing out a coffee cup at the sink. "I can't believe it's April already. We don't have that many shows left to qualify for Washington."

She came over, placed a tall glass of iced tea in front of Cory, and pulled out a chair. Cory winced inwardly. She'd never gotten a taste for the sweet tea people drank here. Tentatively taking a small sip, she discovered, to her relief, it was plain. The weather had turned milder. Gauzy curtains billowed into the room on a breeze and were sucked back against the screens a minute later on the whim of the currents. The scent of lilac wafted in, riding on a tide of warm air.

"Ahhh," Vee sighed, leaning back in her chair. "This morning when I went out to feed, I grabbed my jacket but was happy to discover I didn't need it."

Cory knew what she meant. Sitting in a beam of sunlight, her blood felt like something golden and thick, like caramel, oozing through her body slowly, bringing a sleepy haze to her movements.

"But we can't relax now," Vee announced, as if reading her mind. "We have to keep the pressure on to make sure Epiphany gets to the right shows." With a conspiratorial smirk, she added, "And keep Angela on the run."

The mention of Angela's name filled the room with an almost palpable stink, as if someone had lifted the top off a garbage bin.

"Yeah, that would be an extra bonus," Cory replied but inwardly pictured Regina and Prophet being shut out of the ribbons and going home to face her crazy mother. "And I bet she's really mad after that present you left for her in her truck."

"On second thought, that probably wasn't a smart thing to do. That woman's dangerous, and I don't know if she has any limits to what she might do to get back at me. I assume she's figured it out—that it was me." Vee gathered up a pile of papers from the table and dropped the *To Do* notebook on top. "Grab your drink. Let's move into the living room where it's more comfortable." She added, almost to herself, "I can spend my whole life worrying about what Angela will or won't do, or I can move on."

Cory wondered if Vee had moved on. She noticed how much older she looked in the bright light, but instead of the angry lines around her mouth there was now a softness to her face. She wished *she* could do something to make it up to Vee, something that would change stuff so Vee wouldn't be afraid of whom she ran into at shows and what they were saying behind her back. And Cory knew what that something was—she had to get to Washington. A twinge grabbed at the top of her stomach, and that old urge—the urge to make an excuse, to walk out, or bolt—was hovering just out of reach. God, it would be so much easier just not to try.

They walked through an archway with pocketed double doors to a small sitting room decorated with lithographs of horses and hunting hounds. A leather armchair and ottoman crouched in the corner with what looked like the silhouette of a person still pressing into their cushions. Cory sank down on one end of the couch, shared by Vee's old foxhound, which lifted her head with annoyance.

"Sorry, Mrs. Thatcher," she apologized to the dog.

Vee sat in an odd-looking Victorian chair covered with needlepoint flowers. "Okay." She shuffled through her papers. "I've marked the few remaining shows I think we should hit. The ones close enough for the old truck to make it to safely. Here's what we got." She sat forward on the edge of her chair but turned as Jack walked in.

"Hey, ladies. Vee, brought your mail." Jack slapped a pile of letters with tiny cellophane windows—clearly bills—and a few catalogs and magazines on the coffee table in front of her. He pulled Mrs. Thatcher off the couch by her collar, sat down, and leaned back.

"So, because a lot of the local spring shows were canceled, we absolutely have to do well in the next two . . ." Vee glanced at Jack, who had not shown the slightest interest in her meticulously planned schedule. "I see you don't have a strong opinion on this."

"No, no, I do." Jack sat forward, glanced at the yellow-lined list in front of him. "It looks great."

Vee looked more closely at Jack's expression. "You usually have a lot to say on which shows we should shoot for." She slumped against the back of her chair and gestured with exasperation. "Okay, what is it? Why that shit-eating grin?"

Jack smiled even more and nudged the pile of bills aside to reveal a magazine underneath. Vee leapt off her chair.

"Oh, my God!" She snatched up the magazine and brought it close to her face. "I can't believe it!"

Cory ran around behind Vee to look over her shoulder. "What? What is it?" Then she saw it, too.

The Equestrian Journal. And she and Epiphany were on the cover.

It was a photo from that awful show, the one she did so badly at, but the picture was great—a head-on shot of her and Epiphany sailing over a huge roll top, her head turned, scanning for the next fence. Cory rubbed her sweating palms down the sides of her jeans. She remembered that journalist chasing after her with a photographer and the smug glances from the crowd gathered around Angela. She also remembered signing something at the registration desk about a release, right before they left. She hadn't read it.

"What do they say? Read the article," Cory said. She wanted to tear the magazine out of Vee's hands to study the picture and devour every word inside.

Vee thumbed through the pages to find it, then plunked down on the couch next to Jack. Cory sat on her other side.

"Have you read this?" Vee turned to Jack, who had finally picked up Vee's show schedule list and was acting interested in it.

"I wouldn't read your mail," he said with feigned offense.

Vee's eyes scanned the page. She smiled and made a smug-sounding "hmmph."

"Read it out loud!" Cory wailed. Leaning over Vee's shoulder, she saw a small file-photo of Vee taken ages ago on Pressman but couldn't make out the words underneath.

Vee made some comments about how *The Journal* was nothing but a gossip rag and cleared her throat. "It says, *Silk Purse from Sow's Ear, or Modern-day Miracle Worker*—gosh, I love that title. *Vee Stewart has been gone from the horse show scene for several years, but surely she has not been sitting around watching soaps and eating bon-bons. Judging by the quality of the horse she trained which has burst upon the show scene with a sensation . . .* Blah, blah, blah, stuff about my past show record, you know all that . . . Oh, I love this part, *Vee's former partner, Angela Hamilton, let it be known that this horse, which is burning up the jumper scene, was discovered by Vee at a local livestock auction. Sales prices of Grand Prix-level horses have long been rising through the roof, so this horsewoman is mighty impressed that Vee Stewart has the eye to spot talent and make a jumper out of a rescue horse down on her luck in the sales pens. A true Cinderella story."*

Cory let out the breath she'd been holding. So Angela's plan to make them look stupid backfired. *The Journal* was not only impressed that Vee could spot a good horse and turn it into a Grand Prix-level jumper, they were truly in love with Epiphany, too. The author went on to extol the mare's form over fences, her workmanlike attitude, and her attractiveness.

"Oh, this is great!" Vee stabbed a finger on the page. "Get a load of this. They interviewed that snarky trainer, what's his name, who was at the show. Suddenly I love that guy. Look what he said about Angela.

"Washington may prove to be a much more interesting competition this year with the appearance of Epiphany. It seems her main competition is from none other than Angela Hamilton's horse, Prophet, who, by the way, was also trained by Vee Stewart. Does Angela still need to rely on Vee to train her horses to Grand Prix, as she did in the past? Prophet is being ridden by Angela's daughter in the Junior Jumper competition against Vee's protégée, Coraline Iverson, but rumor has it the sale of Prophet is under negotiation for an undisclosed sum. An amount I've heard has several zeroes behind it."

"Oh, please." Jack laughed. "You've brought lots of horses to Grand Prix that you picked up off the track or wherever."

Vee slapped his side. "Killjoy. This is our moment. Our fifteen minutes of fame, and Cory is going to ride it to glory. Aren't you?"

Cory looked back at them. Jack's arm was loosely draped over the back of the couch behind Vee, who put her hand lightly on Cory's knee. She wanted it to stay like this, in the warm living room with Mrs. Thatcher snoring in the corner, with all the promise of the competition ahead of them, with nothing to spoil it.

"I'll try."

April 15

Everything's moving so fast now it kind of scares me. It was great when it seemed like Washington was almost a year away. Now I kind of wish that Vee wasn't so into getting Epiphany qualified because it all depends on me riding really well, especially tomorrow because we don't have that many shows left. Or else I let everyone down. I wonder if there's more to it than showing up Angela, too. I'm sure it wouldn't hurt to have a horse at Washington for Vee to get some new clients. Seems like she's got a lot more bills lying around lately, and I know the entry fees are pretty expensive. It's kind of like a gamble, and they've put their money on me. Probably not a smart bet.

Chapter
Fifty-Three

CORY TURNED AWAY from her desk and glanced at Jessica's sleeping form under the mound of the blankets. *Why isn't she sweating to death?* she thought, reaching for the computer's switch. As the computer whirred to life, she hoped not to wake her sister. God, Jess had been horrible all day, snapping at everyone and skittering around the house picking at things with the nervous energy of an addict overdue for her next fix. Her big dance competition was tomorrow, and she was clearly a wreck over it. Tomorrow was also one of the last few qualifying horse shows for Epiphany, so Cory felt none too steady herself.

The sound of the computer booting up calmed her. It was a portal to people on the horse message boards, to show points statistics, jumper rider chat rooms, and tonight, most importantly, to her secret friend on Facebook. She logged in, looking for any updates from that friend, Victoria Burr. She smiled when she brought up Victoria's profile. The girl in the glamour shot picture in the corner of the screen wasn't really an image of her friend and was as fake as the name Victoria Burr. She and Regina had planned it all the day they ran into each other at the spring show. Before she left that day, Regina Hamilton confided in Cory that her mom was monitoring everything she did, everywhere she went, and everyone she talked to on her cell or computer email. According to Regina, her mom was crazy and suspected everyone of trying to sabotage her.

"Anyway," Regina told her, "I thought of a way we can keep in touch. My mom would totally burst a blood vessel if she knew I was talking to anyone associated with Vee."

Cory felt a stab of guilt knowing she had been the eyewitness who got Angela banned from the shows. Not that she didn't deserve it.

"Anyway"—Regina always started her sentences with anyway—"I'm a million different people on Facebook. I just make up a person, I use this ancient old email address I was issued for a school project, and I post a fake picture, background, everything. Then, you friend me, and we can talk."

"How am I supposed to find you under a fake name?"

"You'll know who I am. We'll make it up right now." Regina tapped her lip with an index finger, thinking. "Okay, so you can remember it better, you help me come up with the name. Regina means queen. What do you think of when you hear the word queen, quick!"

"Queen Victoria."

"Okay, Victoria, that's good. Now Hamilton. That's harder . . ."

"Burr."

"Burr? Like the sticky things?"

Cory laughed and slapped Regina's arm. "No, you moron. Didn't you ever study U.S. history? Alexander Hamilton and Aaron Burr. The guy who shot him in the famous duel?" Cory's voice rose questioningly at the end, hoping something would trigger Regina's memory. No luck.

"Okay, so you want to name me after a murderer. Kinky, but cool."

Thus, Victoria Burr was born. Cory had been in touch with her friend all through the spring, keeping her up to date on Epiphany's progress and all the stuff with Kevyn. Regina kept her posted on how Prophet was doing and how her mom was getting weirder and weirder.

In the quiet of her room, Cory quickly scanned through some of "Victoria's" old posts and chuckled at the one signed "poopy pants" after the manure incident and the fact that she gave her mother the cover name Mortitia. Cory knew Regina would be just as spun up as she was the night before one of the last qualifying shows and hoped she would have posted something funny to take the edge off. She skimmed through a few more, then stopped. As she read through Regina's most recent post, a slurry gate of adrenaline opened up in her bloodstream, causing her fingers on the keyboard to grow cold.

Mortitia has really been super strange lately. She was mental when that article about you and Epiphany came out, but then she got weirder. Not like usual, not like screaming at me and smacking the horses around, but real quiet, and whenever I come in the room where she's working, she hides stuff. Like I wouldn't notice she's hiding it. So, I went in her desk later, and she has some deal going to sell Prophet. But the guy who's buying him wants some proof he's worth what he's paying, so he has to qualify for Washington or the deal's off. That kind of sucks, 'cuz I'm really getting to like riding him, but, anyway, I overheard Mortitia tell Dr. Killdare that she has a Plan B for Prophet if the sale falls through. I don't know what that is, but I'll find out. Killdare said he would start looking for the replacement just in case, whatever that means.

Cory stopped reading. She was pretty sure she knew who Dr. Killdare was, too. That creepy vet that hung around with Angela— Ward, the guy who wanted to put down Vee's horse. Regina had told her before there was a huge insurance policy on Prophet. Cory remembered Vee's story about Sandy Point, the last "replacement" horse, which ended up dead because he was a twin for an expensive one. Cory glanced at her cell phone and thought about calling Jack and Vee. But what could they do? Prophet was Angela's horse. She could sell him to anyone she wanted—she could even put him down if she wanted—and where was the proof that they might kill him for the insurance money if he didn't sell? It would be a stupid thing to do, even for crazy Angela.

Cory felt the pizza she had for dinner crawling its way back up her throat. A glance at the clock told her it was one a.m. already, so she posted a quick *good luck tomorrow* message to Regina and snapped off the light.

Chapter
Fifty-Four

I N THE MORNING, Cory's eyes felt like she had been out in a sandstorm all night. The coffee she downed roiled like a pool of acid in her stomach as she went through the motions of getting Epiphany ready for the show—braiding her mane, brushing out her tail, putting on the shipping wraps. Every time she started to tell Vee or Jack about Regina's message, she stopped. What could she say? She had no proof, just Regina's suspicions. When they asked her why she was so jumpy, she merely answered, "Nothing, just nervous. And no, I don't want any of my favorite sour cream donuts for breakfast, thanks."

It had warmed up when they pulled into the showgrounds. Jack whistled some Irish-sounding tune as he unloaded the equipment, while Cory conducted her usual scan of the parking lot for the Hamiltons' blue trailer. She worried about Prophet—such a trusting, elegant horse—and imagined Angela sidling up to him in his stall one night. Maybe she'd hand him a carrot, then shove ping-pong balls up his nostrils to suffocate him or have "Dr. Killdare" mix up some bad feed to make it look like colic.

Cory shook her head to derail the crazy nightmare train on which her thoughts had hitched a ride. Why would they kill him just for the insurance? Surely he could be sold for a lot of money, even if it wasn't as much as Angela might want. She took a deep breath, or tried to. Something felt like it was lodged halfway down her chest, blocking the air. Regina had to get him qualified for Washington. That was all there was to it. She was doing as well as Cory—they had been neck and neck for that final qualifying spot all season. Should she let Regina nose ahead into the lead?

"You going to daydream or get that mare warmed up? I'm not impressed that you're a celebrity all of a sudden." Jack gently cuffed Cory on the back of the head as he passed. He was right. She had to snap out of it. A lot was riding on this.

Epiphany came off the trailer with dark splotches of sweat on her flanks and neck. It was warm but not enough to make her sweat up like that. Cory looked her over with a critical eye.

"What's up, girl? You picking up on how much pressure we have on us today, too?" She ran her hand along the mare's neck, checked her legs for any swelling or heat, and stood quietly by her to see if her respiration was elevated. The last thing she needed now was a bout of colic. Epiphany nosed Cory, sniffing her hand for a treat.

"You're a pushy mare. Good thing for you, you're worth it." She slapped the mare's muscled haunches and sluiced a bucket of water over her back to cool her down and wash off the sweat marks.

Epiphany swung her head around, the whites of her eyes showing.

"Too cold? I'm sorry. I can't seem to get anything right today." Cory scraped the water off the mare's back, rubbed her down, and started tacking up.

"A whole lot of people here asking about her today." Jack nodded in Epiphany's direction. "Guess she's something of a celebrity after that Cinderella article." He laughed, casually running a hand along the mare's back. "I'm going to check out the competition while you all warm up."

In the ring, a man riding a big bay gelding was on course. He came down the diagonal line too fast, chipped in to the jump, and had a rail down. Bad timing. Cory turned back to Epiphany. The mare's head was low, her eyes half-closed. One back leg was cocked, her weight shifted, dozing in the warmth of the spring sun.

"You ready?" Vee appeared with her hand wrapped around a paper cup of coffee. "Let's show them what you got."

After leading Epiphany to the warm-up arena, Cory crammed her helmet down over her hair as if she were preparing for battle. Vee gave her a leg up and Cory eased Epiphany into an easy trot, but it felt as if they were moving through deep beach sand. Epi's steps were short and lethargic. Cory took the crop and moved it to her outside hand. Usually the sight of the crop in the mare's field of vision made her perk up, but not today.

"Come on down over this small vertical," Vee called over the other trainers' voices. "You're going to have to move her up some. She looks dead." Vee saw it, too. Cory put her leg on the mare's sides and asked for the canter. Nothing. Cory gave her a little jab with her outside leg and felt Epiphany roll into a flat four-beat canter.

"Wake her up!" Vee shouted.

Cory reluctantly slapped her on the flank with the crop. Epiphany lifted her head, pushed herself up into the next gear, and rolled down to the fence.

"That's more like it." Vee slipped the fence cup up another two holes. "Come on down over it again, then take the oxer."

Cory circled, spotted the raised fence, and rolled down to it as before. This time the mare was late with her front right leg and knocked the rail with a resounding thud. It spun off the cups, causing her back legs to get tangled up in it. Epiphany tripped, struggled to right herself, then raced off on the back side of the jump as if she were furious and ashamed about missing it. Cory pulled her up.

"She's not on her game today. I don't know what's with her."

Vee walked over and stood looking at the horse, then bent to run a hand down her legs. "Nothing's obviously wrong." Vee looked up at Cory, shading her eyes from the glare. "What does she feel like?"

Cory didn't want to sound like an alarmist. They had been working her hard lately. "I don't know. She doesn't seem like herself, kind of sluggish or something. Usually she's really up for shows, but today I can hardly get her to move."

Vee quietly laid a hand against the horse's shoulder. "Tell me she's okay, or we'll go home."

Cory looked down at Vee, whose nose and chin were starting to turn pink from the first strong spring sunshine, then at Epiphany's muscular neck. The announcer blared in the background, but to Cory everything felt as if it were submerged under water. She knew what Vee was asking. The answer meant they either went on and tried to qualify or packed up to go home, possibly kissing goodbye any chance to make it to Washington. She also knew Vee was relying on her to assess the horse's fitness to go on. Vee was trusting her. The unspoken thing between them was the story of Northern Lights. She didn't want to make the same mistake of pushing a horse for the sake of her personal goals. She could quit right now and not worry about it being her fault—if the horse really was unsound. She bit her bottom lip. Vee stood, waiting.

"She just seems kind of dead, you know, not lame or anything." Cory's voice trailed off, hoping that Vee would make the ultimate decision, take the responsibility from her.

"You sure?"

Cory gathered up the reins. "I guess."

"Okay." Vee glanced at her watch. "Put on your coat and get ready."

Vee held the reins as Cory struggled into her show coat and buttoned it. It felt like a straightjacket today, hot and snug around her. Her hands were sweating inside her gloves, and the sun cast a shimmering glare over the dark gray stone dust of the arena. She heard Regina's name announced—another clear round.

"Cory!"

She turned toward the sound of her name being shouted from the other side of the ring. Someone called again, with more urgency. A truck the color of a bruised eggplant rolled up to the edge of the warm-up arena. No one but Kevyn had a truck that color. What was he doing? A show steward jogged toward the truck, flapping his arms to shoo him away from an area prohibited to vehicles. Now Kevyn had gone too far with his defiance of rules. If he started screwing with the horse show authorities, who had no sense of humor, it might get her in trouble.

"Cory!" Kevyn leaned out the driver side window, waving his arm to summon her over.

She thought about ignoring him but noticed Jack sitting beside him in the passenger seat. She turned Epiphany and walked to them. Kevyn jumped out and loped toward her as Jack broad-armed the show steward out of his way. A coldness ran down Cory's arms, ending in a tingling sensation in her fingers. Her brain flashed a warning message: something was terribly wrong. Vee picked up that there was a problem as all three converged from the sidelines. Jack stepped up to take hold of the reins. Kevyn ran up behind him.

"Cory, c'mon," Kevyn said breathlessly. "Your mom sent me to find you. I can drive you to the hospital. It's your sister—she collapsed."

Chapter
Fifty-Five

AS THEY PULLED into the hospital parking lot, the details of the past twenty minutes or so flashed through Cory's head—being helped off Epiphany, Jack leading the mare away. She remembered climbing up into Kevyn's truck and speeding off, the showgrounds becoming smaller and more distant in the side mirror. A twinge of guilt stabbed at her after the thought that her chances of making it to Washington were likewise receding.

"What happened?" she asked Kevyn, his face a mask of concentration, steering into a close parking spot.

"She collapsed at the dance competition. When they couldn't revive her, they took her by ambulance to the emergency room. When you didn't answer your phone, your mom started calling everyone listed on Jess's cell phone, trying to get hold of you. She called me, and I said I'd come find you at the show."

The image of her mother running alongside Jess, unconscious on a gurney, flashed through Cory's mind as she and Kevyn sped through the hospital corridor to urgent care. The hard soles of her riding boots echoed through the hallway as if a storm trooper were invading the hospital wing. Heads turned disapprovingly. Kevyn walked quickly beside her, his hand pushing against the small of her back. When they entered the emergency waiting area, Cory approached the information desk.

"I'm here to see Jessica Iverson."

The duty nurse told her she'd been admitted and to take a seat. She turned back to her computer. Cory didn't sit but remained standing at the desk. Another nurse, wearing a hospital smock covered with smiling teddy bears, summoned Cory to follow her. At the swinging doors leading into the urgent care wing, she held up a hand. "You're both relatives? Family only."

Cory opened her mouth to protest, but Kevyn turned toward the plastic seats in the waiting room. "Don't worry. I'll wait here. Go on."

She followed the nurse in silent rubber-soled shoes past a series of curtained rooms filled with people connected to tubes and machines. The air was sharp with disinfectant and filled with the sounds of sucking air hoses, soft pings, and hushed voices.

The nurse stopped by a curtain pulled closed on its ringed track. She touched Cory lightly on the upper arm. "Remember, visiting hours are over in twenty minutes, dear." She drew the curtain back a few inches and retreated to the nursing station.

Cory stood outside the small, enclosed area, her heart thumping against her chest. Just the edge of the large hospital bed and a big machine with digital numbers and hoses were visible. She drew a deep breath and stepped inside.

Jess was a tiny mound in the huge bed, covered by a thin white blanket. A transparent hose ran across her chest and up into her nose. Tubes were taped to her arms and another to the back of her hand. She looked like she was asleep. Her mother was nearly asleep in a recliner pulled up next to the bed.

"Hey, Mom," Cory whispered.

Roni struggled to stand up. Without a word, she draped her arms around Cory like a dangling rock climber who'd finally found contact with the solid mountainside. Cory staggered back a step, then stood firmly on the spot, breathing in the familiar scent of her mom's herbal shampoo. Cory hugged her mother until a rush of breath escaped her body.

"What's going on, Mom?"

Roni turned away toward Jessica, then looked back at Cory with an intense gaze. "I'm so glad you're here. It was awful."

Words tumbled out of her so fast, Cory struggled to put together the pieces of what happened. After Jess collapsed and they couldn't revive her, Roni rode with her in the ambulance to the hospital. Her mom had been waiting for hours to hear what the doctors had found. The medical team—the doctors and ER nurse—talked about heart damage and had asked some questions that sounded like accusations about Jess's weight and other things.

"I don't know why they're asking me about whether I see her eat three times a day—of course I don't! She's a teenager, not a toddler." She started back toward the chair to sit down but eased herself down on the edge of the bed instead. She rubbed Jess's leg through the thin blanket. "Wake up, honey."

Cory walked up behind her and reached out her hand to touch her mother's shoulder but let it drop. "Jess will be fine. Don't worry." But it didn't look like she was going to be fine. Jess hadn't moved since she'd arrived.

The teddy bear nurse with the stealthy shoes poked her head in. "Mrs. Iverson, some people here to see you in the waiting area. Your sister, maybe?"

Roni looked around as if she'd forgotten where she was for an instant.

"Go on, Mom. I'll wait here. Get some coffee or something."

Roni followed the nurse. Cory left the curtain partially open, taking her mother's place in the recliner. The hiss of air and a soft bleep from a monitor were the only signs that Jess was still alive. Her face was pale and gray. Signs of life beyond the curtain floated in—voices with urgent instructions, the squeaky wheel of a gurney, a slam of a cabinet door. Cory looked down at her useless hands—dirt under her nails, a split cuticle—and wondered if things would have been different if she'd said something months ago.

The drone of the monitor changed. Faster. Cory glanced up and saw that Jess's eyes were open. She looked at Cory, then lifted her hands to examine the tubes running from them. The monitor sped up again. Cory stood and leaned over Jess. She gently pushed her hands down on the bed.

"Jess, it's okay." She spoke soothingly, she hoped. It sounded shaky. "You're in the hospital, but you're going to be okay."

Jess's eyes scanned the room. Her mouth opened and closed like a fish gasping for air. Cory peered out the gap in the curtain. Was there a nurse nearby?

Jess reached up again and tried to pull the tubes out of her nose.

"No, don't do that!" She grabbed both of Jess's hands.

Jess moved her head back and forth on the pillow and pushed Cory away. The monitor squealed a high-pitched tone.

Her head lifted slightly off the pillow. "Don't tell them!" Her voice was brittle and dry. "Don't say anything!"

Before Cory could reply, a medical team rushed into the small room, pushed her out, and slid the curtain shut behind them.

May 5

Jess has been in the hospital three days already, and they're still doing tests to find out what's wrong. I think they know what's wrong, they're just seeing if there's been some permanent damage or something. A social worker's been talking to Mom a lot. Maybe that's good. I missed the show, not like that's what's important now, but I don't have too many left to qualify. But there's next year, I guess. Not sure Jess has a next year for her dancing stuff. Things are going to crap for all of us, it seems. Speaking of which, I don't think I've seen Mom's Bucky the Cowboy around lately, either.

Chapter
Fifty-Six

C ORY HAD BEEN glad when Kevyn suggested they go for a hike to get away from practically living at the hospital the past few days. Now she wasn't so sure. He walked a little ahead of her down the trail as she lagged behind, skirting mud puddles where last night's rain collected in the ruts of the old roadbed.

"This used to be a town?" she called to the back of Kevyn's head. He turned, shifted his backpack, and waited for her to catch up.

"Yeah, Daniels. A textile mill was across the river. The whole town was washed out by a flood."

The Patapsco River paralleled the old roadbed they were following. Stone pillars from the long-defunct railroad bridge stood like sentries amidst the river's slow-moving waters.

"Where are we going again?" she asked, falling in step beside him.

"So impatient," he teased. "Have I ever led you astray?"

Cory stood on the spot and refused to take another step.

"Okay," he relented. "We're going to church."

"Funny guy, no really. Where we going?"

Kevyn didn't answer, but continued walking. Having no other choice and not wanting to be left in the middle of the woods, Cory slogged after him. Her thoughts wandered back to the other night in

Jess's hospital room. Thankfully, Jess had been moved out of intensive care a few days ago but was still being held for observation. Cory hadn't said anything to Jess's cardiologist when she asked certain questions about her sister's health, and more specifically, eating habits. She'd acted clueless when a county social worker interviewed the family about any concerns that might affect Jess's recovery. Her mom sat on the edge of her chair in the social worker's office, her purse perched on her knees, and gave vague answers. That social worker could probably do things that would end Jess's chance of getting into a ballet company, and a whole lot worse.

Cory followed Kevyn down the path, batting a cobweb strand away from her face.

Last night she'd decided she would confront Jess herself, without any outside help, get her to admit to her bizarre binge eating and purging, and make her promise she'd stop. If Jess didn't listen, then she'd go for help. But not to that creepy, overly friendly hospital social worker. Maybe to Ms. J.

"We're here," Kevyn announced.

There was nothing but a narrow deer path branching off to the right, which ran up a steep incline. Cory was tired, it was getting late, and the thought of marching all the way back the way they'd come was daunting.

"Kev, really, there's nothing here."

He walked over to where she stood rooted to the spot. He shrugged out of his backpack, dropped it to the ground, and encircled her in his arms. His hand stroked her hair. The rumble of his voice vibrated against her chest as he spoke into her ear, "I wanted to show you my favorite place. I wanted to come here—with you."

All the tension that had been trapped inside her frame escaped as she leaned heavily into Kevyn's solid body. His lips brushed the outer edge of her eye. When he gently pushed her away and held her at arm's length, he bent slightly to look her squarely in the eyes.

"Okay now?"

"Okay, yeah." Feeling sheepish about being such a whiner, she grabbed the handle of his backpack and hefted it over one shoulder. "Hey, what do you have in here, cement blocks?"

She staggered under the weight of the pack while Kevyn joggled it, making it more unwieldy. "Something like that."

The path narrowed as they climbed a hill moving away from the river below.

"There," Kevyn said with reverence. "That's it."

Across a wooded gorge, perched on another hilltop stood the ruins of a stone church. It was dappled and partially hidden by the trees in the waning sunlight. Vines that climbed up from the forest floor had spread over the bottom half of its ruined foundation. The roof was gone, but its soaring walls and arched windows now led the eye upward—a ceiling that went on forever. The crumbling gray walls were draped in a verdant camouflage, as if the church was being engulfed and reclaimed by the woods. Small saplings had taken root inside, spreading their canopies, creating a new, natural roof. It looked like an ancient British castle being devoured by the forest.

"Oh, wow," Cory breathed. Before she knew it, she was running down into the gorge along a deer path, whipped by tree branches, and up the hill to the church. It drew her like a magnet. She held her breath as she stepped through a gap in the wall under an arched lintel.

Inside, fallen stones from the wall littered the ground. Someone had built a fire pit in the center. Cory dropped the backpack, tilted her head back, and spun in circles, her arms outstretched. The stone walls swirled in a blur of green and gray. When she stopped, staggering a few steps on the uneven ground, Kevyn was squatting by the backpack, pulling out a waterproof ground cover, an afghan, a four-pack of tiny wine bottles, a box of Triscuits, some cheese, and half of a fire-starter log. Cory laughed. He looked like Mary Poppins extracting an impossible number of items out of a carpetbag.

He placed a trio of stubby candles on an empty window ledge and lit them. "My Lady." He gestured to the table he had spread. "Shall I unscrew the wine?"

The sun was setting, touching the top of the tree line, forming shadows in the corner niches of the ruined walls. The tiny candles flickered weakly against the wind that picked up on top of the hill. Cory sat, crushing pine needles underneath and releasing their pungent scent. She clinked bottles with Kevyn and took a tentative sip of the wine. A bird called to a distant mate.

He settled beside her, leaned close, and casually draped an arm around her shoulder. She moved closer, chilled by the cool air.

"I got into Harvard," he announced into the silence.

Cory turned to him. "That's great! When did you hear?" She smiled, calculating how far away Boston was from here.

"March. I've known since March."

"March, really? Why didn't you tell anyone?"

"Because I'm not going."

"Whaaa—?" She stopped. His mouth pressed into a tight line.

"I wanted to tell you, but after I decided what to do first." He looked down at his empty bottle and picked at the label.

Cory rubbed her hand down his back. "What to do about what, Kev?" She tried to make her voice sound gentle when she really wanted to pepper him with a dozen rapid-fire questions.

Kevyn shifted away and propped his back against an opposite wall. "My mom's sick, like I told you before."

"M.S., I remember. I'm really sorry, Kev. Is it getting worse?" She took a slug from her wine bottle.

"Yeah, you could say so. She's losing her sight. She doesn't let on, but I've seen some of the medical reports she's hiding. Between that and her balance . . . She fell the other day. Luckily, I was home. So," he continued, "I can't be miles away in Boston and leave her alone. I can go to some school around here instead, like Howard Community or something, until . . . I don't know."

Cory recalled seeing a cane in the corner of Kevyn's living room when she first met his mother. Lately, she hadn't seen his mom walk at all—she was always either seated at the table or on the couch.

"What do her doctors say?" she asked.

"They don't know for sure, or won't say. Just that this year is crucial.

She was diagnosed about two years ago, but it's getting much worse. And fast."

"I know your dad doesn't live with you guys, but maybe you could get him to help, or your uncle?"

Kevyn dug a little trench with the heel of his boot. "My dad's a plate who runs away with the spoon kind of guy. He was the one who ran away—before they even got married. Mostly because of me, I think. I told you she left him at the altar, but it was the other way around. And my uncle lives in San Francisco and has about a dozen kids now. No way he can help."

"Kev, someone has got to help you. You can't do it all by yourself. So, what did your mom say when you told her about Harvard?"

"Didn't tell her, either."

"You didn't tell her you were accepted?"

"What's the point?" Kevyn scooted away a few inches. "I'm not going, and it would only make her feel bad if she knew I'd gotten in."

"Kevyn, you have to let her know."

"No!" His eyes locked on hers. "And don't you tell her, either." He stood up, took her empty bottle, and placed them back in his pack. He hesitated. "Promise?"

Cory looked down. "Sure."

Another secret. Another promise she shouldn't honor but would. She was going to fall through the earth from the weight of all the secrets.

Kevyn pointedly changed the subject. "How's your sister doing?"

"She's bulimic. Figured you knew that. I knew it." There. She said it to another person. "As long as we're swearing each other to secrecy, you can't tell anyone. Maybe if I had told someone a long time ago, it might have helped. Now she's in the hospital with possible heart damage and God knows what else and an army of social workers crawling up her butt to find out stuff—to maybe put her in therapy, I don't know. Or blame my mom for being a bad mother—which she is, by the way. Sort of." Cory took a breath. She couldn't look at Kevyn. "Did you know that she's looped half the time when I get home so she doesn't even see what's going on right in front of her? Or doesn't want to see it." She felt a tickle on her cheek, and when she brushed it away, was surprised her hand came away wet.

She paused. What was going on? What was this logjam that kept breaking with her blathering stuff to people who couldn't do anything about anything. She searched Kevyn's face for signs he would pull away from her, like she might be too damaged to deal with. He slid over next to her, took her hand, and kissed the palm. He held it in both of his, warming her chilled fingertips.

Cory took a ragged breath. "Sorry," she whispered.

He shrugged. "What for?"

"You know, all that. You have a problem, you tell me about it finally, and I just dump all my stuff on you instead."

"No worries." Kevyn had regained his nonchalant attitude. "There really isn't anything anyone can do to help, anyway." He smiled. "And as long as we're here,"—he gestured to the ruins—"we don't have to worry about it. This is a sacred place, a church. It's used to holding in its secrets. It's protected."

He reclined on his elbows and looked up at the sky. Cory studied his face. The tranquility was there—the same casual grace he carried around with him wherever he went—along with the supreme confidence that had first attracted her. But now she realized Kevyn's confidence compelled him to make decisions without consulting anyone else, even those directly involved. He never asks for help, and he's kept secrets, too.

Cory bowed her head. Maybe he was right. Maybe it was better to keep quiet and go on with your own plans. After all, when you open your mouth, you couldn't control what was going to happen. A released secret was like a tiny virus—you couldn't predict who spread it, who was immune, who got sick or hurt. What if she had told what she suspected about Jessica? Jess would have never spoken to her again. And what if she was wrong? What if she told what she thought was going on with Angela? And Angela got back at her, at all of them? The future was unknown. No one could guess what was going to happen. It all belonged to a reality that didn't exist yet—out there, somewhere, in a place she didn't have to ever enter, if she kept quiet. The real world was here, she decided. Here, in the sacred place where the secrets remained hidden and controlled.

"I have something else to show you." Kevyn stood and walked over to a thick wall in the corner. He removed a loose stone and reached inside a niche. Cory's eyes widened. A secret compartment! She leapt to her feet to join him.

Kevyn extracted a small plastic food storage bin and held it, trying to pry off the cover.

"I discovered this the last time I was here," he explained. "It has a notebook in it and stuff people want to leave, like, to show they were here."

The box contained a faded Boy Scout eagle patch, a pinecone, a condom in its wrapper—weird and gross Cory thought—and two small spiral notebooks. She seized the notebooks and sat down.

As she flipped through the first one, she noticed the pages were covered with different handwriting and styles. Some were small poems, others contained one line "I was here" messages. There were jokes and a rather nice sketch of the ruins itself. The second notebook was even older—its pages were curled and discolored from the damp. Cory thumbed through and found the earliest entry from 1999. The anonymous person who left the notebook in the niche wrote a quote on the first page:

Of all the tyrannies of human kind,
The worst is that which persecutes the mind.
John Dryden

Underneath, in spidery, faded ink, the anonymous hiker had written:

Unburden your mind here and leave your troubles in the embrace of these walls.

Cory fished through Kevyn's backpack for a pen and flipped to the blank pages in the back of the other notebook. She knew what she needed to write. She filled the small page with her prayers for Jess's recovery, for Prophet's safety, for her mom's restored dignity, and for Kevyn's mom's health. She wrote furiously, and as she wrote, she felt the darkness inside her lift and float above the tallest walls of the ruined church, through the open roof, past the treetops, skyward. Finally, the pen fell from her cramped hand. She replaced the notebook and sealed the container with a satisfying snap. Closed, safe.

Kevyn had been watching her. "So, you wrote a novel in there or something?"

"Or something. Never mind." She felt too content now to be bothered by anything. "Hey, Kevyn, did I ever tell you the real reason why I ran out during All-Star Band tryouts last fall?"

He settled next to her. "Nope, but I bet you're going to now."

And she did. The truth. All about how she wasn't the brave leader of a protest movement, like he thought, but rather a mousy new kid who was afraid to play in front of people, afraid even to try. He laughed at her. She laughed, too.

She leaned back against Kevyn, who enfolded her in his arms. She nestled against him, drinking in his earthy scent that matched the woods around them. The candles sputtered out. The pale three-quarter moon competed with the setting sun. As the temperature dropped, a ground fog formed and hovered a few feet above the scrub trees, whispered around the forgotten gravestones, licking at the walls of the church. Her body had no desire to move, and her mind was gloriously free. For one night, she felt unburdened.

Turning sideways, she slid her hand under his shirt, along the taut muscles of his abdomen, to the small grove in the center of his chest covered with fine hair. She could feel his heart underneath her palm. She curled closer and ran her tongue along the outline of his ear. His stomach rose sharply with a sudden intake of air. He turned his face to her, only inches apart, so close she could make out the light amber flecks in his eyes.

"I never want to leave here." Her words were swallowed by the woods.

His eyes grew darker as he reached for her, pulling her tightly to him. His deep voice whispered in her hair, "We don't have to."

Chapter
Fifty-Seven

THIS ROOM WASN'T as bright as the one in the intensive care wing. When Cory arrived, Jess was sitting up in bed with the privacy curtain pulled back against the wall. The other bed was empty. Even though she was still hooked up to a machine, they'd at least removed the tube up her nose, so she didn't look quite so creepy.

"Hey," Cory announced and glanced around the small room. "Where's Mom?"

"Hey back. She left. Finally. Guess she eventually figured she had to eat something, and maybe get some sleep. She spent the last two nights in that chair."

Jess gestured to a faux leather recliner next to the bed. Cory noted the bruising along the inside of her arm as she pointed.

Jess adopted a theatrical voice: "I thought she'd never leave!"

"Looks comfy, maybe I'll try it."

Even Cory could hear the forced cheerfulness in Jess's voice. She dropped into the armchair, which swallowed her in its huge embrace. Jess turned her head toward the ceiling and stared.

"Mom was trying to call you all night. What's up?"

The battery died on Cory's phone sometime last night, and she hadn't bothered to charge it. "Nothing's up, just a dead battery." She pulled the phone out of her pocket and waved it as evidence but felt her cheeks flush.

"Okay, so what do we talk about now?" Jess's voice was flat. "Weather? How're your classes going? And what about them Orioles?"

Cory struggled against the gravity of the chair to move forward. She perched on the edge, her feet flat, ready to bolt if she had to. She didn't want to upset Jess, but she also didn't want to be goaded into her sarcastic game.

"Sure, school. We can talk about that. Not much new there, though. That skater kid who always wears the knit cap is still dealing in the lot behind the donut shop, and Charlene, the color guard captain, is still a big—"

"Doesn't matter. I'm not going back," Jess said, staring at the ceiling.

Cory wasn't sure what she heard. "What?"

"I'm not going back. I decided. Especially not after this." She held out her arms, connected to tubes.

"Okaaaay." Cory grabbed a gossip magazine off the nightstand and thumbed through it. "What are you going to do, then?"

Jess sat up, propped on one elbow. "You know what? I don't care. For once, I don't have a plan. I don't have anything I have to do, and I'm enjoying it. I'm not going to intensive dance camp in Massachusetts this summer—that's for sure, especially not since Dad refuses to let me live with him. For God's sake, it's not like I asked to move in with him forever." Jess slumped back against her pillow. "Asshole."

"That's what Mom says."

"She's right. What a selfish prick."

"You could maybe still find somewhere to stay in Mass. We do have other relatives . . ."

"No." Jess slumped down. "I'm done with that."

"Done with what?" This conversation was taking a strange course.

"Dance."

"What do you mean? You can't be done with dance." The words ended, but the unspoken question, *can you?* hung in the air. Jess turned her face toward the wall with the high windows. The sucking air noise of a machine filled the silence.

Cory shifted in her chair. The fake leather squeaked. "Jess . . ." She didn't know how to finish. She didn't know how to start. She chewed on her bottom lip. "Jess," she began again, "I know you must feel really bad right now, but—"

"Actually, I don't." Jess turned back to Cory, her chin lifted high. "Actually, I feel great. I feel like a huge ton of crap has been lifted off my shoulders. I feel light, like I don't care about anything anymore and I can just sleep all day or get hugely fat or quit school or do whatever it is I *feel* like doing." She took a deep breath. "And I don't feel like doing anything anymore."

"But after all the work, all the stuff you've been through, you can't just quit!"

Jess let out an explosive laugh. "That's funny! *You* telling *me* not to be a quitter. Huh"—she tapped her bottom lip with an index finger in a mock gesture of deep thought—"guess I've finally seen the wisdom in your approach to life."

Cory slid away from Jess's physical presence as if her words, like small ice pellets, had been flung in her face. "What's that supposed to mean?"

"Oh, Cory, don't act all hurt and everything." Jess flipped the covers back and swung her legs over the side of the bed. Her feet, her horribly scarred and calloused dancer's feet, didn't touch the floor but hung like bruised fruit at the bottom of her stick legs. "It's not like you've never quit anything before," she continued. "Oh, except for when you never even try because you're scared of the consequences. Doing nothing is the same as quitting. Maybe worse."

Cory sat in silence. Her throat felt tight. The nurses' voices carried down the hallway. Laughter. Finally, Cory tossed the magazine she held rolled up in her hand back onto the bedside table. The dark ink had bled and stained her palms. She wiped them down the front of her pants.

"Okay." She slapped her knees and stood up. "Guess I'm outta here. I'll talk to you later." She headed to the door and pulled it open but hesitated. Jess sat resolutely silent.

"Bye," Cory said and left.

Outside Jess's room, the corridor seemed abnormally bright. She walked slowly past the open doors of other rooms, past the nursing station, toward the exit sign.

Doing nothing is the same as quitting.

Jess's voice echoed in her head. Cory turned and went back to the desk where several nurses had gathered. A woman with a long gray braid looked up from the computer. Her black nametag was etched in white letters. She had a dimple in her right cheek when she smiled. Every detail seemed burned into Cory's mind as she opened her mouth to speak.

"I need to talk to someone. It's about my sister . . ."

Chapter
Fifty-Eight

K EVYN CRANKED OPEN the window at the back of the band room. A spring breeze rushed into the room, ruffling his hair and sending sheet music flying off the music stands. Cory stood next to him and squinted at the brilliant sunlight.

"How's Jess doing?" he asked.

"She's been home a week." Cory turned to face the band room and shrugged. "And ever since then it's been kind of weird. She's different."

"It's great she's home. I haven't seen her around school, though."

"She's not coming back this year."

Cory didn't feel like explaining, so she slumped over to take her seat with the third clarinets. There, she always had the brass behind her, blasting her eardrums. Kevyn took his seat in front—still the first chair, first clarinet. A stab of sadness struck her when she thought how he wouldn't be in that chair next year but off to college. Somewhere.

The room vibrated with the screech of music stands being shifted around on the linoleum floor and the toots and blasts of instruments warming up. A drum roll provided counterpoint to a light flute scale that drifted over the din.

The room fell silent. Mr. Schroeder, the Hawk, strode in and eyed the assembled students like a border collie sizing up the sheep. He flipped open a large music score on the director's stand and pulled it toward him.

"All right, people, 'Pomp and Circumstance.' Let's try to get it right for a change. You've got two weeks until graduation, the seniors won't be here to carry you, and I don't want to be embarrassed by your playing." He raised his baton. "One, and two, and . . ."

After only a few measures, Cory knew it was off. The rhythm dragged, the brass was drowning out the woodwinds, and the whole thing sounded off pitch. The baton slammed down on the edge of the stand so hard Cory thought it would snap in two.

"Stop!" Mr. Schroeder's face was red. "What's wrong with you people? We've been at this for months now. Brass! If you're going to blast us out of the room, at least do it in the right key."

He descended the podium and walked past Cory to the back row. Waves of frustration radiated off him. He stabbed his baton at the sheet of music in front of one of the trumpet players. The kid's face was as red as his wavy hair.

"Here, Mr. Ryan. It says right here, key of G. Let's hear it. Trumpets only."

The Hawk stood, arms folded. Cory placed the bell of her clarinet on her knee and clutched it to her body. She prayed the trumpets would get it right this time, watching as the terrified redhead raised the instrument to his lips.

The loud, sour notes wafted through the band room and escaped out the open windows.

All at once there was an enormous crash, followed by complete silence. The trumpet players held their instruments inches from their lips, mouths open. Liam Ryan was lying on his back on the floor with his trumpet still clasped in one hand, the music stand on top of him. Everyone stared. Nobody moved. They had all seen Mr. Schroeder smash the back of the stand in a fury, sending Liam Ryan, startled, over backward on his chair.

"Well, get up, you idiot," the director snarled. "I've told you all a million times not to tip back in your chairs."

"You pushed him!" Cory was on her feet.

Mr. Schroeder swung around to face her. "I didn't push him," he barked, then zeroed in on her. "Sit down, Miss Iverson."

Behind him, the other trumpet players scrambled to help Liam up. Cory's legs were shaking. Mr. Schroeder had her locked in his bird-of-prey stare.

"Sit *down*, I said!"

Cory remained standing. She felt a hundred eyes on her, watching. She looked over to Kevyn and saw a faint smile. Mr. Schroeder marched toward her, drawn in by her defiance like a heat-seeking missile. Sweat broke out under her arms. Her hand itched for a crop—she knew what to do with a dominant horse that tried to invade her space and threaten her—she'd back him off with a smart tap of her whip. Mr. Schroeder was in her personal space now, too close. She could see the gray hairs in his dark moustache and the tiny red veins that snaked along the tip of his nose. His voice was steady and low.

"You sit down now or I'll throw you out. And don't you ever—"

"You hit a student!" The words flew out of her. They had the same effect as a stinging rap from a crop. Mr. Schroeder stepped back.

"I never hit him!"

She saw the doubt, the hint of fear in his eyes. "You did. You hit him with the stand." She looked around, seeking confirmation from the others. Only blank stares, open mouths. "You slammed his stand so hard it fell on him, just like you've kicked instrument cases and thrown erasers. You've made us all terrified to come to band."

Mr. Schroeder scoffed but kept his distance. "You're welcome to leave, Miss Iverson. And this time you *won't* be allowed back."

He walked to the podium in the front of the room. Cory pulled her clarinet apart and stuffed it into its case. Kevyn did the same.

"Ah, I see your boyfriend's showing his support. Well, Mr. Kevyn Warfield, you should know that you won't be allowed to walk at graduation with missing credits, do I make myself clear?"

Mr. Schroeder looked smug. Cory envisioned Kevyn's mom learning the news that he'd been banned from the graduation ceremony—because of The Hawk! The blood pounded in her ears as she moved across the room to Liam Ryan, not exactly sure what she would do next.

"Are you hurt, Liam?" she asked.

Liam gingerly touched the back of his head where it had slammed against the floor.

"Get your things," Cory ordered. "I'm taking you to the nurse. Then we're going to see Ms. J."

Liam was like a lamb, following orders. He started packing away his trumpet.

"Our loss!" Mr. Schroeder called in a mocking tone. "A third chair clarinetist and a tone-deaf trumpet player."

Kevyn cocked a thumb at his own chest and smirked.

"Oh, yes, and our lost-cause protester boyfriend who's willing to give up his high school diploma for *love*."

Air quotes around love. Cory hated that. At that moment, she hated Mr. Schroeder more than anyone or anything. He had become the embodiment of all her frustrations, all the self-loathing she'd felt for being a quitter. She was breathing fast, her mind racing, trying to grasp hold of an idea when she seized on the image of the whole band walking out. A mass walkout—the way Kevyn had tried to rally them last fall. A whole band couldn't be expelled. Could they?

Cory turned to Mr. Schroeder. "And the trumpet section. They're coming as witnesses. Right, guys?" She shot the row a hopeful look. As soon as one started to pack up his stuff, the others followed. "Oh, and anyone else who wants to come with us to talk to guidance or Principal Santini."

A roomful of shocked faces looked back. To her surprise, George Thibeault, the shy flute player who was the constant butt of Schroeder's abuse, stood up.

"I'll go."

It was as if a dam had burst. Everyone moved at once, chairs scraped, papers fluttered to the floor, instrument cases snapped shut—and the whole band moved as one toward the exit sign.

May 13

Not sure if I got a teacher fired today, but he so deserves it. At least I know he can't keep Kevyn from graduating. Something had to be done. Someone had to say something. Like with Jess. Doing nothing's the same as quitting.

Chapter
Fifty-Nine

THE OVERSIZED ARMCHAIR engulfed Jess as she sat with her legs tucked under her. Even with her head bowed over the laptop—a curtain of blond hair partially hiding her face—Cory was relieved to see that she was looking much better. After she got out of the hospital, Jess made good on her threat not to return to school but was getting help from a tutor to catch up and take this year's final exams. Cory couldn't blame her for not going back to school. Kids were talking.

Jess glanced up when she walked in. "Hey."

"Hi, Jess." Cory let her heavy book bag slide off her shoulder to the floor and headed to the kitchen to rummage for a snack. When she returned, Jess was still bent over the screen.

"Homework?" Cory asked.

"Hmmm." Jess didn't look up.

"Chip?"

Jess slowly raised her head and peered at Cory through a fringe of overgrown bangs. "Ahh, no thanks." She sighed and added, "Not because—I just don't like that kind."

Cory knew her face must be betraying what she was thinking—the fact that she was walking around all the time afraid of saying the wrong thing. She was treating Jess like a psych patient. She'd felt uncomfortable around her ever since she came home. Even if she hadn't told, the doctors would have figured it out. Jess was lucky. She didn't have heart damage, as they had feared, but *had* burned her esophagus from the vomiting. Jess never said anything about it to Cory, so the enormity of their unspoken words loomed in the room whenever they were together, like a giant cloud of smoke. And the cloud was getting thicker.

Cory thought about saying something as she watched Jess's fingers fly over the keyboard, but instead, for the hundredth time, decided not to. She shrugged, figured *some other time*, and headed toward the stairs.

"Hey, Cory," Jess called. "I forgot to tell you. I found something."

Her foot stopped on the first step. "What?"

Jess gave her a sly look. "Something you'll be interested in."

Cory returned and perched on the arm of the chair as Jess swiveled the laptop so she could see the screen. A dark dappled gray horse dominated the website. Above the image, the banner of a big breeding farm in California boasted its Hanoverian imports, champions, world-class trainers.

Jess searched Cory's blank face. She finally burst out, "It's your horse! Epiphany. I finally found her."

Cory grabbed the laptop and pulled it closer. It looked like Epiphany, only a bit darker. A younger picture of her. She babbled some unintelligible questions to Jess, "How? Why?" In response, Jess explained some equally unintelligible things about web crawlers and Wayback time machines or something. Cory didn't really care about how, she only wanted to know more about the horse.

"Turns out," Jess explained, "that you were right and you *did* see her advertised on Dream Horse. I started there and worked backwards."

Cory nodded her head dumbly. She slid down the arm of the chair and sat squished against Jess's small frame.

"The original owner from this farm in California imported her when she was two to be a broodmare. She has some awesome bloodlines, apparently. Anyway, then this other person bought her."

Cory stared at the image of a very young Epiphany. She saw the resemblance now but puzzled at the name.

"What's with that name she has? How did you know it's her?" The name above the picture of the horse was Dreikonigfest.

Jess laughed. "My German comes in handy, finally. I knew she was advertised for sale as Epiphany, and when I traced her back to the people who imported her, it matched. Dreikonigfest is German for Epiphany."

Cory shook her head. No wonder Vee never found her registration and papers. Her name was in the original German when she was imported, and she was a "D" line Hanoverian, for Dreikongifest, not an "E" for Epiphany. "And look. The auction had the sire's name wrong, too . . . *Die* Eisenhartzen."

Jess took the laptop back and clicked a few keys. "Anyway, like I said, another person bought her. I've got it all marked, what I found out. Here." Jess pointed to an image of a more mature Epiphany next to a woman with short, steel gray hair and a weathered face. "This lady bought her and turned her over to a trainer because she wanted to show her as a jumper. Says here, *the horse shows amazing promise*. So, she lived on a farm in Virginia. What I figured out next was that this woman died soon afterwards, and her husband just kept his wife's horses but didn't do anything with them. For years. Kinda sweet, actually." Jess smiled at the picture.

Cory elbowed her. "Then what? How did a horse on an estate in Virginia end up at an auction?"

"That part's a little harder to put together. I found the obit for the wife but not the husband. However, a real estate sales record showed the farm sold to a developer. A livestock dispersal agent was the point of contact on the Dream Horse advertisement. Maybe the old guy was in a nursing home and a relative tried to sell off all the horses."

"But you don't dump an expensive registered horse at a rinky-dink auction. What happened?" Cory felt a chill run down her back. "You don't suppose she's stolen and the thief dumped her, do you?"

Jess shrugged. "Not likely. No police reports popped up. Hey, maybe she was just meant to be your horse. Stuff happens. Sometimes something lucky's dumped in your lap for no logical reason."

Not likely. She didn't want some long-lost relative turning up to take Epiphany back. She frowned. "I don't know. I don't really believe in fate or destiny or whatever."

Jess closed the laptop and wriggled out of the armchair. She stretched like a huge cat and struck a ballet pose, gracefully tipping forward on one leg. Slowly, she rose. "Then just enjoy the chance you have to ride a nice horse and forget about it. Ride her in that Washington show you're always talking about. Do it! It could end anytime, without any notice." Jess added, "Believe me, I know."

Cory looked up sharply. She only now realized the amount of time and effort it must have taken for Jess to run down all this information for her when she had so many other things on her mind. She stood and silently wrapped Jess in her arms. Bony shoulders, protruding collarbones dug into her arms, but Cory squeezed tighter. Jess stood, silent and stiff at first. Then Jess's arms slid around her waist and pressed Cory hard against her frail body. Her sister's breath brushed against her neck. "Sorry. About the stuff I said. Before."

Cory's vision blurred. "No, I'm sorry. But I'm glad."

For the first time in weeks, the cloud that had been between them disappeared like smoke through a flung open window.

May 20
So glad Jess is home again. She's amazing, and not just the dance stuff. Like she said, sometimes you just have good luck dumped in your lap for no good reason. Sure hope so.

Chapter
Sixty

CORY GATHERED THE dirty clothes from the bathroom floor and headed back to her room. Jess sat cross-legged on her bed, scrolling through the screen on her phone. She glanced up.

"Hey, you must be excited about tomorrow."

"Excited's one word for it." Cory stuffed her dirty clothes in the hamper.

Jess set the phone aside. "What's the matter?"

How could she explain? "I dunno. It's just that a lot's riding on this, and . . ." She struggled into a sweatshirt and zipped it up. The air conditioning was freezing.

"And what? You've been doing great."

Cory perched on the edge of her bed. "Thanks. But that's the thing, too. Epi feels a little weird lately, like not herself. Tonight when we were practicing over some simple jumps, she tripped."

"Maybe she was tired. You guys have been working pretty hard lately."

Cory scooted back and leaned against the wall. "Yeah, could be. But if we don't do well, I'll feel like I let them all down." She thought about the piles of bills on Vee's kitchen table and the fact that Angela was always waiting in the wings to make them—but especially Vee—look bad.

Jess grabbed Cory's leg and gave it a shake. "Hey, you'll do great. What was it you told me once? Oh, yeah, you were born to do this." She stood, opened a dresser drawer and pulled out some clothes. "Did you know Aunt Liv and Douglas are coming, too? Mom talked to them today."

"To the show?" Cory sat upright. "Why?"

Jess shrugged and headed off to the bathroom.

Cory considered picking up the book on her nightstand but knew she couldn't concentrate enough to read it, so she figured she'd see if "Victoria Burr" had left a message for her. *She* had to be just as nervous tonight. Maybe more.

Victoria's dazzling image appeared on the Facebook page with some fictionalized updates and meaningless posts. Cory logged a message.

What's up? You there?

Regina immediately responded.

I'm so freaked out. Tomorrow's the day!

Me too, Cory typed. *I can't believe it's this close.*

Have you seen the rankings? My mother had me jumping Prophet 'til his legs were shaking tonight. My butt is so sore! She's gone insane over this.

Cory stared at the glowing words on the screen. What exactly did Regina mean, insane?

How so? Cory typed.

Didn't I tell you? She has some big fish on the line to buy Prophet IF he can qualify. Big bucks—and we need it. We'll be eating the cat food in the barn soon if my mom's out of work much longer. Guess I should have thought of that before I turned her in at that show. Yeah, I was the "second witness" they needed to get her suspended on the horse abuse thing. God, she'd KILL me if she ever found out.

Cory couldn't believe it. Regina had turned in her own mother. Vee had notified the show stewards about the poling incident, which Cory had seen, but no one ever discovered the second witness who mysteriously came forward.

A knock at the bedroom door caused Cory to jump.

Gotta go—good luck! She exited Facebook and shut down the screen.

"Are you busy?" Roni poked her head in.

"Not really."

Her mother slipped into the room holding something behind her back. Hershey trailed behind her and slumped down on the rug. "Where's Jess?"

"Shower," Cory answered. "What's up?" Her mom hardly ever came to their room. "What's that?" Cory nodded to the item she was obviously hiding.

"Oh!" Roni acted as if the thing had just appeared in her hands and surprised her, too. She pulled it out. "Nothing really, something I made for you." Her face flushed. "Actually, it's not very good."

"Let's see." Cory stood and reached out to grasp a small rectangle of heavy paper about the size of a school notebook.

It was a portrait of Epiphany—her head and neck—sketched in charcoal pencil that perfectly captured her soft gray coloring, her dark liquid eyes. Cory collapsed back down on the bed, holding the picture.

"Mom, you did this? It's perfect!"

Roni sank down beside her on the soft mattress, causing their hips to meet. The older woman leaned over her daughter's shoulder, looking at the portrait with a critical eye. "I copied the image of her from some pictures in that magazine. I liked the way I captured the muscles in her neck but didn't quite get the nose right." As she pointed to the flawed area, Cory leaned over and encircled her mother in a quick embrace.

"Mom, thanks, I love it." She sat back. "When did you do it? And why?"

Her mom moved away slightly and absentmindedly traced the pattern on the bedspread with an index finger.

"I got the idea when I was at the hospital. Did a lot of the preliminary sketch there while sitting with Jess." She sighed. "I had a lot of time to think." Her eyes looked glassy in the dim light of the bedside lamp. "I realized that I'd almost lost one daughter and might just as easily lose the other if I didn't pay attention. Cory, I'm sorry. I'm sorry I haven't . . ." She stopped and shook her head once.

Cory rushed to fill the silence. "That's okay, Mom. I know you've been busy and all."

"No, no, it's not okay." She shifted to the edge of the bed. "I've met with a lot of Jess's counselors, and we've talked."

Cory stood up and propped up the picture on her dresser. She knew what her mother was trying to say, but didn't really want to hear it all. Nonetheless, it felt like a tiny, coiled spring in her chest unwound a few rotations.

"You know, Mom, when Vee sees this she'll be ordering portraits of all her horses from you."

Her mother brightened. "You know, we're all coming to see you tomorrow."

"The whole gang, I heard. Did Bucky get the day off work, too?" Cory knew her mom rarely went anywhere socially or otherwise without a male companion. A while back, she'd resigned herself to having to deal with him being attached to Roni.

Instead, her mother stared out the darkened window. "No, no Bucky." She straightened her back and gave Cory a quick tight smile. "Not anymore."

"What happened?"

Roni lifted a hand and pointed at the picture on the dresser. "That's what happened. He called it a waste of time. Actually, what I think he said was I was spending too much time working on it, instead of with him. But you know something? I felt pretty good drawing it." She lifted her chin. "For some reason, drawing that little picture opened my eyes."

She rose from the bed, walked over to where Cory stood by the dresser, and ran her hand lightly down Cory's arm. "I'm sure you'll do great tomorrow. I'm really looking forward to seeing the show."

Jess appeared in a cloud of warm, perfumed air with a towel wrapped around her head.

Roni moved toward the door. "Well, I'll let you get to bed. Cory, you've got a big day ahead of you tomorrow." She turned to address the small image of the mare. "And you. Promise you'll take care of my baby tomorrow."

Roni left the room and quietly closed the door.

Chapter Sixty-One

ONLY A FINGERNAIL paring of a moon was visible in the dark sky when Cory arrived at the barn. It was chilly enough that she was glad for her ragged barn coat and the loose sweatpants covering her breeches. As she pulled the coat closer around her and fished the stiff work gloves out of the pockets, it released a long-held scent of hay dust and horses. The floodlights over the entrance to the barn set the dark expanse of grass sparkling from last night's dew. A dozen thoughts shot through her mind like electric current, jolting her with renewed doses of adrenaline. What if she didn't do well today at the show? What if she didn't manage to qualify? What if she beats Regina, and Angela decides to . . . to do what with Prophet?

She led Epiphany out of her stall and stood on an old milk crate to reach her mane for the long process of braiding it into a row of tiny, button-sized knobs. She looped a hank of precut yarn through a brass ring in the mare's halter and slipped the required comb and other implements into a pocket. The rhythmic, repetitive motion of braiding accompanied by the steady munching sound of the horses helped to still her racing thoughts.

"You've gotten really good at that." Vee appeared at Cory's side. She tilted her chin toward the row of ten neat little braids along the crest of the mare's neck.

Cory rocked on the milk crate, startled. "I used to hate braiding, but now I think it's okay. Keeps my mind busy before a show."

"Nervous? You don't still get nervous, do you?" Vee teased.

Cory looked down from her elevated perch and gave Vee a *you have to ask?* look. "I've been to the bathroom ten times already, and it's only five a.m."

Vee smiled, dipped her hand in a pocket of her coat, and pulled out a sugar lump for Epiphany. "You've got nothing to worry about. You're both doing great. Besides, I've got it on good authority she's a magic horse."

Cory's fingers stopped braiding. "Huh?"

Vee laughed. "Didn't I tell you? About what Mr. Hammerschmidt told me?"

Cory knew Vee had tracked down the husband of Epi's former owner after she told her what Jessica had discovered about the horse's past. The husband was living in a nursing home in Virginia, but Cory had no idea that Vee had talked to him.

"What did he tell you?" she asked, stepping down from the crate.

"I went to see him. He acted confused and had no idea what I was talking about at first, until I showed him a picture of Epiphany," she explained. "He took the photo and held it close to his eyes. He started murmuring 'Gabi, Gabi, Gabi' and, well, I kind of lost hope, thinking his dementia was worse than what everyone had told me. Then I remembered, his wife's name was Gabriella—Gabi for short.

"His eyes were clear when he looked at me and asked, 'What are you doing with a photo of my wife's horse? Who are you?' That's when I told him everything—about getting her at the auction, the retraining, her success as a jumper . . ." Vee grabbed a brush and ran it through Epi's tail in long, sweeping strokes. "He told me Epi—he called her Daisy—was his wife's favorite horse. The poor guy became so agitated when he learned Epi had been dumped at an auction against his specific orders, I was afraid he was going to get up out of bed and go after his son-in-law right then. Turns out it was his daughter's husband that sold the farm to a developer and handed all the horses over to a dispersal agent. No one knows what happened from there—why the agent would send Epi to a cheap auction." Vee tossed the brush back into the grooming box and let out a long sigh.

Cory flexed her fingers, stiff from braiding. "The poor guy. That's awful. He lost his wife, and then they didn't honor his wishes." She turned to Vee expectantly. "So, what's the rest of the story? The magic part."

Vee poked a stray hair down into her loose ponytail. Her eyes cut away. "Well, it gets a little crazy from this point, probably just a confused old man talking, you know."

"What?" Cory demanded.

"He claimed the horse was magic, like I said." She rushed to add, "Not like I believe any of that stuff, but he told me a really weird story."

They both looked at Epiphany. The mare shifted her weight onto the other back leg and swung her head around to look at them with a bored expression.

"She doesn't look magical to me." Cory gave her an affectionate slap on her hindquarters.

Vee sat down on a large tack trunk and was immediately joined by one of the Jack Russells that leapt up to join her. She stroked the little dog's head.

"Seems it was his wife who was the first to notice strange things happening. She said everything started going better right after they bought Epi. I wasn't convinced until Mr. Hammerschmidt told me this story about a little boy. Gave me chills." The Jack Russell circled on Vee's lap.

A burned-out light sputtered and flashed to life, illuminating Epiphany in a spotlight of flickering light. The horse stood bathed in it, her silvery coat surrounded by a cloud of sparkling dust motes.

"Weird," Cory whispered. "Like perfect timing because we were talking about her."

"I'll tell you what's weird—and you know I don't go for all that animal communicator crap," Vee said with a dismissive gesture, "and don't you dare breathe a word of this to Jack."

Cory sat down on the tack trunk next to Vee and made a show of sealing her lips with an invisible key. Vee adjusted the little dog in her lap and in the cadenced tones of a storyteller started to relay what the old man had told her.

"Well, this is just what he told me. You see, Mr. Hammerschmidt's wife had a niece with a severely autistic child. Really bad, it sounded like. The little boy—I think he said he was about eight years old at the time—never allowed anyone, even his own mother, to touch him. He didn't talk, couldn't communicate. And he started hurting himself, like knocking his head against things. Anyway, the niece was at the end of her rope, her husband had split, and she was in danger of losing her job. By this time, Gabriella had already noticed the weird effect Epi had on people and invited her niece to stay with them, along with the boy. Mr. H said he didn't believe any of his wife's nonsense—'angel talk' he called it at that time."

"What happened with the kid?" Cory was impatient.

"When he arrived, he was unreachable, but they did notice that he would watch the horses, the only thing he seemed to be able to focus on. So, they showed him how to brush one, and that was Epi. He'd spend hours at it." Vee laughed. "Can you imagine her standing still for that? So, one day, out of the blue, he started talking to her. Asked if she was hungry or something. It was a huge breakthrough for him. To make a long story short, the kid started making progress, they got him into school eventually, and it has a happy ending. According to Mr. H's wife, the horse has some magic charm that brings out the good in people, if there's anything good in there to bring out."

Vee brushed the dog off her lap and stood up. "You had better finish braiding our magic mare. We've got to get rolling soon. And remember"—she glanced down the aisle, squinting at the morning sun just coming up—"no telling Jack about my crazy magic horse story, okay?"

Cory nodded and climbed back on the milk crate. "Yeah," she agreed. "Sounds crazy, like just a coincidence." She separated a handful of mane, twisted a strand of yarn through it, and started methodically braiding as her mind wandered. *People don't change for no reason, do they?*

Chapter
Sixty-Two

T HE SKY WAS blue. Impossibly blue. Like a kindergartener drew it with a broad paintbrush, dripping with paint, then added white blobs for clouds. Perched on Epi, Cory scanned the sky, thinking maybe the world really had turned totally upside down. Everyone around her seemed to be changing—her mother's visit last night, her family all deciding to come to her show, Vee's new relaxed attitude. Epi shifted impatiently under her as Cory scanned the grandstands for familiar faces.

There! Douglas and Aunt Liv were in the expensive box seating area with Jack, just beyond the last jump of the triple combination. She and Douglas were dressed in what Cory could only imagine was their idea of the rich horse-owner look: tweed jacket, a silk blouse with a stirrup motif, a stroker cap. Cory didn't care. What baffled her more was the surprising friendship they'd struck up with Jack. Maybe it wasn't too weird; after all, Jack used to be a rich Virginia racehorse breeder. Jack leaned over and said something to Douglas that caused him to erupt into laughter. Cory's mom and Jess were seated behind Douglas, Jack, and Aunt Liv. Her mom raised a small camera and pointed to where Cory sat on Epi at the in-gate.

A hand touched her knee causing a sizzle of electricity to shoot through her. Vee stood at Epi's shoulder. "You ready? You're on deck."

Cory took a deep breath, willing herself to slow the thud of her heart against her chest. Her eyes swept the course again. She had walked it that morning beside Vee, planning their strategy for each obstacle. It was a tough course—it would require a precise ride to negotiate without a rail down or a time fault. The rider in the ring now was a tall guy on a dark chestnut horse. When he came around the turn by the in-gate, the horse picked up speed around the bend and raced into the combination. She predicted it before it happened—too much speed, too far from the first fence. He jumped the first obstacle, but landed so that he couldn't make up the distance and struggled to clear the next jump. By the third fence, he buried the horse into the fence. The chestnut pulled the top rail off with his hind leg. Polite clapping accompanied his exit from the ring. The next rider to go rode past her, entering the arena. She would be next.

"Hey!"

Cory spun in her saddle to look. Regina sat on Prophet a short distance behind her.

"Don't turn around," Regina said. "Act casual."

Cory turned back to watch the rider in the ring. Vee patted her knee and passed final instructions. Cory nodded. As soon as Vee was gone, she spun around.

"You ready?" she asked.

Regina made a face and indicated another direction with the nod of her head. Cory spotted Angela a ways off, talking with a man wearing a navy blue blazer and mirrored sunglasses. Angela's unnaturally bronze tan and lightened hair made her stand out in the crowd.

"That's him, I think," Regina said. "The guy who's buying Prophet." She hesitated. "If we win, that is."

Cory faced forward, trying to follow the horse on course, but instead her attention was dragged back to the mysterious buyer with Angela. They were in a heated exchange. He pointed his finger at her chest, then made a slashing, dismissive gesture with the flat of his palm.

The rider, who had been in the ring, rushed past her. Cory wanted to turn, to say "good luck" to Regina, but noticed Angela heading toward them. The loudspeaker announced the first clean round in the class. Then her name. It was her turn. Cory gathered the reins.

The arena was enormous, the fences huge. After a canter circle to set the pace, she looked for the first jump—a red and white vertical—drawing them into it. The noise from the crowd faded into a low, background hum. As she picked up speed, her peripheral vision blurred like a film tape running by too fast.

Epi levitated off the ground.

The horse's rhythmic breathing floated to Cory's ears. Epi flew over the fences as if she could read Cory's mind, anticipating what she'd ask before she even asked it. The gray horse flew around sharp turns, set herself back, and waited coming into the wide obstacles, and upon landing, immediately sought out the next fence. Cory was giddy with the sensation she had grown wings and could run as fast as a gale-force wind. She forgot about everything and everyone besides her and Epi and the fence in front of them.

In what seemed like mere seconds, she was over the last fence of the course. The crowd erupted with clapping and shouting. They had gone clean. She dropped the reins and swept forward, embracing Epi's sweaty, muscular neck in a huge bear hug. Through the roar of blood in her ears, she heard the announcer's voice. "Another clear round with no time faults for number fifty-three, Epiphany, ridden by Cory Iverson."

Outside the gate, she slid from the mare's back. Kevyn approached with outstretched arms.

"Way to go, sport!"

Cory fell into his arms. "I'm so happy!" Relief flooded over her. "Epi did great."

Vee slapped Cory on the back. "Professional piece of riding. Good job." She took the reins and handed the mare over to Jack.

As more people gathered to congratulate her, Cory looked over Vee's shoulder. Regina mouthed the words *nice job* to her. Without a second thought, Cory walked up to Regina on Prophet.

"Thanks." Regina's face was tense.

"Looks tough." Regina nodded toward the course, her hands gripping Prophet's reins. Regina waited her turn alone at the in-gate.

"Not so bad." She smiled reassuringly. "But the diagonal line is tight—looks like a five-stride but on a big-moving horse rides better in four." She knew Prophet would eat up the distance and she didn't want Regina to bury him into the second fence.

"And don't hold him around the turn into the triple. He hates to be confined and will just get flat and run," Vee said, walking up behind Cory. "Give him his head. He'll be more relaxed." Vee eyed Prophet's nervousness, shifting from one foot to another. Regina had to keep him moving to stay contained. Vee placed a hand on the horse's shoulder to calm him.

"What's going on here?" Angela called, spotting the group gathered around Prophet. She approached at a jog. "Get away from my horse."

Vee's hand dropped from the horse's side as he backed away from Angela.

"We're just . . ." Cory began.

"I know what you're doing, and you can forget it. Regina, I told you—"

"What do we have here?" Moriah Hennisey from *The Equestrian Journal* called as she approached with her photographer in tow.

Cory groaned. The woman was like a shark scenting blood in the water.

"The two contenders who've been going head-to-head all season," Moriah said, "now together with the horses' trainers as well."

"Actually," Vee cut in before Moriah could continue, "I'm the trainer of both horses." She flashed a staged schoolgirl smile. "Prophet was in training with me right before Angela bought him." Vee shrugged in a *whatcha gonna do?* way.

Angela's face darkened under her orangey tan as Moriah turned to her for comment.

"Yes, technically, that is correct, but you wouldn't *show* the horse, isn't that right?" Angela gave a look as if she had lobbed a shot over the net Vee wasn't capable of volleying back.

Vee stroked Prophet's muscular neck. "The horse deserved a better rider than me, like a talented young girl." She looked up at Regina and smiled sweetly.

The photographer stepped in and snapped the photo of Regina looking down into Vee's eyes, returning the smile.

"So what advice do you have for your main competitor, Ms. Stewart?" Moriah asked, no doubt trying to steer the interview toward a confrontation between the women. She glanced at Angela.

Vee said cheerfully, "Oh, I think she's doing great. Just be careful not to pull him too tightly around the sharp turns. It makes him nervous."

Angela pushed her way in front of Vee.

"No one really believes you're here to help my daughter win against your horse." Angela posed in front of Regina, looking the part of the protective mother. "I suppose you want us to believe you'll take it all in stride when we beat you here and take your spot at Washington?"

Vee dropped her chin and peered up under her lashes. Cory could never remember her ever being so calm and self-possessed. She heaved a sigh. "If that's the case, then I guess we'll have a lot more time on our hands. Maybe we could spend it at the beach."

Angela's brow creased, confused.

Vee looked Angela directly in the eye, her expression deadly. "In fact, we can *kill* a lot of time at that Maryland shore you discovered, Angela—*Sandy Point*. Do you remember Sandy Point, Angela, because I sure do."

Angela's smug expression melted. Her face ashen, she backed up a step.

Moriah piped up. "The beach, that sounds great, but back to the competition—"

Cory shifted her feet. "I just wish Regina luck and a good trip. It's a challenging course, but she has a great horse."

Vee gave a curt nod and turned to join the crowd gathering around Jack and Epiphany. Cory jogged to catch up, looking back briefly to give what she hoped was an encouraging glance to Regina. She fell into step beside her, who slipped her arm through Cory's and spoke close to her ear.

"Is she okay?" Vee indicated the mare, surrounded by an adoring crowd that included Kevyn, Roni, Jess, and others.

Cory worried Vee had seen something during the jump round— even though Epi had gone clean and with a great time. Maybe the mare was somehow off her game.

"Not bad. She's okay," Cory said, to convince Vee as much as herself.

Vee's eyes held hers. As they stood, the announcer called Regina Hamilton's name, and they both watched her ride Prophet into the ring.

"Be sure," was all Vee said.

Chapter
Sixty-Three

KEVYN RATTLED THE bag of barbecue chips under Cory's nose. "Want some?" he asked through a spray of crumbs in her direction.

She wrinkled her nose and pushed the bag away. "I hate barbecue. Besides, I can't eat anything." She checked her watch for the hundredth time. It had only been thirty minutes, but five more riders in her class had negotiated the course. Only two others, besides herself and Regina, had gone clean so far. It would be down to the four of them for the jump-off.

Kevyn slung an arm around her shoulder, pulled her close, and blew a stream of warm barbecue breath in her face.

"Ugh!" She shoved him away. "You know I hate that barbecue smell."

Kevyn attempted to encircle her again as she skittered away out of reach. He gave up and slumped down on a seat at the end of the bleachers.

"So," he asked, "what's the rules for a jump-off, anyway?"

Cory's eye automatically cut to the ring to watch the horse on course as she formulated her thoughts. Kevyn's attempt to understand the show jumping rules brought a smile to her face.

"Any rider who jumps clean, meaning no rails down and no time faults, will advance to a jump-off. They usually take out a few jumps, raise some of them even higher, and change the course so it's harder—full of quick turns and sharp-angled approaches. Oh, and they give you less time allowed for it, too." She pointed to the flags and the timer.

"Sounds exciting. What if a lot of people make it to the jump-off? What then?"

"Usually they don't." Cory frowned and squinted into the bright sunlight glinting over the arena's gray footing. "If more than one rider makes it around clean in the allotted time, they can either pick the rider with the fastest time as the winner or hold a second round jump-off, or what they call 'sudden death.'"

Kevyn sat straighter. "I like the sound of that."

Cory chewed at a fingernail. "I don't."

She looked over to where Jack was already saddling Epi. She had to get her warmed up before the jump-off. There was just enough time to run to the restroom once more before she had to get on. As she walked off, Kevyn called to her.

"Hey!"

Cory turned.

"I'll be right here watching you. Watching you kick butt and win!" He smiled and gave the thumbs-up. A wad of nasty barbecue chip was lodged between two front teeth, but she rushed back to give him a kiss—stinky barbecue breath and all.

She jogged across the showgrounds and threw herself against the restroom door. Inside, she dived into the first stall and slammed the door. Darn breeches were so hard to get down! Someone else came in behind her, then there was the sound of a soft click, like the turn of a lock. When she exited the stall, she nearly walked into Angela standing by the sinks.

Cory drew in a sharp breath and bolted for the exit. She tugged at the door. It didn't open. Angela's palm slapped against the door, holding it shut. Her nails were painted a trendy dark blue, but her hands were heavily veined and covered with brown spots. Cory stood, her back to

Angela.

"That's right, it's locked. I wanted some privacy in order to have a little talk with you—alone."

A prickle tingled on the back of her neck, like millipedes were crawling along it. Cory's hand rose to rub the spot as she turned and tried to paste a confident look on her face. She could tell it wasn't fooling Angela.

"Whatever you want to talk about, you'd better hurry." Cory straightened her shoulders and resisted the urge to step away. "I'm out of here in two minutes for the jump-off."

"That's just it, you see." Angela removed her hand from the door. "Regina's going to win because you're going to withdraw."

Cory's heart pounded as if it were banging to be let out. "Why would I do that?" Her voice whispery.

"Because if you don't, someone's going to tip the stewards to the fact that your horse is drugged. And you know, if they do a drug test and find out it's true, you and your trainer are banned for, oh, what is it now? Five years?" Angela strummed her blue-tipped nails over her lips.

"That's crazy! My horse isn't drugged."

"You sure?" Angela stepped closer. "Are you sure because someone could have drugged her when you weren't around." The corner of her mouth turned up.

Someone pounded on the door.

"Closed. Cleaners," Angela shouted, then turned her deeply tanned face back to Cory. Up close, she wasn't very pretty. Wrinkles framed her eyes and around her mouth. A mean mouth, which formed a straight, thin line across her face.

"Someone's with Epi all the time. No one could give her drugs without us knowing." Cory hoped.

"You sure?" Angela folded her arms and rocked back on her heels. "No one could walk by and offer her an apple or drop something into her feed bucket?"

Cory's hands balled into fists thinking about somebody drugging Epi, threatening her life, just to win a class. Angela droned on, her voice bouncing around the tiled walls of the restroom. Cory's gaze was fixed on the chipped enamel sink, the dripping faucets, as the words swirled and her vision darkened.

" . . . so I suggest you go out there and make up whatever excuse you want. Withdraw and save your precious trainer the humiliation of a public drugging charge. You'll probably still place, but Regina will win, and I have a lot at stake, providing she does."

Cory shook her head, trying to shake loose some logic from what she was hearing. This was insane. There were other riders besides her in the jump-off. Did Angela mean to threaten each one of them?

"What about the others? Have you threatened them, too?"

"Don't have to. They made it to the jump-off by dumb luck. They won't be making a clean round. But you"—Angela made a dismissive gesture as if she were shooing away a fly—"you have to go, my dear."

Epi *had* been acting sick lately. Both she and Vee had noticed it. Had Angela been poisoning her all along, at every show, giving her a little dose more of whatever it was? Now the mare was weaker and even stumbled sometimes. The drug might be causing permanent damage, or even killing her. It wouldn't be the first time Angela killed a horse for her own gain. Poor Epi who had overcome so much to come this far. And Jack and Vee who put everything on the line for this.

"Did you hear me, sweetie?" Angela drilled a blue-tipped finger into Cory's chest. "You've got to quit."

The finger poke caused a black veil to come down over Cory's vision. She snatched Angela's bony wrist and twisted it back at an unnatural angle. Her teeth hurt, her jaw was clenched so tight, as she gave an extra crank on Angela's bent arm and shoved her backward until her spine hit up against the wall of sinks. A noise like a cat with its tail caught in something burst from Angela's grimacing lips, but Cory didn't let go. Heat radiated out of her eyes as she stared into Angela's.

"If I ever find out you went anywhere near my horse, I'll come after you. I promise." She released Angela's arm. The older woman cradled it against her chest, rubbing her wrist. "You're pathetic, you know that? You don't have enough faith in your own daughter that she can win the class on her own. She can, you know."

Cory strode to the door, unlocked it, and swung it open with such force that it banged against the wall. A "Closed for Cleaning" sign that hung on the outside fell to the ground. She picked up the sign and flung it at Angela, where it clattered across the floor and skidded to a stop at her feet. "You may want to hang onto that for your next job."

As the door swung shut, Cory relished the shocked look on Angela's face.

Losing no time, she ran toward the show ring. Jack was near the warm-up arena, holding Epiphany tacked-up and ready to go.

Vee, pacing, turned and greeted Cory with a plaintive, "Where *were* you?" as she tossed her up into the saddle.

"You only have time for one or two warm-up jumps before you go in."

The next few minutes flew by in a blur—the warm-up fences, the last-minute coaching—before she found herself again at the in-gate, next to go. The horse in the ring was running flat out, the rider throwing him at the huge fences without setting him up for them. The rails fell down. No clean rounds—yet.

Cory gathered the reins and drew in a deep breath. The swish-swish sound of the bluestone footing echoed with each footfall as she entered the arena. She cantered a circle, eyes searching out the first fence. Epiphany picked up on her focus and aligned her body with the large, airy vertical that loomed ahead. They rode through the start flags, and the clock started. Cory knew she had to be blisteringly fast but accurate. The image of Angela's shocked expression as the door closed, flashed through her mind. But what if Epi was drugged, right now?

The fence was directly ahead, only five strides away. Cory sat back and asked Epi to gather under her, to shorten her stride and prepare for a big effort. In no time, they were at the fence. When she asked, the mare responded. Cory bent at the hips to stay with the thrust as Epiphany lifted off and flew over the top rails.

They landed. Cory turned her sharply toward the next jump, which was almost directly behind them. Epiphany tried to run at the fence when she spotted it, but Cory held her. It was a large, solid wall that would require the horse to meet it directly at its base in order to clear it. Epiphany shortened, compacted all her strength into her hind end, and exploded upward from the base of the jump. Cory's heart thudded. A tingle spread down her fingers as she soared straight up, balanced on the mare's back, like riding a rocket ship. She looped her fingers through some loose mane and held on.

Epiphany landed hard. Her right front seemed to buckle under her, or was it Cory's imagination? The force pitched her forward on the mare's neck, momentarily off balance. She pushed herself up, sat tall, and wrapped her legs around Epi's sides. The bobble had cost them precious seconds. Was she okay? If so, Cory would have to make up for it and go even faster.

Another turn and down the long side, through a double combination, then a treacherous switch back to a roll top. Cory had no idea how she was doing against the clock, she just hoped she was moving fast enough. She bent forward and gunned Epiphany at the first jump of the combination, a wildly colored yellow and black square of rails so tall it could have been an elephant cage. She had to come into the first element strong, but not too fast, in order to land and gather Epiphany enough to clear the second. She resisted the temptation to choke up on the reins and instead sat back, waiting, as the huge fence raced toward them. Epiphany started to lift—*too soon*—and Cory had to just go with her. No choice. She was too far away, they'd never make it over the second. She heard a collective gasp from the crowd.

Cory and Epiphany took off from a long spot in front of the first fence. It felt like they were flying through the air forever before landing. Shortening the reins, she tried to get the mare to gather herself for the split second they had in between the two fences. *Epi is struggling,* she thought. Cory sat up and pressed her heels into the mare's side but didn't feel any response. She pressed harder and prayed.

Epiphany lifted. It was as if she were climbing over the second fence from a deep hole. She expected to hear the thud of a rail drop behind her, but instead, heard a smattering of light applause. She looked across the arena toward the last fence. She could cut the distance of approach through the middle of the arena, shaving off precious seconds, but she would have to approach the jump at an extreme angle. The safer option was to go around and take it straight on.

Cory made a split-second decision and cut across the arena. She could tell that Epi didn't understand where they were headed; her ears flipped forward and back, seeking out the next obstacle. They were racing at an impossible speed that would force the horse to jump it at more than a forty-five degree angle. Epi spotted the fence and hurtled toward it. The approach made the already wide jump even broader. At the base, so close Cory felt she could reach out and touch the top rail, Epi seemed to dig in and rise straight up, over the top. They were flying. The air rushing past her face, cool against her overheated skin. The crowd around them dissolved into a colorful blur, and everything turned deathly still.

She felt the front hooves touch and listened. No thud, no dropped rail. She immediately crouched low over Epiphany's neck, gunning her for the finish line flags. Epi stretched her neck out and flat-out ran toward the end flags. Then stumbled. It felt as if a front leg had crumbled, but then she popped up again at a dead run. Cory lost her balance and pitched forward on Epi's neck. *Why now?* She clung on, an arm looped around the mare's neck. Her cheek bumped sharply against the muscular crest of the horse's neck. Her eye started streaming tears from the pain in her cheekbone and she couldn't see anything going on around her. Epi kept running and Cory held on. Then there was a roar in her ears like a freight train. It was the applause.

When Epi slowed to a trot, Cory sat up, grabbed the reins, and circled Epi around to look up at the scoreboard. A clear round. And no time faults. She reached her hand up to brush away a stream of tears that ran down her face. Tears not from the pain.

Chapter
Sixty-Four

A S SOON AS she dismounted, standing amidst the crowd patting her back and congratulating her, Cory scanned for only one face. Jack took Epi's reins to lead her away.

"Where's Vee? I need to talk to her."

The tone of Cory's voice made the cheery greeting fade on his lips. He indicated the direction with a nod. "She headed back to our stalls the minute she saw you run through the timer flags. Wanted to get the horse comfortable before the next round."

Cory didn't respond but simply took off at a run toward the stabling area. She was out of breath when she found Vee outside the row of stalls, bent over a tack trunk. When Cory called out, she stood, her hands full of leg wraps and liniment bottles. Cory ran and wrapped her arms around Vee's waist and held on as Vee struggled to set the things down on a nearby shelf. She felt the warmth of Vee's hands rubbing her back.

"Hey," Vee spoke softly. "Seems to me a girl who most likely just won the class with a daring bit of riding ought to be a lot more happy."

Cory squeezed harder. She turned her face away and wiped it with her sleeve.

Vee held her at arm's length. "Tell me. What's going on?"

Cory drew a ragged breath. "Angela poisoned Epiphany. She's not acting right!" The whole story of the incident in the restroom spilled out. "I wanted to tell you, but we were so late already. And I didn't believe her then, but now I'm not so sure. "

Vee ran a hand over her forehead and stood thinking. "Cory, that's impossible. I know Angela is bat-shit crazy, but at no time has Epi ever been left alone. And no one has fed her anything. Poisoned apples! Does the woman think she's the evil queen in Snow White?" Vee laughed. "Don't worry!"

"But something *is* wrong with her," Cory took a deep breath. "She tripped twice, and when I put my leg on her, she didn't respond."

Vee's smile faded.

"She's been having a tough time lately, hasn't she? But the stumbling is something new." Vee pulled out her cell phone and started dialing when Jack appeared with Epiphany.

"She deserves a good rubdown and a rest after that performance but seems the show committee has other plans," he announced.

They turned to him.

"What do you mean?" Vee asked.

"Seems our girl and Regina Hamilton both had clean rounds, and get this, had the exact same time for the jump-off. When, in your years of showing, have you ever heard of that happening?"

No one said anything. The only sound was the stirring of horses in their stalls, pulling at the hay and rustling empty feed buckets.

Vee finally spoke. "Jack, we think there's something wrong with Epi. I called the show vet. He's coming over to check her out."

Cory let out a deep breath and collapsed onto the tack trunk. It could be true. Epi could have been drugged, and now Vee was calling a vet who would find out. One way or another. It could mean they would be banned for drugging, if Angela got her way. But at least they would find out what was wrong with the horse.

Jack turned to study the mare. "She seems more tired than usual to me, but then, she's got a right to be."

"See if you can delay the next round jump-off until we get the vet to have a look at her," Vee suggested.

Jack handed the reins to Cory and winked. "Don't worry, I'll take care of it."

Cory wrapped an arm over the mare's neck and dropped her sore cheek against Epi's shoulder. She breathed in the comforting, familiar smell of the mare's skin—a mixture of sweet hay, sweat, and leather oil. She whispered into a cocked ear, "What's wrong with you?"

The show's vet was a thin man dressed in an olive-green coverall with the name of his veterinary practice embroidered on the breast pocket. Cory kept her eyes on the embroidered name and avoided his eyes as he explained in his quiet, patient voice what he had found after examining Epi. His speech was sprinkled with strange words: protozoa, ataxia, nervosa, and paralysis. The words, like black flies, buzzed around Cory's head, never lighting on her consciousness.

Vee kept asking questions. It seemed as if she was trying to make the vet say something they could pin their hopes to, some way to take action, base decisions on. Instead, he demonstrated how Epi circled her foot before she placed it and how she staggered when he pulled her off balance by her tail.

"Neurological symptoms," he explained. "It could be a result of injury, most likely a spinal or pelvic trauma, but it really looks to me like the beginning stages of EPM, a protozoal infestation that causes lesions on the spinal column or brain." He removed a long, clear glove that reached up to his shoulder. He had performed an internal exam, palpating her pelvic area, looking for an obvious reason for her symptoms. "The only way to know for sure is a blood test. Takes a few days to get the results. In the meantime, I'd start treatment. If it is EPM, the sooner she receives aggressive treatment, the better chance she has of arresting further damage."

"Not from drugs, right? She didn't get this from, say, some medicine or something, right?" Cory asked.

The vet looked at her strangely and told her absolutely not. But none of the other words he spoke sounded like any reason for hope, either. Damage, trauma . . . She stood at Epi's head, stroking her face and whispering encouraging words to the mare she herself had a hard time believing. Epi nudged Cory in the chest, a signal that meant she wanted a treat. Cory dumped a pile of sugar cubes into her palm and held them under the mare's nose. Epi's soft muzzle tickled as she swept them up from Cory's outstretched palm.

Jack stepped into the shed row, saw the vet, and looked pointedly at Vee. "They're delaying the second round jump-off. I told them she threw a shoe."

Vee frowned and glanced off into the distance. After a minute, she seemed to have arrived at a decision. She summoned the vet to step aside with her. They moved down the aisle a few feet but Cory could still hear some of their conversation. Vee asked whether the horse could be ridden in the next jump-off round. "Without danger to the rider, of course," she hurried to add.

Cory stepped around the other side of Epiphany, ready to intervene, but waited to hear the vet's answer.

He pulled a white handkerchief out of a back pocket of his coveralls and without unfolding the neat square, rubbed it across his receding brow, then stuffed it away again. His eyes cut back to the mare, then returned to Vee.

"Probably . . . likely." He seemed to gain confidence in his pronouncement. "She'd probably be fine. The ataxia is minimal at this point, although stress does exacerbate the symptoms."

Vee took a furtive glance in Cory's direction, then turned her back to block Cory's view. She lowered her voice more so Cory could only make out a few words " . . . it's just that she's worked so hard to get this far."

Cory hooked Epiphany to the cross ties and stepped up to where they had their heads bent together. "I'm withdrawing."

Vee turned.

"I don't want to put Epi at risk. If she's sick, we'll just bring her home. Get her better."

Vee slid an arm around Cory's shoulder. The vet gave a curt nod, pulled out a prescription pad, and scribbled down the name of some meds. "Get her on this compound right away. If you get the results confirming EPM, I'll put her on the other, more aggressive meds. Unfortunately, they're quite expensive, but the good news is they pose no risk to a fetus."

Cory blinked.

"That's good to know," Vee told the vet, "but we have no plans for breeding her."

The vet looked up from his prescription pad. "Don't you know? Based on my pelvic exam, this mare is already six months into her gestation. She *is* pregnant."

Chapter
Sixty-Five

ESS BURST INTO the stabling area with Kevyn in tow.

"Where were you?" she cried, spotting Cory crouched down by Epi's hind leg, wrapping it in thick bandages. "We looked all over for you afterwards. And then they announced you were quitting!"

Cory stood up slowly. "I'm not quitting." She laid a hand gently on Epi's belly. "I'm simply withdrawing." She shot Jess a look, expecting a smart remark from her, and when she got none, added, "Epi's sick."

Kevyn wrapped Cory in his arms without saying a word. She rested, pressing her body against his. She rubbed the sore side of her cheek against the soft, brushed cotton of his t-shirt, but then pulled back.

"Guys, really, it's okay. It will be okay."

Cory explained what the vet said and about the foal. That little bit of exciting news made the other easier to take.

Jess looked around for a place to sit but thought better of it in her white shorts. Cory eyed her ridiculously girlish outfit and instead of being annoyed, felt a tingle of relief that Jess was taking an interest—a normal interest—in her appearance again. Instead of sitting, she stood as only a dancer would, with toes pointed out and arms hovering gracefully along her sides.

Jess stepped closer, careful to avoid soiling her shoes, and patted

Cory's back. "That Regina Hamilton girl won, which is okay because she did really well, I guess, but her mom! She's giving interviews to anyone who'll listen. I heard her say the horse is sold, that some third party bought him on the spot for an 'undisclosed sum.'" Air quotes.

So, he qualified for Washington. The buyer must have been that blue blazer guy, after all. Cory nodded as Jess filled her in on more details overheard while hanging around the showgrounds. She was happy for Regina. The only thing that really bugged her was the thought that Angela would assume *she* won in the end. That she had intimidated Cory into quitting.

Cory rolled up the spare bandages and tossed them into the open tack trunk. They were taking Epi home to get her well. Even if she had ridden in the jump-off and had qualified her, the mare wouldn't have been capable of making it to Washington in the fall. So what did it matter if Regina went? There would be other years.

She unclipped Epiphany from the cross ties and led her into a stall.

"Speaking of which," Cory looked around, "where is everyone? Where's Mom? Aunt Liv and Douglas?"

Jess shrugged. "Haven't seen them lately. Douglas and Vee's friend, Jack, were by the show office pretty soon after the last jump-off when they announced the winner. Mom and Aunt Liv have been spending most of the afternoon in the gift shops."

"Well, no one has turned up here." Cory looked around to see if Vee or Jack were in another area of the shed row. She was a little annoyed she would have to pack up by herself. Especially after everything that had happened.

"Kev, help me with this." Cory grabbed one end of the trunk. "I want to get out of here."

Kevyn lifted the other end and carried it out of the stabling area, headed toward the truck and trailer.

"Hey," Kevyn exclaimed, "there's Doug and Jack."

Cory, struggling with the weight of the heavy trunk, didn't look up.

"Don't let him catch you calling him Doug," she warned.

Kevyn stopped midstride, dropping his end.

Barking her shins, Cory hollered, "Ow! What are you doing?" She looked up.

Douglas was walking toward them, leading a gorgeous dark bay horse. It was a strange image—Douglas, impeccably dressed, with a horse. Cory tilted her head and puzzled at it. Jack walked along on his other side, whistling a tune.

Something familiar registered. Her eyes widened with shock.

The horse he was leading was Prophet.

Douglas waved at Cory and called, "Got room for one more in that trailer of yours?"

Chapter
Sixty-Six

CORY SAT AT the table in the small L-shaped corner of the living room that served as kitchen table, dining room table, and general dumping-off spot. At least now that school was out, it wasn't covered with books and papers, too. Fingering her horseshoe necklace with one hand, she pushed away a stack of mail and opened Jess's laptop with the other. Cory had worked all day yesterday and today on her new version of the *Desire* essay. She wanted to catch Ms. J before she left for the summer and give it to her, and to fill her in on everything that had happened in the past few weeks.

Jess bounced down the stairs, pulled her purse off the newel post, and called that she was off to dance class. Cory looked up in time to see a blur of gray sweatpants and neatly pinned-up blond hair disappear out the door. Jess had started working at the local ballet studio, just teaching little kids, but it seemed her vow to quit dancing forever was quickly eroding. Cory smiled and bowed her head over the computer to check her essay one more time.

The Desire to Quit, by Cory Iverson

I used to worship false gods. The pursuit after things, ideas, or even other people can become an all-consuming desire—a desire so powerful that stuff such as money, success, fame, or even love can become false gods. Desire is not a bad thing. It is neutral in and of itself. But when desire twists a person with a negative force, driving her to a goal without benefit, it becomes a toxin that poisons one's life.

I saw people chase after things they thought they wanted, but getting closer to their goals did not make them any happier. I watched my sister pursue a dream to dance that landed her in the hospital. My mother abandoned her talents while chasing a romantic ideal that didn't exist. And I lost myself as I idealized other people, thinking they were all cooler, smarter, stronger—well, better—than me. Then I became a quitter. I had always figured it was better not to try at all than to be disappointed with not getting something you really wanted, worked for, or desired. The person I was gradually eroded away and was replaced by The Quitter. And what Douglas MacArthur said was true: "Age wrinkles the body. Quitting wrinkles the soul."

But eventually I found something I wanted and went for it—winning a spot at the Washington International Horse Show on my mare, Epiphany. I wanted to quit a whole lot of times when the competition was hard, but I didn't. When I did quit, it was because my horse was sick, and it was the right thing to do. I thought I would feel bad, but I don't. The shape of my desire changed; its sharp, focused, glassy, clear edges melted and became a desire that was fluid and moldable, flowing, and warm. This desire wrapped itself around me in a protective coat like soft lamb's wool, instead of armor, and shielded my heart from disappointment or fear. I quit confidently, without regret, without second thoughts, and without shame. You quit when it's a choice, not when you're afraid. I guess that's my interpretation of desire, and I think Marcel Proust really got it right about desire when he said: "We do not succeed in changing things according to our desire, but gradually our desire changes."

Cory sighed. It still wasn't quite right, but she hit the print button, just the same.

The high school parking lot was nearly empty. Cory switched off the truck's engine and sat for a while, fingering the envelope containing her essay. She was anxious to tell Ms. J about everything that had happened—how Jess was better and her mom was really getting back into her artwork. Her mom had even talked a restaurant in Ellicott City into displaying some of her pictures. Ms. J would be glad to hear, too, that Kevyn had managed to get a deferment from Harvard, to attend after he sorted things out with his mom. She found out about Harvard—moms always find out—so he had to talk to her. Honestly.

Cory sat forward and pulled at the back of her shirt, already sticking to her. *Kevyn has got to put some air conditioning in this thing! It will be hot riding Prophet all summer.*

Cory had to tell Ms. J all about that, too. The story of how stuffy old Douglas had fooled Angela and bought Prophet for a song through a third party buyer. Seemed Douglas instructed the guy to let it slip that he'd heard rumors about Prophet being drugged. Nothing like a subtle threat to motivate people like Angela. Cory shook her head, recalling how she had been so wrong about Douglas and Aunt Liv. They weren't just posers, after all. And now Prophet was back with Vee in training. Funny how things worked out. At first, she was worried about how Regina would take it, missing a chance to ride at Washington and all, but it turned out she was relieved. Regina hated moving around with the horse show circuit and the constant pressure to win. Cory didn't see Regina much anymore since she moved to Texas to live with her aunt, but they still messaged and emailed each other. She laughed when she read that Regina would be riding reining horses on a ranch. Cory was glad. It would give Regina a change of scenery, especially after what happened with her mom.

Vee finally told the insurance company what happened with Northern Lights. It had been too long so the company couldn't do anything about that case, but after they looked into a few other claims, the investigation uncovered a whole bunch of crimes Angela had been involved in. She was definitely going to prison.

Funny thing was, Vee didn't seem to hate her so much anymore and almost sounded sorry for her. As for Cory's favorite horse—Epiphany, she was getting better every day. Her symptoms were gone and her belly was huge.

Cory was met with a blast of frigid air inside the school's foyer.

One glance through the glass walls of the front office told her no one was manning the visitor desk. Good. She didn't want to bother with signing in. The place was deserted now that the seniors had graduated and school had let out for the summer. When she turned down the short hallway that led to the guidance suite of offices, she saw that Ms. J's door was wide open.

She poked her head into the office and froze. The warm Oriental carpets, the colorful tapestries, and the shelves of books were all gone. Scarred cinder block walls, empty shelves, and a cracked linoleum floor assaulted her eyes. It was as if every shred of Ms. J had been stripped from the room. Could she have left the school for summer break already?

"She's gone."

Cory spun to see the school's custodian standing behind her—a tiny woman with unnaturally black hair. Around her neck was a badge with the name *Mary Margaret Canavan* in large black letters.

"She was fired," the woman added. "Or, as Miss Fancy Pants in the front office says, she was *let go*."

"But why? She was the best teacher here."

The small woman lifted a huge string mop out of a bucket of grayish water and slapped it against the floor. But instead of mopping, she leaned against the handle. "You're telling me. Seems the good ones are the ones they get rid of." She moved closer and whispered, "I heard they got some complaint in the front office."

"But where did she go? Do you know?"

Mrs. Canavan sighed. She smelled of menthol cigarettes and bleach.

"I hear a lot of what goes on here. She's gone to teach at that Catholic school near Baltimore. They're smart enough to grab up a good teacher and don't care about her breaking rules."

"What school, Bishop Spaulding?"

"No, no." Mrs. Canavan shook her head back and forth, staring at the floor. "Not named for a saint or nothing . . . Mount something . . ."

"Mount St. Mary's?" Cory suggested.

"Nah. No use. Can't recall it." She plopped the mop in the bucket and started rolling it back down the hallway. Cory dropped her hand down by her side, still clutching the big manila envelope.

Mrs. Canavan spun around. "Mount de Salle! That's it. Ms. J's gone to teach at Mount de Salle!"

Cory thanked her and rushed down the hall toward the front office. When she pushed open the door, the administrator shot her an unwelcoming glare. She was a huge woman with a double chin and protruding eyes. She loomed over the reception desk, its surface covered with fussy little statues of frogs in various positions. She looked like a frog herself surrounded by her little hatchlings. Her wide mouth opened.

"Students are not allowed on school premises after—"

"I'm dropping off an envelope from Vice Principal McCutchins." She knew Froggy would hop-to if she heard his name. All the students knew she had a thing for him. "He wants it to go out immediately, in fact, today."

"Over there." The frog princess pointed to the outgoing mail bins.

After depositing the envelope in the bin, Cory walked outside to the truck and sat for a moment, wondering what Ms. J would think when she read the essay. She had added her home address and phone so Ms. J could contact her. If she wanted. After a minute, she shifted the gearshift into reverse and turned to pull out of the parking space. A streak of dark gray fell from above and landed with a loud thud into the bed of the truck. Cory slammed on the brakes. A pair of sneakers—or what used to be sneakers—had fallen, their insides facing each other as if nestled, new, in their box.

She laughed.

That pair of sneakers that had meant so much to her at the beginning of the school year now lay in the bed of the truck. Dirty, worn, exposed to the harsh elements for nearly a year, they had nonetheless survived—a lot worse for wear, but still intact. She looked up at the wire that had held them there, constantly hanging over her head. It was empty, except for the remains of the rotting laces, fluttering in the light breeze. They had finally returned to Earth.

Acknowledgments

I thank all who read early drafts of *False Gods* and offered valuable comments: Barbara DeBoy, Diane Danielson, Hannah Robare, and especially my writers group friends Susan Yanguas, Liz Rolland, Deliah Lawrence, and Michelle Paris. Also, huge thanks to Suzanne and Emilie Forest not only for their valuable insights into the world of ballet, but also for their encouragement and belief in me as a writer. I also would like to acknowledge Kevin Bruce, a friend and consummate horse trainer. Additionally, without the help of such skilled writers/editors as Amy Harke-Moore, P.J. O'Dwyer, and Joyce M. Gilmour of Editing TLC, this book would still be languishing in my computer. As an added note, any errors in this work, especially facts pertaining to horse show rules and regulations, are entirely the fault of the author and were likely truths sacrificed for the sake of plot. Lastly, I thank my horses, who taught me everything.

About the Author

L. R. Trovillion grew up in Massachusetts and earned degrees in Russian Language and Literature. Since then, she's worked as a translator, language teacher, editor, and reporter. These days, when she isn't writing, she spends time riding and taking care of her horses on a farm in Maryland she shares with her husband, daughter, a tuxedo cat, and several spoiled dogs.

The story continues . . .

Turn the page to read the first
chapter of L.R. Trovillion's new novel

The Horse Gods

The second book in the Maryland Riders series

One

I'M TOLD WE'RE going to prison. I expect it to look awful, but when we turn the corner and the brick building comes into view, a little furry creature with scrabbling claws starts doing laps inside my stomach. Maybe the Taco Bell breakfast burrito I scarfed down a few hours ago was not a good choice. My God. The fence is about a hundred feet tall with rolls of barbed wire coiled all through and over it, which could keep an army of stampeding elephants in there. On second thought, considering who's inside, that's not such a bad thing.

Brenda pulls into the parking lot not far from a squat building in front with the name Maryland Correctional Facility for Women over the doorway like a college or something. She undoes her seatbelt and reaches into the backseat. I get out. I'm tired of smelling the strawberry air freshener she uses to cover up her menthol cigarettes. Rather smell the cigs.

It's warm for November. The sun is just coming over the guard tower, but for some reason my hands are really cold. Brenda calls something like "wait for me" from the other side of the car. Sure, like I'd go in there alone.

"Regina,"—she walks around to my side, breathless from digging that huge pocketbook out from the backseat. Dark half-moons of sweat already stain her pale blouse. "—I want you to know that you don't have to go in. If you decide not to see her, I can meet with her alone." Brenda squeezes my arm above the elbow and smiles. I hate that.

"Nah, I'm okay." I smile back. She's only doing her social worker job. Give her a break, I figure. I step toward the entrance.

Inside, I'm hit with a blast of stale air. A guard right by the door stops us. The black butt end of a pistol is sticking out of his holster. I've never seen a gun, a real one, up close. Brenda fishes around in that Mary Poppins bag of hers and pulls out her ID and some letter. The guard waves her off to the metal detectors.

"Put your items on the belt," he says in a way that tells me he's repeated that line a million times this week already. "All items on the belt, empty your pockets of any change and loose items, and step through, please."

I pull my phone out of a back pocket and drop it in the plastic tray. Brenda's purse vomits its contents all over the bottom of its tray. On the other side of the metal detector, a lady, also in a guard uniform, waves us over to the desk. Her face sags like a bulldog. No one here smiles, that's for sure.

She takes our phones and pushes visitor badges across the desk to us. Good, because I sure wouldn't want them mistaking me for someone who needs to stay here. Then another lady guard walks us to the other door. She holds it open and announces, "This way to the visitation block," like she's giving a tour. I was really hoping that something would be wrong—improper ID or not a visiting day after all—and they'd turn us back and I could go home. Instead, this lady is taking us to the big building. The real prison. Where *she* is.

I look up at the sun before stepping through another set of doors. Inside, it's just how I imagined—cinder blocks painted in baby poo green and furniture that makes the stuff at school look like Martha Stewart picked it out. More guards. The lady guard keys in some numbers and a heavy door opens with just a *click* and a *whoosh*. No clanging bars or jangling locks. The door closes with a whisper behind us.

"In here." She pushed open the door. "Have a seat. The matron will bring the prisoner."

The prisoner. That's what she's called now. Funny, until now, I always felt like I was *her* prisoner.

The visitors room has some inspirational posters on the wall and a fan of outdated magazines on a plastic coffee table. There's a water cooler against the far wall behind two rows of chairs. I think they're bolted to the floor. The room's empty, but on the other side of a Plexiglass wall, there's another little room. While I'm standing, looking, the door to this room opens and she walks in. I haven't seen her for more than a year now. Under the fluorescent lights she looks more orange. More than her usual fake-tan orange. Maybe it's the mud-colored jumpsuit. There's an inch of dark roots where her hair has grown out. She turns to a woman behind her, waves her hand like a queen, and the other woman sits in a chair in the far corner. Our escort punches a code into a keypad by the door and leads us into the Plexiglass fish bowl, where she's waiting. The lady guard announces, "Your visitors are here."

She turns, spots me. Smiles at first. Then her face creases in on itself. "Regina, your hair!" Her lips pull down into a clowny frown.

My hand floats up to run fingers through my shorn-off curls, but I stop it in midair.

"I don't like it. Makes you look like a patient or . . ."

She struggles to find more insults to hurl at me. Maybe "prisoner," I think, but keep the thought to myself. Instead, "Hi, Angela" are the only words I allow past my lips.

"Angela! What happened to *Mom*?"

She comes at me, arms spread wide, but the lady guard steps between us.

"I'm sorry. No physical contact."

"That's absurd. She's my daughter." Angela tries to step around, but Lady Guard is a linebacker. "We haven't seen each other for a year."

Angela uses her imperious queen voice around here, too, it seems, but Lady Guard doesn't back down. Instead, she pulls out a chair from the table. Even though I think she meant it for me, Angela takes the seat and pulls out the one beside her. I take the one across the table.

"I'm so glad to see you, dear." She places her hands on the table and leans in. Her nails are short, unpainted. I don't think I've ever seen them that way. "I want to hear all about how my sister is treating you down at that dust bowl she calls a horse farm. I've always hated Texas."

Angela takes a deep breath, ready to continue. Her attention has already wavered from hearing about how I'm doing, when Brenda walks in clutching a folder to her chest.

"Who are you?" Angela asks.

"Nice to meet you, Ms. Hamilton. I'm Regina's caseworker, Brenda Grossman." Brenda holds out a chubby hand.

Angela shakes with only the tips of her fingers, turns her chair sideways away from Brenda, and crosses her arms and legs. "My daughter is not a case, Miss Grossman."

"Of course not!" She blushes to the roots of her hair. The room is overcrowded and hot. Brenda dumps the folder on the table and takes a seat next to me. I smell that fake strawberry smell oozing off her clothes now, too. "I've been appointed by the State of Maryland to ease the transition, you know, answer any questions and go over the rules governing custody."

I don't usually listen to Brenda much, but now I've heard a word that makes that furry rodent in my gut start scurrying around again. Did she say *custody*? "What's going on?" My voice is loud in the little fish bowl.

"Now you've ruined my surprise, Miss Grossman." Angela spins toward me. "Regina, I've got good news."

The back of the chair is pressing on my spine as I lean as far away as possible. Angela's eyes are on me. Mine are on the folder on the table between us. Brenda must have known about this. Why didn't she warn me?

"I'm getting out in ninety days. Isn't that great? The State has come to its senses finally, it seems. And you'll be back with me. You won't have to live with Sophia in Texas anymore. Isn't that wonderful?"

She keeps asking me if this is wonderful and all I want to do is throw this damn table through the Plexiglass window and escape. Why didn't someone tell me? Aunt Sophia flew up with me and never said anything. We've been in a rented room together for days and she never said a thing.

"Why?" My voice cracks.

"Why?" A small laugh bursts from Angela. "Because they made a mistake after all, I guess. I should never have been stuck away here for so long."

Angela assumed I was asking a different question, a question about her, of course. Brenda is shuffling papers in that stupid folder and doesn't say anything.

"Five minutes," Lady Guard says.

"Get going, Miss Caseworker, so my daughter will be ready to come home with me when I'm released." Angela slaps the table. "And Regina—" my eyes lift to meet hers. "You can call me Mom, not Angela. What kind of a way is that for a daughter to talk?" She looks around the room for agreement. The matron nods.

We stand. Lady Guard goes to the door and that's when Angela takes two steps across the room and wraps me in a hug. She whispers, "And we'll pick up where we left off. You understand?"

72197288R00203

Made in the USA
Columbia, SC
13 June 2017